Korean Winter

Book 12 in the
Combined Operations Series
By
Griff Hosker

Published by Sword Books Ltd 2019

A CIP catalogue record for this title is available from the British Library.

Cover by Design for Writers

Prologue

I thought my war was over in 1945 but when the Korean conflict flared up, I was called back to the colours. I had been sent to the Pusan Peninsula where my team and I had spent a couple of months raiding behind enemy lines. My last mission, unfortunately, resulted in a wound which had been potentially life-threatening as a piece of shrapnel had come within an ace of crippling me for life, but an American surgeon had saved my life. While I was recuperating, I had been ordered to Hawaii to meet with British and American intelligence. My wars were never simple. A mysterious American woman whom I had first thought was a sergeant clerk but who turned out to be a major, had whisked me to a Japanese Airbase and I was on an aeroplane heading for Hawaii. I confess that I was bemused. I know that I could have made a fuss and said that my wound and the terms of my service meant I could return home to England, but I had always been a team player. I was asked to go and go I did. Major Aitkens, the CIA agent who had taken charge of me, had read my character well and knew that I would not abandon a job half done. My father had had the same problem for he had served in World War One, in police actions between the wars, and had only retired from the R.A.F. at the end of World War Two. I could only hope that my sons, William and Samuel, would not be called upon to go to war! If they were like me and my father, they would make sacrifices which, I knew, others back in England had avoided! I had spent almost as much time away from my wife, Susan, than I had with her! It was only because she had served in Intelligence and was a wonderful lady that she had understood and stood by me. As I looked out of the aircraft's window at the Pacific below, I wondered what the future entailed.

Chapter 1

I was asleep and I was dreaming that I was flying one of our company Dakotas. I enjoyed flying. In the air all appeared peaceful and the sky was relatively empty for there were few other aeroplanes and, if you were a good pilot, then it was safer than driving. My father and I had set up a charter business which flew cargo all across Europe and it was a choice I had made when I stopped being a warrior. I would be a pilot and enjoy the company of my father and other ex-servicemen. The dream was so pleasant that when I was woken, I woke with a scowl!

"Tom, Tom."

I looked up at the stunning Major Aitkens, "What?"

She laughed, "Ah, I see you wake up grumpy!" She pointed at the airman who had a trolley with snacks. "The airman wondered if you might like something to eat or drink. We are halfway through the flight." I looked at the trolley, seeking the whisky. The Major said, "This is a USAAF aeroplane, it is dry."

"Then I take it a cup of tea is out of the question?"

The sergeant grinned, "That is not a problem, sir. When I knew we had a British officer on board I made certain we had some tea."

"Then a cup of tea and a sandwich would be splendid."

"Pastrami or ham sir?"

"Pastrami. Have you any English mustard?"

"Sorry sir, American."

I nodded, "We must all make sacrifices in war."

The sergeant said, "I will be back soon, sir! Anything for you Major?"

"Coffee and a cookie if you have them."

"Coming right up Major, we have some freshly baked chocolate chip!"

The Dakota Skymaster had forty-nine seats and three quarters were occupied. Most of those on our flight were wounded servicemen returning home. I looked at the Major. The uniform looked brand new. When I had first met her, she had been in the uniform of a sergeant. "I am guessing that you are not even a Major."

She had an enigmatic smile, "I am like a chameleon, Tom. Let us say that it was easier to travel in the uniform of a Major than a sergeant. You are a Major and this allows us to chat as equals without '*sirring*' each other all the time."

"And I take it we cannot talk about the reason I am flying to Hawaii?"

"For the purposes of this flight, you are a wounded man being sent for further treatment in Hawaii so we will keep our conversation to chit chat."

"Even though the noise from the aeroplane means it is unlikely that anyone can hear?"

"I forgot that you are a pilot and know such things. Will it be so hard to talk to me, Tom, as a woman rather than..." she smiled, "an officer?"

Her perfume was intensified in the confined cabin and I shook my head, "Major," she frowned, "Kathleen, I have already told you that you are a very attractive woman but I am a happily married man."

She laughed, "Even though you are half a world away from your wife and she would never know?"

"I would know."

She nodded, "Are all Englishmen as ridiculously noble as you?"

"Probably not. So, can we talk about my men? I know that Callow has been repatriated and Captain Poulson promoted but where are they now and will I be returned to them?"

"What makes you think I would know?"

It was my turn to laugh and the return of the sergeant with the trolley delayed my answer. He put two trays on our laps. I drank the tea first. It was weaker than I would have liked. Sergeant Major Dean liked tea that you could stand a spoon in and that was my preference too. The mustard on the sandwich was not hot enough and although there was plenty of meat, I found myself missing England. True, we still had rationing, but you grew used to the taste of home. I had had just five years of life in England after the last war but I had made the most of it.

When the trays were taken away, I said, "Kathleen, I know that you know where they are and what they are doing. Without compromising their security, what can you tell me?"

"They are still operating behind enemy lines using the MTB and that is all I can tell you. However, if I was a gambler," she laughed, "actually, I am a gambler! As a gambler, I will predict that you will not be returned to them. You impressed a great number of people with… well, what you did. Those skills will be needed if we are to bring this war to a speedy conclusion and then you can get back to your very lucky wife."

That was all I could get out of her and we spent the rest of the flight talking about our respective countries although she learned more about my background than I did about hers.

We landed, in Hawaii, at Hickam Air Force base where a car was waiting to whisk us off into the hills. We arrived at a compound surrounded by barbed wire and with some serious looking, well-armed sentries on the gates. We were inspected closely before they admitted us. There were a couple of accommodation wings and a building which had guard towers and wire around it. I guessed that was where Jeremy Blair, spy and traitor, was being held. I wondered at that for he was still a British citizen. Perhaps that was why the spymaster known as L, was coming over. He was MI6 and he would understand the diplomatic protocols better than I could. The last time I had seen him had been when we had been sent to bring Blair back from Uiseong-ro. Then he had used the title of Colonel Churchill. Like Major Aitkens that would not be his real name.

The accommodation block had a front desk which was manned. When the Major handed over documents, I saw the desk sergeant stiffen. She was senior and had far more power than I had assumed when I had first met her. He quickly handed us two keys, "Here you are majors. Do you need help with your bags?"

I had a small holdall with toiletries, pyjamas and a spare uniform. Both the uniforms I had were dress and not combat uniforms.

The American Major answered for me, "No thank you, sergeant. Are the arrangements for dinner still the same?"

"Yes, Major."

"Good and if you would let me know when the British Colonel arrives."

"Yes, Major. What is his name?"

She smiled a cold smile and said sharply, "I doubt that you will be inundated with British Colonels so let me know if any British Colonel arrives. Clear, sergeant?"

"Clear, Major." The man was almost shaking. He was obviously not combat trained but I understood his reaction, Kathleen Aitkens, or whatever her real name was, was a force of nature.

She turned to me. "Dinner will be at seven-thirty. I will knock on your door at seven." She smiled, "Is that soon enough?"

I knew what she meant and I nodded, "Yes Major, quite soon enough."

My room was simply furnished but comfortable and it was a bed and not an army cot. I saw a dressing gown hung behind the door and there was a bathroom complete with a shower. For a serving soldier, this was luxury. There was a wardrobe and I changed out of the uniform I had used for travelling and laid my best uniform on the bed. I was not as tired as I thought I would be for I had slept for half the flight but I needed refreshing. I took a shower. One thing about American bases, they had good showers with hot water. In England, I had showered in cold water more often than hot! I donned the gown and, as I had some sheets of notepaper with me, I began to write a letter to Susan. I had one already started but that was in Korea. I had no doubt that Brevet Major Poulson would see to my gear. I had the shower first and then wrote a letter to my wife. I kept it simple and there was no reference to my wound or the action which had led to it. I spoke about Korea, the food and the people. I had learned to write carefully as my wife knew how to read between the lines! She had worked at Combined Operations and knew the form. I wondered when, if ever, my letters from home would reach me. Four pages later and I glanced at my watch. It was close to seven. I dressed quickly and, as I tied my tie there was a knock on the door.

The CIA agent was stunning! She knew how to dress. I guessed that here she could, quite literally, let her hair down. She had no need to hide who she was and what she did. I smiled, "Beautiful as ever, Kathleen."

She beamed. "Am I breaking down your resistance, Tom?" I could not tell if she was teasing me or if she meant it and I just smiled. We walked down the corridor to the stairs, "Your L is not here yet and so we have a couple of days to see the island. You might as well recuperate and the sights will give you something to put in the letter you are writing." I stopped and stared at her. She laughed, "There are no spyholes in your room, Tom. I am well trained and when you opened the door, I saw the unfinished letter on your bed and, besides, it is just the sort of thing I would expect you to do."

"Then you should know that the one thing I will not do is to tell Susan that I am in Hawaii. I wrote to her that I was recovering from my wound."

"You are thinking all the time, Tom. We shall eat alone tonight. I will bring you up to speed on Blair. He has been interrogated and we know a great deal already. The rest must wait for British interrogators."

We had entered the dining room. It had linen cloths laid on wooden tables and the chairs were good ones. The stewards were military but, other than the uniform, this could have been a restaurant in Washington! A sergeant took us to a table. I saw that the tables were arranged for even numbers, two, four, six and eight. We were taken to a table for two. A few of the others were occupied by officers. This was the equivalent of an officers' mess and I saw that there was a bottle of wine on the table. As we sat the sergeant steward poured us a glass each.

After he had left us, she toasted me, "Cheers!" We drank and I smacked my lips for the wine was good. "Californian. Prohibition destroyed most of the wineries but they have been getting better and the war meant we needed to produce our own wines. I chose a good one as I know that you Brits are such snobs about wine."

I shook my head, "Some are but not me. I grew up drinking rough wine at our holiday home in France. This is good. It is a little sweet for my taste but good."

She nodded, "I took the liberty of ordering food. I assumed you would like steak and that is what I ordered."

"I like steak. We are still rationed in England so this will be a real treat for me."

She ran a red fingernail around the rim of her glass, "I guess you and your people had it far rougher than we did. We just saw the air raids on London on the newsreels."

"Not just London; Liverpool, Newcastle, Portsmouth, Coventry, Scotland... the Germans bombed wherever they could and those rockets they had by the end of the war, well goodness only knows how far they could have reached."

She looked surprised, "You knew about them?"

It was my turn to smile, "Let us say, Kathleen, that you are not the only one with secrets." I had helped to destroy the base which manufactured a vital part of the rocket.

The steward brought soup; it was chicken and sweetcorn. After we had eaten and while we waited for the main course she said, "Let me fill you in on our friend, Blair. When he was taken to the house where you recovered him, we knew that he was more than just a socialist in a Commando uniform. Blair is not his real name. His real name is d'Aubigny and his father is landed gentry. When

Blair, we might as well use that name, went to University at the start of the last war, he was recruited by a Russian spymaster. With a war on there was less scrutiny at universities. There was a professor there who worked for Russia and he was subverted. His personal lifestyle helped. Your L is not sure if Blair was blackmailed but whatever the reason when he left University, he changed his name and joined up. The professor disappeared at the end of the war. By then your MI6 was investigating the professor. That is the reason L has not arrived yet. He is gathering as much information as he can."

"It all seems a little elaborate."

She shook her head, "Blair is what we call in our trade, a sleeper. He was put in a Commando unit because they are elite and, most importantly, are sent behind enemy lines. You can do real damage if you infiltrate elite units like that."

"But the U.S.S.R. were our allies!"

The steaks arrived and we stopped talking while the food was placed on the table. When the waiters had gone, she continued, "The Communists are pragmatic. They needed the capitalists of America and Great Britain to defeat a common enemy but their avowed intent was always world domination. When the Nationalists were defeated by the Chinese Communists then the Russians joined with them. The map of the world used to have great red swathes that was the British Empire. Now that is Communist red and it is spreading!"

"Okay, I can see that placing Blair in a Commando unit would jeopardise missions behind the lines but when he was found out he ceased to be of importance, surely?"

"That is why he is here. It makes no sense to us but he was in Uiseong-ro for a reason and he was protected and treated as though he was important. The men you killed were North Korean elite soldiers! So, you see why we brought you here. We need to find out why he was there and if we have succeeded in cutting out the cancer or is there more out there that we know nothing about?" She leaned forward. "You should know that General MacArthur is about to land troops close to the original border between North and South Korea. Brevet Major Poulson and your unit will be involved. They are, even as we speak, being dropped behind enemy lines along with Major Rogers and his men."

So, Captain Rogers had been promoted too!

"But Blair has been a prisoner so he can't hurt us!"

"Who else is out there, Tom? Where are the other sleepers? Think of all the men who joined the army towards the end of the war and after. No, we need to know the extent of all this. Blair was in Uiseong-ro for a reason. You got in and out quickly. What if there had been radio equipment? What if Blair was talking to men in other units, not just the Commandos? These sleepers are clever men and radio operatives are well trained."

I thought back to my radio operators. She was right and they were very clever. A memory hidden in the deep recesses of my mind surfaced. Blair had tried to be given responsibility for the radio. What might have happened if he had succeeded?

The coffee arrived and I leaned back, "What I can't understand, Kathleen, is why Blair went out of his way to be so obstructive."

She lit a cigarette and said, "I have thought about that too. There are two reasons, neither of them is mutually exclusive. His personality and the fact that no one would expect someone working for another government to be so high profile. You British like the underdog. You feel sorry for them and give them every chance. I think Blair was so clever that he played on that. He was the son of a lord and understood privilege. Just a theory." She finished the cigarette and stubbed it out. "Anyway, you have had a long flight. L's flight is due in tomorrow evening and so we have a day to see Oahu."

I smiled, "I would like to see Pearl Harbour."

"I thought you might. It is a reminder to Americans never to be complacent again! We were caught out once but never again!"

I had a surprisingly pleasant day although the sight of the Arizona in Pearl Harbour was sobering. Dad had spent some time in the Far East during the war and we had spoken of the loss of the American battlewagons as well as the British ships sunk by the Japanese. When it came to the men from the east it paid to look for surprises.

When we returned to the complex, we heard that L had arrived and would be joining us for dinner. We were in the officer's club bar when he arrived. As usual, he was chain-smoking. It seemed to be an occupational hazard. Since my time in the hospital, I had smoked my pipe less. He gave me a thin smile, "Well done, Major Harsker. Your operation was successful and the rescue of Sergeant Callow might have resulted in a Victoria Cross under normal circumstances but as you have one and the mission was a delicate one…"

I nodded, "I understand, er, Colonel?"

He smiled, "We will stick with Churchill. I have a fondness for the name. As for your records, the incident was noted and I dare say a promotion might be forthcoming."

I shook my head, "This is my last foray, Colonel. When I am done here, I go back to my family!"

"That is a pity. You appear to have a knack for it." He turned to Major Aitkens, "Has our little red said anymore?"

"He keeps demanding a lawyer and since he has realised that this is an American base, he has the effrontery to demand to speak with someone from the Consulate."

The man known as L laughed, "You have to admire his cheek. We learned a little more while I was in England. His father died at Dunkirk and the rest of his family were killed by a V1 rocket at the end of the war. The estate simply disappeared. No heir was found as Blair had changed his name. That may be another reason for his bitterness towards the British establishment."

Major Aitkens nodded towards our table which was now ready, "We can eat and tomorrow morning we can begin the real interrogation. It is a pity that our hands are tied in terms of the methods we might use. Our enemies are not so concerned about their methods."

We sat and the two Intelligence Officers talked of how they would approach it. We were drinking our coffee when L said, "You have been quiet, Harsker; is it the wound?"

To be honest I had endured worse pains from other wounds and I shook my head, "I still don't know what use I will be. You people seem to know your business, I will just be a spare part!"

L shook his head and lit a cigarette, "When we had some psychologists look at Blair's profile, they saw things that we didn't. They seem to think that you are someone of interest to him. You joined as a private and rose through the ranks yet your father was well off. You are seen as a humanitarian officer. You lead from the front."

I was confused, "And ...?"

"And you make him question what his Communist masters have told him about British officers. You proved them wrong and he resents you. Perhaps he worries about his sexual preferences and you are a threat there. Happily married and attractive to the opposite sex, it may be that he is attracted to you too!" he shrugged, "One of the mind doctors told me that."

My eyes widened, "But..."

Kathleen put her hand on mine, "This is all conjecture, Tom, and may not be true but the point is we can use you if we have to. First, we try our old-fashioned techniques. You are the joker we play if it is needed."

I was not needed for the next three days. I decided to get fit for I knew I would be returning to action at some stage. They had a PX on the base and I managed to get some gear to use for running. I could not leave the base as it would have entailed too many problems at the gate and so I had a circuit around the buildings. When it became obvious that I would not be needed soon I increased the length of the runs. The nature of my wound meant that it did not impair my running. In fact, the opposite. It was sitting which caused me discomfort. When I ate with the two Intelligence Officers at night, they were circumspect about what they had discovered. I guessed, from the cigarettes they smoked and their general demeanour, that they were not getting as far as they might have liked. What I did learn was that Blair thought I was dead and had succumbed to my wounds.

I was sent for, as I came back from my run, on the fourth day. "Major Aitkens asked if you would dress, sir, and join them at the cell block. If you wait outside with your ID you will be admitted. No firearms are permitted, sir."

I put on my travelling uniform and took my pipe. I don't know why I did that but, I suppose, it was something to hold and with which to fiddle. The room in which Blair was being questioned was in the heart of the building and there were no windows. An armed guard stood next to the door.

The Staff Sergeant who escorted me to the room said, "The room is soundproofed, sir, and, as you might have noticed there are few windows in the whole building. It means the prisoners can be disorientated. We manipulate the days so that they lose all track of time. Right now, the prisoner thinks it is the middle of the night. Someone will be out for you in a short while. Until then you will have to be patient sir. This one is slippery!"

So, Blair had had an effect on the Americans too.

I did not have to wait long and I was just filling my pipe when the door opened and a corporal, complete with sidearm said, "Major, if you would like to come in." He spoke quietly and, as I entered, I saw that the two Intelligence Officers were facing Blair whose back was to me. The corporal closed the door quietly behind him and Kathleen waved me to a seat next to her. Blair did not turn as I passed him but, when I had passed him, he looked up. His face showed great surprise and then blackened to show shock and outrage.

"You are dead! They told me you were dead." He jabbed a finger across the table at the two of them. "Typical lies!"

I saw now one of the reasons I was here. Blair had been, seemingly, in control, but the sight of me set him off and made him unstable. They could exploit that.

L said, as he stubbed out a cigarette, "We said no such thing. You assumed he had been killed and we merely allowed you to continue to think so. Sit down, Major."

I could see that Blair was rattled. I took out my pipe and continued to fill it. I knew that it would annoy him. Blair said, "Can't bear to look at me, eh? Still guilty about the men who died following your orders." I tamped down the tobacco and took out a match. "You are a heartless bastard! I should have let Roy slit your throat like he wanted." Roy, that had been Marsh's first name, and Marsh had been a simple lad taken in by Blair's lies. "You will get yours one day."

I had the pipe going and I let the smoke out slowly and looked him in the eyes for the first time, "But not by you, eh, Blair? You will be tried and you will be hanged."

His eyes widened, "I will have my day in court then and this travesty of justice will be remedied. I will never be hanged. I have friends and they are in high places!" He jabbed a finger at L, "one of the men who command you is one. I will never hang and you cannot make me talk! Now let me return to my bed."

He had already said more than he intended. The sleep deprivation was working. I decided to use something that L had said. I would mention the radios and see what effect it had on him. I smiled, "Don't worry, Blair, or whatever your real name is, we have replaced every radio operator in every British unit in Korea. Your plan has failed!"

It was then that he lost his temper. He lunged over the table at me. I had been watching him carefully and I anticipated the move. The guard on the door grabbed for his gun but I merely moved to the side. He was tired and he was slow. He knocked the cups to the floor and he ended up cracking his head from the tiles. The sentry reached him and pinned his arms behind his back. I took my pipe from my mouth, "You were always a poor Commando, Blair."

Major Aitkens stood, "Take him back to his cell and the next time we interrogate him he is to be handcuffed!"

"What about my head? I am bleeding!"

She smiled, "When the doctor can find the time have him stick a band-aid on the wound, eh corporal?"

When we were alone the MI6 man became serious, "There was a rumour that there was someone high up in MI6 who was a spy. This confirms it. Very effective, Harsker, and well-done Kathleen, you chose precisely the right moment to bring him in." He nodded at me, "That was inspired about the radio operators. We wondered how we would be able to track down potential enemy agents. This is manageable. I will send a coded signal to the units both in Korea and on their way. With the offensive about due to start the time is crucial." We can check the backgrounds of the key radio operators much easier than going through every man's file."

Later, the next day, I ate with the Colonel and Kathleen. "You have impressed people back in England, Tom. These are important people. I have been given permission to ask you to join us."

"Us?"

He smiled, "Those who fight the enemies of the west but choose not to wear a uniform. You have the right skill set. You are clever. You speak a number of languages and I have yet to dine with someone who can use weapons as well as you do."

I took out my pipe. I needed thinking time. I was flattered, of course I was. In addition, part of the job excited me. I would still be fighting for England. I lit my pipe and nodded. I saw Kathleen smile, she thought they had won. I was merely nodding at the satisfaction having lit the pipe with one match. "I am happy to fight for England but it will be in this uniform and it will be alongside Commandos. I am here to do a job and when Korea is over I shall go home and be a dad once more. Sorry. I am flattered but I will go back to Korea."

L knew he was beaten but Kathleen was like a dog with a bone. "The war in Korea will be over soon."

"Then I will get home all the sooner."

Her face became a mask of anger. "You are a fool!"

I smiled, "I think, on that, we are all agreed!"

I was kept at the base for another week. I did not get to speak to Blair again but they still needed me as insurance. However, the coded radio signals to the regiments yielded results. They were not as bad as we had thought. Of those in Korea, only two had men whose backgrounds did not match and they were whisked back to Blighty. When the word spread in England that radio operators were being scrutinised five men deserted. Kathleen was surprised the number was so low.

I understood why and I explained it to her. "It is hard to be a loner in the British Army and these men have to be the ones who can operate alone. I am not surprised but I am worried that Blair will get off because he has friends in England. I had a man murdered by Blair and others whose lives were put in danger. What happens when he gets representation?"

Kathleen showed a cold side I had not seen before, "Tom, the only people who know that Blair was recaptured are the men of your unit and the MTB. If Blair were to disappear who would ask about him? He has no family and, as you have just pointed out, no friends. His story will never get out." I opened my mouth, "Better that you do not ask any more questions. This way you have plausible deniability." She smiled, "Besides, in a week's time you will be returned to Korea. The offensive is beginning and when your men return from their first mission under Brevet Major Poulson then you will resume command!"

Having seen the harder side of the intelligence agent I was more than happy to leave Hawaii. There was something about this that did not sit right with me. All wars were dirty wars; this seemed to be filthy.

My last few days on the base with the two Intelligence officers were polite and nothing more. I saw them only at mealtimes for they sensed that they had a way into Blair's head. I was still in Hawaii when MacArthur landed at Inchon with forty thousand men. I felt like a spectator at a football match played out on the radio. I heard the news along with the rest of the base, relayed through the radio. In four days, the army was racing to relieve Seoul and my unit had broken out of Pusan!

Major Aitkens took me herself to the airbase at Hickam Field. This time it was not filled with wounded men but replacements for those lost in the advance towards North Korea. "Thank you for your help Tom and I am sorry… well, let us leave it at that. The word 'sorry' covers a lot of territory. Good luck when you get to Korea. It might be a new start for you." She took my head in her hands and gave me a full-blown kiss. The other men waiting to board the Dakota cheered and wolf-whistled. The Major did not seem to care, "Your wife is a lucky woman and Tom, take care and keep your head down." There was something in her words which made me wonder if there was a hidden message. I dismissed the thought. I had been around the shadowy world of espionage and spies too much. It was time to get back to my men. Her last words had a hidden meaning and I could not decipher it. I put the Major from my thoughts. That episode was over.

I slept most of the way and, after we had landed, I had to find transport to the base at Donbaek-ri. I knew that it was unlikely that the men would still be there but it was a starting point. My orders were vague; I was to rejoin my unit. I was lucky. Most of the American replacements were heading north and would have to pass through Donbaek-ri which was our base before the offensive. My back complained all the way along the potholed road.

It was dark when I arrived and the place seemed deserted. Of course, before I had left it had been a war zone and at the forefront of the action. Now it was a backwater. There was still an American base nearby but it had just an admin staff. There were ten men who had travelled with me bound for the base and we all shared a truck. I just had my holdall with me. I headed for our quarters where I assumed there would be some sort of caretaker. What I did not expect was Sergeant Major Thorpe. After being allowed through the compound gate I walked up to the barracks and opened the door. I heard voices within and Sergeant Major Thorpe beamed at me, "Well sir, they said you were coming but I didn't know when! This is good timing. We leave in two days." He put his pipe on the table and snapped a salute.

I had not expected this. Behind him, I saw new faces. They were Commandos but not my team.

"Good to see you, Sarn't Major. Are we going to join Brevet Major Poulson?"

His face fell, "They didn't tell you, sir?"

"Tell me what?"

"The lads were sent behind enemy lines when the push started. They haven't been heard of since but two days ago we heard that we were not to expect them back. These ten are replacements. The rumour is they were either captured or they are dead. Sorry, sir, I thought you knew."

The Major's last words suddenly made sense. She had known and she had not told me; new start indeed!

Chapter 2

It seemed that the raid had been attempted during a chaotic time; the Americans were landing at Inchon and men were being dropped behind the lines to cause as much mayhem as possible. The Rangers had been used as well and it was Major Rogers who had reported that the Commando side of the raid had gone wrong. None had returned from the mission and, as it was behind enemy lines, no bodies had been recovered either. This was nothing short of a disaster. I had one experienced man, Sergeant Major Thorpe, and ten new men who were now my unit. Sergeant Major Thorpe told me that more men were being sent from Britain but it would take them more than a week to reach us and we had been ordered north. It was a lot to take in. "And what about Lieutenant Drake and Petty Officer Flynn?"

"Sorry sir, they went north too but I think they are still active; they are based closer to the front line but we are making so many advances that it is hard to say where that is. When I was up at the American base, they were talking about invading the north." He gestured with his pipe towards my kit bag, Bergen and weapons. They were on my cot, "We have all your gear and your letters. We knew you would be back so the Captain, er Major, said to watch over them. He thought it would be a cakewalk, sir, after we heard about Inchon."

That was the trouble. Polly was ever an optimist and sometimes it paid to look at things half empty.

"And where have we been ordered to?"

"The capital!" He smiled, "Just two hundred miles to Seoul, sir. It appears that the Americans are heading for North

Korea and they want us close to them. We have a lorry but no jeep."

"An interpreter?"

"Sergeant Bo-yeon Heon went with the lads. We are still waiting for his replacement."

"Well, we don't wait here for one. We will have to rely on our basic Korean. Rations? Ammo?"

"Plenty of both."

I lowered my voice, "And the new lads?"

"A little green, sir. No World War 2 veterans amongst them apart from Corporal Dixon who was with Number 3 Commando on D-Day. But they are all keen as mustard."

"I will talk to them tomorrow before we leave. I shall read the letters from home first."

The Sergeant Major went to the admin desk and took out a single envelope and a number of others held together with an elastic band. Mr Poulson said to give this back to you. He said you would understand."

I nodded. It was the letter I had written to Susan in the event of my death. Polly had been right. I didn't need it.

I lay in my cot and read my letters. Mum and Susan had sent two. Mary and Dad just one. They made home seem a little bit closer. It was late when I finished reading them for I had read each one twice in case I missed anything. I finished the letter to Susan and then began one to Mum. I felt guilty that I hadn't begun one on the long flight.

The next morning was a new day and I determine to throw myself into my new command. I changed into my overalls for the journey and packed everything into my kitbag. The winter gear I had brought might prove useful. It already felt like Autumn at home and it was only the end of September. I knew that we were just a little further south than my home in England but the mountains here made it feel colder. The Sergeant Major drove and he turned off at the American base. "I told them we would call in when we were leaving. You know what the mail is like. The staff sergeant said he would send it on."

I nodded as we drove through crowded streets. The port was busy once more and men and material were being sent north as soon as they arrived. The ports we had captured further north appeared to be too damaged to use at the moment. We stopped at the gatehouse and the Sergeant Major went in. He was there longer than I had expected. The reason became clear when an American Captain came from the Admin block. He came to my side of the lorry and saluted, "Major Harsker I have a message for you from a Colonel Wilding in Seoul. He is a liaison officer between the American and Commonwealth forces. Apparently, you are now seconded to the American sector. It has all been cleared with your commanding officer. He said to go to the main base north of Seoul. I have a map." He handed the map to me. Without an interpreter, it would be vital.

"Thank you, Captain, and if you could send any mail to us, we would be grateful."

"Will do. We will miss you guys and this place will be a lot quieter now!"

As we drove off, I asked, "What was all that about?"

"Sorry sir," He looked and sounded embarrassed. "When the lads got the news that you had pulled through, they sort of celebrated. It was a little wild."

I was relieved; I thought something far worse than a simple booze-up had occurred.

We only had two hundred miles to cover but it might as well have been two thousand for the roads twisted, turned, climbed and fell. The roads were crowded with people returning to their homes in Seoul now that the Communist threat had abated. There were the remains of the fighting all the way along the road. The roads had been cleared but neither the damaged vehicles nor, in at least four places, had the bodies been removed. It was getting on for dark when we finally reached Seoul. After crossing the bridge, we had just four miles to go to reach the base. The Sergeant Major and I had shared the driving and I handed over to him for the last

section. We reached a traffic jam of trucks and vehicles. I had
expected such confusion. The problem was that there were
vehicles arriving from the south and leaving for the north and
Seoul was a bottleneck. The North Korean Army was fleeing north
as quickly as they could.

"I will walk ahead and do the paperwork, Sergeant Major. It
will make it easier to get in."

"Aye, sir. I will just have a pipeful."

I climbed down from the cab and immediately regretted not
wearing my greatcoat. There was a chill in the air. I walked along
the side of the largely American trucks. We were half a mile from
the gate. I saw the problem immediately. They were allowing a
convoy to leave for the north and as there were tanks and self-
propelled guns it was taking some time. I reached the gate where a
corporal and two privates were waiting to examine the papers of
the vehicles entering. Two MPS directed traffic. The three snapped
to attention when they saw my crown.

"Sir!"

"At ease," I jerked my thumb behind me, "We have just driven
from the Pusan area and I thought I could expedite our entry." I
handed the Corporal the papers.

"You still have to wait until the others are checked, sir,"

I smiled, "The difference is, Corporal, that when you see my
lorry you will simply wave us through eh?"

I saw realisation dawn, "Yes sir." He read my papers and then
handed them back. "Thanks, sir, they appear to be in order but we
will still have to look in your truck!"

"Not a problem, Corporal."

One of the privates said, "You are the first Limeys, er British
soldiers, we have seen for a while, sir. Your guys are further east."

I nodded, "I think the sudden collapse of the North Koreans
has made for a confusing time."

I think they were bemused by my accent. They were young
soldiers. Older ones who had served in Europe had grown used to
it. The Corporal said, "Yes sir and the North Koreans are running
faster than jackrabbits! We even caught some of the Russkies too!"

I had not heard that, "The Russian advisers?"

"Yes, sir. They were brought in yesterday." He leaned forward conspiratorially, "We have heard a rumour that Old Doug is going to invade China! End the red threat there too, sir!"

Doug was General MacArthur. The ordinary American soldier had a great affection for him after the Philippines. "I doubt that Corporal. Any idea where we will go?"

"Yes, sir, from the designation on your paperwork you need to be at the northeast end of the compound, Dog sector. There are MPs at all the crossroads to direct you." He grinned, "Just like New York on a busy Saturday!"

Just then the last truck left the huge compound and the MP sergeant said, "Right, Mac, get this traffic moving!"

The Corporal said, apologetically, "Sorry sir."

I stood to the side. The three of them knew their business. The Corporal held his hand out for papers while one of the privates covered the driver with his rifle. The third went to the back and checked it. The truck was only admitted if the papers satisfied the Corporal and the soldier at the rear gave a wave. The traffic moved more quickly. I stepped onto the running board of our cab as the rear was checked. The Corporal waved us through. The camp had been built hurriedly but it had been organised by Engineers and the roads all ran north-south and east-west. It looked like the area had been chosen as it had been badly damaged during the attack for Seoul. I leaned out of the cab at one crossroads, "Dog sector?"

"This is it, sir. Are you the British Commandos?"

"Yes, Sergeant."

"Those are your tents to the right. The guys who had them have just left for the front." He pointed first, ahead and then as he pointed in the opposite direction, he added, "And there is a tent there which is operating as an officer's club, sir."

"I smiled, "As much as I would like a drink, Sergeant, my men will need food. Where is the canteen?"

He looked confused and then smiled, "The chow house? Right next to the Officer's Club."

We pulled in to the tented area and Sergeant Major Thorpe quickly organised the men. I took the tent which was slightly smaller than the rest and I began to lay out my gear as I knew the value of organisation. I had a whole bag of weapons and, unlike the new lads, I still had my original Bergen and battle vest; they had served me well in the last war and I saw no need to change. Even though I knew I was something of a dinosaur but unlike those prehistoric beasts, I had survived! I saw that there were four cots in my tent and I used one as a storage area where I laid out my weapons and equipment so that I could pack it quickly when it was needed.

Once we had all unpacked, I led the men in the direction the MP had indicated. With men still arriving the cooks had food on the go the whole time. The men had never eaten American style and, after British Army cuisine they were impressed. I was asked if I wanted to eat in the Officer's mess but I declined. I needed to get to know these men and I did not have the luxury of a long flight from England to do it!

I already knew their names and so I listened as they spoke. I would then ask them more pertinent questions. They all struck me as very young but then that was a sign of my age. Sergeant Major Thorpe was older than I was so they would appear as children to him. There was a hierarchy in the Commandos and the two NCOs sat together. The rest sat in friendship groups. I saw that one, John Lofting, sat almost apart from the others. I remembered the issues I had had with Blair and Marsh and so, as he was at the end of the table, I took my plate of food and sat opposite him. The NCOs did not react for they knew my purpose but the others all stared.

"John, isn't it?"

"Yes, sir."

I recognised an East Anglian accent, "Fen Country?"

He laughed, "Yes sir, well near enough, King's Lynn."

"What made you join up?"

"I knew I was due to complete National Service sir and, to be honest, I was not keen on farm work. The only job I liked was gamekeeper and my father has that job. My dad is still working so it was either leave home and try to be a gamekeeper somewhere else or join up and, well, the Commandos do things differently don't they, sir?"

"They do indeed. You are a good shot then?" He shrugged, "No false modesty, John, in my experience gamekeepers know their way around guns."

He grinned, "Yes sir. I was top of the class at Commando school."

I now understood why he was a loner. He was not anti-social nor did he have issues which needed resolution. He just liked to be on his own and I could respect that.

"Sir, is it true you have a VC?"

The man next to John had plucked up the courage to speak to me, "Ralph Smith isn't it?"

"Rafe Smith, sir, from Manchester."

"To answer your question, Rafe, yes." He nodded. "Tell me why did you join up?"

"Me dad." I smiled. I recognised the peculiar grammar of the North of England. "He was in the Commandos. He died on D-Day at Sword Beach."

"I was at Sword Beach."

"I know sir, that was why I was made up when I found I was in your section!"

That unlocked the doors and the conversation flowed around me as I was asked questions. I discovered strangely useful nuggets of information such as Smith's affinity for dogs and Hall's interest in gardening. They were a disparate bunch. The questions and their reactions told me much about the men I would be leading. None was older than twenty. I could not remember such a young group. Nor had they had the same training as I had. It had moved on. Some things were for the better but some of the old ways still had much to commend them. Of course, they were now Royal Marine Commandos.

The Sergeant Major and I were amongst the few remaining Army Commandos.

Phil Hall came from Halifax and his family had a farm which raised horses. When I asked him why he didn't join the cavalry, he told me that the only regiments who rode horses were too posh for him. He was a typical plain-spoken Yorkshireman.

Bert Entwhistle came from a village near to Wigan and was a Lancashire lad through and through. As most of the lads where he lived went into the mines and he did not like the thought, he had joined up. He loved the outdoor life.

Archie McKenzie was a Scot from Dunbar whose uncle had been in the Royal Marine Commandos and lost a hand in Sicily. Like Rafe, it was a family connection.

Peter Powell came from a family of fishermen from Hartlepool. He liked the sea but he liked fighting. He had been an amateur boxer. I looked forward to seeing his close combat skills. He had also been training to be a doctor! Somehow that did not seem to agree with his love of boxing.

Jack Fox and Harry Ashcroft were friends who joined up together and they came from Bristol. They looked so similar that they could be brothers and the others mocked, in a good-natured way, their West Country accents. It did not offend them.

Sam Williams was an only child whose parents had both died in an air raid at the start of the war. He had been moved from London to a children's home close to Wolverhampton, Codsall. I think he had grown up in an atmosphere of discipline and order. The Commandos gave him a chance to continue that but he also had a temper. He told me when the two of us chatted on the way back to our tents, that he had had to learn to use his fists in a children's home filled with all sorts of boys. He had learned to survive and to look after those who were weaker than he was. In many ways, he was the perfect Commando for he knew how to battle.

As we stood outside of their tents I said, "I do not know what our mission will be yet but I doubt that we will be fighting on the line. We have to go behind enemy lines. For that, we need to be as fit as we can. We rise at 0500 and we will have a run inside the compound." I grinned at the Sergeant Major, "That means all of us. Then, after we have had breakfast, I will go to the admin office and find out when the rest of our men will be coming and what arrangements have been made for our ammunition. Get a good night's sleep. Your war begins tomorrow."

I watched them head to their tents. I waited with my two NCOs, "What do you make of them?"

The Corporal, Matt Dixon, nodded, "A good bunch, sir. They are green as grass and have no idea, yet, what the job entails but they will get there."

The Sergeant Major gave a sad look, "If they get time, sir. Some of the lads who went with Mr Poulson had potential and now they are either dead or in the bag!"

"And it is up to us three to ensure that does not happen with these boys."

As I lay on my cot, for sleep would not come, I wondered just what had happened to my men. Our advance had been so rapid that the North Koreans had not had the chance to put them in camps yet. Indeed, with our tanks and men racing towards the border they would have to keep on running. The question was, where could they run to?

We received some strange looks as we ran an improvised five-mile run. I knew I was unfit but it surprised me when I was the first one back. My NCOs had brought up the rear to assess the problems.

I shook my head as the last one, Harry Ashcroft, puffed his way in, "Disappointing, lads. I have had a wound and been in a hospital yet I beat all of you back. I will put it down to the journey here. We go out again after lunch, so make it a light one." I tapped my watch, "I know the time I have to beat and yours will be the same one. We do this twice a day until I am happy with you."

Just then an air raid siren sounded. I had no idea where the shelters were located. I looked around and saw the other personnel heading for a sandbagged area, "Over there!"

The fact that so many troops had left the previous day meant that the shelter into which we dived was relatively empty. The men inside burst out laughing as we dived in for we wore vests and shorts. "Are you guys lost?"

"Are you training for the Olympic games or something?"

Sergeant Major Thorpe recognised that the speaker was a Marine sergeant and he snapped, "That is an officer, so watch how you speak, Yank!"

The American looked at me, "Sorry sir. You the Limeys who arrived yesterday? The cloak and dagger boys?"

I smiled, "We do go behind the enemy lines, yes." I waved a hand at the sound of aeroplanes above us and the rattle and crash of anti-aircraft guns, "Does this happen often?"

"Regular as clockwork. Six Yaks fly over at exactly the same time, strafe and bomb us and then skedaddle before the aircraft from the carriers can be scrambled and then reach us."

I realised that jet aircraft were not the aircraft to use as an umbrella. "Do they do much damage?"

"Not really, sir. If they do hit anything it looks to be pure luck." Just then the all-clear sounded and we made our way out of the shelter. "Good luck, sir. My unit moves up the line today so I doubt I will see you again. My wife will get a kick out of this when I tell her I was talking to you guys. You sound just like Cary Grant you know!"

As we made our way back to our tents, I realised that we were the only British unit in this camp. It explained why we were such a novelty. I ate in the Officer's mess but the only reason was in the hope of seeing Colonel Wilding. No colonel was to be seen and so I headed for the admin building. Security was high and I had to show my papers. I was sent up some stairs and I waited in an ante-room where a sergeant and three female typists worked away. I did not have to wait long. The American was an older man He looked to have served in World War 2. He smiled and held out his hand, "Pleased to meet you, Major Harsker, welcome to Seoul. Sergeant, have a pot of coffee brought in."

We sat down and he smiled, "I worked with your unit in the last war. I have to say they impressed the hell out of me and now to meet someone with not only a V.C. but also a Distinguished Service Cross, well I am tickled pink!" The pot of coffee was brought in. The sergeant laid it and a sheet of paper on the desk and the Colonel said, "See that we aren't disturbed." As the sergeant left the Colonel said, "How do you take it?"

"As it comes sir, black."

He nodded approvingly, the only way to drink coffee. Now I am your liaison officer as well as, temporarily, your commanding officer. You are the first of other Commonwealth units. My job is to orientate you. In your case that is unnecessary as you have been in Korea longer than me! At the moment there are many officers who believe that we will be home by Christmas. Even some of the brass think that; they have begun an operation called 'Home by Christmas'. Stuff and nonsense. They kept saying that in the last one." I warmed to the Colonel. He was straight-talking and knew his business. He saw my look and smiled, "You will find, Major, that I am plain talking. I should have retired this year but they kept me on for this little shindig. So as long as I am here, I will do the best that I can! You have been attached to us to give us the ability to drop behind the lines. We are waiting for the Rangers to return and the 18th Airborne to arrive. This will only be a temporary appointment but we have a mission for you." He turned and took a wooden pointer and rapped a map behind his head. "A map of Korea before this little police action started!" He shook his head, "What fool came up with police action? As you can see the north of the border is a little light on detail and our forward units, when MacArthur gets the green light to invade, are going to find it a hard land. I know from your record that you don't need telling that. When the advance starts the roads are going to be jammed with the enemy. It took us six days to mop up the men in the area you crossed to get here."

"I saw evidence of heavy fighting."

"And that is why we are here. Seoul is a mess. This place was earmarked as a POW camp for Americans and other foreigners captured so far and there were a lot."

"What about the South Korean soldiers, sir?"

"You are thinking of your interpreter who was captured?" I nodded, "Don't hold your breath. Most are shot."

"So, we are going to invade?"

"We are but we await the UN to make the decision. If we do then we have a mission for you. There is a small town at Pyonggang. It is ten miles from the border and is an important crossroads. If we get the go-ahead then you will parachute in and place demolition charges on the road to Bokke which is just a couple of miles north of Pyonggang. You hide in the mountains until the advance reaches you." He smiled, "I suppose you could walk back south through the mountains."

"It would have to be a night-time drop in mountainous country. I have done those before, sir, and they are fraught with dangers. Won't our damaging the road slow our advance?"

"We are using tanks and half-tracks as the spearhead. We just need to slow down the North Korean reinforcements."

"When will we know, sir? I mean we need a time scale for this."

"Good question. I will give the order for the transport to be ready October 1st."

"Sir, that is two days away!"

"I am sorry. Major Rogers and his team are earmarked for another mission and this one was supposed to be Brevet Major Poulson's."

I sighed and sat back in my seat, "And from which direction will our forces be advancing?"

"The road comes from the south and west."

I nodded. That would help us. If we waited to the south and east, we should be able to avoid being hit by friendly fire. "And the airfield?"

"In Seoul; it is being repaired even as we speak. He spread his arms, "Look, Major, this is a tall order, I know that, but you of all people should know that the planners do not worry about small details such as how the hell can we do this? They just expect the job to be done. We have a good pilot. He dropped SOE behind the lines in France and we have good equipment. Have you a demolition specialist?"

"I know my men's names, sir, and that is about it. I need to get back and see them now. You will keep me informed, won't you?"

"As soon as I know anything then you will. The situation is dependent upon New York and the UN."

I stood, "If you could send the ordinance and equipment to our billet, sir, we can check it out and I will let you know of any shortfalls."

"Of course." He picked up a piece of paper, "And here is some good news. There are another ten men, including another officer, on their way to you. They landed last night."

I saw nothing on the way back for my mind was still reeling. Every Commando could operate a radio and set demolition charges but, in every section, there was one man who was a specialist. Scouse Fletcher had been my radioman for most of the war and Roger Beaumont was a genius with explosives. Commando Blackwood had been a competent radioman and I had had high hopes for Black and Hope. Now the three new men were dead or captured. As for the new men, they would be of little use until I was able to assess them. If they arrived the next day it would be too late to brief them but, at least, another officer would be handy

Commandos are not, by nature, lazy men and all of them were busy with their weapons when I arrived, "Cup of tea, sir?"

"Good idea Sergeant Major and bring one for yourself to my tent. We have a mission. The three of us need to talk about it first!"

He could tell, from my tone, that I was concerned, "Right sir. Corporal, go and get the Major a brew and bring it to the Major's tent."

"Righto, Sarn't Major."

When the two sat down on two upturned packing cases we had found I said, "Well we have a parachute drop behind enemy lines in two days' time." They both looked stunned. Both had served in the last war but this was hasty even by those standards. I smiled. "And it gets better. We have to drop in the mountains at night and blow up a road. Then we have to hide and wait until the advance reaches us."

Ken Thorpe nodded and he took out his pipe and began to fill it, "Then the rumours are true; we are invading."

I took out my pipe and began filling it too, "It looks that way. We need to know the skills of our men. So do we have a radioman?"

"Harry Ashcroft. He liked to mess about with short wave before he joined up. He was talking to me about it on the way over here."

"Good and an explosives specialist?"

They both sipped their tea as they wracked their brains. Ken Thorpe said, "As I recall Sam Williams did well on the course. It was in his file."

"Doing well and being a specialist are worlds apart but, unless there is someone better, then he will have to do and then we have the crucial question, who can make the jump?" We all knew that while all of us had trained to jump most regarded it as a box to tick and then forget about. I saw Ken Thorpe flush and look down. "Sergeant Major, the truth."

"I will be honest, sir, I am not keen but if I have to, I will come."

"Thanks for being forthright, Ken. How about you, Matt?"

He grinned, "I joined for an exciting life and I have completed six drops but none were in a war zone."

"Well, the first thing we need is to find six of these lads who can and want to jump."

"You aren't taking the whole section, sir?"

"No, Ken. It is not necessary. A radioman, someone to set the charges and a couple of lads to keep watch. That is all that I will need. Right, let's go and speak to them." We stood, "And we have ten men and an officer arriving in the next couple of days. Ken, until we see what he is like you had better keep being the adjutant."

"Right sir, and I am sorry about the jump!"

"Forget about it. That is why we have paratroopers."

All of the men were keen to jump, that much was obvious as soon as Corporal Dixon returned but I also realised that some of them were afraid for I saw it in their eyes. I did not need all of them and so I chose just five. I included Ashcroft and Williams as they had been identified as having skills but I was not certain that Sam was as confident as his answer suggested. I had learned to look in a man's eye and see the hidden terror. I softened the blow for the others.

"We will have other parachute drops but this one needs a small number of men. The rest can help us prepare."

Sergeant Major Thorpe and I sent them away to prepare their Bergens. We might have to sleep rough for a couple of nights and that meant camouflage netting, food and plenty of spare ammunition. I had chosen John Lofting and I gave him my sniper rifle and scope. You would have thought he had won the football pools. In the middle of the afternoon, a truck appeared and our equipment was delivered. When I saw Sam's face, I knew he was not confident about the explosives. I now regretted that I had allowed Roger Beaumont so much control over the demolitions. He was good but I should have kept my hand in. It could not be helped. The good news was that not only was Harry Ashcroft good on the radio but also his oppo Jack. I was glad I had chosen both of them. The afternoon flew by and I still had so much to do. I sent most of the men to eat while I sat with Sergeant Major Thorpe and Harry Ashcroft and went through the signals and codes we would use. They had to be right or we might risk being shot by our own side.

I ate in the Officer's Mess to enable me to speak with Colonel Wilding. He had told me, when I spoke to him, what time he ate. He was with a Major Jones and I saw the Intelligence flashes on his uniform. I could speak. "I have chosen my men, sir, there will be five of them. All that we now need is the time to check your equipment and then get to the airfield as early as we can"

"You aren't taking all of your men?" It was the Major who spoke.

"No Major, the more men you drop the more you risk losing. At the airborne drop on D-Day, one man tripped as he was heading along the aircraft and by the time he got up the stick was five miles from its drop zone. No sir, the fewer the better."

The Colonel nodded, "You know what you have to do better than any. I still have no further information but I will have transport to take you and your men to the field tomorrow afternoon. You might as well wait there. The code and passwords have not changed, it is just the timing of the operation which is in doubt."

"And when we are done, we return here?"

"For the time being this is your base. We are close to the airfield. This terrain makes travelling overland hard. Using an aeroplane is easier."

As I ate, I reflected that Sergeant Major Thorpe and the others who were reluctant to drop would have to get over that reluctance. We could afford no passengers. "And is there any word on the replacements you said were on their way?"

"As far as I know they are still on their way. You travelled those roads and know how clogged they are. They could be here tonight or in three days' time. Sorry Major, this is Korea!"

When I got back to our tents, I told the team what we would be doing. We went through all of the maps and I gave detailed instructions for the whole operation. It was another reason for taking the smallest team possible. They asked me questions and I saw that as a good thing. I made it clear that our task was very specific and also highly dangerous. If the advance was held up for any reason we could be hung out to dry and we had to be prepared to march all the way home!

"Sergeant Major, you will command until I return. The replacements will be here anytime and this will be our base for a while. Winter is coming and these tents will be chilly, to say the least. We had better scrounge and improvise."

The Sergeant Major nodded, "I have a feeling, sir, that the Americans will have huts brought here. They had them at Donbaek-ri but you are right, it will be cold and we had better prepare. Could you ask the Colonel if we are being sent winter uniforms?"

In normal circumstances, we would have our quartermaster requisition such equipment. "I have a feeling that we will be using American equipment."

Ken Thorpe nodded, "They have good gear, sir. Right lads, early night, we have a lot to do tomorrow. Are we going on the run again, sir?"

I nodded, "We did not manage a second one today so, yes, we go for a run at 0500!"

Chapter 3

The good night's sleep was interrupted at 0400 when a lorry pulled up outside our tents. I was woken by the noise and went outside in my shorts and vest. A Lieutenant snapped to attention, "Sir, Lieutenant Jacob Morrison and the replacements reporting."

"Major Harsker," I smiled, "At ease, Lieutenant, you are a sight for sore eyes." Sergeant Major Thorpe had emerged from the NCO's tent. "Sarn't Major, sort the men out. Lieutenant, this luxurious tent is the officer's quarters."

"I will get my gear, sir."

I went back in and lit the lamp. The tent was meant for more and was spacious, the Lieutenant had two beds to choose from. I began to dress for the run as I knew I would not be able to get back to sleep and, this way, I could chat with the Lieutenant. I could hear him outside shouting commands. He knew his business. I was sitting on my cot filling my pipe when he entered. I took him to be in his early twenties. He was dark and shorter than most men. I saw that he had a broken nose. Many Commandos had such noses; it came with the training. As much as I wanted to tell him of the mission, I knew this was not the right time. He had had a long journey and his mind would not be sharp. He needed to sleep.

I got the pipe going and said, as he unpacked, "Was it a bad journey?"

"Slow, sir. We ground through villages slower than we could have walked. Is the whole country like this?"

I realised he had just come from England and would have no idea of the terrain. "I am afraid so; Korea is made up of lots of mountains and little twisting roads. Did you join after the war?" I knew the answer would be yes but his reaction surprised me.

He stiffened, "Yes sir, I did!"

His tone had changed and I decided to discover the reason sooner, rather than later, "Is there a problem, Lieutenant?"

"Sorry sir, no sir. I am just tired."

"Listen, Jacob, is it?"

"My friends call me Jake, sir."

"And I hope that we can be friends. I am Tom. You and I are, at the moment, the only officers in this section. Tomorrow I will be leaving you in command while I drop behind enemy lines, so we need to be on the same page. I will ask again, Jake, is there a problem? My question was harmless. I asked all of the new men when they joined and why. I joined because we were fighting the Germans. That war is over so, why did you join?"

"Sir, I am a Jew!"

He said it as though he expected a reaction. I nodded, "Good for you but what has that to do with my question?" I saw that I had confused him. He was tired and I regretted beginning this conversation now.

His tone softened, "During the war, I encountered a lot of anti-Semitism, sir. I was called a Jew boy." He tapped his nose, "This was a result of a fight in school and not Commando training. My father was killed in the war. He was in the paratroopers and he was captured at Arnhem. When they found out he was a Jew he was taken away from the rest of the airborne division and shot. I decided to join up." He must have sensed another question for he added, quickly, "The Commandos have more chance of action and I wanted action."

My pipe had gone out and I took out my penknife to clean it. "Why?"

"Why sir? I wanted action and the Commandos seemed my best chance to get it."

"Why do you want action?" The last thing I needed was a death or glory boy as my second in command.

"Sir, I am twenty-two. When my enlistment is up, I will get a job and get married. I know that the North Koreans are not the Germans who killed my father but they are as close as I am going to get. I would have revenge. An eye for an eye."

I shook my head, "You are right they are not the same and if you think that killing North Koreans will exorcise whatever ghosts you have then you are wrong." I put the cleaned pipe on the spare cot and stood, "I am going for a run with the rest of the section. You get your head down. I will be leaving here sometime after noon. I will wake you before I go and give you your orders."

"Yes, sir. I can come on the run too, sir!"

I smiled, "I did the same journey you did. Sleep. You and the new men can run to your heart's content while we are behind enemy lines."

Corporal Dixon's voice came from outside the tent, "Major, the lads are ready!"

"Be right there." I turned to the Lieutenant, "Get some sleep." I joined my men, "Sarn't Major, join me at the front!"

As we ran, we talked. I kept looking at my watch to ensure that we were keeping good time but by speaking I kept the pace manageable. "Well?"

"The two NCO's know their business. Both joined after the war but they seem like good lads. The young lads are just that, young but the two of them reckon they are keen as mustard."

I sensed a but in his words. "Are you happy then, Sergeant Major?"

He looked behind him, "Perhaps we could chat later, eh sir?"

I knew that he wished to talk about the Lieutenant. "Quite and now we can pick up the pace."

We knocked eight minutes off the first time but Ken Thorpe was out of breath! I still had breath, "Well done, lads. Now have a shower, breakfast and then get your Bergens packed!" When they had gone, I gestured for the Sergeant Major to accompany me down the road which led to the rest of the, as yet, unoccupied tents. "I take it there were some comments about the Lieutenant?"

"Yes, sir, and I wouldn't mention it but I know the way you operate. The Lieutenant is more than a little standoffish. Sullivan and Lake, the sergeant and lance corporal, tried to offer him advice on the way over. They were on a transport and the Lieutenant kept his distance from the other officers. Admittedly they weren't commandos, but still."

"Thank you for confiding in me, Ken. Let us not judge him eh? It is up to us to make him part of this family. I will have a word with him before we leave."

After my shower, I headed for the Officers' Mess. Colonel Wilding was there and he grinned and held up a thumb. He had to have learned that from our lads in the war. "It is a go! You drop tonight and…"

"Tonight? We have not had time to check the chutes and speak with the aircrew."

"Nevertheless, it will be tonight. The transport will be here at noon. You have all afternoon to speak to the pilot. It is only a short flight. The ground troops are at their jumping-off points already and they will be going in at 0430. General MacArthur is worried about leaks of information. There are North Korean sympathisers here in the south and by acting so quickly he hopes to catch the North Koreans off their guard. There will be an aerial attack on the town at 0500 so you and your men need to be under cover before then. Set your charges to go off at 0505."

I hoped we had better timers than the ones we had used in the last war. I sighed, "Yes, sir but, for the record, in future, I would like more time to prepare."

"As I said, Major, this is just bad luck. The men who were earmarked for this would have had a whole week to get ready for it."

Those men were my men and I wondered how many had survived. I had put them to the back of my mind but I had not forgotten them. I gobbled my food and hurried back and when I arrived at our camp I went into my tent and began to pack my Bergen. The Lieutenant stirred and then woke, "Sorry, Lieutenant, I didn't mean to disturb you."

"I managed to sleep in the truck yesterday. I was not as tired as you thought, sir. Something up?"

"As I said last night, we have to drop behind enemy lines and plant demolition charges on a road."

He nodded, "You have a good man for that, sir?"

I shook my head, "Marine Williams is the best we have but this will be his first solo attempt."

"My background is engineering sir and I was top of the class when it came to demolitions."

"So was Williams."

"With respect sir, he is a Marine and I am an officer."

"Listen, Lieutenant, every man in my command is the same in my eyes. I began life as an enlisted man and worked my way up to officer."

"Sorry, sir, that came out the wrong way but I would be an asset on this raid and you know it."

He was right but I did not like it. It was always dangerous to introduce a new element, especially at this late stage.

His eyes pleaded with me and he used another argument, "And I have made ten parachute jumps. I was a member of a club before I joined up."

He looked keen and I confess that the thought of a more experienced demolition specialist not to mention an officer was appealing. His argument decided me. I nodded, "Get your gear sorted and then find Marine Williams. He has the explosives. You can share the load. I will speak with the Sergeant Major."

Ken Thorpe was surprised but he agreed with me that two demolition specialists could only help. "And one of the new lads, Tomlinson, is a radio specialist. I will give him the codes and passwords and he can talk to Ashcroft before you go."

We spent the rest of the morning checking that we had everything and ensuring that we all knew what everyone was doing. I took my Colt and its silencer. I made certain that I had plenty of grenades. I also took my Thompson which was well stocked with ammunition as I had been to the armoury. This was an American base and .45 bullets were plentiful. The men now had the Lee Enfield Mark 2. We had two Sten guns which were a little crude and nowhere near as good as the Thompson but we took one with us. We just needed the two guns as a back-up.

As we waited for the truck the Lieutenant and Williams were still checking the detonators and timers. Sergeant Major Thorpe looked worried, "Are you certain about this, sir?"

"The planners have already tied our hands by sending us out so quickly with inexperienced men. In a perfect world, I would refuse to go, Sarn't Major, but we both know that this is an imperfect world. You and I have a hard task ahead of us. We have to turn these keen young men into professionals, without getting them killed."

He nodded, "Just come back safe, sir. I am getting too old to lose good officers!"

"Don't worry, Ken, I will do my best! I have three children to watch grow!"

Just then the truck arrived. I turned and shouted, "Come on Lieutenant, we have an aeroplane to catch!"

As I climbed in the cab the driver said, "The Colonel is at the field already, sir."

"Good."

The field was close and we were there within twenty minutes. I saw transports, fighters and fighter bombers. It had taken some time to recapture Seoul and MacArthur did not intend to relinquish it easily. There was a Quonset Hut which the driver drove towards. "The Colonel said to have your men put their gear in there and I am to take you to the tower."

"Right." I clambered out and said, "Lieutenant, take the men into the hut and have my gear unloaded. I will be back shortly."

"Don't worry sir, Marine Williams and I have plenty to do yet!" I saw Williams roll his eyes.

We drove the two hundred yards or so to the tower. I left the cab and climbed the stairs. A flight sergeant pointed me to a room. The Colonel and the two pilots were studying a map. "Ah, Major Harsker, this is Captain Waring and Lieutenant Stonebridge. They are taking you in tonight."

They saluted and the captain said, "This is all a bit sudden, eh sir?"

"You could say that. What height are you flying in at?"

"Not as high as we would like, sir, the mountains are a little high but we appreciate that you have to be low to make certain that you hit the target."

"What strength is the wind?"

"That is the other issue, sir, the North Koreans do not share their weather data but we estimate that it will be twenty to thirty miles an hour when you drop and it will reduce to five or ten by the time you are on the ground."

I had been studying the map while he had been talking, "I know it is asking a great deal but if you could fly south to north and use the road as a guide it might make our job easier. We can march down a road faster than down a mountain. We might well be a mile or two out. My lads are fit and we can run."

"We can try that but what we don't know is the strength of the air defences."

I laughed, "Captain, what we don't know would fill a hanger full of Dakotas!" He laughed too. "Whatever you can do to get us close would be appreciated."

The Colonel said, "It will be the 1st Marine Division which is the spearhead of the attack. They have been warned to look out for friendlies but…"

"I know, sir. Don't worry, we will be circumspect."

"Well, I will be off and leave you chaps to go over the finer details. I will be listening on the radio although as there will be radio silence until contact is made, I am hoping that I just listen to static. If not, it may presage a disaster!" With that cheerful thought, he left.

When he had gone, I said, "Look, Captain, if we are dropped too far north it will not be a disaster. We just have to stop reinforcements from the north. Just get us close to the road and not in the town and we will be happy bunnies!"

He laughed, "Don't worry, sir, I know my business. We will head west when we leave the field. We believe that the North

Koreans are watching the airfield. This way was can deceive them and gain height so that I can bring her around to the right course. It adds time for the flight but we are close enough for it not to matter." I nodded. It was a sound strategy. He lit another cigarette, "Sir, I think I have heard your name before. Wasn't your father an ace in the Great War?"

"He was."

"Then your brother must be the pilot he set up that company with."

"No, I have no brother, I am a pilot too."

"That explains a lot!" He laughed, "You know the problems we face, then?"

"As well as anybody. I am happy to be in your hands, Captain, and I will go and see my men. We have a long twenty-four hours ahead of us!"

I returned to my men who looked up expectantly when I entered, "It could be a little windy up there. "First things first and then we will check and pack our chutes." I had learned that packing your own parachute was the best way to ensure that it opened. I made certain that I had their attention. In my head, I had a checklist and I ran through it. "Lieutenant, make sure that you and Marine Williams split the explosives. detonators and timers between you then if we are separated we have a chance of pulling off this magic act." They nodded. "To that end, Williams you will be right behind me at the front. Lieutenant, you will bring up the rear."

"Sir."

"Ashcroft, you and the radio will be behind Williams. Corporal, you will be next, then Smith, Lofting and Fox. When we go out, we try to do it so that we are as close together as possible. I have asked the pilot to take us from south-east to north-west along the valley and the road we will be using. It means if we are strung out, we can use the road as a marker. Marine Lofting, you will be northern lookout along with Fox. You watch the road to the north. Corporal, you and Smith will watch the road to the south. I hope we are undisturbed but with our air cover during the day I know that the North Koreans will move men during the night."

The Lieutenant said, "And if that happens, sir?"

"Then we think on our feet! Now pack your chutes."

There was total silence as we packed our parachutes. I noticed that a couple of the men watched and then copied me as I packed mine. I had been the same the first time I had done this. They had all done this, at least once, but it was more reassuring to watch a veteran do it. When they were all packed and stacked, I said, "I know it is a little late for this but we have been pressured into this operation. Were you all taught to improvise booby traps from hand grenades and parachute cord?"

Their blank looks gave me the answer.

I nodded, "When we land, do not throw away your parachutes." I went to my Bergen and took out some parachute cords. "These are from my last jump in World War Two!" Taking a grenade from my battle vest I showed them how to use the cord to trigger the grenade. "You can use paths, stones, vehicles, anything. Booby traps saved me and my men on many an occasion. We are few and the enemy is not! The parachute itself makes great cover in snow and, remember, winter is just around the corner. In addition, you can use it for bedding." I reached into my Bergen and took out some summer camouflage netting, "And I have this from the war. When we get back, I will have the Colonel source us some."

The Lieutenant said, "Why did they not teach us this in training, sir?"

"For the simple reason that we were never taught it either. We learned in the field and when new men came, we passed it on. You, as you progress through the ranks, will pass it on to others and, I have no doubt, you will learn new skills. We play a dangerous game, Lieutenant, for we are behind the lines more than any other unit. If you want to survive then use any means at your disposal."

Corporal Dixon nodded, "The Major is being modest, lads. In the last war the Germans had an order, the Hitler Order; all Commandos, even in uniform, were to be shot!"

Sam Williams said, "So you were never caught then, sir?"

"Oh, I was caught, in North Africa by the SS but I escaped!" I made it sound simple but Bill Hay and I had been lucky and we both knew it. "Anyway, check your bags and then get some rest."

My words had the effect of focussing them on the mission. All of them assiduously packed their bags. I repacked mine and then applied the camouflage to my face and hands. That done, I sat on my chute and lit my pipe. Would this be the last team I would lead? I had thought that the section which I had first led at Donbaek-ri would have been the last but I was wrong. Where were they? There was no Hitler Order but I doubted that they would be treated well. As our men in Burma had discovered, the eastern mentality and attitude to war was different from that of the west.

My pipe had just gone out when Lieutenant Stonebridge and the Flight Sergeant came in, "It is time, sir." The windowless building had hidden the fact that night had fallen.

"Come on lads. Chutes on," Matt Dixon took charge and watched each man for me. We all donned our parachutes and we each checked the next man's. We would do so again before we jumped. You could never check the parachute too many times.

We walked across the tarmac to the waiting Dakota. I entered first and jammed my Bergen and machine gun under the bench. Williams sat opposite me and Matt Dixon next to me. We had plenty of room. The Flight Sergeant waited until we were all seated before he closed the hatch and took his seat. There was lighting but it was, perforce, dim and just cast an eerie glow on the interior. When we were close to the target it would change to red.

Corporal Dixon could see the nervous looks on some of the faces and he tried to make it easier for them, "You know that the Major can fly?" Their faces all turned to me. "That's right, isn't it, sir? You can fly one of these."

"Yes, Corporal. They are a solid aeroplane but hopefully, I will not be required to give a hand!" They laughed and the tension was eased. "If we had longer in the air, I would be so confident I would have a nap but, as it is…"

Just then the engines fired up. I saw the Flight Sergeant plug in his headset. Conversation would be difficult for a while. The pilot knew his business and we were soon in the air. I felt the aeroplane bank and heard the engines working hard as we climbed. We had mountains to cross and then he would descend. It was a relatively short journey and we would not be in the air for long. When we heard the steady beat of the engines, I knew we were at the right altitude. I looked at my watch. I estimated that we would have less than forty-five minutes of flying time.

I saw the Flight Sergeant nod and then stand. I put on my cap comforter and parachute helmet. He unplugged his intercom and after walking to the hatch he turned the light to red. I stood and slid my Bergen and gun from under the seat. I took my hook and clipped it on the rail. Then I hung my machine gun from my battle vest and put my Bergen so that it was before me with the straps behind my arms. The Flight Sergeant checked my hook and nodded. I heard a click behind me and then Marine Williams tapped me on the shoulder. My chute was fine. I turned and checked his. The Flight Sergeant came back down the line and plugged his intercom back in. He gestured for me to move towards the door. We all shuffled down. I could feel Williams' Bergen in my back and knew that my words had been heeded. I knew when we were getting close for the Flight Sergeant opened the door and there was a rush of cold air. Through the open door, all that I could see was the black of night. The red light above the door would turn off and the green one light when it was time. With my arms wrapped around the Bergen, I stood as close to the door as I could. The American's arm was across the door and I could hear the wind whistling. The sergeant was listening intently to the pilot.

No matter how many times you did this it was always a critical time just before you stepped out in to darkness. You relied on the skill of the pilot and his crew. The Flight Sergeant grinned, nodded, and, as the light turned green, moved his hand away. I was ready and I stepped out. The shock of the cold and wind hit me. I resisted the temptation to watch for the chute opening; I looked, instead, at the ground. I could see nothing yet. I heard the crack as the chute opened and, as I was jerked upright, my descent slowed. There would be little point in looking above me for all I would see would be the canopy. If all had gone well then my men would be behind me and following my flight. I took hold of the cords I would use to steer. The wind was from the south and I saw below me something which indicated buildings for a light flashed and then darkened. That would be a door opening. That helped me to locate the long black snake which was the road. I realised that I was being taken too far to the east and I adjusted my parachute and saw that I was now following the road. I had to hope that the light I had glimpsed had been Pyonggang. It did not really matter where we landed on the road so long as we reached it.

I must have been five hundred feet or so from the ground when I saw, in the distance far to the north, a dim glow. It had to be vehicles coming down the road. This would be a race to land, gather our parachutes and then hide! I concentrated on my landing. I adjusted the cords so that I was aligned with the road which was mercifully straight although I had no idea what the surface would be like. I braced myself and as my feet hit the ground began to run. The wind behind caught my parachute and I began to reel it in. As soon as it deflated, I was able to stop. I could not see the headlights any longer but they were coming in our direction. I bundled the chute and then, after dropping my Bergen, I took off my harness and put the whole lot into my Bergen. I slung my Tommy gun over my back and took out my Colt. I fitted the silencer as I turned. Williams was off to the side and was struggling to get his parachute under control. The Corporal and Ashcroft had also made the road.

I ran to the Corporal, "Dixon, there is a convoy heading down the road. Get the men under cover. I will go and help Williams."

I ran and grabbed Williams' parachute which was in danger of inflating again. "Sorry, sir. I came down fast and I thought I was going to hit you."

"Don't worry. It is my fault. I should have realised you had more weight with the explosives. Put your chute in your bag and take cover. There are trucks heading down the road."

I ran back to the road. I saw, way in the distance. the dimmed lights of North Korean trucks. Corporal Dixon ran up to me, "All the birds have landed. They are all taking cover."

"Then let us join them."

We hurried to join Williams who had found a jumble of rocks behind which to hide. I risked looking down the road and I was gratified that I could not see my men. I could now hear the trucks as they laboured up a slight slope.

I could not see my men but I hoped that they could all hear me. "They are close. Cock your weapons but don't use them until I give the command." I had no idea how many trucks there were. If it was just one or even two, we might have risked an ambush but that would jeopardise the operation. I ducked back down and listened. The engine noise grew louder and then there was a sort of echo as they neared us. I was able to count the trucks from their engine noise. There were six trucks and the last vehicle sounded like a GAZ, the Korean equivalent of a Jeep. I had driven one and knew the sound. Then the trucks receded south. I risked standing and could see nothing so I said, "On me!" I hurried back to the road. "Corporal, gather them here. Set the vanguard and rearguard. Williams, when the Lieutenant arrives bring him to me."

I hurried up the road. I knew what I was looking for but not where to find it. I had to estimate where I had heard the echoing noise. It had been a culvert or bridge. I went to the side of the road where I found the drainage ditch. It would be a perfect place to leave charges. The Lieutenant and Williams found me when I dropped to the bottom of the water-filled ditch.

"Sir?" I heard the urgency in that one word. It was now 0300 and we had less than two hours to plant the charges but I had found the perfect place.

"Here, Lieutenant, we have a culvert under the road. There is a stream. I heard the corrugated iron echoing when the trucks drove over it. You won't need to dig and you can use the rocks to channel the explosion upwards. Can I leave you two to it?"

His teeth shone white against his camouflage as he grinned, "Yes sir! This will be the work of a moment."

"Take all the time you like, Lieutenant, but get it right. When they are set, head back to Ashcroft and the Command Post."

I ran back down the road. I was wearing my rubber-soled shoes rather than my boots. When winter kicked in, they would be redundant. I passed Lofting and Fox, "You two can wait up ahead where the Lieutenant is laying his charges. When he is done follow him to the CP."

The rest of my men apart from Smith and the Corporal were with Ashcroft. "Did the radio survive?" They were a lot less bulky than the ones we had used in the last war.

"Yes, sir but the proof will be when I try to use it."

"This is the Command Post. Cock your weapons and keep watch. I will not be long."

"Where are you off to, sir?"

I could hear the worry in his voice, "Don't worry, Marine, I am just going to find us a way out." I took out my compass and began to walk eastwards. We had to get as far away from the road as we could. I saw the side of the valley rise rapidly to some peaks. I took a course to the south and east. It was a risk but I wanted to make certain that we would be close enough to the town to be able to see when the Marines had captured it. This was rough ground and had, as far as I could see, never been farmed. I suppose animals might have grazed but there appeared to be more rock than things which grew. I kept turning to keep an eye on the road. We had to be far enough away so that we would not be seen but close enough so that if the explosives failed to go off then we could do something about it. I reached a steep part. There was no trail to be seen but there were some enormous boulders. I guessed they must have fallen from above at some time. There was no direct way in and so I had to climb over them. I found a perfect place to hide where the huge boulders circled a void; it looked like an animal den. I climbed back out and headed back to the road. I checked my watch. It was 0345; the attack would be starting in forty-five minutes.

To my relief, all but the Corporal and Rafe Smith were at the CP. "Marine Fox, go and fetch the men watching the road. Well, Lieutenant?"

The charges are set, sir. I used four timers. They will go off at five-minute intervals starting at 0505 hours. I thought that would guarantee an explosion. If the first one fails to detonate one of the others must. I didn't fancy returning to see why they hadn't gone off."

I saw the fear on his face. Had he made a mistake? I smiled, "Good thinking, Lieutenant. Now we have a thirty-minute hike to somewhere we can watch the fireworks. It will soon be dawn and I am not certain if they have a sky watch." A sky watch was an aeroplane which patrolled. The last three men joined us and I pumped my arm and led them to the jumble of rocks. It did not take me as long as it had the first time as I knew where I was headed.

"Fox, up on the top rock and you have first watch."

"Sir." The West Countryman scrambled up the rock.

I opened my Bergen and began to cut the cords from the parachute. The others saw me and copied my action. I did it to keep us all occupied. Waiting was hard enough but waiting for explosives to detonate was nerve-wracking. When the crack came from the south, it made us all start. The single crack was followed by the sound of artillery and tanks. The attack had begun. This would be well south of Pyonggang but soon there would be men heading from the north.

"Fox, you had better come down. The air attack will start soon and night bombing is never as accurate as daylight bombing." To be fair it was better than it had been and this would be dawn but a jet travelling at more than six hundred miles an hour can miss a target by a mile if the pilot makes the slightest of mistakes.

The sound of combat grew and I looked at my watch. I heard the jets at 0455 as they screamed from the south. Sam Williams had found a crack in the rocks where he could see the road and he shouted, "Sir, I can see trucks coming from the north and a tank!"

We could do nothing about this. We had set our charges to go off at the right time but the reinforcements might have passed the culvert before they exploded. Then we heard the bombs dropped from the aeroplanes as they exploded. I had my hands over my ears but some of the young lads had not. They would find it hard to hear for a while. The air attack lasted less than ten minutes and the Lieutenant's strategy paid off. Sam was watching the road and his watch. He shouted above the noise of the bombs and the firing from the town, "The first timer has not exploded, sir, and the leading jeep is almost over the culvert, sir!"

I saw a nervous Lieutenant staring at his watch as though he was willing the next detonator to explode. The last jet screamed away south and suddenly there was an explosion.

An excited Sam Williams shouted, "The tank sir! We blew up a tank and the truck behind has caught fire and is in the crater."

"How many vehicles got across?"

"A jeep and a truck sir. They have stopped and they are rushing back to help the others."

"Ashcroft, get on the radio and give them the code word. Smith, climb on the top and use the glasses, Williams has a restricted view." I handed him my binoculars and he clambered up.

It took him a minute or two to get up and focus the glasses. "There are three trucks and a second tank, sir. It looks like they are going to try to cross that stream. Hey up!" There was an enormous explosion.

"What was that Smith?"

"Looks like the ammunition in the damaged tank exploded, sir. The tank was a mess before but now it is destroyed and it looks like the shrapnel tore through the canvas of the trucks."

I felt relief. That meant just one truck, a GAZ and a tank had escaped. I should have known that our luck could not last. Perhaps Smith was careless and light reflected from my binoculars, I will never know but he said, "They have seen something. The tank is coming over here! Heads! The tank has fired!"

We were now trapped. The truck and the tank might not get to Pyonggang but they would make do with us!

Chapter 4

Our little hidey-hole had now become a potential death trap and we had to get out quickly. "Everyone, get out!" We had no weapons capable of taking out a tank. Our only hope was to climb where the tank could not get us and then try to pick off the infantry as they attempted to winkle us out. "Climb up the slopes and find places to hide!"

The tank's gun fired again and its machine gun began to fire but they were firing blindly at our position. The ground was uneven and the bullets and tank shell flew into the air and smacked into the valley side. The men in this convoy were not veterans. I made certain that I was the last one out of the den. I took out two hand grenades and some of the parachute cord. My men had taken the natural route up the slope and I followed them; it looked like a path and I could use it. The bullets were still being fired wildly and I was confident that they would not hit me.

"Hurry up, sir!"

"Corporal, don't worry about me. Get them under cover. It is the infantry we worry about." I placed one grenade under a rock and tied some cord to its pin. I tied the other end to the pin of a second grenade and jammed that in a jumble of rocks on the other side. It was at boot height. Stepping over it, I took my Thompson and Bergen and raced up after my men. The infantrymen were now catching the tank and their bullets, as they stopped to fire, were more accurate. I saw that the Lieutenant and the Corporal had found some shelter behind a few large boulders. As I climbed the slope which was quite steep at this point, I shouted, "Marine Lofting, use the sniper rifle! Take out the officers and sergeants!"

"Sir!"

The .303 cracked and I heard a cry from below me. That was the difference between novices and veterans, Peter Davis would have already downed three or four! Gaining in confidence my sniper sent four more rapid rounds. Corporal Dixon shouted, "Right, lads, give the Major covering fire." Bullets from the tank's machine gun now grew closer to me. It had stopped and with a stable platform was more accurate. I looked up and saw that the ground above my men was covered in scrubby shrubs. It was not loose soil.

I threw myself behind the rock; Sam Williams sheltered there. "Have you no ammunition, Williams?"

"Yes, sir!"

"Then use the gun. Fire at the sergeants and officers."

"But sir, there is a tank!"

"And we can't do anything about the tank so let us deal with the infantry eh? The tank can't drive up here!"

"Right, sir, sorry sir."

"Ashcroft, get on the radio and give our position. Tell them we are under attack from a tank and ask for air support."

"Yes, sir."

"And the rest of you, fire at the infantry!"

I took out my Thompson and cocked it. The infantrymen were approaching the rocks behind which we had sheltered. It was about four hundred feet from us and my Thompson did not have the range. I sent a burst anyway to distract them and the bullets made splinters fly from the rocks. The tank's gun fired and hit the hillside above me. Soil, branches and leaves cascaded down. It was as I thought, they were novices too. I pulled a grenade from my battle vest and hurled it high in the sky.

"Grenade!"

It had a six-second fuse and it exploded in the air above the infantrymen who had just reached the rock. The shrapnel scythed through them and made half take cover while the other half ran for the path. As the booby trap was triggered the two grenades cut down half of the ones close to the path. My men gained confidence and I saw their training kick in as they aimed and fired without panic.

Ashcroft shouted, "Sir, they are sending aeroplanes!"

"Good, now remember your training and think back to how you were taught. Breathe, aim and fire; one man at a time! We have cover and we have better weapons. We are Commandos!" I had half a magazine left and I aimed the gun over the top of the rock behind which I sheltered and fired a burst at the path which led up the slope. It was optimistic but the ricocheting bullets made the survivors take cover. I could see that Lofting was good. Each time a sergeant or an officer raised his head a bullet hit him. It demoralised the others. Then the tank got lucky. It hit the undergrowth above us and brought down a small landslide of small rocks and soil. All of us were showered with it. None of us were hurt but all were unsighted and that allowed the North Koreans to advance closer. I put the Thompson over the top and sprayed, blindly. I took a grenade and hurled that over too. I knew in that moment that I had much work to do with my section. I was the only one who had reacted.

Then I heard the roar of jet engines and a Lockheed P80 Shooting Star screamed in from the south. It gave a burst from its guns and then climbed. I knew what he was doing. He was assessing the threats. The North Koreans wasted ammunition firing after him. I shouted, "Get your heads down!"

The jet had banked and turned. He came in on exactly the same alignment except this time he used his bombs. They must have straddled the tank for there was an enormous explosion. The ground shook and it was hard to hear anything for the concussion. As soon as I could I raised my head. I saw the jet make its last run and start to strafe the tank and the GAZ.

I shouted, "Pour it into them!" I had a few bullets left in my magazine and I fired at the North Korean survivors who were still at the bottom of the slope. Lofting's rifle cracked and men fell. The dozen or so survivors fled north. "Anyone hurt?" It was only as I asked that I realised I had not assigned a medic. John Hewitt had been my medic in the war. I was slipping. Perhaps coming back to the Commandos had been a mistake.

Corporal Dixon shouted, "No, sir."

As I changed my magazine I shouted, "Right. Let's get down from here. Lofting, you watch us until we reach the road. Watch for Koreans playing dead. When we reach the road then you can join us!"

"Yes, sir! Nice rifle and scope, sir!"

I led the way down through the smoke from the burning tank. The bombs must have exploded both the ammunition and the petrol tank. There were more than thirty dead men. I am not sure how many we killed and how many were collateral damage from the exploding tank but the operation had been worthwhile. Had we not damaged the road then there would have been two tanks and four truckloads of reinforcements for the town. The Americans would still have taken it but it would have been harder. In my head, I was writing the report. It was important for Intelligence to know that the North Koreans were moving men at night. There were none left alive between us and the road. A few carrion birds were already picking at the pieces of flesh littering the ground by the exploding culvert. After I had ascertained that we were the only ones left alive, I signalled for Lofting. Had this been the last war we would have scavenged weapons and ammunition from the enemy. The North Korean equipment as not worth taking.

"Ashcroft, get on the radio and tell base that we are at the site of the ambush and that we will wait here."

"Sir."

I waited until Lofting joined us before I slung my Thompson and took out my pipe. Ashcroft said, "Sir, they say that we have taken the town and the Marines will be heading up the road soon."

"Then we might as well walk back to the town. We have to find some way to get back to Seoul."

The Lieutenant, who had not spoken since the charges had exploded asked, "Won't there be transport for us, sir?"

I shook my head, "In a perfect world, yes, but we are one small unit in a foreign army. I am guessing we will have to improvise."

As we marched down the road, I reflected that the operation had been a success in other ways. I had learned the strengths and weaknesses of my men. Lofting, Dixon and Ashcroft were the successes. The Lieutenant and the slow reactions of my men were the failures.

Smith was on point, a hundred yards ahead of us and he shouted, "Vehicles, sir, coming up the road. They look like tanks."

"They are ours so sling your rifles over your shoulders. These lads might shoot first and ask questions later. Move to the side of the road."

I recognised the M4 Sherman. They had been the workhouse in the last war and they were more than a match for the tanks the North Koreans were using. The tank halted next to me. I saw that they had armoured personnel carriers and half-tracks. The Captain in the tank saluted, "Are you the British Commandos we were told to watch out for?"

"Yes, Captain. The remains of the convoy are a mile or so ahead."

"Thanks for clearing it, sir." He leaned into the turret, "Right, McGinty, let's get back into the war."

The column heading north seemed to go on forever. Sabres appeared overhead and raced north. They would be heading for Bokke. I saw the smoke rising from the buildings in Pyonggang and already the Americans were clearing bodies. A rough compound had been fashioned and there were Korean prisoners being herded. I sought an MP. There were some of them directing traffic.

"Lieutenant, we have been behind enemy lines and we are heading back to Seoul. Is there any transport available?"

He shook his head, "The prisoners will be taken back tomorrow, sir, but everything is going north."

I had been expecting that. "Are there any North Korean vehicles?"

He looked perplexed but his sergeant said, "Yes sir, there are three of four of their little pieces of junk that look like a jeep."

I nodded, "GAZ! Where are they?"

"Follow me, sir. I will take you." As we walked, he talked. "Were you the guys who blew up the road?" I nodded. He looked at my handful of men. "You guys are like Rangers then eh sir?"

I smiled, "Yes, Sergeant, we are like your Rangers."

He took in the weapons my men carried and said, "I think I would like a little more firepower if I was behind the lines."

"We improvise, Sergeant."

We had reached what looked like a military building. It had been shelled and there was a burned-out North Korean tank and two damaged trucks but there were also three GAZ vehicles which looked intact. "All yours, sir, but they don't look like they would get very far."

"You would be surprised, Sergeant. Thank you." I turned as he left to return to his unit. "Take off your packs. Let us see if any of them go. Anyone good with engines?"

Rafe Smith said, "I had a motorbike, sir, and I like messing around with engines."

"That is a start. While Smith and I check out the transport the rest of you find food and fuel. Lieutenant, Corporal, I leave that to you." Once again, I saw the hesitation on the Lieutenant's face but Matt Dixon took charge. I dropped my Bergen and machine gun and went to the nearest GAZ. I opened the filler cap. It had fuel and that was a start. When it started first time, I knew that we could get back to Seoul. It was more than ninety miles but even if the others did not work, we could cram ourselves in the GAZ. Luckily the GAZ looked almost identical to the American jeep and with no markings I hoped that our uniforms would prevent friendly fire.

Rafe Smith grinned, "Well done, sir."

It took time but we got the second one going too. The third refused to start and so I had Smith syphon off the fuel and fill the tanks of the other two. It would be cramped but we would be able to fit our gear as well as the men in the two vehicles. The men began to arrive back. "Sorry sir, there was no fuel but we have some food." Matt Dixon shook his head, "It is Korean. One of the Katusas said this one was called Kimchi." He opened the lid of a metal tin and shook his head, "It stinks like it has gone off but he reckoned it was like gold!"

I nodded, Sergeant Heon had explained how they made it, "It is just cabbage, spices, vinegar and other ingredients. They ferment it for six months."

"Cabbage? It looks disgusting, sir."

I nodded, "We are Commandos, take it. Lieutenant, we will eat now and then split the food which remains between the two vehicles. Marine Smith will drive your GAZ and I will drive the other."

"Yes, sir."

We ate the fresher food first. There was some bread and we had four tins of bully beef. The Korean food was left untouched. I smiled; they would eat it when they had to! "I will lead. If you have a problem, Smith, then honk your horn or flash the lights although I am not sure how efficient either of them are. The roads have only just been cleared of North Koreans so keep your weapons handy."

The Lieutenant asked, "What about the bags?"

"Pack them around yourself or tie them to the bonnet." I needed to have a serious word with the Lieutenant when we reached base for he had much to learn. The journey back was not quick. There were columns of men and materiel heading up the road to exploit the breakthrough and we had to keep pulling over to allow them to pass us. We had seventy miles to go to reach the border. All the way along we saw evidence of the fighting. The Americans had used almost surgical skill to destroy potential strong points. The air superiority we enjoyed had made all the difference. We were stopped by MPs at every checkpoint. That was not a surprise. It was my English accent, rather than paperwork, which facilitated our passage. That and the fact that our uniforms showed signs of fatigue. It took six hours to travel the seventy miles. We had used some of the enforced stops as toilet breaks but, even so, by the time we pulled into the compound I was weary beyond words.

We were admitted a little more quickly this time, partly because there was now less traffic coming in. I said to the sergeant, "Tell the Colonel we are back but, unless he is desperate, I would like to save the debrief until tomorrow."

"Yes, sir."

We parked the two Korean vehicles behind our tents. They were a handy little runabout and despite their condition had not faltered during the ninety-odd miles home. "Clean and check your weapons before you go to get some food. Well done. The mission went as well as I might have expected but there are lessons to be learned."

"Sir!"

The rest of the men crowded around the team to ask questions. Lieutenant Morrison headed into our tent and Sergeant Major Thorpe approached. He was tapping the ash from his pipe, "I wasn't expecting you back so soon, sir. I can see you haven't lost your touch."

I smiled, "Yes, Ken, we were lucky."

He lowered his voice, "And how did they do?"

"Alright, but they don't have the reactions of the original team. We need to drill into them that they have to be ready to fight no matter what happens." I told him about the North Korean attack. "We need lessons in setting booby traps and we had better have a few hand to hand sessions."

"Sir, I will head to the canteen and make sure they have food for you."

I went into the officers' tent and closed the flap. Lieutenant Morrison had lit the lamp, "How did you think it went, Jake?"

He looked me directly in the eye and shook his head, "Not good, sir, and I am speaking personally."

I smiled, "Then that is a start. Had you thought it all went well I would have been worried. Corporal Dixon is a good man but he is an NCO. We get paid more to be officers and to lead. I didn't see you leading."

"I was afraid of getting it wrong, sir."

"Hesitation means you have got it wrong. The men need you to lead. What would have happened had I been incapacitated? What would you have done?"

He shook his head, "I hope the right thing, sir, but I don't honestly know."

I appreciated his honesty, "You are the only other officer. You have to be ready to take command if I fall." He nodded. "How did Williams do?"

"Keen but even greener than me, sir."

"Then work with him every chance you get. If you are shot, we will have a replacement."

He looked shocked and said, "That seems a little harsh, sir."

"It is the way of the world, Jake. I will spend time with you and try to give you some tips but your best bet would be to watch and then emulate. Now when your weapons are cleaned off you go and get some food."

"What about you, sir?"

"I have a report to write." It was one aspect of leadership I did not like. I put the pen and paper on the side table and then cleaned my guns. It helped to clear my mind and I liked having perfect weapons. When I picked one up, I knew it would fire!

The Lieutenant was finishing his meal when I arrived. The cooks had saved me pork chops, gravy, potatoes and sweetcorn. I ate it all and used some bread to mop up the gravy. The young Lieutenant watched me patiently, "Sir, when that avalanche came down weren't you afraid?"

"What of?"

"Being buried alive, sir."

"It could have happened I suppose but a greater threat was the enemy. I was the only one who used grenades; why?"

He shook his head, "I don't know, sir."

"They are a handy little weapon and the closer you are to an enemy the handier they are for they spread shrapnel and can take out as many men in one go as a magazine fired from a Lee

Enfield. Remember that. Always take at least half a dozen with you."

"But the weight!"

"Will save your life."

As we walked back, he said, "You know sir, I am not certain how useful our training was! I feel ill-prepared."

"That is because you are remembering the parts and not the whole. When they sent you on your long run and asked you to get back to base that was the real training."

"It was a game, sir."

"And there you are wrong. It was giving you the opportunity to practice something which is very dangerous in a safe manner. Tomorrow is a new day. Let's all start afresh eh? We have a run at 0500!"

His mouth dropped open and I laughed.

Chapter 5

I confess that I was not ready for a run but I had the whole section to think about. The run was not just about becoming fitter it was a way to build a team; when you ran together it was as though you became one being. Our time was three minutes slower than the last one. The men who had been with me on the raid had an excuse, but not the rest.

When we got back, as they huffed and puffed, I pointed an accusing finger at them all. "Not good enough! We will be out again this afternoon. I have to go to the debrief. I will leave the NCO's to work with all of you on basic skills such as setting booby traps, hand to hand combat and hiding in plain sight. When I return Lieutenant Morrison and Marine Williams will work on demolitions and I want the rest of you to come with a list of the five best skills you have as a Commando!"

I saw the perplexed looks on their faces. Sergeant Major Thorpe and I had discussed this and he would give them some pointers. I needed specialists and fast! Colonel Wilding beamed when he saw me, "Like a knife through butter, Major! You and your guys did well and our advance elements are already closing with the North Korean capital! The optimists may well be right and this might be over by Christmas!"

The words did not inspire me and my heart sank. I had heard the same optimism in World War Two and it had always been misplaced. The plan had been a good one and we had caught the North Koreans unawares but they would fight back. I nodded, "Yes sir. I thought I would give you my oral report first."

"Of course, and then you and your men can enjoy a few days' rest."

Shaking my head, I said, "No sir! No rest for us as we made too many mistakes."

"Mistakes? But you achieved all of your objectives."

"And we were lucky! I have learned, Colonel, that a man has only so much luck and it is better to save that for the times when the training and the preparation do not help." He nodded and I gave him my report. I left promising him the written version by the next morning. The meeting had taken a couple of hours and I saw that Sergeant Major Thorpe had all of the men working. The raid had injected urgency and purpose into the section. The ones who had been on the raid had told the others of the action and it acted as a spur. The exception was Lieutenant Morrison. Marine Williams was studying the field manual and I saw a pile of unused demolitions close by him.

I said nothing to him about the Lieutenant as that would be unfair to both of them, "How is it going, Sam?"

He grinned, "I reckon I have sussed out why that first charge did not go off." He proffered a timer. "See this one, sir, if you look at it closely you can see a tiny kink in the cover. I think that caused the problem. It was the way we carried them, see, sir. They were crushed together in our bags. Now if we had packed them separately then it might not have happened. Anyroad up, next time we use them I will know what to look for. You feel such a fool when something like that happens, eh sir? Sorry I didn't spot it."

An ordinary soldier had spotted what an officer had not, "It is not your fault Williams. Well done. "

"Will we have to jump again, sir?"

"Why, Williams? Are you afraid?"

He laughed, "No sir! It was fun! It is just that if we do, I will need to work out how to protect the gear when we drop."

"Well done, carry on." I entered the tent and the Lieutenant was lying on his bed and smoking. I closed the flap. It was not perfect but it would have to do. I sat on my bed and took out my pipe. Cleaning and filling it would keep me calm when I spoke with Morrison. I waited until I had the pipe going before I took out my Colt and disassembled it. There was an order to the cleaning of a gun which I found calming.

The Lieutenant sat up and stubbed out his cigarette. I laid the parts of the Colt on the bed and took the pipe from my mouth, "I thought I asked you to work with Williams on the demolitions, Lieutenant."

"We had a look, sir, and I saw nothing that would have indicated a problem. Probably a faulty fuse."

I nodded and sucked on the pipe. This was the last of the rum-infused tobacco and it was smoking well, "Williams has found the fault while you were resting."

"What sir?" he sat bolt upright.

"A kink in a timer. It happened because they were not packed well enough. Williams saw that and apologised but it should have been you who saw it." He hung his head, "When you were at school, did you do well?"

"At school sir?" I nodded and he beamed, "Always top of the class, sir. The same at Officer Training!"

I used my penknife to loosen the ash at the top of the pipe and drew on it, "All of which shows that you are a clever man but you are not transferring that to the job in hand. Sergeant Major Thorpe is out there ensuring that the men are all on task and you are sat here doing nothing. You are my deputy whether you like it or not. If I had been killed out there would the mission have succeeded?"

I saw him begin to retort and then he paused and he ran through the raid. Realisation set in and he shook his head, "No, sir, but it is different when there are real bullets flying around!"

"They used real bullets when you trained!"

"We all knew they were over our heads. The other night was different. We could have been killed."

I laid the pipe down and began to clean the Colt's component parts, "We can all die, Lieutenant. I buried enough friends in the last one to know that. When a soldier goes to war then death is always a possibility. It is the extra weight you pack in your Bergen. If you worry about it then you increase the chances of it coming true." He nodded. "Now get out there and find out what every man is doing. You need to know these men as well as any of your family, for that is what they are, your family. Get to know Williams. He is a good Commando and he can handle the demolitions but he needs you to help him."

"Yes, sir. Sorry, sir."

"Sorry does not get the job done!"

I cleaned all of my weapons and then went outside. Sergeant Major Thorpe had a brew going and he handed me a mug as I stepped out of the tent. He smiled, "The lads have taken your words to heart." He looked pointedly at Lieutenant Morrison, "All of them, sir." To the Sergeant Major, we were all lads.

"Good. The Americans seem to think this is going well and that it will be over by Christmas."

He laughed, "Aye, sir, and we have both heard that before, eh? The Koreans fought well when they charged us. They are not cowards; we just caught them with their pants down. It will get harder, sir. Any more missions planned?"

"Not that I have heard but I suspect that when the advance is held up then they will need us again. Until then we keep up the training. We will take the men out after two."

Sergeant Major Thorpe gestured up at the clouds which were gathering, "And I reckon we will have a drop or two of rain too. We are heading for winter sir and this country looks like it might be rough when that happens. The lads are all on task, I will nip to the Quartermaster and see if the winter gear has come. If the Americans think it will be over by Christmas, they might not bother to collect theirs. I will see what I can scrounge."

"Thanks."

As I walked around the men, I sensed a more purposeful attitude. The risk of death did that to a man. Training was one thing but no one knew how they would react under real fire until they experienced it. I was still concerned about the Lieutenant but I was stuck with him and I would have to try to mould him whilst in action. The Sergeant Major procured everything that we needed for a winter war as well as replacement ammunition and guns. He even acquired a couple more Thompsons. The two of us knew the value of such weapons and we were able to replace the clunky Sten guns. We had a problem with grenades. We had to use the American ones. They were a good grenade but I was used to Mills bombs and I knew that under fire I would not be as confident in their use.

We had been back three days when trucks began to arrive at the camp and I was summoned to a meeting with Colonel Wilding. The trucks and jeeps arrived in the morning and I was sent for in the late afternoon.

Lieutenant Morrison had taken on board my comments and he said, "While you are gone, sir, I will take the men for a run. It may well be we have another mission in the offing."

"Good!"

As I entered the building, I saw an American Lieutenant General and his staff leaving. The airborne wings on his uniform told me his unit. Something was happening. I was whisked in to the office where there was a British Captain of Intelligence. From the piles of papers and the fug of smoke, I knew that the officers I had seen leaving had held their meeting in this office. There was a map of North Korea on a wall and some intriguingly positioned red pins.

The Colonel looked harassed and lit a cigarette, "Good of you to come so promptly, Major. This is Captain Warwick from British Headquarters. He will act as your liaison for this next operation."

I nodded and shook the outstretched hand of the Captain, "I have heard a great deal about you, sir. This is an honour."

Nodding I said, "Colonel, would this have anything to do with the 187th Airborne Infantry?"

The Colonel smiled, "Sharp as a whip, eh Major. Yes, the 187th is going to drop behind enemy lines. We are pushing north really quickly now and General MacArthur wants to try to capture as many North Korean officials as he can. In addition, the North Koreans are trying to take their prisoners of war towards the Chinese border. You know what that means."

My ears pricked up; my unit could be prisoners of war. This protentional mission suddenly became personal, "Yes, sir, they become bargaining chips. I take it from my presence and Captain Warwick here that we are involved too?"

The Colonel nodded to the Captain and went to pour himself some coffee. "Yes sir, there are few British prisoners of war but we have photographs showing at least twenty being marched a few miles behind larger numbers of Americans. They are not with the American prisoners; they are kept separate but heading north. They are being marched and we are estimating where they will be."

I knew what was coming.

"We believe that at least half of the prisoners of war are Captain Poulson and the remnants of your section."

"Brevet Major Poulson."

"Yes, sir, sorry sir. I believe he was a friend of yours."

"He is a friend of mine." The Captain looked embarrassed. "Captain, have you seen action yet?"

He looked embarrassed and said, "No sir."

"Then you should know that any man with whom you fight is your friend. It is not just the Major who is a friend, the men are too. And Major Poulson is still a friend of mine." I emphasised the word, is.

"Yes, sir. Sorry, sir. Headquarters want you to go in with the Americans. The British prisoners are heading for Sunchon while the American prisoners and the officials are at Sunkchon. They are close, it is just sixteen miles between the two towns but there is a mountain range between and not close enough for the Americans to guarantee getting to them."

"So, our job is to land, recapture them and then what?"

The Captain looked at the Colonel who sighed and lit another cigarette, "That is the hard part I am afraid, Tom. You will be too far north to make it back to our lines. You and the prisoners will have to hole up and wait for the advance to reach you."

I nodded, "If they have been prisoners for a couple of months then they will be in no condition to move anyway. I doubt that the North Koreans will be any less harsh than the Japanese were."

"You are right. Lieutenant General Trapnell who commands the 187th was a prisoner of the Japanese and he echoes your words." The Colonel stubbed out his cigarette.

"Major Poulson and the men were in summer gear when they were captured. It is October now and I do not doubt that the weather will get worse. We need greatcoats for them and we will need food."

The Captain said, "But sir, you are dropping by parachute!"

"And we can drop containers too. It will be tricky as the valleys are narrow. We will have to make a lower drop than is desirable but it can be done. And the opposition, sir?"

"North Korean regulars; there is half a company guarding them and a company garrisoning the town."

I nodded and took out my pipe, "So that means we will be outnumbered by ten to one."

The Captain looked shocked, "They are impossible odds!"

I smiled as I filled the pipe with the last fragments of rum-infused tobacco, "Of course they are but the alternative is to leave my men in the hands of the North Koreans. The odds are acceptable." I lit the pipe whilst studying the map. When I had it going, I said, "Colonel, we have no heavy weapons. I need two mortars and a heavy machine gun.

"We have the Browning M1919A4 or the Browning M1919A6."

I smiled, "The former, I think. I heard some of your men complaining about the A6 in the last war."

"You know your guns. I can get all of the gear you need but your men will have to practise with the new equipment today. You leave tomorrow night."

"I thought we might. Captain, could you get the equipment for us? I will need copies of these maps and then I will have to brief my men."

The Colonel said, "Captain Waring will be your pilot." I was relieved. He had done a good job the last time. "Come along, Captain. I will take you to Sergeant Jones, he will get what you need."

By the time he returned I had examined the map more closely and seen the size of the problem. The Colonel lit a cigarette and said, "This is a tall order. You are doing that which needs a battalion."

"I know but we are the only ones who can do this. We have infantry in Korea but we are the only ones who can go behind the lines. Don't worry, sir, I do not have a death wish but I will not let my men down. We will do our best and, God willing, keep our friends safe."

As I walked back to the tents, I heard the sound of singing. It was my section and the Sergeant Major had them singing as they ran.

That's my brother, Sylveste (What's he got?)
A row of forty medals on his chest (Big chest!)
He killed fifty bad men in the West, he knows no rest
Speak of the man (Hell's fire!), don't push (Just shove!)
Plenty of room for you and me

He's got an arm like a leg (Lady's leg!)
And a punch that would sink a battle ship (Big ship!)
It takes all the army and the navy
To take the bra off Mae West

He thought he'd take a trip to Italy
He thought that he'd go by sea
Jumped off the harbour in New York
And he swam like a man from Cork

He saw the Lusitania in distress (What'd he do?)
He put the Lusitania on his chest (Big chest!)
Drank all the water in the sea
And he walked all the way to Italy

That was my brother, Sylveste (What's he got?)
A row of forty medals on his chest (Big chest!)
He killed fifty bad men in the West, he knows no rest
Speak of the man (Hell's fire!), don't push (Just shove!)
Plenty of room for you and me

I was not sure that the Lieutenant would have known the song but it was popular with all three services. My young officer was leading and singing as loudly as the rest. The section was becoming a team and it was none too soon. The Captain had been correct, the mission sounded almost impossible. The Lieutenant was grinning when he halted the men, "Right lads, quick shower, eh? Then the Major can tell us what our mission is going to be!"

They chorused, "Yes sir!" It filled me with hope.

"Sergeant Major, Lieutenant, join me in my tent before you shower. I will give you a heads up before we speak with the men."

Ken Thorpe was an old hand and he knew the score, "That bad, eh sir?"

"Pretty much, Sarn't Major; up there with the Cockleshell Heroes I think!"

The two of them sat on Jake's cot and I went through the main points. The Colonel had given me four copies of the map and I gave them one each as I explained the mission. When I had finished, I said, "And to make matters worse there is a North Korean Air Base to the west of the town. Even if we escape the ground troops the airmen may well pursue us and this time, we would be too far from our own air force to call in a strike."

"It has to be done though, sir, we can't leave our lads with the Koreans."

"I know, Ken, but the trouble is we are unsure of exactly how many men there are. The aerial photographs show that the numbers of prisoners are growing the further north they march. It could be twenty or thirty more by the time we get there. We will need a medic. In a perfect world, we would have a doctor but…"

"Powell did two years training to be a doctor before he jacked it in to join up and Wally Bridges was a volunteer in the St. John's ambulance."

"Good. I have two mortars coming and a Browning."

The Sergeant Major nodded, "Those Brownings are big buggers, sir, if you will pardon my French. They need a couple of big lads. Bates and Lowe are likely lads and they are pals."

Jake lit a cigarette and said, "Timkins and Nesbit are also close friends and they scored quite well on the mortar."

Just then I heard a truck. "This might well be our supplies. We will sort out the rest as and when. We leave tomorrow morning. The rest of the afternoon is getting to know the weapons. Ken, you take one Thompson and Jake the other."

We stepped outside. The men were just coming back from the shower block and there was much horseplay. I heard Sergeant Sullivan and Lance Corporal Lake shout at them to calm down.

I said quietly, "Sergeant Major, we need another couple of Lance Corporals. Smith and Williams did well. What do you think?"

"Aye they will be alright and it will give us the opportunity to assess them."

"Jake?"

He smiled. "I was going to say that Williams was a little young but I am guessing you two think that about me!"

Ken Thorpe kept a straight face as he said, "Of course not, sir!"

Captain Warwick jumped down from the cab. "We have everything I asked for, sir, and I got on the radio to the airfield. They are procuring some canisters to use for the drop."

73

I was relieved. I had tried jumping with equipment tied to my leg and it was not an easy thing. "Good! Sarn't Major!"

"Right my lovely lads. Now that you are all nice and clean get this gear out of the lorry. Be careful with it because we will be using it and soon!"

The Captain said, "We have two belts of blanks and eight practice mortar shells. Sergeant Horowitz here will take the mortar crews and machine-gun crews to the range."

"Sergeant Sullivan."

"Sir."

"Bates and Lowe will be operating the Browning. Tomkins, Nesbit," I looked around, "Foster and Fox will take the mortars. Take them to the range and make sure they know how to use them. Those three weapons are our heavy armour!"

"Sir!" he turned to shout at the six men.

"Ken, I will let you give the good news to Williams and Smith. Jake, after your shower, you and I will go back into my tent with the Captain here and try to come up with a plan which has half a chance of success."

Jake shook his head, "A shower can wait, sir!"

Once inside we lit the lamp for soon it would be getting dark. I lit my pipe, "Smoke if you like." They both took out their cigarettes. "Now then, you say they are still being marched north?"

"Yes, sir. At the moment they are here, at Pyongyang, the capital. The Americans were there too but when we began the push, they started them marching."

"How do you know that the two sets of prisoners will be kept separate?"

"They have been kept apart all the way from the border and there is a new camp at Sunchon. It looks like they are going to hold them there."

"So, they might be north of Sunchon by the time we land? It might only be a temporary holding camp?"

I saw him chew his lip and then he shook his head. "The further north they go the slower they are travelling. The roads are cluttered with civilians as well as the military."

I looked at the officer, "Remember Captain, this is not a training exercise. If we get it wrong it is our backsides hung out to dry. I want your most confident guess."

He stared at the map, "They will be at Sunchon, sir." He pointed to a compound. "We think they will be there. It is a small garrison and they have a stone wall, as well as new wire, to protect them."

"And the airbase?"

He smiled, "Believe it or not they have eight biplane dive bombers, the Henschel Hs 123 as well as two Lockheed Hudson bombers. I think we can dismiss them as a threat."

I turned to the Captain, "My father flew biplanes in the Great War and let me tell you that they can be highly effective. In many ways, a piston-driven aircraft is better than a jet as it has longer over the target. However, I am more concerned with the personnel at the base. Twelve aircraft would only need a dozen or so guards for the airfield. So, where should we have our drop zone?"

The Captain volunteered, "I think that Headquarters has identified the landing zone, sir."

I did not look up but continued to smoke my pipe and stare at the map, "Unless someone from intelligence is coming with us the drop zone will be in my hands!"

Jake said, "Sir, how about the same sort of place as the last time. If we land north of the town, we have less chance of being spotted and if they have left Sunchon already, we should be able to catch them."

Jake was learning, "A good idea and, as the river valley runs from north to south it will make an easier landing."

The Captain shook his head, "And what do you do, sir, if you do manage to rescue them?" I gave him a sharp look, "No, sir, I am genuinely curious. How will you get out of the town if you are north of it?"

I smiled, "There is a river and the river runs south. There are mountains too. We hide and hope for two things. One, that the advance continues at the same pace and two, that the North Koreans are more interested in escaping than hunting down a few prisoners of war. From what I have been told the attempt to take politicians might be seen as a more serious threat." I tapped my pipe out, "And who knows, we may find some vehicles again. It worked before." I pointed the pipe stem at the Intelligence officer, "The radio will be vital. I want someone on the radio at this end. I have two operators and I intend to take two radios."

"Don't worry, sir, I will man the radio myself. I shall sleep by it for the duration of the mission."

I stood, "Right, then as I could eat a horse, I shall dress and go to dinner. I shall leave you two in charge." With that, I strolled off to grab my towel and take a shower. To be truthful I was nervous but I wanted the two of them to think I was supremely confident. It would permeate to the men. Troops liked following a confident leader, even if he was not confident!"

Chapter 6

I made certain that the truck taking us to the field was early. We had much to pack and I wanted to speak with the Colonel of the 187th as well as our pilot. We left an empty camp and there would be no caretaker for we needed every man we could muster. We had all of our weapons as well as winter clothes. We would be laden and that was not a good thing but this time there was no certainty that our troops would reach us in time. When we reached the busy airfield, I left the Lieutenant and Sergeant Major Thorpe to organise the packing of the canisters with the heavier equipment and the winter clothes for the prisoners of war.

"Captain, come with me, let us find this Colonel White."

There were a number of hangars at the airfield and we had one to ourselves. The 187th were using the rest. I saw a Colonel wearing his fatigues speaking with some officers and the Sergeant Major of the regiment. I headed for them. I snapped a salute as I was wearing my beret, "Major Harsker, sir!"

He turned and smiled, "Good to meet you, Major. I have heard a lot about you. I am Colonel Walter White and these are some of my officers. We are the Rakkasans!"

I frowned for I had never heard the word before, "Rakkasans, sir?"

"When we were in Japan, after the war, an interpreter tried to explain our function to the locals. Rakkasan means umbrella man. We kinda like it!" He turned to his men, "Give us some space, gentlemen, I am sure you have things to occupy you."

I saw that Captain Warwick was hovering nearby and that the Colonel wanted privacy, "Captain go and give the lads a hand! You can pack anything but my parachute!"

Disappointed he gave a salute and said, "Sir."

When he had gone the Colonel said, "You have done this before then?"

"Just a few times."

"You really have been given the shitty end of this stick. When I saw the single truck pull up, I thought they must have made a mistake. We are going in with a battalion!"

I shrugged, "We are the only commandos in Korea and the men I am going after are mine."

"Ah, now I understand. Well look, we will try to push east to reach you but I can't promise anything. The powers that be want the North Korean officials. I want the POWs."

"Thank you, sir. My aim is to rescue the POWs and see that they are safe. We have a river we can use as well as the mountains and, as I said, this is not my first time hiding out from an enemy. Don't risk your men coming for us. We are good at improvising."

"And you will need to be. Listen, I need to stay in touch with you. We both know that sending a radio signal all the way back to Seoul can be tricky. I will send my communications officer and chief radio operator to talk to your guys. That okay with you?"

"Of course, sir, and thank you."

"If it is any consolation, we have been told that they have a battalion with three tanks guarding the town and there are more than three hundred POWs." I nodded. "I know that we will get the job done but good men will die." He shook his head, "Can't leave our boys behind, can we?"

"No, sir. I just wanted to come to meet you. I like putting a face to the name and when you shake a man's hand you know something of his character."

"A man after my own heart." He held his hand out and we shook. "Good luck, Major, and if we both make it back; we will have a drink in the Officers' Club! I take it you do drink?"

"Of course, sir. I look forward to it."

I strode directly to the aeroplane we would be using. Captain Waring and Lieutenant Stonebridge were with their flight sergeant examining the door trim, "Is there a problem?"

"Not really but I don't like the state of this door trim and we have time. We will replace it. See to it, Harry." The Captain turned to me, "I thought they might have given you a rest, sir."

"The men we are going to extract are my men, Captain."

He nodded, "Then I understand. Your Captain Warwick said that you wanted to be dropped north of the town, is that right?"

"Yes, and I want us to come in as low as we can. I do not want to be strung out over miles. We have canisters with important equipment in this time."

"The brass wanted you south of the town, sir."

"Where there is a road as well as a river. The road will be clogged with men and they will shoot first and ask questions later. North of the town is just a river. There is no road and that suits us."

"Then I will get you in as low as I can. Do your men know what to do?"

I grinned, "I will tell them and I will be the first out. If anyone is going to hit the ground hard it will be me. Once you give us the signal make a slight slow climb. The canisters will be at the end and we can always find them."

"Right sir. Well, you get some rest. The days are shorter and we will be leaving as soon as the sun goes down. I guess you will need to reconnoitre "

"That we will."

The men had all packed their parachutes and were organising, under the watchful eyes of Sergeant Major Thorpe, the canisters. I saw my parachute waiting on the table and, dropping my Bergen and Thompson, I went to pack it. I took all the time in the world and when I was satisfied, I laid it down. I then went to my Bergen and unpacked it before repacking it.

Captain Warwick said, "Sir, why pack the Bergen twice?"

"If I had time, Captain, I would pack it a third time. It is reassuring to know what you have with you and now is the time I can fetch something I have forgotten." I had plenty of ammunition and in my Bergen were ten grenades. Four were Mills bombs. I had my silencer and my Colt. My Commando knife and sap were also on my battle jerkin. I felt like a dinosaur wearing it but it had served me well before. I then looked at Sergeant Major Thorpe, "Al Jolson time?"

He laughed, "Aye, sir!" We knew that if Marine Harris was here, he would be singing, Mammy! I wondered if he had survived and was on the road to Sunchon.

We both applied the camouflage make-up to our necks, faces and the backs of our hands. I smiled as I saw the section suddenly retrieve their own and begin to apply it. I waved over Jake and Sergeant Sullivan. "I want a radio operator, the machine gun and the mortar crews to come and see me. I need Lance Corporal Lake too. Fetch them would you, Barry?"

"Sir."

When they arrived, I said, "You eight are our insurance policy. When we land you are going to make Fort Zinderneuf! The rest of us will be coming in hot with the prisoners. Your job will be to keep the Koreans off our backs until we can get them behind you. You will have most of the night and some of the morning to do so. Lance Corporal, can you handle it?"

He nodded, "Aye sir!"

"Ashcroft, the Americans are sending their radio operator. I want you to be able to talk to him as well as Seoul. They will be closer to us."

"Yes, sir!"

We spent the next hour going over what we knew and the vague plan. As I stressed to them, we needed to be flexible for the aerial photographs only told half of the story. We needed boots on the ground. "The main objective is to get the prisoners out of Korean hands. When we land, we will recce and that will be when I decide on the final plan. This time there will be no barrage and no column of friendly tanks just a few miles away. The big battle is for the North Korean capital so we, to all intents and purposes, are on our own. When we open fire, it will alert the enemy to our presence. From that moment on the clock is running and every Korean within ten miles will be racing to Sunchon to squash us like bugs! Colonel White has enough men to hold his town. We do not." I saw their faces take in the seriousness of the mission.

There was hot food for us and we all ate heartily for our next hot meal could be many days away. I had some tobacco. One of the officers I had met at Seoul had been a pipe smoker and he told me of a new American tobacco called White Rum. I had bought some. It was flavoured with rum and moist but it was not as good as my navy enriched tobacco. I had enough with me for a week and I enjoyed a pleasant pipe in the hangar as I listened to my men talk of home. We had not been together long enough for all of us to know all that there was to know about each of our lives and families. That would come but for now, the conversations remarked on the coincidences in our lives. Men discovered places and events they had both shared, albeit unknowingly. There were football teams they had in common and others which were great rivals. It would provide ammunition for banter. Much of the talk was down to nerves. Outside I saw that the sky had darkened and the predicted rain was beginning to fall. At this time of year, it could turn so easily to snow.

Captain Warwick sat next to me while the Lieutenant and my NCOs moved around the men to check that they were prepared. "They seem a good bunch, Major."

"I started fighting in '39, Captain. By and large, the men with whom I have served were all a good bunch. I have visited the graves of many of them and told them so since the war ended."

He was silent, "I didn't think there would be another war, sir. When they dropped the atomic bombs on Japan, I thought that was the way of the world and the days of the soldier and his rifle were gone. My family has a tradition of serving. I can trace the officers in my family back to Marlborough. I thought that if I was going to serve then Intelligence would give me the best opportunity to make a difference."

I shook my head, "Britain will always need soldiers holding a rifle. Our navy keeps the island safe but aeroplanes make it vulnerable. Look at us. We are going to fly deep into enemy territory and take a couple of towns. We need Intelligence Officers but we also need intelligent officers who can lead men and, when the going gets tough, help them out of a tight spot."

"Like you and Major Poulson."

I nodded, "I have known Paul Poulson a long time. Alone of all of the men I served with in the last war he stayed in. If I hadn't been wounded then I would be with him and a prisoner."

The Captain lowered his voice, "And it would be Lieutenant Morrison who was coming to rescue you."

Something in his voice made me turn, "If you have something to say then spit it out, Captain."

He sighed, "I read the files on all of you. Lieutenant Morrison has an uncle and a brother who went off to Israel in 1947. They both fought in the war. His uncle is now a general."

"So?"

"There was a rift and Lieutenant Morrison was caught in the middle. His brother was wounded last year by Arabs. He joined up soon after and they have not seen each other for three years. He could be fragile."

I laughed, "Whatever issues the Lieutenant may have he is a Commando and he was trained as such. We all have, what you call issues, Captain, but when we fight, we put them from our minds." He nodded, "But thank you for the information. It may help."

He looked relieved, "Perhaps I shall retrain, eh sir?"

"Perhaps but give it a little more thought. Not all of these commandos will be coming home. Think on that."

The Captain had been caught up in the moment and I saw realisation set in. "Sorry, sir. You seem so confident I thought…"

I nodded, "As I did when I first started. Events rarely turn out the way we plan." My subordinates had returned. "Any problems?"

"No, sir, they are raring to go."

"I will have a quick word. Once we are airborne then it is impossible to talk."

Sergeant Major Thorpe put his hands on his hips and said, "You heard the Major, front and centre!"

They stood around me, "This will not be an easy drop and it will not be an easy mission. If it was any other mission, I might question it but these are Commandos we are rescuing, our Commandos. Remember that. We are going in low so I will be first to jump. Watch my chute. The ones who dropped with me before will follow me. The rest of you watch and jump as closely as you can. We have a plan but it may change. Listen to the NCOs, they will know what you have to do. We have two new ones this time," I gestured to the two of them, "Williams and Smith did well the last time. If you do well on this mission, who knows? Now check your pockets. We take no papers at all and your dog tags are all the identification you will need." As they busied themselves, I said, "When they are done get the bus loaded. I am certain the flight sergeant would appreciate it and it will keep the men busy."

We were all successfully boarded as the sun set in the west. I waved goodbye to the Captain. The transports carrying the Rakkasans were already loaded and we would take off with them. We would follow the same course for the majority of the journey and a couple of flights of Sabres would accompany us. However, the bulk of the North Korean Air Force had been neutralised. The Henschels at Sunchon probably represented the most potent weapon they had left. We had just over one hundred and forty miles to go and the journey would take longer than the last one. I closed my eyes to rest them to listen to the reassuring noise of the Pratt and Whitney engines. I knew that many of the men were nervous but I could do little about that. The noise from the engines drowned out almost everything else. The engines built up to a crescendo and then, as the pilot and co-pilot pulled back on their sticks we rose into the air. We were on our way!

The Flight Sergeant would act as drop master. When we parted from the 187th he tapped me on the shoulder. I stood with my parachute on and clipped the line to the rail which ran down the centre of the aircraft. I attached the Bergen and machine gun by clips from my belt. The others stood. The ones who had dropped with me before moved efficiently. They had done this and survived. The NCOs were spread out amongst the others and they were helping them. We had time yet although I felt the movement as the pilot began to drop to the correct height. We had been told that there were no anti-aircraft guns but the last aerial photographs had been days old and who knew what changes had been made?

I turned so that Williams could check my chute and he turned so that I could check his. I shuffled forward, moving my Bergen with my feet until I reached the door. The Flight Sergeant was listening intently to the commands from the cockpit. We hit a little turbulence and the aircraft lurched a little. The pilot was good and he soon corrected for the disturbed air. I turned to look down the line of jumpers and saw that all the chutes were hooked up and Sergeant Major Thorpe gave me the thumbs up. Immediately behind him were the canisters with the mortars, machine gun and other vital equipment. I could rely on Ken to watch their descent. Turning back, I saw the Flight Sergeant slide back the door and a wall of icy air hit us. Flecks of rain showered me but what I noticed was the flickering lights from ground fire. Men were firing at us. They were using machine guns and the odds on hitting us were remote but they might see us. If this was a hot landing then it would be a baptism of fire for the new boys!

The light turned green and the hand on my shoulder propelled me into the dark. I kicked my Bergen and it dragged me into the night and the sleet flying in my face told me that the rain was coming from the north. We would land closer to the town that I would have liked. That could not be helped and, as my parachute jerked me, I began to scan the land below me. There was no road to guide me but, to my right, was the black snake which was the Taedong River. So long as I kept that to the east, I would be hitting somewhere close to the optimum landing site. I had to hope that Lance Corporal Williams was right behind me and following me. A good landing depended upon everyone keeping eyes on the man ahead and following him. This was not the massed parachute jump of D-Day. This was a tiny incursion by an elite group. We could not afford to lose a single soldier!

The rain mixed with flecks of snow was not helping and the lack of features on the ground was worrying. The aerial photographs had not shown any trees but the landing surface was still an unknown. I had nothing to alert me to the ground and it would be down to my quick reactions. It was the years of experience and my sixth sense which saved me. I saw the field of winter barley just moments before I hit it. This would not be a soft landing. I braced myself and took the impact with my knees. I did not fall but the pain in my knees told me that it had not been a good one. Even as I stood, I was gathering my parachute and scanning the area for lights or the unmistakable flash of a gun. There was nothing and I heard a double thump as Williams and Ashcroft landed. We had a radio on the ground and that was a start!

Had there been anyone close by then they would have heard my men as they hit the ground hard but there was no one and, as I rolled and bunched my parachute, I saw my line of men landing in a roughly straight line. I looked at Ashcroft, "Is the radio intact?"

"It didn't hit the ground, sir, but I will have to wait until I can check it."

I nodded, "Do so now and tell Captain Warwick that we are down. Nothing more. As soon as he replies then shut down."

I took off my chute and jammed it into my Bergen and then, as I slipped it on to my back, ran back down the line. I saw that my original parachutists were already storing their parachutes but some of the newer ones were still struggling. I shouted, as I passed, "On me!" Ashcroft would make his signal and then he and Williams would join us.

By my estimate, we were just a mile from the town. The sleet had turned to snow. If I had not had adrenalin rushing through me,

I might have felt the cold but the combination of low temperatures and snow might well keep the Koreans indoors. They would be expecting the aeroplane they had seen above them to drop bombs and not parachutists. At least, that was what I hoped. I saw that the men were all down and where they should be but the canisters had, inevitably, drifted offline and Sergeant Major Thorpe was already organising men to fetch and open them. Lieutenant Morrison was also organising men. Since our talk, he had made a real effort. I was relatively happy for things were going well. Then I saw Marine Allenby. Powell and Bridges were with him and the commando was injured. I ran to him, "Problem?"

Allenby looked up and shook his head, "Sorry sir, bad landing. I hurt my leg."

Powell had trained briefly as a doctor but Wally Bridges had been a St John's ambulance man. It was he who spoke, "A really bad sprain, sir. He can't walk."

Allenby shook his head, "I can manage, sir!"

I shook my head, "These lads are the experts. They say you can't walk then you can't walk." I looked up and saw that the Sergeant Major and the rest of the section had retrieved the canisters and were dragging them closer. "Powell, fetch one of those empty canisters and some parachute cord. We can make a sledge and you two can pull him."

"Sir!" Powell ran off. "Allenby you can be with Lowe and feed the Browning."

"Sir!"

I stood, "Don't worry, Allenby, accidents happen and this could be worse." I cupped my hand, "Officer's call!"

After a few moments, the Lieutenant and my NCOs joined me. I looked at the luminous dial on my watch. It was just after midnight. Already I was modifying my plan. "We have a wounded man. I am taking Bates off the machine gun and putting Allenby there instead. We use the canisters as sledges and I want them dragged to the outskirts of the town. When we get there have them filled with soil. They will protect the mortars and the machine gun."

They nodded. I took heart from the fact that they looked confident despite the conditions. The snow was not yet lying but it soon would; winter was coming.

"We can use the parachutes for camouflage; by morning this will be a white world let us use whatever advantage we have. Lieutenant, you are in charge of building a defensive position. I will take you, Smith and you, Williams with me. I will leave Lance Corporal Williams at the place I intend to be the site of Fort Zinderneuf. When the rest of you get there, make a hide for Lofting; our sniper might well prove to be our ace in the hole."

"Sir." Lieutenant Morrison looked worried, "Are you sure about this, sir? Surely one of us could go in. It is too great a risk to send you."

I shook my head, "I have done this more times than I care to think about. I have the silenced weapon and I am the one who knows the men we are seeking. Keep to the plan. I want a defensive position and I will be away for no more than an hour. This weather is a godsend to us as it will hide our movements. With luck, we can get in before dawn. I would rather rescue the men while the town is asleep."

They nodded. I took out my Colt and fitted the silencer. "Ready?" The two newly-promoted men nodded and I headed towards the dark shadows that marked the town.

The barley field had given way to an area which looked like a market garden of some type. There were still the remains of the last beans and winter cabbages were in neat lines. We picked our way through it. There was a hut at the end and I stopped there, "Williams, this looks a good place to use as our defensive position." I pointed at the house I could see through the sleet and snow. It was less than half a mile from us. "We are close enough here. When the others arrive ask the Lieutenant to send a couple of scouts out to find the river. By my reckoning, it is less than four hundred yards east of us."

"Sir."

87

I turned to Lance Corporal Smith. "Sling your gun and take out your sap. I want no noise. We hide if we see anyone and if we are disturbed then I will deal with them. Got it?"

"Sir!"

As soon as we left the hut, I saw that there was a path of some sort which led to the nearest house. That made sense as they would need to visit the area each day. The cabbages would be used to make the Korean staple, kimchi. It was a desperately cold night but our speed kept us warm. However, it also caused our breath to crystallize before us. That was not good, it meant we could be seen. I knew, from the aerial photographs, that the compound was at the junction of a main road and a smaller one which led north. I led Smith past the solitary house and saw, immediately beyond it the buildings of the town. This was not a western town. Most of the buildings were single-story and I saw, in the distance, a watchtower. That had to be the compound and it looked to be less than four hundred yards from us. I could hear some dogs barking but they were in the distance. They had not sensed us. This was the middle of the night for it was barely one o'clock. Even the early risers would not be roused until four. We had time.

When we reached the buildings, I walked in their shadows. The snow had begun to lie on the open areas but here the buildings afforded some protection and it was drier. The buildings felt warm as we passed them. The people would keep fires burning all night. I heard a dog bark ahead and a Korean voice shout; there was a yelp from the animal. There were guards ahead and I held up my hand and, leaving Smith to watch, I moved slowly to the edge of the building. Ahead of me, I saw the compound; it was eighty yards from us and the ground around it had been cleared. There were two watchtowers at the opposite diagonal corners and I spied the dog and handler as they patrolled the perimeter. They were outside and heading away from me. I had been lucky. Beyond the wire, I spied the tents which we assumed were being used by the prisoners and I saw two guards, on the far side, sheltering under the eaves of a building and smoking. They would have to be dealt with. They were in an open area and further towards the centre, there were buildings. That would be where the garrison slept. The watchtower closest to us was just twenty feet or so high and I saw a machine gun protruding from it. The glow from two cigarettes identified the guards there. The wire could be cut but the guards would have to be eliminated.

I headed back to Smith and gestured for him to follow me. I now had an idea of the difficulties we would encounter and I, once more, changed our plans. We needed a diversion to affect our escape from the compound. When we reached the hut, I saw that the team had been busy. My NCOs and Ashcroft approached me, "Sir, I contacted the Captain. The radio works and he knows we are here. I also got in touch with the Americans; they are down too."

"Good. I want you here when we rescue the prisoners. Lieutenant, take the explosives we brought. I want the bridge ready to demolish. Take Williams with you. I want it exploding at precisely 0520 hours. I expect North Korean reveille to be at 0530. I want them asleep when we attack. I intend to break in at 0500 hours. Wait close enough to the bridge to see that it is demolished and then get back here." I did not add that he ought to check his timers. That lesson had been learned.

"Yes, sir."

I looked at my watch. It was 0210. "We leave here as soon as we can. We leave the Bergens in the hut and carry as many grenades and ammunition as we can. Whatever else needs doing can be completed by Lance Corporal Lake and his men. The two medics sole responsibility will be to look after the prisoners who are in a bad way. The rest of us will do the fighting. Get to it and send Lofting and Smith to me."

Sergeant Major Thorpe nodded, "Sir."

Our sniper arrived. I was pleased to see that he had his rifle wrapped and protected. "Lofting, I want you as close to me as my Bergen."

"Sir!"

"I intend to use my Colt to eliminate the two guards in the tower. Your job will be to keep watch for any Korean who tries to raise the alarm."

"Won't my bullet do that, sir?"

"Yes, but a single shot will just make them curious. A shout which tells them they are under attack will rouse the camp. There is a second watchtower on the north-west corner. You will need to take those out." He nodded. "Smith, you take out the dog handler. I don't think that he and his dog get on. You like dogs."

He nodded, "Aye, sir, and I have some pemmican I bought at the PX. That should do the trick."

"You will have to use your knife."

"I know, sir, I am ready!" It was one thing to stick a commando dagger into a stuffed dummy and quite another to tear into a man, ripping muscle, veins and tissue whilst scraping off bone.

"Right, dump your Bergens with mine at the hut. We won't be needing them."

The Lieutenant and Lance Corporal Williams ghosted next to me. The snow was now falling so heavily that visibility was becoming difficult. "Ready to go, sir."

"Remember, you don't need to destroy the bridge just make a noise. Save some explosives and timers in case we need them later." They nodded, "And Lieutenant, if I don't make it back, you have to extract the team."

"I know, sir. I will be ready!"

I smiled. He was getting better.

Chapter 7

There were just fourteen of us who headed through a world of white. I had seen the increasingly bad conditions and ordered the men to make ponchos of their parachutes. They not only disguised us they afforded us a little protection from the biting wind and arctic cold. The Sergeant Major and Tomlinson with the spare radio brought up the rear. They would not enter the compound until we had the prisoners in our hands. Along with Lofting they would be our back up and provide covering fire for us. I had my Thompson slung beneath the poncho. Hall and Entwhistle had the wire cutters and their task would be to get us into the compound. The snow was lying and our footprints on the virgin snow would alert the enemy to our presence. It did not really matter as the gunfire and the explosives would tell them sooner. We moved more slowly than when I had made the recce and it took much longer to reach the compound.

We reached the edge of the last building before the compound. I saw the two sets of footprints in the snow. They looked to be the sentry's and his dog; they led east. I turned and tapped Smith on the shoulder. He peered up at the tower to make sure that the sentries were looking in a different direction and then he sprinted off to the wire. Walking next to the wire was the safest method of avoiding detection. I turned to my two wire cutters and nodded. With my Colt held before me, I led them to the wire. Lofting would cover us. I had seen, on the recce, that the ground was flat and I ran whilst watching the tower. I saw no faces peering down and, again, that made perfect sense. To peer out meant getting a face full of snow! It was better to stay beneath the parapet. When I reached the wire and turned, I was gratified to see that I could not spot Lofting. The parachutes were a good disguise. While I aimed the gun at the tower, I heard the clip, clip of the cutters. To me, it sounded loud but the noise would not be heard in the tower. I glanced at my watch. The time was ten to five and we were on time. It took ten minutes to cut through the wire and remove a piece big enough for us to pass through. My two cutters picked up their rifles, slithered through and took up defensive positions. The snow was easing off and soon it would stop.

I stepped into the compound, I walked slowly to the tower, checking all the time to see that I was not observed. It was a metal ladder and, after tucking my Colt into my belt, I began to climb. It was a risk but I hoped that the men would not look over the side and, if they did, the snow and the parachute would disguise me. I still had no sight of my men. That meant the camouflage worked. There was a light in one of the buildings to the east of me. I could now hear the two North Koreans talking above me. I had enough Korean to pick out the odd word but that was all that it was, an odd word. I saw an open hatch above and a glow. They had a brazier of some sort and that would help me. It would spoil their night vision and I knew that their attention would be on it. I was acutely aware of the time but haste might cause me to make a mistake. The voices helped me to identify where they were. The two of them appeared to be on the south side of the tower. That explained why I had not seen them. As I neared the top I drew and cocked my Colt. It was now or never. I pulled myself up with my left hand and saw the two Koreans seated on stools playing cards. I fired two shots. They were less than five feet from me and they died instantly as the two bullets struck their foreheads. I checked there were no other sentries and descended. When I reached the bottom, I tapped Entwhistle on the shoulder and pointed to the tower. I mimed for the two of them to use the machine gun. As they clambered up, I waved for Corporal Dixon to bring over the rest of our men. The first part was done; now I had two more sentries to kill and then we could start our rescue.

I did not wait for my men to follow me as time was of the essence. I ignored the tents and ran, instead, to the smaller building to the right of the main one. I was hidden by the tents and although I could not see the sentries, I doubted that they would have moved. As much as I wanted to take them prisoner, I had the lives of almost forty of our own men in my hands. The sentries were soldiers and sudden death was an occupational hazard. When I reached the smaller building, I glanced at my watch. It was 0515. I had taken longer than I had hoped. As I headed to the main building, I saw that it had a large door on the eastern side. As I began to creep along the side of the main building suddenly the sky to the west was lit up by a huge explosion. The Americans had detonated something. It mattered not what it was the garrison would be alerted. The two Korean sentries obligingly stepped out and both died without knowing whence the bullets had been fired.

I ran to the tents knowing that the bridge would soon blow. I was not a moment too soon for I heard an alarm within the main building and a searchlight from the north-west tower began to sweep across the compound. Lofting had wrapped the barrel of his gun in parachute shroud and that not only hid the muzzle flash it dampened the sound a little. I knew the sound but I doubted the North Koreans would. He sent a whole magazine at the tower. The light went out and there were cries. A final shot eliminated the threat. I shouted, "Commandos coming in. Grab your gear!"

The tent flaps opened and I saw Lance Corporal Pike emerge. He saw me and grinned, "Get the lads! It is Major Harsker!"

Faces appeared in the tent doorways. I shouted, "Corporal Dixon!" Pausing only to fire at the open door of the main building my sergeant ran to me. "Get the men back to the camp, Dixon!"

"Sir!"

"Smith, you and I will cover them!"

Just then the sky to the east was lit up as the bridge blew. I glanced at my watch and saw that it was on time, to the second! I jammed my Colt in my belt and swung around my Thompson. A North Korean officer stepped out of the building only to be struck in the chest by one of Lofting's bullets.

"Right sir!"

"Come on lads, you heard the Major." I heard Sergeant Grant's voice.

My sergeant and my men poured out of the tents. I could see that some were having to be supported by others. Time was of the essence and I could not afford the time to scan the faces to see if Polly was still alive.

I heard the Korean machine gun, operated by Hall and Entwhistle, open fire. It was a heavy gun and huge holes were torn in the door of the building. Smith knelt next to me. I saw that the North Korean watchdog was with us and lay in the snow next to my Lance Corporal. I cocked my Thompson and watched the side of the building. As I had expected men had left the side entrance. I fired a short burst as soldiers appeared. Three of them fell and the others took shelter; I was buying time for our men to get to the camp. Behind me, I heard my men as they encouraged the prisoners and helped those who could barely walk. I was desperate to turn and see who, other than Godfrey Pike and Sergeant Grant, had survived. There were too many North Koreans before us.

"Smith, pull the pins on two grenades. Send one to the left and one to the right." I sprayed the west corner of the building and then the right. I had less than half a magazine left.

The din from the building as men fired at us and orders were shouted was so loud that I barely heard Smith as he shouted, "Grenade." I threw myself to the ground and covered my ears. The air was filled with flying shrapnel. As I stood, I emptied the last of my magazine and pulled two hand grenades. They were American ones and I shouted, "Grenade!" as I threw them and then hit the ground. As the concussion washed over me, I changed magazines and looked behind me. Smith and I were alone, with the dog! I fired a short burst and said, "Run! I will be right behind you."

Our grenades had hurt the North Koreans but I heard the sound of motors. They had vehicles and that spelled disaster for us. I fired a second burst, drew a grenade and threw it. This time I ran for the gap in the fence. The wall of concussion had largely dissipated by the time it reached me. I had run so fast I could have represented Great Britain in the Olympics!

As I ran, I shouted, "Hall, Entwhistle, Lofting; time to go!"

Hall had the presence of mind to throw the machine gun over the side of the tower rendering it useless when it smashed on the ground. They slid down the ladder and were waiting for me at the fence. Smith and Lofting were also there. "Can't any of you obey an order?"

Smith grinned, "Couldn't go without you, sir!"

I pointed to the north and then threw a grenade under the tower, "Run!"

We were safely behind the building when the grenade exploded. I heard a crash and knew that something had fallen; I hoped it was part of the tower. So far all had gone well but we now had a company and a half on our tail. Faces appeared in the doors of the town as we ran but when they saw our guns they ducked back inside. I stopped as we neared the edge of the town and the solitary building which marked the end of the inhabited section. I could hear vehicles behind us. I saw that the rescued men were still shy of our defences. "Right lads, let us hold them here for a while."

They lay down on the ground; it was easier for them with their rifles. My submachine gun meant it was easier for me to stand. I heard the GAZ as it hurtled from the compound. "Lofting, empty a magazine through the engine block. You other two get grenades ready."

They had a machine gun on the Gaz but it was bouncing and sliding on the slippery road and the bullets were striking the building and the road rather than us. I fired a short burst. The Thompson was inaccurate but the bullets zipped over the vehicle, making the driver swerve. I heard Lofting's Lee Enfield and then the crack as they hit the North Korean vehicle. They did not damage the engine block but the cloud of steam from the front told me that they had hit the radiator. "Throw your grenades and then run back to the lads!" I emptied my magazine, spraying from side to side and then ran. We used the building for cover and the exploding grenades did us no harm.

I heard as we covered the ground to Fort Zinderneuf, the sound of Lieutenant Morrison's voice, "Wait for my order to fire!"

Behind us, I heard the sound of a truck. I had used one and recognised its sound. We could have used a bazooka but hindsight was always twenty-twenty! We did not have one. We threw ourselves over the snow-covered, soil-filled parachute canisters. "Lofting, you know what to do."

"Yes, sir!"

I turned to Sergeant Major Thorpe and Lieutenant Morrison, "Any casualties?"

"None, sir, but half of them are in a bad way."

Sergeant Major Thorpe nodded, "Pikey has been their only doctor. Major Poulson might well lose his leg. We have fifteen wounded and another five who have, like the Major, more serious wounds."

Although I was relieved that Polly was alive this was becoming depressing, "Any unwounded who can fight?"

"There are twelve, sir. They are mainly our lads but Major Poulson is the only officer. The others are from the 1st Middlesex."

I looked at Ken Thorpe, "Have spare weapons issued to the twelve. They can use the guns from the mortar crews, machine gun crews and medics. They are looking after Major Poulson, aren't they?"

"He is their priority. Powell's training might help, sir. If we get a moment, he will need to speak with you."

Just then Lofting shouted, "Here they come, sir."

My friend and the medics would have to wait. I nodded at Jake who shouted, "Wait, for it, wait for it!" The Korean truck barrelled towards us and fifty or more North Koreans, screaming and waving their weapons charged at us. I aimed my Thompson. The Lieutenant judged it well and shouted, "Open fire!" when they were just a hundred and fifty yards from us. Our defences absorbed the odd bullet which struck us while the mortar shells, sent as fast as Fox and Foster could drop them, scythed through the infantry. We were lucky in that one shell managed to hit the truck and explode its tank. The vehicle lifted in the air as it blew up. It was the end of their attack. They fell back to the safety of buildings and the edge of the town. More than seventy of their men lay dead, dying or wounded. I saw some crawling back. John Lofting raised his rifle, "Let the wounded go, Lofting. If we shoot them it will anger them and this way they have to look after them."

"Sir!"

"Sergeant Major, feed the prisoners. I want to move as soon as we can."

"In daylight, sir?"

"If we have to." He left to obey my orders.

"Well done Jake. Do you have explosives left?"

He grinned, "Yes sir, and, while we were setting them, Marine Williams found some boats on the river, sir. They were barges and they are north of the blown bridge. He said they might be a way out and I think he might be right."

"Is the river navigable?"

He shrugged, "The boats must go somewhere." My lack of enthusiasm dampened his spirits. "It was just an idea, sir."

I smiled, "And a good one too. Don't mind me, Jake. I am just worried about my friend."

"He looked in a bad way when they brought him in but he was still smiling."

I said, almost to myself, "That is Polly for you!"

"Polly, sir?"

"A nickname."

I looked at my watch. It was still early in the day but the snow had stopped. What would the North Koreans do next? I had no doubt that the airwaves would be filled with chatter. They had to know that the Americans were the greater threat in addition to which there was a push towards Pyongyang. Even now the North Korean capital might be in allied hands. I had to trust my men. If the Sergeant Major thought that the men were too sick to move unless there was no alternative then I would have to believe him. I might be forced to delay our departure until dark.

"Make sure everyone eats. Keep a watch for the North Koreans. Can you take charge, I would like to see my men?"

Jake's face suddenly looked almost ancient as he nodded, "Of course, sir. Take all the time you like. I have this."

I took out my pipe and began to fill it. I had cleaned it on the aeroplane as it had kept my hands occupied and my mind focussed. Wally Bridges was just coming out of the hut, which we had cleared. He shook his head, "Sir, it is not right what the North Koreans did to our lads. They have had nothing but rice water and stale bread since they were captured. They all have the galloping shits." He shook his head, "Sorry sir, dysentery." His eyes pleaded with me, "Will we get them home, sir?"

"Bridges, I don't make promises I can't keep but I will do my best. These are good lads."

"You are right there, sir."

I opened the door and stepped in. It was dark and it was Stygian. There was a smell of antiseptic in the air. Corporal Lowery stood, somewhat unsteadily and saluted, "We knew you would come for us, sir. These foot sloggers didn't believe me but I said Commandos never leave men behind."

"And you were right. Now sit down and rest. We are not out of the woods yet.

Powell and Lance Corporal Pike approached me as he sat. Their faces told me all I needed to know. Waving them to join me outside where we could talk, I stepped to one side and said, "Give me the worst."

Godfrey nodded, "The Major is a game 'un sir, He kept us together and fighting even when he was wounded but his leg is infected. I am just a medic but I knew something needed to be done. I asked the gooks, sorry sir, North Koreans but they played dumb." He sighed, "He has to lose the leg below the knee. We have used the penicillin the lads brought but it will not be enough. If the infection spreads then…"

I nodded. Polly had always been a fit man and his life was the Commandos. I could not envisage him with life outside. I trusted my men. I turned to Powell, "Your opinion?"

He nodded, "He is right, sir but it might be too late, it should have been done much sooner."

I did not need this distraction but I owed it to my friend. I knew he was just one of many but I had a chance to save someone and I was damned if I would ignore the opportunity. I had lost too many friends I could not save. "If you take the leg?"

Powell took a step back, "Me sir? I…"

"The alternative is a St. John's ambulance man and Pike here. Answer me. If we do not take the leg then what happens?"

His shoulders sagged and he shook his head, "He dies, sir."

"And if we operate and take his leg?"

"He might live."

I nodded, "Then there is no argument. Do what you have to do to prepare. We take the leg and we take it now! We leave here after dark and the North Koreans will come as soon as they are reinforced." I stared at Powell and knew I was being unfair. He nodded, "Pike, get Bridges and clear a space. I will go and speak with the Major."

He gave a wry smile, "That is all he has been asking for. He is a tough one. I will get a fire going. We have to cauterize the wound or the operation will be a waste of time."

"I know." I turned to Marine Powell, "Thank you, Peter, I know I put you in an impossible position and I apologize." I think he was in shock for he just nodded, dumbly. I went back inside. I walked over to the pile of parachute bags my men had made for a bed for Polly. I smiled as I approached the pale shell of the man I had known for almost five years. "Well, look at you! A bed fit for a King."

He nodded, "I am sorry, sir. I have let you down! I lost so many men!"

"Look at the ones you saved. Pike told me what you did. This is bad luck."

"Williams, Barton, Smith. They died. Wilberforce, Tenby, Golightly, Caygill, Inns, Gowland, they were the new lads and they all died."

I nodded and held his hand in mine, "And that is not your fault. They were thrown into a conflict for which they were unprepared."

He winced, "This bloody leg!"

He opened his eyes and I held his gaze, "You have to lose the leg below the knee or you will die."

His eyes closed and his head fell back. I saw a tiny tear seep from his eye and I gripped his hand. He just said, "Bugger."

I laughed, "Bugger, indeed. It is not as bad as it sounds, Powell trained as a doctor."

He opened his eyes and said, "This means we can't leave. I won't be the cause of more men's deaths!"

"Hey!" I forced steel into my voice, "I am still in command! We leave when I say and not before! You are a brevet major and don't you forget it." He nodded, "Besides, it would be suicide to leave here in daylight. We will take whatever they throw at us and then try to leave after dark. The new Lieutenant has found some boats. We can take a Korean cruise."

He relaxed and smiled, "Just so that it is not me who holds things up."

I nodded, "You won't be."

"When will they…"

"As soon as they are ready. They have no anaesthetics; just some morphine."

He stared at me and then grinned. He was Polly once more. "You know I always fancied being a writer. This could be the start of a new career. I should look at all of these experiences as a challenge."

I looked into his eyes and saw both fear and pain, "If I can I will be here for you."

He shook his head, "Knowing that you are on the line fighting, sir, will be enough. You are worth a whole section. Sir, if this goes tits up, I want you to know that serving under you and with you has been a privilege and..."

I stood, "None of that, commando! You are not going to die on my watch and that is an order!"

He laughed, "That is it, sir, never change. It is what we love about you! I shall do my best." He raised his right hand and saluted. I returned it and left. I felt lower than I had ever felt. Once I stepped into the snowy sunlight Corporal Dixon approached and saluted, "Sir, we have heard engines. They are back."

I smiled, "Right Corporal, have the men stand to. Make sure they all have ammunition. Have someone watch the ground to the north."

"Ground to the north, sir?"

"There are North Koreans there. The last thing we need is to be attacked from the north."

Sergeant Major Thorpe handed me a mug of soup and a hunk of bread, "Here, sir, eat!" I nodded and obeyed. "Major Poulson?"

"He is going to lose his leg. We stay here until the operation is over."

"Of course, sir."

"What I am worried about is the north. There is no road but they could send tanks."

He looked north, "Aye, sir, you are right."

"Have Williams and Hall take the rest of the explosives and a few grenades. I want them to mine the ground half a mile from here. At least we could have a warning."

"Right, sir. We will be alright. We have good lads."

I hoped he was right! As I ate I watched Lance Corporal Williams and Marine Hall heading north. It was open ground and all that they would be doing was putting explosives and booby traps where they through the enemy might pass. We were not trying to kill large numbers nor even slow them down. We just needed a warning that they were approaching. We had too few men as it was to defend the perimeter.

While eating the bread and soup, I went to Harry Ashcroft, "Get on the horn to Captain Warwick and tell him we have the prisoners but there are more wounded than we had expected. Give him the precise numbers and tell him that we can't leave yet. Ask the Americans their situation too."

"Sir."

I saw Marines Harris, Collins and Haynes; they were wearing the greatcoats we had brought and were clearing some snow behind one of the canister parapets. They looked up at me as I approached. Harris said, "We thought you would be back in Blighty, sir, after that wound."

"What, go home and miss your smiling faces?"

Haynes asked, "Will Mr Poulson…?"

"Live? I hope so. We have three medics who will do their best to see that he does." These were like family and as family deserved to know the truth. "He will lose the leg below the knee."

They all knew what that meant, "It is not fair, sir, he is a good officer! It is all the fault of those Koreans!"

"What do you mean, Harris?"

"When he broke his leg, sir, Pikey used the last of his powder on the wound and set it as best we could. He asked for a doctor to look at it but they just laughed. That was the real reason we surrendered, sir. We had almost run out of ammunition and when Sergeant Bo-yeon Heon was killed we had no interpreter." He shook his head, "We should have kept on fighting sir, or tried to get home. You would have tried, wouldn't you, sir?" I was not sure and I said nothing. To have commented might have implied criticism of Polly. "We were put in the bag with the Middlesex lads. There were a lot more of them then."

"And then the bastards made us walk." Haynes shook his head. "Mr Poulson was going to try but we took it in turns to carry him. And even then, they whipped us when we went too slow. When the officers from the Middlesex regiment objected, sir, the two of them were shot!"

I had felt guilty about shooting the four Koreans; now I did not. Even the Germans would have treated our wounded. He would lose a leg because the enemy had not adhered to the Geneva Convention. I realised that we were in an even worse position than I had thought. We were outnumbered and trapped. If we were overrun then we could expect draconian treatment. I mopped the last of the soup from the mug with the crust of bread and looked along the line. The rescued prisoners were interspersed with my men. There were some from the Middlesex regiment. I did not know them but I had no doubt that after their march north and losing their officers the way that they did, they would fight as hard as my men.

"Hall, Entwhistle, do you think you could nip over the parapet and collect some of the Korean guns, ammunition and grenades?"

"Aye, sir!"

"Stand to! Cover these lads while they try to get some weapons. Lofting, eyes front!" I could not see Lofting for he had a hide. He was our secret weapon. I heard his voice.

"Aye, sir. It looks clear!"

They clambered over, leaving their own weapons behind and ran the eighty or so yards to the closest Koreans. The ammunition would not fit our guns but we could use their weapons to augment our own. The two of them worked quickly and efficiently. Bodies were unceremoniously searched and flipped over. Suddenly I heard the crack of a Lee Enfield and a Korean tumbled from the roof of the building. Lofting had the advantage of a telescopic sight and he shouted, "Best hurry up lads! There is movement."

They were coming.

Chapter 8

This time they were led by a small tank. It had a two-pounder gun. It was a poor tank but we had no anti-tank defences and so any tank was a threat. "Mortar crews, your target is the tank!"

"Sir!"

Behind them came North Korean soldiers. There had to be at least two hundred of them. I wondered if Intelligence had miscalculated or had they been reinforced?

I looked at the crew with the Browning machine gun, "Allenby and Lowe, you have our best weapon. Use it wisely."

Williams and Hall ran in, "Sir we have planted all the explosives. They are half a mile north of us. We could have used more, sir."

I nodded, "The mantra of every soldier since the Romans. We never have enough but it will have to do. Now take your positions and use your bullets judiciously!"

The North Koreans in the tank were either too eager or inexperienced. Their first shot soared beyond our defences and exploded two hundred yards behind us. I saw the two mortar crews carefully adjusting their weapons. They would work together. One would fire and the other would watch the fall of shot. In theory, they should do no damage as they were using high explosives but these old fashioned light tanks were more fragile than they appeared. A sudden flame could ignite fuel or ammunition. Only Lofting was firing and his rifle was picking off officers and NCOs as they approached. The men would wait until they were closer. We were relatively safe from their bullets as we had the snow-covered canister defences before us. We were also harder to see as we all wore the parachute

ponchos. I lay next to Marines Williams and Hall. I missed the Lee
Enfield I had given to Lofting. I always felt I had more control
when I used it but the Thompson was deadly. We had three of
them and they, along with the Browning, would winnow the
Koreans when they were closer.

The tank fired again but the gunner had not seen the dead body
he had driven over. The barrel rose as he fired and instead of
hitting our lines it landed a hundred yards behind us. This time we
suffered a shower of snow and soil. Then the first mortar fired and
the shell exploded just behind the tank. The effect was devastating,
the body of the tank helped deflect some of the shrapnel and a
swathe of soldiers were cut down. The second mortar exploded
directly in front of the tank and it made it swerve.

I saw that they were now in range and I shouted, "Open fire!"
The heavy Browning thundered and the three Thompsons chattered
a deadly chorus. The Lee Enfields and the North Korean automatic
weapons we had taken from the enemy dead filled the air with the
smell of cordite and deafened us all. The machine guns were all
firing short bursts and when we stopped, I heard the double pop of
two mortar shells. One was a lucky shot. It hit the body of a North
Korean who lay close to the tank. He must have had a couple of
grenades on him and they exploded. The track on one side was
damaged and as the tank slewed around the second mortar hit the
top. They had not buttoned it up. Two more shells were sent in
quick succession and one of them struck either the fuel or
ammunition for the tank suddenly lifted into the air and then
exploded. Pieces of metal scythed towards us but we had all taken
cover when we had seen the strikes. The North Koreans had no
such shelter but they were game. They began to fire back from
their prone positions. It was a waste of ammunition.

"Open fire!"

We fired again and the mortars sent their shells towards the
Koreans and it was the last six mortar shells which finally defeated
the enemy. They fell back leaving more than half of their number
dead.

"Cease fire!" I looked around. "Casualties?"

Matt Dixon shouted, "Hall has been hit by shrapnel but it is a scratch."

"That is a relief. Keep a good watch!"

I saw that my medics had brought Polly into the open and he was on a table behind the hut. I saw why they had done this. They were close to the fire Pike had started and they had better light. I wandered over. There was a pot of boiling water and there were commando knives in the bottom. I saw wire cutters which would be used to pick the sterilised instruments from the bottom of the pot. Pike said, "We have cleaned up as well as we can. Sergeant Major Thorpe had a flask of whisky and we used that to sterilise our hands." I nodded and looked at Polly. He looked to be asleep. "We gave Mr Poulson the morphine to dull the pain and a couple of tots of whisky. He fell asleep."

Powell said, "We had better start, sir."

I nodded, "And you want me out of the way."

He smiled, "If you don't mind, sir. This is hard enough without a senior officer watching over my shoulder."

"Right. Good luck." I touched Polly's hand, "Take care, old man!"

I went to join my men. The tank was still burning and the air was filled with the smell of burning flesh. It was not a pleasant aroma and I saw some of the younger commandos had reacted badly to it. Sergeant Major Thorpe joined me. He pointed to the northern sky, "Those clouds suggest more snow, sir."

I nodded, "That might help us."

"Are you still planning on using the boats Lieutenant Morrison found, sir?"

"It strikes me as the safest option but we do not know the condition of the vessels nor if they have power. I don't fancy travelling down the river with no power."

"Is there an alternative, sir?"

I pointed south, "We could fight our way south. The Marine Division is marching up that road. We might only have a day or so to travel before we find them." I turned to look north, "But if the weather deteriorates..." I did not finish the sentence as I saw a dot in the distance. It could be only one thing, an aeroplane and if it came from the north then it was an enemy aeroplane. "Take cover! Incoming!"

I grabbed my gun and knelt. It was not in my nature to take an attack lying down. I would fight back. I heard Allenby shout, "Swing the Browning around!"

It was at that moment that I realised this was a jet and a fast one. The North Koreans did not yet possess jets. This one had to be American, Chinese or Russian. When I saw the spurts from the aeroplane's guns, I knew that it was not American. Even as I opened fire, I knew that the odds on my hitting the aircraft were slim. The Browning and the other guns chattered a feeble response. The enemy shells struck as the jet screamed overhead. I felt them whizz past me. When I heard screams, I knew that some of my men had been hit. I prayed that the three medics and Major Poulson, not to mention the rescued prisoners, had not been hit. They had been through enough. I tracked the jet and emptied my magazine. I saw the star on the side which identified it as Russian. It was a MiG. As it banked, I saw that some of our bullets had done some damage for I saw a tendril of smoke coming from the wing. It continued its turn and headed north and west which confirmed that it had come from Russia. I heard cheers from the town. They must have called in the strike.

I looked at the devastation it had caused. It had torn a line down my men. Allenby, Lowe and the Browning had all been hit. None had survived. Archie Mackenzie had also been in the line of fire as were five of the Middlesex regiment we had rescued.

"Lieutenant, go and check on the men in the hut." I shouted, "Is anyone wounded?"

Corporal Dixon shook his head and pointed to the eight corpses, "Just these lads who are dead! Sir, what are the Russians doing in this war?"

I have no idea." I suddenly remembered the medics. I ran around the hut. There was a great deal of blood but the three of them were still tending to Polly. Godfrey shook his head, "We were lucky sir." He pointed four feet to the right of them. Their Bergens had been piled up there and were now shredded.

"How is the operation going?"

"The critical part, sir. Do you need any of us?"

Shaking my head, I said, "An undertaker is all we need!"

I went back and saw that Sergeant Major Thorpe and the Lieutenant had organised the men to begin digging graves. Jake handed me the identity disks. He said, "Sergeant Major Thorpe said to get them in the ground while we can, sir." He pointed to the sky. "Snow is on the way!"

He was right and even before we had finished digging the graves, we were enduring a blizzard. Pike had rigged up a parachute as an awning and to afford some protection from the elements. Corporal Dixon had kept men watching for a North Korean attack but they seemed broken. After dark it would be a different matter but, by then, I hoped we would be away. By the time the men were buried, it was two o'clock.

As much as I wanted to be around to see how the operation went, I knew I had to recce the river. "Ashcroft, get on the radio to base and tell them that we have been attacked by a Russian MiG and we hope to make our escape south tonight."

"Shall I tell them how, sir?"

I shook my head, "Better not in case the enemy soldiers are listening. Lieutenant, take charge here, Williams, come with me. I want you to show me the boats. Sergeant Major, if you need me then send up a flare."

"Sir." He took out his pipe and wagged it at me, "and sir?"

"Yes, Sarn't Major?"

"Be careful."

I took just my Colt and I left my Thompson with Marine Harris. We had just under a mile and a half to go and as Williams led me, I was assessing the chances of making it to the river with so many injured men. Luckily the snow had flattened everything and with more snow falling we would have a relatively solid, albeit slippery surface. I saw that just one end of the bridge was destroyed and, as we drew closer, I saw that the barges were moored to the north of the wrecked bridge. Would there be debris underwater? Would the boats have engines?

We moved cautiously and that caution was justified. I saw movement close to the river bank. There were North Korean soldiers there. I counted just five of them. I drew my Colt, having already removed my silencer and I took out a grenade. I said quietly, "Williams, we are going to have to shift those North Koreans."

"Yes, sir. What if there are more of them?"

"Then we will have to go back and find another way out of this fix. Wait until I tell you before you fire. You start with the soldier furthest south and I will hit the one furthest north. Take it steady and make every bullet count. I am hoping that these white ponchos will make it harder for them to see us. And now we crawl." We had three hundred yards to crawl through the snow. The falling snow made it hard for us to keep our eyes on them and so I was confident that they would not know that we were closing with them.

We got to within eighty yards of them. The range was not good for the Colt but any closer and we risked being seen. I tapped Sam on the shoulder and I levelled my pistol. I was resting on my elbows with a two-handed grip just as I had been taught all those years ago. I did not look at Williams, I just said, quietly, "Are you ready?"

"Sir!"

"Then open fire!"

I squeezed the trigger as I said the word and my bullet spun one Korean around and he fell into the water. Sam's shot hit a heartbeat later and my second hit one in the shoulder. The last two looked around for their attackers and two more bullets ended their confusion. I quickly rose and ran. I was looking for anyone else. When we reached them, we found just two bodies. The other three were floating down the river and I was able to gauge the speed of the current. "Williams, take their guns, grenades and ammo."

I slithered down the bank to the boats. They were not big, perhaps twelve feet wide and thirty feet long; they looked to be barges used for transporting material up and down the river. They would not have to travel far. There was a cabin at the stern of each one. I had just clambered up on the nearest one when I saw a rifle emerge from the cabin. As it swung towards me, I raised my Colt. It was like a gunfight in the wild west. Which bullet would reach its target first? Although it was me and I hit the man in the chest, I sensed, rather than saw the bayonet which lunged towards me from the side. There had been another on the boat. Although I flicked the bayonet aside with my pistol it still scored a deep cut across the back of my hand and I dropped the gun. I drew my dagger with my left hand and grabbed the barrel of the Korean rifle with my right hand. I knew there might be more men on board and so I slashed my dagger across the man's throat. He fell spurting blood. I retrieved my Colt and went into the cabin. It soon became clear that there were just the two men. I saw that the one who had used the bayonet had oily hands. He had been in the engine room.

I saw the open hatch and I went down into the engine room. There was a light which suggested power of some type. I had seen naval engines before and I recognised a big red button. I pushed it. The engine turned but did not fire. I cursed myself. "You idiot! It needs priming!" I saw the priming level and I pumped it seven times just as I would with my petrol lawnmower back in England. I pushed the button again and, although it complained, it fired and began to chug. I was unsure of how much fuel we had and so I turned it off. One boat worked. Did the other?

I climbed out of the cabin and saw Sam's face as I emerged, "Sir, are you wounded?"

I looked down and saw the blood on my poncho. "No, Sam, this is the Korean's and I just have a scratch on my hand. This one works. Let's have a look at the other."

As soon as we stepped aboard the second barge, I knew there was trouble. It was lower in the water and, when we stepped into the engine room, we stepped into water. There was a leak. Despite priming the engine, it refused to even turn over. I shook my head, "Unless we have a mechanical genius, we are in trouble." He nodded, "I want you to stay on the other boat and guard it. If North Koreans come then fire three shots and we will come running. While you are here, see what you can find on the two barges which might be useful."

"Yes, sir."

I discarded the poncho. The blood on the white made it useless as a disguise. As I ran back to Fort Zinderneuf I saw that the sun was setting in the west. It had a couple of hours to go but it would soon be dark and when it was then the North Koreans would come and come mob-handed. Every man in the town would be armed and they would swarm all over us. We had to leave by sunset at the latest!

Jake and the Sergeant Major were waiting expectantly for my return. "We heard gunfire, sir."

"There were Koreans aboard. We have one barge which has an engine. It is a go. Sergeant Major have the prisoners of war escorted there along with food, weapons and ammo. Load the barge with Williams on it. Keep the mortars here. Put a good man in charge in case they come again."

"That would be Sergeant Grant. He may not be fully fit but he has a mind as sharp as any and he knows what's what!"

I nodded. "As soon as they are aboard, Lieutenant, begin to send the men over. One mortar crew first and then half of the men. I will go and speak with the medics."

Their faces told me that they were not confident. I fearfully stepped around the back of the hut where I could smell burned hair and flesh. They had cauterized the wound. They were smoking and that told me the operation was over. I looked at Pike, "Well?"

"We took his leg and he is not bleeding. He is sleeping and that is a mercy as he woke up during the operation." That explained the looks my subordinates had given me. "Now it is in the hands of God."

I took a deep breath and stepped close to the bloody sheet which covered my friend. I touched his hand and was gratified that it felt warm. I turned to them, "And now the big question; when can he be moved?" I looked at Powell; he was the nearest thing we had to a doctor.

He stubbed out his cigarette, "Are you asking me as a medical man or a commando, sir?"

"There is no easy way out of this one, Powell, both!"

"As a doctor, I would say that he should rest here for at least twenty-four hours but, as a commando, I know that is impossible. They will attack again and when we lose, he will suffer and he will die. All I will say, sir, is to leave it as long as possible."

"A good answer. We leave when the sun sets. Rig something up to carry him. I will get another man for you. There is a barge and it has an engine; that should ensure that he has a smooth journey but you have to carry him for more than a mile, in the dark."

They looked at each other and Pike said, "We will manage, sir."

"Whatever you need on the barge send it now. We just take the Major when it is dark."

"Sir!" He looked at my hand, "before you go, sir, let me deal with that. The last thing we need is for you to be wounded."

They tended my wound and I went around to the other side of the hut. Already half of the men had gone. "Smith!"

"Yes, sir!"

"Go to the medics. You will be carrying the Major."

"Sir!"

Ken Thorpe said, "He is alright then, sir?"

"Perhaps but they want as long as possible. When the sun sets, they will carry him. Send Dixon to tell Grant and the others. We need the engine ready to run. There is spare fuel on the damaged barge. Have it transferred to the one which works."

Marine Harris came up to me and handed me my Thompson, "Here y'are sir."

"Thanks. Is there a brew on?"

He grinned, "If there isn't, I will make one, sir!"

"Good man." I stood with the Sergeant Major and the Lieutenant and took out my pipe, "They will come after dark."

Lieutenant Morrison nodded as I reamed my pipe, "I have put some booby traps amongst the bodies, sir. I used the Korean grenades."

"Good." I began to fill my pipe. "Sergeant Major, I want the men to be a screen for the Major. The medics have done a great job, we can't allow them to get hurt carrying the Major to the barge."

"Right sir."

"Lieutenant, you know the way so you lead. Lofting and I will bring up the rear. Ashcroft, get in touch with Captain Warwick and let him know what we are doing. You follow the stretcher!"

"Sir!"

I had chosen Rafe Smith as a stretcher-bearer because he was resourceful and he helped the three medics to use a canister as a stretcher. With half of the men now on the barge, we no longer needed the defences. I was watching them attach the parachute cords to their makeshift stretcher when I heard Lofting, "Sir, they are coming again!"

It was twilight and a little earlier than I had expected but it was inevitable that they would try again." Stand to!"

I grabbed my Thompson and ran to the parapet. It was now devoid of the heavy machine gun and we had just one mortar. Timkins said, "We are down to twelve shells, sir!"

"Then make them count." Just then I heard an explosion from the north. The first of Williams' booby traps had been triggered. They were attacking from two directions and we did not have enough men to cover both! "Pike, get the Major out now!"

I heard a distant voice, "Right, sir!"

There was a cheer from the town as the Koreans, emboldened no doubt by the lack of numbers facing them, charged. Lofting's rifle barked and I saw a leader, hand raised in exultation, fall to the ground. A second, carrying the North Korean flag fell to Lofting's skill and one who tried to pick it up was also slain. There were more explosions to the north. "Timkins, open fire and spread your rounds. As soon as you have fired the last one, pick up your mortar and follow the others."

"Sir!"

Slipping my Bergen on to my back I ordered, "Lieutenant, go!" I stood and sprayed a whole magazine as Timkins and Nesbit sent their last twelve mortar shells to decimate the Korean line. As they picked up their mortar, I changed magazines and fired another burst. "Lofting, time to go!"

"Sir!"

I picked a grenade from my belt and hurled it as I followed Lofting. A fusillade of bullets thudded into the parapet and there was another explosion from the north. Then my grenade exploded slowing down the pursuit. The sun had, just to say, set as we ran towards the river. The snow had stopped and the clouds cleared a little. There was enough light to see the ground but no more and the Koreans were charging an undefended camp. They fired blindly as they ran towards what they thought was a defended position. We should have laid booby traps but I had not thought of it. I was slipping. The two of us zigged and zagged knowing that to turn and fire again would invite disaster. Sergeant Grant had the side of his barge defended and they sent mortar shells to the south of us followed by machine-gun bullets as we closed with them. I saw that the mortar crew, Williams, Ashcroft and Geoff Bates, along with Corporal Dixon were standing on the bank.

"What is wrong?"

"The working barge is full, sir. If we hadn't got out then the Major and the medics would not have been able to board. Any more on board and it would capsize. The injured lads take up more space than we thought, sir, and the stretcher… We put the Korean dog in the barge too."

I waved my hand. I did not need to know the details and I trusted his judgement, "Lieutenant, set sail. We will follow!"

"No, sir!"

"That is an order."

Williams said, "Sir, there is a rope. We could tow the second barge. It has no engine but…"

Dixon said, "It is worth a try!"

Williams grabbed the rope and threw one end to Rafe Smith who tied it to the first barge. Already the Koreans were closer and the Lieutenant and Sergeant Major Thorpe were sweeping their machine guns from side to side.

"Take the first barge away but if we get in trouble then leave us and that is an order! Right Sergeant Major?"

I heard his weary reply, "Yes sir."

"Get aboard."

We had no sooner clambered aboard than bullets rattled into the wooden hull. While Dixon secured the tow the rest of us fired into the dark at the fireflies that were the muzzles of the North Korean guns. The other barge moved into the centre of the river and I heard the rope creak. I wondered if it had enough power to move us. Suddenly we were sucked from the mud and followed the other barge.

"Cease fire! They can't see us if we don't fire."

I could barely see the other barge as it headed downstream. I did not know who was steering but they wisely kept to the centre of the channel. I went to the stern and took the tiller. It felt loose but I was able to follow the other barge. I knew that the bridge was close to the town and that they would have men there and that they would fire. We would have to endure whatever they threw at us.

"Williams, get below and check on the level of the water."

"Sir!"

"We were nearing the bridge and men on the bank began to fire at the other barge. My mortar crew must have had mortar shells left for there was an explosion on the river bank and by its light, I saw men falling. If we could get beyond the town then we would have a chance. As we slipped past the ruined bridge, I put the tiller over a little to take us away from the bank. We had travelled twenty yards when I heard a horrible noise and Williams suddenly appeared. "Sir, the water was already rising but we hit something and it is flooding in. We are sinking!"

I was paid to make hard decisions and make them quickly, "Dixon, cut the tow and tell the other barge to proceed without us, we are sinking."

"Righto, sir." He was calm and his matter of fact voice told me he had confidence in me. I don't know why.

I began to put the tiller over to drift us closer to the shore. "Ashcroft, make sure the radio is dry."

"Sorry, sir. It was hit in the last attack and it is beyond repair. Tomlinson has the only working radio and he is in the other barge."

There were more men on the other barge and we could improvise. "Well, that is the best place for it. Grab everything you can. We are on our own and in a few minutes, we will be scrambling ashore. Until I say so we use hand signals. Stay close and I will try to get us out of this." My voice had a confidence not shared by the inner me. At least there were just eight of us and the majority had a chance to make safety. As for us? It seemed to me, a choice between prison camp and death!

Chapter 9

The stricken barge actually touched the bank before the water filled her and we were able to scramble ashore without becoming soaked. No one had seen us land for the night was a filthy one with snow flurries all around us and, for the moment, we were undetected. The snow was lessening and that would make us easier to see; we had to move quickly. I signalled for Lofting to prepare his gun and then, Colt in hand, I crawled up the bank. I saw, more than half a mile away, the town and the bridge. There were lights and a great deal of activity but it appeared to be along the river bank further north. The damaged barge had brought us further south than I could have hoped; we were south of the town and the road lay open before us to the south. I risked standing. I no longer wore my white poncho but it was dark and I hoped all the attention was further north. Just forty yards from the river was the main road running south and that would soon have men upon it. I saw more lights to the west, about a mile away. It was the airfield and, even in the snow, men were working on the aeroplanes. A mad thought came into my head. We could go to the airfield. It was one place they would not think to look for us as we were fleeing them. There had to be vehicles there even if they were just petrol bowsers, small trucks, ambulances and fire engines. There were just eight of us and we only needed to get forty or so miles south and we would reach our troops. It was a mad plan but the best that I could come up with. I slithered back down.

I waved my arm for them to close up with me. The snow stopped and it was now much colder; my breath crystallized before me as I spoke, "We are going to head to the airfield. With luck, we can steal a couple of vehicles. I plan on driving us south if I can. Lofting, you are my shadow. Corporal Dixon, you are tail end

Charlie. If we have to use a weapon, make it a grenade." I handed my Thompson and my spare magazines to him. "I will stick with my Colt."

They nodded their understanding. The trust they were giving me was a heavy weight upon my shoulders. "Let's go."

We sprinted across the road. The snow was more like slush on the road showing me that vehicles had been using it and I saw, to the north, a pair of dim lights which told me that another vehicle was coming down the road. It spurred me on and I ran across the snow, hoping that they would not notice the footprints in the recently fallen snow. My men followed in my footsteps which minimized the trail we left. I kept glancing to the north as we ran west. I could hear the vehicle now. It was a GAZ. I waved the men to the ground and we lay on the ground as it came down the road. I held my breath as it neared our footprints which seemed, to me, to be a sign that they could not miss but they did and continued south. It was as they passed that I saw why. They were looking to their left watching for moving barges. They had a heavy-duty torch which they played in the centre of the river. The sunken barge was hard against the bank and could only be seen if they left their vehicle and walked to the edge of the river. The Lieutenant and my men would be far to the south by now. They would still be in danger but only if the North Koreans on the west bank of the river were watching for them. I put that unpleasant thought from my head. We had cast the die and the barge was beyond my help. I rose and waved my men forward.

We were crossing a field of some sort of spring crop. The snow had made it all flat and it was relatively easy to cross. When daylight came then our footprints would be a clear marker but by then I hoped to be away from here. The lights on the airfield helped us for, illuminating the field and the aeroplanes, they made us invisible. Even so, I approached gingerly. I could see them working on two of the Henschels and the Hudson. I saw that the Hudson had been Chinese, I could still see the red star on the fuselage, but they had attached a North Korean flag. I saw that they had vehicles. A petrol bowser was filling up the Hudson and there was a GAZ and an old truck next to it. We would head for the Hudson for those two vehicles might just suit us. I waved my men to spread out on either side of me. We moved slowly, crouching whenever I thought a head had turned but they were too busy with the engines of the aircraft. I saw a pile of bombs on a cart ready to be loaded. I wondered why they had not used them to bomb us but the reason became obvious when we were just three hundred yards from the field. There was no fence around it and I waved for the men to lie in the snow. They were all invisible for they wore their white camouflage but I was exposed. I heard voices shout and I saw that there was someone in the cockpit of the Hudson. He waved and they tried to fire the engines. One started and there was a cheer. That had been why they had not bombed us. The engines had failed. The second one refused to start and they shut down the starboard engine and continued to work on the port one. The two Henschels they had been working on did fire their engines and there was another cheer. I heard what I assumed was Korean banter from the two sets of mechanics. Then they began to load twenty-five-pound bombs under the wings of the old German biplanes.

An idea began to form in my head. They would not take off at night; only a fool would do that especially with a slushy and slippery runway. Once they had finished repairing and loading the aeroplanes they would retire for the night. If they managed to get the Hudson repaired, we could steal it. I had flown one once. My father and I had been down to a sale of ex-RAF aircraft and that had been one we had considered. My father and I had liked the bus but our mechanics had preferred the Pratt and Whitney engines of the Dakota to the Wright R-1820 Cyclone 9-cylinder radial engines of the Hudson. I had once stolen an aeroplane from Germany but that had been German, I hoped that this would be easier as I was familiar with the layout and design of the aeroplane.

We lay still in the snow and watched. The night was getting colder and I felt it getting into my bones. My men would be warmer as they were lying on their ponchos which would give some degree of insulation. I was getting too old for this sort of thing. I looked at my watch. We had been there for thirty minutes and it had been at least ten since they had tried the engines. The North Koreans who had loaded the bombs on the biplanes now cleared the snow from around the aeroplanes. That made sense. It was beginning to freeze and they could grit the runway in the morning. They would not want to chip off the ice and frozen snow first. The Henschels were loaded and their crews left leaving just six mechanics working on the Hudson. The petrol bowser left and then the GAZ. Another thirty minutes passed and then they tried the port engine again. It coughed and spluttered twice before it barked into life. The mechanics cheered and they ran both engines for five minutes to make certain that they worked.

It was now well below freezing. The mechanic in the cockpit switched off the engine, then climbed down the ladder from the hatch and they managed to load the bombs in the bomb bay in less than thirty minutes. They loaded eight twenty-five-pound bombs. I suspected that was far less than the maximum payload and might indicate that the North Koreans were short of ammunition. No doubt spurred on by the cold, they drove the old truck off towards the main buildings. Their laughter showed the relief they felt. That ended my idea of stealing vehicles. It was now eleven o'clock. They had not left a guard on the aeroplanes for they were within sight of the buildings just one hundred and eighty yards away. We could approach from the river side and we would be hidden from the control tower by the aeroplane. I gave the base an hour to quieten and then I rose and waved my arm. I pointed to the aeroplane. I dared not give my men verbal instructions as their voices would carry in the night. They would have to trust me.

The North Koreans had cleared the snow from the runway which made it easier for us to run across the tarmac which had yet to freeze properly. I led them to the aircraft and sheltered by the wheel. I kicked the chocks from the port wheel and, gesturing for my men to stay where they were, I ran to the other wheel and did the same. When we reached the fuselage, I went to the hatch and opened it. I signalled for them to enter. They had questions written all over their faces but their training kicked in and they obeyed. I dropped my Bergen in the rear of the fuselage, well away from the bomb doors and said, "We are going to steal this aeroplane. Ashcroft, find the radio and find out how to work it. The rest of you make yourselves as comfortable as you can. There are neither seats nor harnesses. There may be a seat on the dorsal turret and there is a seat behind the cockpit where the navigator sits. It will be the take-off and landing where problems might occur. When and if we land, I cannot guarantee a smooth one. This could be a bumpy ride."

Corporal Dixon asked, "You can fly this, can't you, sir?"

I grinned, "We will soon find out. Dixon, take charge and tie down what you can. Williams and Ashcroft come with me to the cockpit!"

They followed me and dropped their bags while the others took the bags to the safe place behind the cockpit before exploring the interior of the aircraft. The moon had come out and bathed the airfield in light. The control tower and the buildings were in darkness. I saw the glows of two cigarettes which marked the sentries. They were at the main gate barrier and at least four hundred yards from us. I pointed to the radio and Ashcroft sat on the seat. "Williams, take the co-pilot's seat. Just do exactly what I do. I just need help to get the beastie in the air!" I pointed to the throttles. "You will be pushing those with me and," I pointed to the joysticks, "then pulling back on these with me. Now strap yourselves in and hold on tight, it will be noisy and we will slip and slide all over the place!"

We would not have the luxury of headphones and flying helmets except for Ashcroft as there was a set attached to the radio. This would be seat of the pants flying. I intended to head south until we reached an allied airfield and try, if I could, to land. I knew that the runway would be slick. I doubted that it would have been gritted. Once I was ready, I fired the starboard engine. It was still warm from the test run and it fired. The port one struggled and hunted but eventually, when I tweaked the fuel, it fired. I saw lights come on in the building; they had been alerted and we were now on the clock. The wind was from the north and the runway was east-west. It would be a crosswind take-off which was always risky and I would not have the luxury of a long taxi. I nodded to Williams, "Hands on!"

I began to push the throttles and the pitch of the engine grew. We began to move along the runway. I did not want to go too fast and risk a skid. The danger was that the North Koreans would find some way to stop us. There were at least two of the biplanes which could fly and they had machine guns! I took us all the way to the western end of the runway and turned the Hudson so that we had the full length of the runway for the take-off; it also meant we were as far away from the men with guns as we could be. That would change when we tried to take off. I saw men racing from the buildings. They were armed and they would not let us leave without a fight.

"Ready, Williams?"

"Yes, sir!"

"Off we go then!"

We pushed the throttles and we began to bounce down the runway. I had my hands ready for the flaps but I concentrated on the joystick. The aeroplane wanted to slip and slide and I had to fight it. I saw the muzzles of the North Korean rifles spit flame and heard bullets strike the fuselage. Then I heard the chatter of the twin Brownings in the dorsal turret. Corporal Dixon had placed someone there. The North Korean fire stopped as they took cover. We were halfway down the runway and picking up speed. I knew that we were laden with bombs and would be heavier than we ought to be. Timing the take-off would be crucial. If I missed it then we would end up in the river! Suddenly the Brownings fired again and this time, whoever was firing them, fired at the Henschels. They had been fuelled and the two recently repaired aeroplanes burst into flames, setting alight the others. I had no time to look for the end of the runway was approaching. When I heard the explosions, I knew that the bombs had exploded.

"Williams, grab the joystick and be prepared to pull!"

He was quick and he held on to the joystick as though his life depended upon it.

"Now pull back!"

We both pulled back although nothing seemed to happen. The end of the runway was less than eighty yards away and beyond that lay the road and the river. We bounced up and down. My father would have tutted at such a poor attempt and then we started to lift. I do not think we had ten yards to spare but we rose above the ground, then the road and, finally, the river. I was aware that the river was the best marker we had for it led due south and so I banked towards the south.

"You can take your hands off now, Williams. Well done."

This time the dials were in English. The Hudson had been a gift from the Royal Air Force and I was able to use the information before me to climb above the height of the mountains and to get the airspeed up. We had a full tank. That was a mixed blessing. If we crash-landed then it increased the chances of a fiery end. In addition, we had eight bombs aboard! I would use maximum fuel and climb to burn off as much fuel as I could. As I retracted the wheels and the flight became smoother I realised my original plan would not work. I needed to rid the aeroplane of the bombs and that meant heading out to sea first.

"How is the radio coming on, Ashcroft?" I glanced over my shoulder and saw that it was not a British radio. It was Chinese and had Chinese characters. There was a headset with built-in mike and Ashcroft had the headphone over one ear.

"Sir, I can't read it."

I shouted, "You don't need to read it. Just keep turning the dial until you hear English and then transmit."

"Sir."

Williams, looking out of the starboard windscreen, shouted, excitedly, "Sir, I can see the barge!"

I was relieved. The Lieutenant and his precious charges had not been attacked, not yet anyway! We were ten minutes from the field when we reached two hundred and thirty miles an hour. She was flat out but this was not the top speed she had had when new. This was a tired old bus at the end of her life. I knew that it was over a hundred miles to the sea and I intended to fly south until we reached the sea and then turn east and head for Seoul. I turned to Williams, "Go under the cockpit, through the hatch behind us. Crawl to the bubble at the front of the aircraft and see if there is a bomb door release and bomb release device."

"How will I know if I find it, sir?"

"You might not in which case we won't be able to dump the bombs at sea but have a good look and then come back and tell me. You might check on the lads in the back and see if any were hurt when the Koreans fired at us."

"Sir!"

One advantage we had was that we were flying at night and I did not expect too much air traffic. The river turned west by Pyongyang and it was just after there that anti-aircraft fire sent flak into the air. They missed, for we were high and alone. We were soon in darkness once more. I would now have to use the compass for direction. It would be slightly out but that did not matter. I had enough margin for error; I was aiming for the sea!

Williams returned, "Sir, the lads are all okay and I have found the bomb switch. It is red! There is a sign that says bomb doors. It was covered in a piece of paper with Chinese writing. I tore it off and found it."

"Good, now sit back in the co-pilot's seat. When we get over the sea and it is clear I want you to dump the bombs!"

"Sir!" he seemed excited at the prospect.

We flew over a dark land. There were no landmarks, except for the river, to be seen. There was a blackout in place from both armies and I had to hope that the compass was accurate. There were soldiers below us and no doubt some were fighting but up at eighteen thousand feet it was peaceful.

Sam suddenly pointed ahead and shouted, "Sir, the sea!"

He was right. "Get below and tell the others that I am going to descend. Then get into the bubble and wait; you shout when the sea is clear below us and I will give you the orders." I would get well away from the coast before I dropped my bombs. It was safer that way and would burn off fuel.

"Right sir." He disappeared through the hatch.

"Sir!"

"Ashcroft?"

"I have found some English chatter, sir, but I am still looking for the transmit switch."

"When you find it, speak in clear language. Identify us and tell them that we are flying a Lockheed Hudson with North Korean colours. I will lower my wheels when we are near allied airspace." Lowering the wheels while in the air was a universal signal of surrender.

I saw the land slip by and we were over the water. We were down to eight thousand feet when Williams shouted, "Clear!"

"Open bomb bay doors." I heard the electric motor groan as the doors opened. "Bombs away!" It was only two hundred pounds we dropped but the aeroplane rose a little as we did so. I began to bank towards the east. I would fly towards the rising sun. I pulled back the throttle to slow down. I wanted a landing in daylight. If I had to, I would circle Seoul until I found an airfield in daylight. I knew there were two: a military and a civilian. We had taken off from the military one and I would prefer to land there. However, the important thing was to get down; I would land at either! I had pushed our collective luck enough already! As we banked, we saw the bombs explode as they hit the water. Some lucky fisherman would be able to collect fish from the surface.

My compass told me we were heading east but I wanted daylight to land. I had been lucky in the take-off and it would not do to count on it for the landing. We had almost half a tank of fuel left. I intended to climb when we neared the coast and burn off more fuel. Williams rejoined me. He was grinning like a child on Christmas day. "I got to drop bombs!"

"Well done! Now keep your eyes peeled for the coast."

"Sir!"

Silence filled the cockpit. We were accustomed to the drone of engines and when Ashcroft suddenly shouted it came as a real shock, "Sir! I have a contact! It is a battlewagon off Inchon."

"Good, then tell them we are coming in from the west. They should find me on the radar at, "I checked the altimeter, "at ten thousand feet and I will climb to fourteen thousand when we near the coast. Use Captain Warwick as our identification."

A few minutes later and Sam said, "Sir, I can see a line I think might be the coast."

"We will wait until we get a little closer."

"Sir, the battleship has confirmed that she can see us on radar. To confirm that it is us that they see they want you to climb to twenty thousand feet and then descend when they give the order."

I nodded. It made sense. We could be a threat to the fleet. Blair had been a Communist agent and Colonel Churchill had told me that they were using radio operators. Twenty thousand feet would make it harder for us to bomb the fleet. I climbed and levelled out; it did not take long as the Hudson had a good rate of climb. I flew straight and level for a minute.

"Sir, I can see the coast."

Before I could respond to Williams, Ashcroft shouted, "They want you to descend to eight thousand feet and take a heading of 275. They are sending a couple of P51 Mustangs to escort us in."

"That is to be expected. When they come, they will close with us to make sure we are who we say we are."

Dipping the nose, I began a gradual descent. I saw the sun begin to rise in the east as the two Mustangs came on either side of us. Williams and I waved, showing our Caucasian faces. The pilots waggled their wings and gestured for me to lower my undercarriage. I did so and felt the drag immediately. I increased the power. They made the sign for us to descend. When we did so they followed us, one on each side of us. I breathed a sigh of relief. The flight was now uncomfortable but it was safe.

"Sir, I have the pilot of the Mustang. He said we are heading for the field we used when we took off."

I nodded. That too, made sense for Captain Warwick was there. I almost cheered when I saw Seoul in the distance and the Mustang pilot instructed me to land! "Brace yourselves, lads, we are going to land and this could be bumpy!"

"Right sir!"

The Dakotas which had taken us were now in their hangars and I brought the Hudson down on an empty runway. It was not the best landing I had ever made but when the propellers stopped and we did not burst into flames, I smiled. I took out my pipe. "Get the hatch open! Not a great landing but any landing you walk away from is a good one!"

My men cheered. They could not have expected this outcome when our barge had sunk!

Chapter 10

There were armed guards facing the aircraft but they did not point their guns at us. I filled my pipe and waited for someone to come to us. Being stationary seemed the best option. I struck a match and drew on the tobacco. Captain Warwick and Colonel White rushed out to greet us. The Colonel shook his head, "When we received the first message, I was certain that it was a trick! I can see there is a tale here but, first, where are the others? Not…"

I shook my head, "We had two barges, sir. The majority were in the first one which was powered. Ours sank and I improvised. I estimate that they should be approaching Pyongyang. Is it still in North Korean hands?"

The Colonel shook his head. "It fell as you were heading north in the Dakotas and the Marine Division defeated a large force which was being sent to relieve the city. I am not certain yet about the security of the town but I will get on the radio and warn them to watch out for a barge filled with Commandos." He pointed to a truck with an American corporal behind the wheel. "That is the transport for you and your men."

"And there are some survivors from the Middlesex Regiment. Sir, if I could see to my men and then I can give you all the details!"

"Of course, and I have a bottle of rye to help us celebrate!"

Captain Warwick said, "I will walk with you, sir." I had my pipe going and I saw that my men were unloading Bergens from the fuselage. "You can fly a plane then, sir."

I nodded, "My father and I run a small charter company. It would have been easier with a co-pilot but Lance Corporal

Williams did well." We reached my men, "Well done, lads! You can have a couple of days off. There is your transport."

Corporal Dixon spoke for them all when he said, "The others, sir? What about them?"

"We have no word yet but I believe they should be safe. Pyongyang has fallen and that is the largest place they will pass. The Colonel has sent a message. However, if they are lost then I will go back out and find them."

They all nodded, "And we will come with you, sir!"

They headed for the waiting truck. I would make my own way back. I knew that this debrief would be a long one. What I had learned from the prisoners of war was disturbing. The Captain lit a cigarette as we headed back to the Colonel's office, "The Americans are racing for the border, sir. I believe that they intend to cross."

I stopped, "Into China?"

"I think so! I mention it here because, well I am not sure of the views of the Colonel on the matter. This is just something I picked up in the mess."

"Suicide! The North Koreans are one thing but the Chinese! Let us hope that someone sees sense before they try that." What worried me was not so much that MacArthur might attempt to invade China, there were enough level heads in Washington to stop that, but that the Chinese might suspect that the UN-led forces might do so. The sleeping dragon that was China was best left asleep!

"When I reached Colonel White's office there was just the duty sergeant at the desk. He beamed at us, "Step inside sir and the Colonel will be with you momentarily. Congratulations, sir. That sure was ballsy."

Captain Warwick asked, "Ballsy?"

I nodded, "An American expression and I think it is complimentary. Thank you, Sergeant. Is that coffee?" I gestured to the pot.

He nodded, "I think the Colonel has some rye waiting for you as well, sir."

"And I will enjoy that but I have been awake for almost forty-eight hours and if I am to be in any way coherent then I need coffee."

"Of course, sir!" He leapt to his feet and poured me a mug. "Cream and sugar, sir?"

"Just the way it comes."

He returned to his desk, picked up the phone and dialled, "Have a plate of ham sandwiches brought up to the Colonel's office, pronto!"

The coffee was good and I had drunk two mugs by the time the Colonel appeared, "Good news, Major, your boys made it. They are with the Marines and Major Poulson is being airlifted to the hospital here in Seoul. They have good people. The others are being sent south by truck. You did fine work. The aerial photographs of Sunchon came in. It was a truly remarkable piece of work. You held off half a battalion and your losses were minimal."

I poured myself a third cup and shook my head, "Not in our opinion, sir. There are eight brave men buried there."

Both the Colonel and the Captain were desk men and they could never understand the bond between fighting men. There was an embarrassed silence which was, thankfully, broken with the arrival of the sandwiches. There were enough to feed a platoon! The Colonel gestured for us to enter his office and the Sergeant brought a spare chair. He had a stenographer's note pad with him.

"I thought that Sergeant Houlihan could take notes, it will be easier than you writing a report."

I smiled, "Thank you, sir." As I ploughed my way through the ham sandwiches I went through the events in order. I gave the facts and tried to avoid any emotive language. I finished with our landing. I saw the Sergeant shake his head.

The Colonel said, "Get that typed up, Sergeant and the Major can read and amend it."

"Sir." The Sergeant looked at me, "This would make a helluva movie, sir."

I shook my head, "It is too far-fetched to make into a film."
He closed the door and I lit my pipe.

The Colonel beamed, "Well, it looks like this war is almost over. The 1st Marine Division and the 1st Cavalry Division are driving for the border. The 8th Cavalry is at the Chosin Reservoir already! That is just a hop and a jump from China."

I said nothing but poked a match into the ash in my pipe to loosen the fibres beneath.

My silence was eloquent, "Major, I take it you do not agree?"

"Sir, the last thing you need is for the Chinese to become aggressive. There was a Russian MiG which strafed us. The Russians provided advisers and the aeroplane I brought back was Chinese. The tank we destroyed was Chinese. If they come over the border, sir, they will come mob-handed!"

He smiled, "I understand what you are saying but this is way above our pay grades. I think it is a case of bluff and double bluff. We have the threat of the atomic bomb. The Chinese will sue for peace and we will have a unified Korea."

"And General MacArthur will go home a hero." I could not keep my words neutral. I knew I had gone too far from the Colonel's reaction. The general was something of an icon amongst the American military. I had met him. He was a competent general but he an ego the size of Texas. "I am sorry sir, that was uncalled for. I have had no sleep for forty-eight hours and most of my men are still too far away for me to be happy about it."

The Colonel smiled, "You are quite right and I understand. Here let us have a glass of rye. This is a fifteen-year-old Maker's Mark. I think you will enjoy it." He poured us a generous glass each and said, "Here is to an early end to the war and home for Christmas."

We echoed his sentiments but I knew that we would still be in Korea come Christmas.

It was lunchtime by the time we had finished. There was much to tell him, especially about the treatment of prisoners of war. Sergeant Houlihan typed it up and I signed it. No amendments were necessary. Captain Warwick had managed to acquire a jeep and he gave me a lift back to the camp. The Colonel offered me lunch but I was exhausted and I wanted to give my men the good news about the rest of the team.

"Well, Captain, is your work done now? Do you move on now that this mission is over?"

"I am not sure. I think I am being moved to Pyongyang but I shall miss working with you chaps."

"You hardly know us!"

"You would be surprised. Talking to Ashcroft on the radio showed me the regard your men have for you. You are almost a lucky charm. Even when you were surrounded and attacked by the Russian aeroplane, Ashcroft still believed that you would get them out of there and he was right. You are a reservist and yet you have such a professional attitude that it astounds me."

"Thank you for that, Captain, but it is down to my mother and father. They brought me up this way. I just hope that the next generation is brought up in the same fashion."

None of the men had gone to bed and they were all outside the tents, despite the cold. They huddled in their greatcoats and smoked. When the Captain pulled up, they surrounded us, "Well, sir?"

"They are safe and the Major is being airlifted to a hospital here in Seoul!"

They all cheered and the Captain, as he put the jeep into gear, shook his head, "I will never experience this sort of esprit de corps."

I was not sure if he was talking to me or himself but I said, "You, will, at least, survive the war. Take that, Captain. We have chosen our route and we can't go back now, even if we wanted to. This is our fate and we have to live with it."

It took two days for the men to reach us. The 1st Middlesex had rejoined their own regiment and the men who were still injured and wounded were hospitalized. For the rest, it was a homecoming like VE day. Commandos old and new greeted each other like old friends. The fourteen or so hours we had spent in Fort Zinderneuf had been enough. They were one unit. I had been to the American PX to buy some American whisky. I had two bottles for the enlisted men, one for the NCOs and one for the Lieutenant and myself. We would not drink it all but whatever was left I would give to the enlisted men.

We sat outside our tents with snow falling. We had found two oil drums and they made a good fire. With Marine Harris back we had our singer and he regaled us with Al Jolson songs. Jake and I said little. We listened to the men as they bantered and spoke of the battle of Sunchon. We had won and done so against the odds. Our two escapes had been quite remarkable and we knew that the legend would grow with the telling. Many other units had heard of our escape and it gave hope. If you were trapped then there was a chance that you could survive. We were living proof.

Jake tapped my glass, "Cheers sir."

I said, "Cheers!" and raised my eyebrows.

He laughed, "What must you have thought of me when I first arrived. What a pompous little man I was. That man could not have sailed a barge down an enemy-infested river. It was you and the Sergeant Major who made it possible."

"Sergeant Majors have been doing that since Waterloo. You just needed time to find yourself."

"Don't do yourself a disservice, sir. You know how to lead and that is a rare skill. I can see that. Now that it is almost over what will you do next? Stay in or go back home?"

"Jake, this is not over. I will go home when it is and that will not be for some time."

He nodded and sipped the whisky. "I hope the Major is alright. He is one tough Commando!"

"They all are but I hope he can cope with the loss of a leg. He is lucky to be alive but he lived for the Commandos. He will have to find something else."

"It is in your blood though, sir. I mean, you will go back to your business but this is part of you, isn't it? You can't just shed it like an old uniform."

I laughed, "You suddenly got wise, Lieutenant! You are right but this little war has taught me that it will be my last one. I am getting slow; at Sunchon I missed things that five years ago I would have seen. This is a young man's game. It is your time. This will be my last war and I hope that you and the Colonel are right and that it is over but I fear it is not!"

The Lieutenant could not handle his whisky and a short time later he began to snore. Sergeant Major Thorpe and I put him to bed. When we emerged from the tent the Sergeant Major said, "Right lads, better think about hitting your beds."

I threw the bottle with the remains of the whisky I had been drinking with Jake to Rafe Smith, "Finish this off and then bed. No run in the morning but the day after..."

Rafe adeptly caught the bottle and said, "Thank you, sir."

Ken Thorpe said, "The lads did well, sir when we came south and the Lieutenant, well he is a different bloke now from the one who joined us a short time ago."

"Did you have much trouble?"

"They had a couple of manned bridges and we were fired at but the Lieutenant held his nerve and we suffered no casualties. To be honest we were all more worried about you. We had escaped but we thought you were in the bag. If we hadn't had the Major and the other wounded, I think that the lads would have landed and come back for you."

I gave the Sergeant Major a stern look, "But you and the Lieutenant would have stopped them, right?"

He chuckled, "Probably, sir, but it did not come to that so we will never know, sir. What are the orders for tomorrow?"

The snow had begun to fall again. It made me think about the next weeks leading up to Christmas. The Americans thought that the majority of the troops would be home by Christmas. We had to make plans for a longer stay. "We can't live in tents over winter. I will see the Colonel tomorrow. What say we use local buildings in Seoul? I mean there must be empty buildings and I would prefer something sturdier than tents especially in a Korean winter."

"A good idea, sir. I mean this American food is all very well but the lads have been asking for Shepherd's Pie and Bangers and Mash. They like cooking for themselves."

"And we had better get winter uniforms for Sergeant Grant and the other lads we recovered. We need to check for mail. It seems like weeks since we had any and letters from home will lift the spirits of the lads."

"Will do. It isn't all about fighting is it sir?"

"No indeed."

I had passed the point of sleep. The whisky had if anything, woken me up and so I went to the tent and, after ensuring that Jake was covered by blankets and had a bucket close to his head, I wrote a letter to Susan. When I had finished then I was ready for bed and I slept. My dreams were haunted by the faces of the men killed by the MiG. Allenby's injury had meant he was on the machine gun and not Bates. Bates had survived and Allenby had not. Such were the threads of our lives which determined life and death. The dreams were a warning to me.

I rose late, woken by the sound of retching from the Lieutenant's bunk into the bucket. I stood, "Are you alright, Jake?"

"Yes, sir, sorry, sir. I am not much of a drinker."

"Don't worry about it. It was a celebration." I grabbed my towel and coat. "I will go and take a shower. Listen, the Sergeant Major and I were talking last night. Winter is not the time to be in a tent. I will see the Colonel. If we can't get accommodation here, we will see about renting digs in the town. You might as well come with me to the meeting. It will be good experience for you."

I then sat down to write the letters to the families of the men who died. It would not have been right to do it while drinking. This needed sober reflection and the correct choice of words. That done I stepped out into a white world and a cold one at that. Sergeant Grant was feeding wood into the oil drums and Sergeant Major Thorpe and the other NCOs were drinking tea, "Morning sir!"

"Morning lads."

Lance Corporal Pike shouted, "If it stays like this, sir, we will have a White Christmas in a few weeks' time!"

"I always think that Christmas cards are the best place for snow."

After I had showered, dressed and breakfasted, Jake and I went to the admin office. Sergeant Houlihan was on duty and he shook his head when I asked if the Colonel was available. "Sorry, sir. There is a big push up north and he is with the other senior officers planning what to do when we have the whole of Korea. It looks like you have done with fighting, sir. I heard the Colonel saying that he doubted your specialist skills would be needed again. You could well be home for Christmas." He also told me that all the accommodation was being used. I would find something in the town.

I doubted it but we left the office anyway and headed for the motor pool. I asked the duty sergeant for a jeep but he shook his head, "Sorry, sir. Your Captain Warwick took my last jeep to the airfield yesterday. He was on his way north. We will have to wait until someone brings it back."

I could not sit around and twiddle my thumbs. The Sergeant Major had set an itch in my head and so Jake and I wrapped up in our greatcoats and left the camp to walk into town. When Seoul had fallen to the North Koreans there had been much damage to the town. We had driven up the road many times but I had not looked closely at the buildings. Most of the buildings within forty yards of the main gates had been demolished by the Americans but beyond that, they had been left, no matter what their condition. I knew that when the war ended there would need to be a great deal of work to remedy the damage done. The buildings were all empty. The first three we looked at looked structurally unsound but then we came to a block which had obviously been shops and restaurants. The doors hung from them; that was blast damage and snow had blown inside but when we entered the first one, a food shop, I saw that although the windows had been blown in the walls were sound. We went up the stairs and saw that there were two rooms and they had been the bedrooms of the family who lived there. We went out of the back where there was a yard which

was protected by a wall. Looking down the row of houses and
businesses we could see that the roof had been damaged in
only one place and there were even some windows remaining at
the rear while at the front the shattered windows could be boarded
up.

"If the other shops are in the same condition this might well
suit, Lieutenant. We are close enough to the compound and the
base. I think this might do nicely!"

He looked dubious, "It would take a lot of work, sir!"

"And that is precisely what the lads need." I did not want
bored Marines.

We found four habitable dwellings. One had been a café of
some kind and had a kitchen. Like all Korean kitchens, it used
large wood-burning stoves. There was no electricity but then again,
we had none in the tents. If the Colonel agreed we would move in!
After we had assessed the buildings we headed back to the base.
The Colonel was still busy when we returned to the office and I
told Sergeant Houlihan what we intended.

"Sir, I can get you a Quonset hut! You don't need to move into
a bomb site!" I could tell that he was appalled at the thought.

"Sergeant, as much as we enjoy your hospitality my men are
used to fending for themselves. I will just need to get in touch with
British Headquarters to arrange the funding. I do not think it will
be a problem. Asking is a courtesy really."

He shook his head, "Sir, I know you are our allies but I
sometimes understand the Koreans more than I understand you
guys. No offence, sir!"

"And none taken."

We returned to the camp and I gathered the NCOs to explain
what I intended. Had there been a wave of disapproval then I might
have reconsidered but they were overwhelmingly in favour of it.
Lance Corporal Lake rubbed his hands, "You know, sir, when the
19th Infantry bugged out a couple of weeks ago they left a
generator. It is still there, covered with a tarpaulin. I am sure we
could find it a good home!"

I adopted a blank expression, "You know, Lake, that as senior British officer on this camp, I could not possibly condone such behaviour. Of course, if I know nothing about it then it becomes an act of God!"

He tapped his nose, "Righto, sir. Message received and understood!"

"First things first; Sergeant Major Thorpe, I suggest you take the men to the building and begin to clean it out. We may be squatting but we do have standards."

"Sir!"

"And the Lieutenant and I will see about getting some supplies until HQ can contribute to our housekeeping."

I took the Lieutenant to the canteen. I did not see the duty officer, instead, I found the Master Sergeant who was in charge of cooking. "I just came to thank you, Master Sergeant, for all the fine food you have served us."

"You are leaving, sir? You just got back from your last raid."

"We are not going far. We have decided we would like solid walls around us for the winter. We will be fending for ourselves."

He smiled, "Then you could still come here for your meals, sir."

"True, but we will still require food and other supplies. I suppose we could go to the Seoul market."

I saw the expression on his face; like most enlisted men he mistrusted local markets. "Sir, let me give you some basics!" He turned, "Allen, fetch a side of Canadian bacon." He smiled, "We got this in for you guys anyway. A tray of bread, the canisters of tea we bought in and a box of dried milk and eggs." He smiled, "That should keep you going for a while sir and I will find some fresh food. If you send your guys along, later on, we will have it all ready for you."

"Thank you, Master Sergeant."

He wagged a playful finger at me, "But you come along for dinner tonight, sir. We have some porterhouse steaks just flown in and in a week or so we have our Thanksgiving dinner! You guys will enjoy that: turkey, honeyed yams, sweetcorn and pumpkin pie!"

"I look forward to it and thank you, Master Sergeant."

"Sir, after the two missions you guys pulled off, it is the least we could do."

As we headed back to our tents Jake shook his head, "Where did you learn to do that sir? It isn't in the manual."

"Most of the useful stuff isn't. Remember when you were training and you were dumped somewhere to find your way back home?"

"Yes, sir."

"This is the same thing. You improvise. I think this move will be good for the section. It will make us all feel more like British soldiers. Start to pack away your gear and I will go and get on the radio to Headquarters."

I was lucky. When I managed to get through to someone it was a lowly lieutenant and he was a little intimidated by me. He agreed to send the funds to pay for our food as well as more ammunition for the Lee Enfields and Mills bombs. As he was so acquiescent, I pushed my luck. "Those four Bren guns we requisitioned have still to arrive."

"Sorry sir, I will expedite them immediately."

Sadly, my request for our back mail was not granted as there was some sort of issue at the British end but I felt pleased with what I had achieved. By the time I reached our tent, the Lieutenant had packed all of his gear. "I will just pop down to the new quarters, sir, and give the lads a hand."

I smiled. He was now one of the lads and that was a massive improvement in the young officer who had come to us. Before I packed, I filled my pipe and read the letter I had written to Susan. I was happy with it. Sometimes, especially when I had been drinking, I tended to be a little maudlin and sentimental. I was pleased that I had not. I sealed the letter. I would post it before I joined my men. Then I packed all of my gear.

By the time I headed to the new quarters it was noon. I saw a great deal of rubbish outside the buildings. The men had been busy. I saw Haynes and Collins refitting the doors and Carter and Campbell were boarding up the broken windows. The snow had turned to sleet and it would be cold in the buildings. I saw that Lake had the generator rigged up and he was frowning. "A problem, Lake?"

"We will need fuel, sir! Leave it to me and Batesy, we will sort something out."

I shook my head, the only fuel they could obtain would be from the Americans and that meant stealing! I watched the men as they busied themselves. We had our own cots and bedding but we would need food to augment that which the Americans had provided. I waved over the Sergeant Major, "Have some men go to the canteen. The Master Sergeant has some supplies for us."

"Well done, sir. This will all be shipshape and Bristol fashion by tonight. We can stay here if you like."

I nodded, "We will eat in the mess tonight. They have steak and it would be a shame to deprive the men of that. Are there fireplaces?"

"Sort of but I am not sure how effective they will be."

"Then, for tonight, we rough it. It will be warmer than in the tents anyway! I will pop into the market and buy some fresh food. I will see if we can get some pots to use for cooking." We had plenty of tinned food but my men liked to have fresh produce whenever possible.

He shook his head, "You don't need to buy pots, sir, we found some, sir, and some dishes in what must have been the caff!"

"Good."

I headed into town. I had passed the market on numerous occasions but I had yet to visit it. The bombing of the town, the evacuation and the reoccupation meant that normal methods of shopping were difficult but the old market survived. I had some local money. It had been in my Bergen. When we had been sent in to extract Blair, I had been given it in case it was needed. It was not and now I would put it to good use. Even though my Korean was rudimentary, I felt confident that I could use a mixture of Korean and signs to buy what I needed. The market was still busy and I took a moment or two to orientate myself. We needed fresh fruit and vegetables. I knew that some of the men had a sweet tooth and so I wanted some pastries. I was not sure what would be available. What I would not be buying were kimchi and the fiery hot sauces. I might quite like them but I knew the taste buds of my men would not cope with the heat.

For some reason I found myself drawn to a stall with a one-armed market seller. He seemed loud and ostentatious. He was a true showman and he had attracted an audience. I waited patiently for him to finish; it was an English trait. When he had finished and served his customers, he turned to me and surprised me by speaking American English.

"You are an English soldier! What brings you to Seoul?"

I laughed, "The war."

He held up his left arm, "And the war brought me home and I lost this. My name is Ji-hoo Hwang but you can call me Joe. I got used to it when I sailed the Pacific in a freighter."

I nodded, "And I am Major Harsker, Tom."

He held out his good hand and I shook it. "I lost this when the bastards from the north attacked us in summer! Can you believe that they won't let me fight?"

I nodded, "I can understand it. And, of course, you can't go back to sea."

"I don't want to. This is not over Major. Until we destroy every communist in the peninsula the war will go on!"

There was real venom in his voice. If there were more like him then this country was in for a long war!

He smiled, "Anyway, the rant is over, how can I help you, sir?"

"My section has just taken over some houses close to the compound and we are fending for ourselves." I held out a wad of money. "We need fresh food and supplies."

"Then you have come to the right man!" Like a magician doing a trick, he whisked the roll of notes from my hand. I will send my boys with your goods! They will be there by the time you reach your new home."

"Boys?"

He gestured to about eight boys none of whom was older than ten, "Orphans. The North Koreans killed their parents. I have taken them under my wing. I will teach them how to fight in case the Commies come back!"

"How do you know what we want?"

"I know you need fresh fruit and vegetables. Your men will want something sweet and some alcohol. I served amongst Americans and Limeys! I know what they want. Do not worry, sir, you will not be disappointed."

For some reason, I trusted him and I gave a half bow, "I am in your debt!"

He smiled, "And we will keep an eye on your property for you. It will be safe!"

By the time I reached the new quarters they were clean and they were secure. They were also bare. My new friend was wrong and the boys did not beat me back. Sergeant Major Thorpe said, "Well we just need our cots and gear. The generator is purring like a kitten so we have power when we need it."

Just then a Korean voice shouted, "Hey mister!"

I turned and saw Ji-hoo Hwang's boys. I gestured with my arm and they marched in and began to pile up boxes. Lieutenant Morrison said, "What the…"

"Don't worry, Lieutenant, I have just met the Korean equivalent of Fagin but I think he is on our side."

When the boys had gone, giving us a cheeky wave as they did so, I said, "Let's go back to the compound and have a shower before dinner. We can bring our gear back later."

"Will it be safe, sir?"

"I think so, Sergeant Grant, I think so!"

Chapter 11

By Thanksgiving, we had made dramatic improvements to our new home. We had one of the houses as officers' quarters, one for the NCOs and two for the enlisted men. Jake and I each had our own room. We had cobbled together some furniture so that we were quite comfy. We had brought the cots from our tents. The lack of windows did not matter as we had electricity and it meant we did not need to bother with blackout curtains. A bonus was that we had had mail from home and the chastened Lieutenant at Headquarters had sent us the Bren guns and money for food. We still ate most of our main meals at the base for we were not fools and the food was good but we enjoyed cooking our own lunches and breakfasts. We had proper bacon!

Each time we visited the base I asked Sergeant Houlihan about our transfer back to Commonwealth control. However, MacArthur's advance meant that we were almost forgotten and we all became fitter as we ran twice a day and the newer men received more training from old hands like Sergeant Major Thorpe and Sergeant Grant. The Colonel had not been happy with our decision to decamp, as I discovered a week after we had made the move, but three weeks later he was too busy to worry about us due to the bad news from the north. The sleeping dragon had finally woken and China had sent over two hundred thousand men across the border to strike without warning the most advance units of the allied army. The 8th Cavalry was surrounded at the Chosin Reservoir and other elements were trapped behind enemy lines and a Dunkirk type evacuation looked like it would be needed soon in the northeast of the country. MacArthur's gamble had failed. The Thanksgiving dinner was enjoyable for my men but there was a mood of doom and gloom amongst our hosts. Operation Home for

Christmas seemed to stick in men's throats. All the gains we had made were as quickly lost and the roads were clogged with units retreating towards the 38th Parallel and the original border.

I was aware that we would be needed again just as soon as someone remembered that there was a section of Commandos who could be used behind enemy lines. Even though winter had set in and we had to endure both rain and snow not to mention cold, I took the section out twice a day for two five-mile runs. In addition, we continued with our training. We were now a much stronger unit. The old hands had endured incarceration and it made them stronger somehow. We had a backbone of NCOs that would be the envy of any unit. We had kept the North Korean weapons we had taken and they were disassembled and then reassembled so that we knew how they worked; who knew when that skill might be needed. We replaced the mortar shells and prepared for the day when we would have to fight again.

On the last day of November, the Colonel sent a jeep for me. Major Poulson was about to be repatriated and he was at the airfield waiting to board his aircraft. I was given the opportunity to say goodbye. I was relieved to see him in a chair with a pair of crutches. It showed that he had not given into the loss of his leg. He also looked healthier than when I had last seen him after the operation. I saw the medical transport standing by and others were being loaded on stretchers. The Chinese initiative had already begun to hurt.

He tried to rise, "Sit! You have earned it! I grabbed his hand, "You are looking well."

"For a one-legged man."

I thought of Ji-hoo, "None of that; we both know of lads buried in French cemeteries who would swap a leg for the cards they were dealt."

"You are right, sir, it is just that this was so unnecessary. If I had had medical treatment, I would not have lost the leg."

My voice softened for he was right, "I know. So, what will you do?"

He shook his head and looked terrified, "I don't know, sir! That is the plain truth. I have spent the last ten years as a soldier. I know nothing else."

A flight sergeant said, "Sir, the Major is the last to board."

"Alright. Listen, there is always a job for you with our company."

"Charity, sir?"

I shook my head, "You know me better than that. You are a soldier and we need security. There must be other ex-servicemen who need jobs and you could manage them. You know how to organise and you know the sort of skills we need. We have been lucky but I know of other charter companies who have had consignments stolen." I saw the flight sergeant tap his watch, "Be patient, flight. You owe the Major that, at least, and I am a pilot. I know that five minutes here or there will not hurt!"

"Sorry, sir."

I turned back to Polly. "All I am saying is think about it. They can give you a prosthetic and that might change your life. You don't know. When you reach Blighty give Dad a ring. You know him. I will write to him and tell him about your situation. Promise me."

He nodded, "I owe a great deal to you, sir, but I won't take charity."

"And this won't be charity. You will be earning your money." He nodded acceptance. "Now you had better go before Flight here has me on a fizzer." I winked at the airman. He smiled.

I clasped Polly's hand, "Thank you, sir, and you take care. You are the last of the originals."

"Don't worry. I will."

He used his crutches to pull himself upright and then headed to the Dakota swinging his damaged leg as he went. It showed he had been practising and that was Polly all over. The self-pity would pass and he would become the commando I had known for the last ten years. When we returned to the base I went into the office and asked to send a telegram. I must have sounded serious for no objections were put in my way and I sent a telegram to Dad. I felt much better that night as I lay in my cot.

I was summoned, the next day, to the compound where there was a great deal of activity. I saw sandbags being unloaded from trucks and heavier weapons strategically placed. Sergeant Houlihan handed me a mug of coffee when I entered the office, "The Colonel is in the briefing room, sir."

"What's up Sergeant?"

"The Chinese have attacked all along the front and pushed our boys back. It looks bad, sir, but the Colonel can give you more details." He was a loyal sergeant and he knew more than he was saying but I respected his attitude.

The briefing room was already thick with smoke and I slipped my unlit pipe back into my pocket, I would not add to the fug. I was not the last officer to arrive and I took a seat next to an Air Force Colonel. I vaguely recognised him from my visits to the airfield. He must have recognised me too, for he spoke first, "I'll bet you are glad to be back here and not up in Indian country."

"You mean now that the Chinese have thrown their cap into the ring? Then yes, you are right. The Chinese have a little more firepower than an old Hudson and a few biplanes."

"You did a good job flying back the Lockheed and you are right. We have seen more Chinese jets lately. At the moment their bases are north of Korea but once they get their act together then we could be in for some serious dogfights."

Just then Colonel Wilding stood, "Gentlemen, come to attention please."

We all stood and a General with two aides appeared. He took off his hat and stood with his arms behind his back and his feet apart. This was a soldier! "Gentlemen, I am General Matthew Ridgeway and President Truman has sent me here to gather facts about the conduct of the war and our ability to stop the Communist threat. What I have discovered so far tells me that we are in a grave and serious position. Captain?" His aide pulled back the cloth hiding the map and handed the General a pointer. He tapped a port on the north-eastern side of North Korea, "We have just evacuated over a hundred thousand men and civilians from Hungnam. They were in danger of being captured." He tapped various other points further south. "Here, here and here, our men have been forced back. General MacArthur's gains have all been lost. We are back to the 38th Parallel." He allowed that to sink in. It meant that they were less than thirty-five miles, as the crow flies, from Seoul. What had gone wrong?

A hand went up and Colonel Wilding said, "There will be time for questions later. The General has not finished."

"We cannot allow what happened in summer to be repeated. We have to stop the North Koreans and their Chinese allies here. We have to endure what they throw at us. But I have to warn you of a new tactic which has caused some of our units to panic. The Chinese often preface their attacks with loud trumpets and gongs. I have not witnessed it but believe that it is truly terrifying and many men and units have broken and run before such an attack. Your men must steel themselves. I am now leaving to meet with General MacArthur. Colonel Wilding has the orders for this area. I leave you with this message; make them bleed for every inch of land they try to take. We will prevail. We have better soldiers, sailors and airmen. The enemy may have more but we have better. Until the line is stabilised then we defend and blunt their attack. Do not worry we will go on the offensive once more but for now, we hold!"

I liked the General for he had less bluster than MacArthur. I knew his reputation for I had heard his name before. The Colonel allowed the General's party to leave and then, sitting on the edge of the desk said, "Pete, what was your question?"

"Why don't we nuke the bastards?"

I heard murmurs of approval. The Colonel lit a cigarette and shook his head, "We know that the allies of the Chinese, the Russians, also have nuclear weapons. We know from Major Harsker that Stalin has deployed MiGs in North Korea. We cannot risk a nuclear war no matter how many people wish it." I wondered then if some senior officer, perhaps even MacArthur himself, had discussed the idea. The Colonel was right, a nuclear war was a step too far.

A voice shouted, "So what do we do, Colonel? Sit on our butts and wait?"

The Colonel smiled, "When the North Koreans attacked in summer the army here was unprepared and they sliced through like a knife through butter. We will blunt their attack. The United Nations are bringing in more troops but it takes time to get here and we have to buy that time. We make this city into a fortress. The sandbags which are being placed now will just be the start. We build bunkers for our guns. The airfield will also be defended. The troops who landed there in the last four days will defend it." He picked up the General's pointer and tapped a spot just south of Seoul, "And here, south of Suwon, there will be a second line of defence." He put down his pointer and picked up a sheet of paper. "Here is a list of the precise positions for each of your units."

He read through them and when he had finished, I realised that he had not mentioned the Commandos. I knew him well enough to know that was not an oversight. We were dismissed and he waved me over, "Tom, come to my office."

The door closed and I began to fill my pipe. "I saw you noticed that you were not mentioned and there was a reason for that. When you left the base, I was not best pleased but, in hindsight, it might be a clever move. You and your men are now in a position to protect the southern approach to the base and to give covering fire if and when we retreat. I want you to strengthen your quarters. I have four Browning 50 Calibre machine guns and explosives for you."

"Explosives, sir?"

"Yes, we want you to mine the buildings so that if you have to leave you can slow them down. The main road south passes by their front."

"And if we do retreat?"

"Then you will make your way to Suwon. It is just fifteen miles south of Seoul and you and your men have already shown that you know how to move behind enemy lines."

"Then you want us to cover a retreat?"

"It is a lot to ask and you can say no but I hope that you will not. All we need is forty minutes or an hour to allow us to get across the bridge. That will be a busy crossing as almost every unit in the area will be heading for it. It is a choke point and we will need time to get across. I hope that you and your men can buy us that time."

He knew that I would not refuse but I would not commit suicide. "It will be my decision when we leave."

It was not a question and the Colonel nodded, "Of course. No one doubts your courage, Major, but we expect you to try to live."

We discussed the logistics until we were interrupted by Sergeant Houlihan, "A telegram sir, for the Major."

I looked at the Colonel who nodded. I tore it open.

OF COURSE STOP PAUL IS MORE THAN WELCOME
STOP YOU TAKE CARE STOP DAD

I smiled, "Good news?"

I nodded, "Not unexpected but reassuring. And now, sir, if you will excuse me I have much to do."

As I walked down the road I now viewed it, not as my way home, but as a place to ambush. The houses and businesses opposite had been destroyed in the summer attack. The rubble there would afford cover and would have to be mined. The difficulty was that we could not fit detonators until we knew that an attack was imminent. Although our new home faced the road, we would have to create a gun emplacement to face north and the compound. That would be easiest from the roof. I would have to get a couple of bazookas from the Colonel and find men to use them. I stopped in the middle of the road and looked back. If the Americans were driven out, they would have to drive south down the road and that meant we could not mine the road. They would be followed by eager Chinese. We would have to find some way of blocking the road once the Americans had gone. I walked to my quarters. The problem would then be for us to escape south too. We would have the advantage that there would be less than thirty of us and we could split up. I needed to do a recce south. I was suddenly aware that I was soaked and cold. The snow had stopped falling a few days ago but that did not mean the weather had improved. It was still very cold and melting snow was equally unpleasant.

When I entered the quarters, I found the Lieutenant cleaning his gun.

"Gather the NCOs and men in the men's mess. I have news for them."

We had used the upstairs of one of the buildings as a mess. For one thing, it was warmer and it was also large as the internal wall had just been made of lath which we had removed. We could all squeeze in. I did not sugar the pill but told them what I had been told. I outlined my plans so that they would all know the ultimate goal.

Sergeant Grant said, "We are the rearguard then sir? Just us?"

"Probably." He nodded. He just wanted clarification. I had my pipe going, "I was in the retreat to Dunkirk. This will not be like that as the Americans are already building a second line of defence south of here. Winter is here already and that will slow down the advance but be under no illusions there are two hundred thousand Chinese troops already in North Korea and they have more than a million just waiting to follow. We will need all the ammunition we can muster and then some. We use the strengths of this building and the fact that we are in a perfect place to ambush the enemy. Trucks will bring our extra gear but I want you to bring it inside before we unpack it. The North Koreans will have spies and I don't want them to know what we are about. Lieutenant, when you and the Lance Corporal plant the explosives in the rubble you will do so at night. Right, if there are no questions then I will have a short meeting with the NCOs and we knuckle down to some work."

As the men were leaving, Lance Corporal Pike asked, "And when do we expect them, sir?"

"That, my friend, is the unanswerable question. It could be tomorrow or it could be in two months. It depends on how much they are held up on their drive south so the sooner we are done the better."

Once the men had gone, I said, "Sergeant Grant, I want an opening making at the north end of the gable end. I want a Browning there and, when I get them, a bazooka. Corporal Dixon, we will use the north yard for the mortars. They will be hidden and we can use a spotter to give them fall of shot. We need every distance marking on paper so that when we fire, we know what we will hit. This is a static position and we can prepare. I want firing slits in the rooves of the attics. We have little enough going for us, let's use what we have. Lieutenant, you take charge, I want to see Ji-hoo. I think he may prove useful."

He was at his stall and, as usual, it was busy. He saw me and bent to speak with one of his helpers. He sidled over to me and lit a cigarette. He did it so adeptly you would never have known that he had only lost one arm months ago. "It is not the day you normally come to market and I am guessing that you are not here to buy food."

"You are right."

"Then this must be about the news you received from the General this morning." My mouth opened involuntarily. He shrugged, "You should not be surprised for there are many of our people who work on the base."

I nodded, "And that is why I need your help. There may be North Korean spies."

"Undoubtedly there are."

"And can you do something about them?"

"Probably but I am unarmed." A sly look came over his face. "Now if we had weapons then…"

I knew what he wanted but it was taking a huge risk. "Suppose I could get you some weapons; what then?"

"Then the threat of a North Korean spy knowing what you are doing would disappear."

"Come to the house tonight, after dark."

"Of course."

I would let them have some of the captured North Korean handguns. We had limited ammunition for them anyway. If Ji-hoo was discovered with them then it could not be traced back to the Allied army. Once I had seen him, I felt better. I never saw his watchers but I knew they were there. We did not miss the North Korean weapons and when the Americans left he would be the resistance against the invaders.

We worked hard right up until Christmas and each day we expected an attack which did not materialise. The retreating United Nations forces were making it hard for the Chinese to make the rapid gains they had in the summer. The wintery conditions aided our forces. From what we heard, when we ate meals at the base, the Chinese were using the sheer weight of numbers to overwhelm positions and, more ominously, Russian fighters were now involved. The allied pilots were still superior to the enemy and bringing down more of their aeroplanes but my father had told me that in aerial combat a good pilot could still be brought down by a lucky shot from a bad pilot or, as in the case of the Red Baron, a fluke rifle bullet from the ground. One such bullet had driven off the Russian MiG when it had attacked us. We now had two bazookas and Carter and Collins operated those. We had spare Bren guns as we now had the Browning 50 Calibre. For the first time, we had serious firepower. We also had plenty of ammunition and explosives.

When Christmas Day came, we took our first day off. Of course, if the Chinese had been clever, they would have chosen that day to attack although some of the Allied forces were not Christian and did not adhere to the Christian traditions; the Thai and Turkish elements would not celebrate. It was, however, a muted celebration. MacArthur's much-publicised plan, Operation Home for Christmas, had failed and the truckloads of wounded troops who passed through Seoul was a testament to that failure. The bright spot was the appointment of General Ridgeway to the 8th Army. I had liked him and his words. With him, it was all about the plan and not the ego.

I dined with the Colonel and his officers. The base was now ringed by heavy and light guns and sandbags. The garrison walked around with helmets and even in the offices, the admin staff kept their helmets and guns close by.

I drank sparingly and enjoyed the wine, which was served, all the more for that. "Well, Colonel, the Chinese have missed a trick. Had they come today, then we would have been unprepared."

"I disagree, Major. We have men watching the north and the radar is constantly manned."

"But are the men prepared?" I waved the stem of my pipe around. Although the mood was muted the officers were drinking and eating as they would at home.

He nodded, "Well, they didn't come and the celebrations are over now."

"And New Year?"

He looked appalled, "You think they might come then?"

"If they don't then they will have made a fundamental error. The days are now at their shortest and their gongs and trumpet tactic works best in the dark when soldiers are at a low ebb anyway. General Ridgeway is improving the morale of the 8th Army and fresh troops are arriving almost daily. Each day's delay works to our advantage." I stood, "My men and I will return to our camp. Everything is prepared and we constantly monitor the radio. As soon as you know anything…"

"Don't worry, Major, you will be the first to know."

As we walked back to our camp I wondered at the lack of tanks around the base. The American M46 Patton tank was superior to anything the Chinese and North Koreans had. The British Centurion was also a powerful tank. Even the Sherman could give a good account of itself. The Colonel had just four and they could be surrounded by fanatical troops and taken out. Not for the first time I wondered at the events which had led us to be brigaded with American forces.

As we neared the houses, I saw the three figures wave and then disappear. Ji-hoo's watchers were diligent. No matter what the weather they were always there. We had boarded up the front entrances to the houses and we used the back passages to gain entry; that way we would not be seen by an attacker. It was an old fashioned sally port. The wooden doors we had replaced were now backed by corrugated iron and braced with iron bars. If we had to leave in a hurry then we would find it easier to get out through the alleys which crisscrossed the rear of the line of buildings. While the Lieutenant checked the rest of the buildings, I went up to the new gun position at the north gable. I saw Sergeant Major Thorpe leading the rest of the men down the hill. They marched and showed that they, too, had drunk sparingly. I waited until the duty NCO came up to relieve me before I left. Corporal Lowery was in command. Each night we had four men on watch; one of the men would listen to the radio. I did not want us to be caught with our trousers down.

The Lieutenant was reading. After I had washed, I picked up the letters which had arrived three days earlier. The Allied Postal Service had realised the morale-boosting effects of mail. I had a hand made Christmas card from Izzy, Sam and William. I ran my hands over it as though I was, somehow, feeling them make the card. Then I re-read the letters from Susan and my mother. Dad was not the greatest letter writer. England was a month behind the war here and they were still reading about MacArthur's advances to the north. The letters spoke of my imminent arrival home. By now they should know the truth for I had written to them just after Thanksgiving and warned them not to believe all that they read. That done I folded the letters and put them in my battledress pocket. The card I propped up on the wooden crate which served as a night table. I kissed the card and said, "Goodnight, kids. Daddy will be home as soon as he can." I had been away for just over half a year and I knew that I would have missed so much. Depressingly I could not see me getting home any time soon. I wondered if Major Poulson had made it home in time for Christmas or was he stuck in some hospital? At least he was out of it.

The next day Ji-hoo came after dark. We had given him guns and he was a happy man. He had a piece of cloth which looked bloody, "We found one of your North Korean spies. He told us of two others." He removed the cloth and I saw the head of the North Korean spy. "We will leave this close to the place we suspect the other spies gather. Soon they will all be dead."

If I thought our war was vicious it was nothing compared with that of Ji-hoo and the North Korean spies.

The weather which had been wet became colder. Sergeant Major Thorpe, who had a nose for such things, predicted snow and thus far he had not been wrong. Certainly, the houses were becoming colder and we were lucky to have the oil drum fires and braziers to keep us warm. The snow began to lie on New Year's Eve. Normally we would have celebrated. In England, people would be first footing. All past ills would be forgotten and doors would be open to allow complete strangers in to partake of a nip of whisky or rum. Many would still carry a lump of coal, a sign of good luck and the old year would be swept away when the back door was opened. Even in wartime, it had still been celebrated but not this year. We all went to bed at the normal time. I had volunteered to be duty officer that night. The others protested but, in truth, I wanted to. I had Ashcroft, Williams, Harris and Bates as my team. Ashcroft fiddled on with the radio. He was less than happy that others operated 'his' radio and he would grumble on about the state in which it had been left.

"They all fiddle with the dial, sir, and there is no need! I mean the base is not going to change the frequency, is it, sir? They all like to think they can be radio operators! It is all very well monitoring signals, sir, but using it? That is the real test!"

We all let him chunter on. It was his way and it kept him occupied.

"Lance Corporal Williams, are you and the Lieutenant happy with the explosives across the road?"

"Oh yes, sir. Until we attach the wires, they are safe as houses. We ran a channel between the cobbles and used a piece of pipe. It means the wires can't be damaged by tanks and the like. As soon as we attach the wires, we hit the plunger and kaboom!" He mimed with his hands and Harris smiled. Williams had an endearing innocence about him and the whole of the section regarded him as a kid brother.

The air was so cold that we could see our breath as we spoke. Here in the old loft, there was no heating and we wore our greatcoats, comforters, balaclavas and gloves. When we fought, we would have to take off some layers but until then we would keep as warm as we could. We had had hot cocoa an hour into the watch and that had helped. I wonder if Mr Flynn was still making stoker's cocoa.

Geoff Bates had been quiet since Sunchon. "It's funny sir, if Allenby hadn't hurt his ankle then he would be here and it would be me in that grave."

"That is a hard road to travel, Bates. If I dwelled on every time someone died or was wounded when it should have been me then I would be locked up in some sort of asylum. One of my first sergeants, Daddy Grant, had a way of explaining it. He said, '*It is like God is playing dice but he doesn't look at the roll. He just rolls and sometimes your number will come up and at others, you survive. Live your life for the man who died instead of you. Be the best at what you do.*'"

"That is not a bad idea, sir. I will do that. Poor Eddie would be dead no matter who was with him." He rubbed his chin. "At least it was quick."

I saw Ashcroft start but before he could speak, I saw the sky light up to the north and heard the scream of 122 mm shells as the Chinese began their New Year Offensive.

Ashcroft said, "Sir, it is the base! They are under attack! There are thousands of Chinese and North Koreans.

"Right lads, time to wake the others up. Bates and Harris see to it. Williams, go and attach the wires. I want those explosives live!" We were about to feel the full force of an attack by almost two hundred thousand men. How long could we hold on?

Chapter 12

We had planned for this and there was no panic but the blind firing of the artillery shells was disconcerting. What had I said about the roll of the dice? The only protection we had was a double pile of sandbags. I took out my binoculars. The Chinese had a better view of the base than the city and already there were explosions from inside the compound. Had we still been in the tents then the odds were we would have been killed already.

Ashcroft said, "The Chinese have tanks as well as thousands of infantrymen, sir. The radio operator sounds worried."

"They just need to do their job." The trouble with the garrison was that they had not had any fighting to do and it now showed.

Lieutenant Morrison climbed the ladder to our lofty eagle's nest, "Everyone is in position and buttoned up. Lance Corporal Williams has wired up the explosives. We are good to go."

"Let us hope that they are not needed for a while." I was not as certain as I sounded. There was a battalion of fighting men on the base and the rest were the equivalent of paper pushers. They knew one end of a gun from the other and that was about it. The handful of tanks they had were their only real defence. They certainly didn't have the firepower of the Chinese. As if to make the point there was a huge explosion from the centre of the base and then the shells began to scream over our heads. They were changing target to the city and with all their guns. There were shelters but I was not certain how effective they would be.

Harris had returned and he had good eyes, "Sir, I can see movement. It looks like the sea. My God, it is the Chinese; there is a sea of them!"

They flooded down the road which led along the side of the base. I knew that Colonel Wilding had some machine gun pits there and suddenly the air was filled with the sound of twenty heavy machine guns. The fires burning in the base must have made the Chinese think that the base was about to fall but the Colonel's clever strategy meant that hundreds of Chinese fell as they were mown down.

"Do we open fire, sir?"

"No one fires, Lieutenant, until I give the order. The minute we fire then they know where we are. We only fire when the base is about to fall and they need covering. The exception is Lofting." Just then my sniper appeared. He had camouflage on his hands and face and he wore his comforter. The end of his rifle was wrapped in layers of black material. It would silence the gun slightly but we needed him to be able to mask his muzzle flash. "Are you ready?"

"Yes, sir."

He lay down in the gable end opening. The Chinese had spread around the southern end of the base and were just two hundred yards from us. The end of his barrel rested on a piece of six by six. "Remember, you go for the officers and the sergeants. If you could get those men with the damned trumpets and gongs then it would help!"

"Yes, sir." He carefully placed a pile of clips next to him.

I used my binoculars. The Chinese were wavering. They were fanatical but fanaticism only takes you so far. I saw an officer raise a sword. He was next to a soldier with a flag. It all looked medieval. The officer spun around as Lofting's bullet took him. The Chinese were all watching the base and when the flag fell to my sniper's next bullet the Chinese waved their fists at the Americans. The machine guns continued to scythe down the Chinese and I saw them begin to fall back. An officer who tried to rally them was hit by Lofting and that opened the flood gates. They streamed north. I knew they had vast numbers of men but I also knew the effect of demoralized troops. I had seen it in the Low Countries. Someone would have to rally the troops and that would buy the Colonel time. When dawn broke, he would be able to call in an airstrike. I could still hear the duel between the Chinese tanks and the Pattons. Behind us, the shells still fell on Seoul. We could not see the city from our vantage point but I knew that there would be fires and many people would die. Others would be fleeing south. The Americans had planned for this and there were Military Police at the various crossroads who would keep the road clear for the Americans when they retreated. The Colonel had told me that they could not hold on to Seoul; too many would die to hold on to something which had no strategic value. Pyongyang had fallen easily as had Seoul the first time. The Colonel was buying time for civilians and other troops to get south of the river and reach the UN lines. The defences south of Suwon were designed to stop men and tanks. Their artillery was massed to pound an enemy into dust. We were just making them bleed and to allow more units to be drafted in to strengthen the line.

"Sir, the Colonel has sent a message. He says that as soon as it is daylight, they are going to send the first of the wounded south. He is calling in an airstrike."

"Tell him good luck."

In the distance, beyond the base, we heard the crack of tank guns as well as sporadic rifle and machine gunfire. I turned to Lance Corporal Williams, "Ask the Sergeant Major to make a brew and get some food for the lads and have two of the Brens brought up here."

"Sir."

"Lieutenant, go down to the ground floor and your detonator. Have Tomlinson and his radio with you."

"You think we will be exploding it soon, sir?"

"I don't know but we might as well be prepared. I just scanned the battlefield and I counted over seven hundred dead men out there. We might run out of bullets before we destroy this army."

"Sir!"

Smith and Hall brought up their Brens and they flanked Bates and Entwhistle who had the Browning. This now meant we could keep up a continuous rate of fire. When the Browning needed a new belt the two Brens could throw their .303 bullets at the Chinese. Thorpe accompanied by Williams brought up teas and bacon sandwiches as the sun peered in the east and the firing died a little. It was almost like the end of a round when the boxers retire to their corners. I knew who was hurting the most. We had lost fewer men but we had fewer to lose.

Then we heard the Sabres and Gloster Meteors as they screamed in from the west. They came from the darkness and their rockets, machine guns and bombs were dropped to the north of the base. At the same time, four trucks appeared at the south gate and hurtled down the road.

"Sir," Ashcroft waved at me, "The trucks will be returning tonight. The Colonel wants us to make sure they are not interfered with."

Sergeant Major Thorpe was still with us, waiting to take down the mugs and tray. He laughed, "Makes them sound like a little old lady. Interfered with!"

The trucks made it down the road without incident. The first flights roared home and for the rest of the day, the Air Force kept a flight of four aeroplanes above us all the time. For part of the day they used six Mustangs which could stay aloft for longer and, I suspect, deliver a more accurate strike. Then at about two in the afternoon black clouds rolled in and I knew that meant the air cover would be grounded. When that happened, the Chinese would attack. The Sabres stayed as long as they could and their presence allowed the four trucks to return.

"Pass the word, I want one man in two to get some sleep. This is going to be a long battle. Ask Sergeant Major Thorpe to join me. We will share a watch!"

Ken nodded at me when he entered the loft. "You get your head down, sir. We all had a couple of hours last night, or was it the night before?"

I handed him the binoculars, "Your guess is as good as mine. Wake me when you need to. A couple of hours would be perfect."

Already confusion over time was kicking in. It often happened in combat. You were so attuned to being alert that time seemed to cease to exist. It was cold in the loft but I lay down next to the internal wall; it was the furthest from the opening. I pulled my balaclava down to cover my face and I entered a world of darkness. The men were silent. They would be respecting the three of us who were trying to sleep.

When Ken shook my shoulder, I was awake instantly and I pulled off my balaclava. "Have they come again?"

"The last Mustang left their airfield an hour ago and the base said that their outposts had heard the sound of tank engines coming from the north." I nodded and yawned. I could have done with more sleep but it had been enough. "Sergeant Grant is organising some food; just tea and corned dog sandwiches but it will fill a hole."

I went to the opening and peered out. It was a shining world of white. The freeze had made the snow whiter and the road blacker. Would that everything was as clear as that. The plan of the General was the only one which gave a chance of success but there were many flaws in it. If the base was overrun before the Colonel could escape then the loss would be incalculable. I saw Ashcroft return to his radio and look at the dial suspiciously. He put on his headphones and listened.

Harris brought up my mug of tea and a stack of sandwiches. "Batesy is bringing the rest, sir." He chuckled, "The lads with the mortars are freezing their bits off outside!"

The Sergeant Major shook his head, "Dozy buggers! They have no need to! I will go down, sir and tell them to light an oil drum. There are walls all around their position and they can't be seen from the north!"

He had just descended when Ashcroft said, "Out!" He took off his headphones and shook his head, "The airfield has been overrun, sir. The Mustangs which just left have had to fly south to the airfield south of Suwon. They got most of the personnel out on transports."

He left unsaid the most obvious comment. We might have lost our air umbrella, at least for the time being and the Chinese would take advantage. The Colonel would also know that he was without air cover and that would affect his decisions. Our plans were in place; when I gave the command, Dunkirk, then the heavy equipment would be booby-trapped or disabled. Everyone would leave their posts immediately that was done and head for the back passages with whatever they needed. Sergeant Grant and the Sergeant Major would bring up the rear and I would lead the section through Seoul to safety. I had walked the route twice. It avoided the main road but was still fraught with danger. The Chinese would be using vehicles and we could be trapped. We would only escape if I was cleverer than the Chinese and if our luck had not totally deserted us!

We needed no radio signal to tell us that the Chinese were attacking. There was a sudden artillery barrage which pounded the base. It stopped after five minutes and we heard the trumpets and gongs. They were coming.

"Stand to!" I cocked my Thompson. This time there would be no screaming jets to drive back the enemy and they knew about the machine guns along the east and west of the base. They would use armour to drive through the centre. We had learned to differentiate between the guns of the different tanks and when the Patton's guns could no longer be heard we knew the end was coming. One of the Shermans must have been dug in for we heard its 76 mm after the Patton ceased to fire and then we just heard the sound of Chinese tanks.

Ashcroft had his headphones on and he shouted, "The Americans are bugging out, sir!"

"Ashcroft, go around and warn everyone. Wait for my command!"

"Yes, sir!"

He disappeared down the ladder. I peered through the binoculars. I saw movement. The defenders were abandoning the

machine guns along the east side. The Colonel would have
ensured that they would not fall into the hands of the Chinese.
We still heard firing and then we heard the sound of trucks.
There were just seven of them and, as they emerged through
the open gates, we saw that men were clinging to the outside of
them. We also heard a roar and that meant the Chinese had
overrun the rearguard. The last vehicles which left the base
were five overloaded jeeps. Each had a machine gun pointing
behind them and, as they chattered their defiance, I saw
Chinese troops racing to get at them. The Colonel would have
placed obstacles in the way of the Chinese tanks. They would
get by them but men on foot would manage it first. The
machine guns on the jeeps cut down the first, eager Chinese
and North Koreans. We had to buy them as much time as
possible. I hoped we could delay them by an hour but the sheer
weight of numbers made me doubt our ability. Our only hope
was surprise. Ashcroft returned and I pointed to the opening
we had made in the roof on the western side. He would stand
there and direct the mortars until they were ranged in. He
peered out. The crews and Lowery would be watching.

The Chinese aided us for, as they flooded through the
camp, they triggered off the booby traps left by the Colonel.
We saw bodies flung into the air as they tried to grab the guns.
I watched an officer use the flat of his sword to beat the men
around him into some sort of order. It was tempting to ask
Lofting to shoot him but that would have ruined the surprise.
He formed them into a column and they began to run through
the open gates and down the road. In the distance, I heard the
engines of tanks and small explosions as the enemy found
booby traps.

"Right lads, now wait for it. Ashcroft, the mortars will fire
first. As soon as the first shell hits then let them have it.
Williams, go and join the Lieutenant." We had firing slits in
the windows and most of the men would be using those. We
had placed white stones amongst the rubble to help me

estimate the range. When the column of men was three hundred yards from us, I shouted, "Now Ashcroft!"

He shouted, "Shoot! Shoot! Shoot!" Sergeant Sullivan was there with the four men and he was experienced.

I heard the double pop of the two mortars. The sound of the feet of two thousand Chinese troops drowned out the command and the sound of the mortars. Even as they landed Lofting had shot the sabre wielding leader. The mortars landed in the middle of the column and as we opened fire with Thompsons, Bren guns and the Browning I shouted, "Perfect, Ashcroft, now join the party!"

He shouted, "Bob on!" He grabbed his weapon and came to fire through an improvised hole in the roof.

We could not miss. Smoke poured from the opening as the column was destroyed. As the survivors pulled back, I shouted, "Reload!" Lofting kept up his relentless decimation of officers and NCOs. I put the half-empty magazine in my Bergen. If we had the chance, I would reload the magazines.

Ashcroft looked out of the opening and shouted, "Check! Check! Check!"

I looked at my watch. We had bought the Colonel a precious fourteen minutes already. "Keep your heads down. They know where we are and they will react soon enough." I was aware that it felt a little warmer and I put it down to the heat from the guns until the first flurry of snow drove through the opening. A blizzard was on its way. Would that help or hinder us? The next Chinese attack was not a column. Another battalion or so ran to the east. They would attack us from behind the rubble. Lofting dropped six men before they were out of range. I heard tanks as they came from the camp. There were three of them. I did not know them well enough to be able to identify them but they each looked to have a 78 mm gun. Our lofty position meant that Collins and Carter had the chance to hit the top of the turrets with their bazooka. Tanks had their strongest armour on the front. The Sherman had almost two inches around the front of the turret but the belly and the top was half that thickness, one inch! If the Chinese were built the same way then we had a chance to surprise them.

Right, lads, now you have the chance to see what you can do with a bazooka from above."

"Yes, sir. Don't worry, we have a plan." The two of them had been prisoners and they would not return to that state easily!

We needed the tanks closer. Troops moved along behind them and I knew that we could hit some. "Open fire. Ashcroft, the mortars are in range."

"Sir, Shoot! Shoot! Shoot!"

We all opened fire at once. One mortar shell hit the rear of the second tank but it did not penetrate. However, the shrapnel scythed off at all angles to slice into the Chinese troops behind. Our bullets also ricocheted off armour and killed men. The tanks fired. The crews had been too eager and still had armour-piercing rounds in the breech. They hit the side walls and the rounds raced through the houses before exiting. I hoped none of our men had been hurt but there was no time to find out. The crews must have realised their error and they reloaded with high explosive. They headed down the road to get a better angle on the front of the building.

Carter tapped Collins on the back of the head. The bazooka's fiery trail showed it race unerringly to the top of the leading tank's turret. Bullets from the troops on the ground hit the roof above our heads. Our lofty position made it hard for them to hit us. The rocket must have struck the ammunition or the fuel for the whole tank suddenly lifted into the air in a fireball. The second tank was set on fire and the two remaining tanks hastily retreated. They drove over some of their own men in their haste to escape. The crew of the burning tank opened the hatch to try to douse the flames. The first two were shot by Lofting and the tank, still burning, headed back to the compound. The second tank headed east to join the Chinese who were there.

I looked at my watch. We had bought forty minutes. "Cease fire!"

"Check! Check! Check!"

I went to the ladder and shouted down, "When I give the command, Lieutenant, set off the charges and then prepare to bug out!"

"Sir!"

I knew that they would be bringing artillery to end our resistance and the building would be destroyed. There was little to be gained from our sacrifice. I had promised an hour and, by the time we left, we would have given the Americans more than that.

Ashcroft shouted, "Sir, they are bringing around men to attack from the north-west."

"Get the mortars to switch targets and spot for them!" I fired a burst through the open window as Chinese troops ran past the burning tank. The Browning had jammed and Bates was clearing the jam. We had a hole in the roof facing east and through it, I could see the Chinese as they gathered their men ready to assault us. The tank was in position and it fired its first H.E. shell at the building. It punched a hole through and then there was an explosion beneath us. I hoped no one was hurt. "Carter, Collins, get the bazooka over here and fire a couple of rockets at the tank. It might distract them."

The Browning was now firing again and I heard the whump of the mortars as they began to fire at the new threat. Ashcroft called, "Bang on lads! Keep them there." His head turned. "Sir, I can see artillery being moved."

"Right, tell them another few rounds and then bug out!"

The rear of the bazooka flamed as the first rocket raced towards the tank. I peered through the opening. It had hit the glacis but not penetrated the armour. "Again, and then outside. Tell the others 'Dunkirk!' You lads fire your last belt and magazine and then disable the Browning and get the hell out of here with the Brens."

Suddenly there was a salvo from the artillery followed by screams. Ashcroft said, "Bugger! The mortar lads have bought it, sir. They stood no chance."

"Right, get the radio and join the others. Tell the Lieutenant to blow the explosives." I moved away and patted Carter who sent another rocket at the tank. It hit a track and the tank slewed around. The Chinese troops rose as one. "Carter, Collins, Lofting, time to go!"

I heard a single shot and he said, "Righto sir! I got another officer."

I was left alone and I watched as the Chinese flooded over the rubble. The Lieutenant had detonated it perfectly. Suddenly they were all lifted as one. Even the tank was raised. Debris and rubble rattled against the walls and then the Chinese artillery opened fire at the gable end. I was knocked from my feet but miraculously survived, even though the end of the building was now open.

"Sir!"

"Coming, Sergeant Major Thorpe. I grabbed my Bergen and gun and slid down the ladder. I descended the stairs and raced out to the open area in the middle of the row. My men were waiting. "Who did we lose?"

Sergeant Grant had a bandage around his head, he said, "The mortar crews and Sergeant Sullivan. They never knew what hit them, sir. I have their tags!"

Brian Foster, Norman Timkins, Gary Nesbit and Jack Fox would not be going home.

Lieutenant Morrison said, "Sir, we had best get a move on. Williams and I had spare explosives. We have used timers and this lot will be going up in," he looked at his watch, "eleven minutes!"

Bearing in mind how erratic the timers could be I just said, "Move!" I ran towards the open gate. The Chinese shelling had blocked the northern entrance and so we ran south. I knew that the Chinese would be swarming down the road and I ran with my Thompson cocked. At the end, I almost shot the South Korean boy who stepped out. It was one of Ji-hoo's lads, "You come with me, mate!" Without waiting he turned and ran down the road to our right. I had to trust him for the explosives were nine minutes away from detonation.

The boy was fast and he had to keep stopping to ensure that we were keeping up with him. After a hundred yards he dived into a back yard. When we followed him, we saw that there was a hole in the ground. A second boy waved for us to descend. We were like Alice going down the rabbit hole but we had begun and had to continue. We followed. I cracked my head on a low beam.

Shouting, "Watch your heads!" I put my hand up. There was blood. I spied a light in the distance as we made our way through it. This was obviously a building destroyed in the initial attack by North Korea but a path had been cleared through the rubble. I just wished that they had put some candles in!

The lighter area proved to be the exit and we clambered up. I looked at my watch. The explosives would go off in two minutes. By my estimation, we were still just six hundred yards from them. Ji-hoo stood smoking a cigarette. One of his men, wearing North Korean garb, was behind the wheel of a North Korean truck. The one-armed soldier grinned. "You give me a Thompson and I will give you a ride out of the city."

Without hesitation, I handed him my Thompson and my magazines. I could always get another.

He grinned, "Get in the back and stay quiet! There are Chinese and North Korean bastards everywhere."

I nodded to him, "And you?"

He smiled, "We still have a war to fight. We knew this day would come and we have prepared holes like the one through which you came. We have weapons and we will get more. You will return, won't you?"

I nodded. Just then the explosives went off and the sky to the north of us was lit up. Rubble and debris showered the buildings close to us.

Ji-hoo said, "Your work?"

I said, "Yes, a little leaving present!"

"Good, now go! My man will get you beyond the last of the enemy. He can speak a little English. When he tells you to get out then you are on your own."

"Thanks, Ji-hoo!"

Lieutenant Morrison held out his arm and hauled me up. Ji-hoo banged on the side of the truck and I was thrown to the ground as it lurched off. I was helped to my feet. The canvas at the rear was lowered and we bounded along rubble covered roads. I took out my Colt and fitted the silencer. It was in the dark but I had practised this many times before.

I addressed them all in the gloom of the lorry, "Have grenades ready. We don't use our guns. The Chinese are all over the city. We just held up some of their men; others were already attacking the city. We are going to be dropped where it is safe and then make our way south."

Pike said, "Let me look at your head, sir. It is bleeding."

"It can wait." All around us I could hear the sound of explosions. Lieutenant Morrison's little present had made them wary. They would blast first and investigate later. They would think that every building was booby-trapped. "Well done, Lieutenant. That was a nice touch."

"Thank Lance Corporal Williams, sir, it was his idea."

When the journey was less bumpy then I knew that we were beyond the area of shelling. I began to hope that we might, perhaps, have escaped when the truck squealed to a halt as the brakes were jammed and I heard voices. They sounded Korean but, equally, could have been Chinese. I heard a rifle bolt sliding back and then voices headed towards the back of the truck. I raised my pistol. As the flap was lifted, I saw two Chinese and our driver. My gun fired twice and the two men fell. The driver caught one before he fell to the ground. I jumped down and the driver pointed to the left-hand side of the truck. Rafe Smith was at the back and I signalled for him to join me. He had a grenade in his hand. I pointed to the right.

A Chinese voice shouted from the front of the truck and the driver answered. I stepped out with my Colt levelled. Rafe dropped to the other side. There were four men before me and I emptied the magazine at them. Then I heard Smith shout, "Grenade!" and I dropped to my knees. There were screams.

Rafe appeared, "Better shift, sir!" He pointed the way we had come and there were more men running towards us.

The driver said, "Good job! I drive. Not long now!"

Rafe and I clambered aboard and the truck was put into gear. We seemed to be moving very slowly and the Chinese soldiers, all ten of them who were chasing us, began to fire. "Sergeant Major Thorpe roll a few grenades behind us."

"Sir!"

I was counting on an eight-second fuse in each of the grenades and the fact that our driver would soon pick up speed. The grenades were rolled from the back and we all lay down with our heads covered by our hands and Bergens. Erratically fired shots ripped through the canvas roof but missed us. We picked up speed and I heard the explosions. I lifted the bullet-riddled flap and saw that the men had all been cut down.

Fifteen minutes later we pulled up and the driver came around. "We are here!"

I saw that we had managed to get across the bridge over the Han river. I had been worried that the North Koreans and Chinese would have beaten us to it. "Everyone out!"

He seemed unconcerned that he would have to go back into Seoul. He had no idea who might have seen him. He was a brave man. He said, "You have cigarettes?"

Sergeant Grant handed him two packs. "If we had more, we would give them to you. We owe you, pal."

His accent defied the Korean and so I said, "Gowamo!" Korean for thanks.

He said, "Okay, mate, now go!" He pointed south, not down the road but along a trail which led up and into the trees. We could see that others had used it for the snow was heavily trampled and although the tracks would soon be covered it was still easy to mark the route. The blizzard which had begun when the attack had started showed no signs of abating. It would be a long hard slog.

"Let's go. We have more than thirteen miles to go and I don't think the weather will be getting any better." I pumped my arm and led the way. I considered telling Ashcroft to get on the radio but I doubted that anyone would be listening and, besides, it would do us little good anyway. Until we hit the lines beyond Suwon we were, effectively, behind enemy lines.

Chapter 13

We were all fit men and the only injuries we had were Sergeant Grant's and mine. Both were minor and we pushed on through the blizzard. Our fitness was shown when we began to overtake refugees from Seoul. They were hardy folk in this area and we saw women and children carrying very heavy loads. When we offered to help, we were shooed on our way. One old man who spoke English told us that we had to help fight the Communists and that they would manage. We trekked through the hills and along local trails. I suspect that had we used the road we would have had to fight our way south. As it was, we just fought nature and the elements. It still took us until dawn to reach the defences south of the abandoned town of Suwon. The trail we had followed had twisted through hills and valleys but it brought us out on the road which led into what would be our new, temporary home.

There were two Patton tanks on either side of the road and sandbagged machine-gun emplacements. On both sides of the road, there were lines of American soldiers who were dug in. The blizzard had covered their sandbagged positions but these looked like fresh troops and not the exhausted ones who had been driven south. As I expected our papers were checked but, fortunately, I was recognised by one of the men who had been on duty at the base the first day I had arrived. He shook his head, "Did you come down the road, sir?"

I pointed to the trail, "No, Corporal, we came over a trail. There are many refugees on the trail and I think you are going to be inundated soon enough."

It was almost as though he had not even heard me, "I thought not. The Commies caught up with the last truck out of Seoul. There were no survivors."

The Korean driver had saved our lives. The cigarettes had been an incredibly cheap price to pay for our safety.

"Where do we go now, Corporal?"

"All the new units are being directed to one of two camps which straddle the road. I think they are putting the non-American UN troops in one."

"Right."

We tramped down the road. I took the opportunity to light my pipe. While we had been trudging through the snow, I had not allowed myself that minor pleasure. Now, behind the front line, I would enjoy a pipeful. The traffic on the road had turned the snow to slush. When night came it would freeze into jagged, sharp, icy spikes and would be a nightmare for the drivers. The lads were in a better mood. They had not forgotten the five men we had lost but they had been put to the backs of their minds. It was their way. Harris began to sing. He had a good voice and our men enjoyed singing together. Even Lieutenant Morrison joined in. I smiled at the singing but, while I was walking, I was examining the defences. There were bunkers, dug in artillery and tank traps. This would not fall as easily as in the summer. As we neared the town, I saw the tents which lined both sides of the road. An MP. said, "You are British, sir?"

"Yes Lieutenant, Royal Marine Commandos."

He pointed to his right. Those tents are for U.N. personnel. Only a few are occupied and they are by a Turkish unit so take your pick, sir. We have messes but they are closer to the town." He looked at my men, "You came from, Seoul, sir?" I nodded. "Then you will need a hot meal. When you have found your tents then I would suggest you head to the mess tent. I will send one of my guys to ask them to hold some ham and eggs for you."

"You are a good man, Lieutenant."

The first four tents were occupied and so we took the next five. The Lieutenant and I would share one, the NCO's a second and the next three by the others. There were eight cots in each tent and pillows and bedding on the top of each cot. We dumped our Bergens on the cots we would use but kept our guns. Sergeant Major Thorpe addressed them all as we lined up outside the tents. "We are representing the British Army here so let us look and march like soldiers."

He organised them and when he nodded to me, I said, "Right, Sarn't Major! Let's go!" As we reached the road I looked back and saw the refugees. They were being closely questioned. It did not seem fair to me but I knew the MP's had to be scrupulous. The last thing we needed was to allow infiltrators into the new defences. We marched, in step, down the road.

We reached the mess tent. I could see that most of the men had already eaten but there were men still seated around the trestle tables and I recognised some of them. They were from the base. Their heads were down, staring at the half-eaten mess left on their metal plates and they showed all the signs of men who had been to the absolute limit. As we walked down the line of cooks each tray was loaded with ham, eggs, hash browns and bread. I was also offered a stack of pancakes which I declined but I took the mug of coffee gratefully. The rest of our men gave the Lieutenant and myself some space. I drank half of the coffee before I began on the food.

I had just picked up my knife and fork when Sergeant Houlihan appeared at my side, "Sorry to bother you, sir, but I just wanted to thank you and your men. I know that without you guys less than half of us would have made it. Did you lose any men, sir?"

I nodded, "Five; a sergeant and four men."

"Sorry about that. I will say a prayer for them." I had not noticed it before but now that he had no tie his crucifix hung out of his shirt. Someone once said that there were no atheists in the trenches. Perhaps they were right.

"The Colonel?"

He shook his head, "Didn't make it, sir. He was killed at the start of the last attack. He was cut in two by the machine gun on one of their tanks."

"I am sorry. He was a good man and I liked him."

"The feeling was reciprocated, sir. Anyway, I just thought I would thank you personally."

"And what next for you, sergeant?"

"Office work is out of the question for a while. We have all been assigned to combat units. When I had to fire my rifle, I didn't realise how out of practice I was. I mean, I hunt at home in North Carolina, but combat is different." He laughed, "What am I telling you for, sir? It must be second nature to you."

I shook my head, "Sergeant, you would be surprised. You take care now and don't try to be a hero."

"I leave that to you and your men, sir."

He saluted and left. A steward came along and topped up my coffee. "Don't let that food go cold, sir."

Thus admonished I wolfed down the plateful of food and wiped it clean with some bread. I pushed the tray away and said, to no one in particular, HP sauce, that is what the Americans need. It makes all the difference."

Lieutenant Morrison had finished some time ago and he laughed, as he lit a cigarette, "Yes sir, you are right." As I cleaned out my pipe he said, "Will we be working behind the lines or doing the same as Sergeant Houlihan?"

"I think, Lieutenant, that for the next week or so we will just try to stop the Chinese making more gains than they already have. I for one intend to get as much sleep as I can today just in case we are woken tonight." I had the pipe going and I emptied the mug of coffee. The steward made to come to refill it but I shook my head. I stood, "However, before I get my head down, I have five letters to write and a report to begin."

"I can do that for you if you like, sir."

I shook my head, "You will have time enough when you are the senior officer. Don't rush back on my account."

Back in the tent, I took off my greatcoat. It was cold enough for me to continue wearing it but I would not be able to write that way. I had paper in the bottom of my Bergen and I took out the Birome pen my father had given me. It was hard to believe that we did not need a nib and ink any longer. When he had been given the pens in 1945, they had been both rare and expensive. Now they were more commonplace. I spent an hour writing the letters. I guessed the rest of my men were talking about the events of the last couple of days.

I had just finished them and was about to lie down on my cot when the flap opened and a Lieutenant Colonel stood there. "Major Harsker?"

I stood and clicked my heels together. I was not wearing a hat. "Sir."

"At ease and I am sorry to bother you. I am Lieutenant Colonel Thomas Coulter in command of the 95th Infantry regiment. You and your commandos are attached to my unit until further notice and I thought I should meet you and, if you don't mind, let me show you your position in the line."

I grabbed my greatcoat and comforter. "Yes, sir."

He saw my Colt. "I see that you use an American weapon."

I nodded, "I had a Thompson too but I gave it to the Korean who helped us to escape from Seoul."

He laughed, "From what I hear that was a fair swap. I will get you another. Guns we have; men who know how to fight is another matter and a friend of mine, Major Rogers of the Rangers, told me that you have more medals and experience than any man he knows."

"He is too kind. I hope he is keeping safe."

"Last I heard he was in Indian country!" We crunched through the snow, "Those words show me that you are a warrior. We do not need your men to stand a watch at night time but, during the day, you will be in line with us."

I stopped, "With respect, sir, it is night time when we will be needed. So far that is when they sound their trumpets and gongs. The noise they make terrifies men. Also, we have air support during the day but not at night. We will be on the line at night. We will be sleeping at other times but ready to fight when the Chinese come."

He nodded, "I won't argue with you. From what I hear you are the expert in all of this." We had reached the front line. There was a long trench behind which were sandbagged bunkers. The long trench had snow-covered sandbags and was wide enough to use mortars. I spied four of them on each side of the long trench. There were four heavy machine guns too. He pointed to the sandbagged bunkers behind the main trench. "Those are the places we use for sleeping between watches." His men stood to attention as we used duckboards to cross the trench. He pointed ahead. "Here we have our firing pits. Each one accommodates four men." I saw that they had four sets of firing pits and they were staggered so that they had a continuous line of fire. "Every other trench has an automatic weapon of some type." He pointed to the barbed wire. "That is to slow them down."

I shook my head, "Except that it won't."

He frowned, "Won't?"

I sighed and, fastening my greatcoat across me, ran at the wire and, with my cap covering my hands, threw myself upon it. "Feel free to use me as a bridge, Colonel."

I heard him laugh and I stood up. "I guess you have done this before?"

"Just a few times, sir. The trouble is the snow. It stops you putting mines down. The enemy can see where you have put them. Now if you attached grenades to the wire you would have warning of an attack and kill a few too."

He turned and led me back to the trench. I saw the soldiers there grinning at the mad Englishman. "So, this is where you will be. We want your men to occupy every other trench. I want to make your unit part of mine."

"Good idea."

"You can be with me, in the command trench."

"No, sir. I will be here, with my men."

"I can see how you won so many medals but a commanding officer needs to have the whole picture."

"And you are the commanding officer, not me. I lead my section. I only have twenty-four men left. I would like to be close to them."

"Your call. We will give you the rest of this day and night off, Major. You have had a hard few days."

"Don't worry, sir, if we hear gongs and trumpets, we will be in those firing pits with the rest of the battalion!"

By the time I reached my tent the rest of the men were back. I sighed, sleep would be denied me a little while longer. "Sergeant Major, bring the sergeants and corporals. Lieutenant, put on your coat. I will show you where we are fighting."

I took them back to the trenches and summarised what the Lieutenant Colonel had said. "We sleep in our tents tonight but I said we would be on the line for the next few nights. We can always sleep in our tents during the day. We all know they will attack at night."

"Yes, sir!"

I want one officer or NCO with each group of three. See to the rota, Sergeant Major!"

"Right, sir!"

I was proud of them. None complained and none were dismayed at the situation. They were soldiers and would just get on with it.

When we returned to our tents, I took off my boots and just wrapped myself in my blanket. I slept. I was woken by trumpets! I sat bolt upright and then realised it was just reveille. I felt such a fool. When we had walked to the mess, the previous night, I had seen the showers. I knew that it was unlikely I would stay clean for long but a shower would make me feel more human again. The snow had stopped, albeit briefly but I saw thick black clouds to the north. More was on the way and that could only help the Chinese and the North Koreans. After a shower and a good American breakfast, I felt like a new man.

We had spare cots and I laid out my equipment to check it over. I was halfway through when a voice from outside said, "Major Harsker?"

I stepped outside, "Yes Corporal?"

The American Corporal held out a Thompson machine gun and a dozen magazines. "The Colonel said you might like this sir."

I could not help grinning, "Tell him he is a gentleman!"

The Corporal said, "I am not sure some of the guys would agree with you, sir, but I will tell him."

I had checked over the gun and repacked my Bergen when I heard firing from the north. My training kicked in and I grabbed my new gun, pistol and greatcoat. "Sergeant Major! Stand to!"

"Sir! Come on my lovely lads! We have had a day off! Back to work eh?"

The fact that they were all outside in less than a minute complete with weapons and greatcoats told me that they were eager. We ran to the gun pits. I had Ashcroft, Hall and Lofting with me. With a Thompson and a Bren gun, we had some serious firepower. As I passed the Colonel in the main trench I shouted, "What is happening, sir?"

"They have overrun the men at the crossroads!"

As I ran to our slit trench, I saw the two Pattons reversing across the snow. The sentries from the crossroads were clinging to the back. The tanks were firing their machine guns and main gun as they retreated; the commander of each tank was using his Browning .50 Calibre. Behind us, I heard the crack of the 155 mm heavy guns further south as they opened fire. Snow and flames belched into the air as the shells struck. They were using high explosive and the Communists would be taking heavy casualties.

Behind me, I heard the American Regimental Sergeant Major shout, "Prepare to fire but wait for my command!"

Lofting shook his head, "And I thought Sergeant Major Thorpe was terrifying!"

Ashcroft laughed, "The Sarn't Major is a pussycat! Isn't that right, sir?"

"Let's just say that I would not like to prove the point. Cock your weapons and aim them but don't fire."

The Chinese also had artillery but it was made up of lighter pieces. Someone must have been spotting for the American artillery for as the two tanks reached our lines the 155 mm began to fire in salvos. When the Chinese guns ceased firing, we knew who had won the battle of the big guns. We stayed in the trenches for two hours. Then it became obvious that the Chinese had stopped this particular attack.

The RSM shouted, "Thank you, gentlemen, you may stand down!"

We headed back to our tents. We had not had to fire our weapons yet we felt we had been in a battle. Some shells had fallen short and we saw medics attending to some wounded further down the line. Sergeant Major Thorpe said, "We had better make sure the lads eat, sir. This is going to be a long night and I suspect there will be more snow." He gestured behind him with his thumb. "It will make crossing the wire much easier for infantry, sir."

"You are right and try to get them to sleep too."

That was easier said than done. I lay on my bunk and tried to close my eyes. The trouble was that I had slept too well the night before and an undisturbed night felt unusual. I sat up and rolled my legs off the bed. Morrison sat bolt upright. "You couldn't sleep either sir?"

"No, but you should get some rest, Jacob."

He laughed, "You sound like my mother, sir. She always used what she called my Sabbath name when she was telling me off."

"I am not telling you off. It is just sage advice."

"I am thinking about tonight, sir, that is all. They will be coming over. Today was just a push to see if we were defending the line. Tonight, will be another of their wild charges and it might succeed. We have, what, nine hundred men to defend just over half a mile? The Chinese will have ten times that number. We have to defend the whole line but they can throw their weight against any single point. Night-time means the artillery will not have spotters."

He had changed since he had first arrived. Then he had been fearful now his caution was derived from experience. His evaluation was a good one although flawed. "The Colonel and his senior staff will not be in the trenches with us; they will be in the command bunker and they can act as artillery spotters. They have the measurements and coordinates. You are right, the Chinese will come mob-handed but the very size of their army is a weakness because it is easier to hit. Now if we had no artillery support and we were surrounded then it would be a different matter. I can see General Ridgeway's hand all over this plan. This is his army and he is trying to build morale ready for when we push north and we will push north!"

"You are confident then, sir?"

"About the ability of this army to hold off the enemy? Yes. Now if you are asking me if we can win this war then that is a whole different, as the Americans say, ball game. As soon as the Chinese and the Russians came in then they changed the rules. This becomes a battle between the east and the west. Our Communist friends will not wish to lose face. They will support North Korea come hell or high water. Neither Stalin nor Mao Tse Tung will worry about losing men; to them, face is far more important."

He was silent and I began to clean out my pipe. I used one of my precious pipe cleaners to remove all the tar from the stem. I took out my penknife and reamed the bowl. I could afford to use as much tobacco as I liked. The Americans had a good PX and I knew I could buy as much tobacco as I liked. I had just begun to fill the pipe when the Lieutenant spoke.

"You know, sir, this has helped me clarify my mind. I joined up because, well, my brother was wounded and I just wanted to hit back at someone."

"And you have yet you have discovered it doesn't help."

He laughed, "You are mind-reading, sir. This is a war we can't win. You are right there, sir. The South Koreans are good people but this is now a battle between the Communists and the rest of the world. It is a battle which needs fighting but it is not my battle."

I struck a match and puffed on the pipe. This was an epiphany and he did not need me to interrupt him. I tamped down the end with my finger. The pipe was drawing well.

"I didn't follow my brother and uncle to Israel, well, there were lots of reasons but mainly because I was afraid. The new nation of Israel is taking on huge numbers of enemies but, you know what, sir? They are winning. What this has shown me is that if you are well trained and well-led then the odds don't matter." He shook his head, "Less than thirty of us held off modern tanks, artillery and over five thousand men for an hour! I think I would like to go to Israel and fight for something I can believe in. You probably thought I had some sort of chip on my shoulder when I first came, sir and you might be right. At school, until I went to a Jewish school, I was called names. Gangs would taunt us when we did go to our Jewish school. This section has shown me that most blokes are not like that and that a small group can be stronger than the component parts. When my enlistment is over, I will go to Israel. There must be an Israeli version of Sergeant Major Thorpe, thanks to you and the lads, I now have skills I can use there and with my uncle as a general I feel happy that I can ask him for a commission knowing I have got my boots dirty already!"

I took a matchstick and loosened the ash at the top of the pipe, "But you know that you will lose some of those men with whom you intend to fight. That is inevitable. There are five good men in a yard in Seoul who are a testament to that. You might be one of them."

"But I would be dying for something worth dying for. You are right, sir, we can't win over here, not with the Chinese against us but Israel? That is a battle we can win."

"Well if your mind is set then I will support you."

"What about you, sir?"

"As long as this section is here then I am bound to be with them but I would rather be at home with my wife and family. This is my last war, Jake. I also suspect it is Sergeant Major Thorpe's last one too but we will both stay here until the section is recalled. You are different for you are young."

"I won't go until you do, sir!"

I tapped the pipe out on the floor, "We will see, Jake, we will see."

The American RSM shouted, "Stand to!"

We gathered our gear and left the relative comfort of our tents. The blizzard began again as we trudged to our gun pits. I saw that Lofting had made some fingerless gloves. He was a sniper and he needed touch. I decided I would try to get him some mittens. He could use those to keep his hands warm until the action began. Dad had told me that in the Great War women in England had all knitted such items for their men in the trenches. I doubted that any, except for those with husbands and sons fighting, would even know there was a war on. We were remote and they were safe yet the war we fought was for them. I had seen enough of Communism to know that it did not have tolerance as one of its virtues. It wanted the whole world to be red and the dead which still lay before us showed that they did not care for the individual in any shape or form.

The blizzard made it hard to see anything. I knew there were men ahead of us, to the left and right, but I could barely see them. The cleverly designed defences meant that the machine guns behind us could fire over our heads and we could fire over the heads of the men in the trenches before us. We had the firepower of a whole battalion. That did not guarantee safety. They could still overrun us but, if they did so, then they would lose many men. Once the inevitable initial chatter of entering the trenches had ended silence fell. We all knew that there could be Chinese crawling over the snow in white camouflage. None of us doubted the courage of our enemies nor their fanaticism. They would happily charge knowing that they might die. It was one reason the Crusaders had failed in the Holy Land!

Lofting used his telescopic sight to scan the ground ahead. He could see little more than we could but it kept him happy. I had stood many watches in the last war and I would fix my eye on one spot and look for movement before moving my eye along. The wire, in which the Colonel had placed such faith, was now invisible. It was covered by snow. It was no longer an obstacle. I was glad I was not one of those in the gun pits in front of us. One moment's carelessness and Chinese could be upon them. I looked at my watch. It had just passed midnight. We had another six hours, at least, to watch. There were reinforcements for us if we were attacked. The men who had watched during the day were now abed and if there was any firing would race to join us. There was also a reserve battalion but that would be sent only when a breach had occurred and that would be a disaster. We had to fight with the men around us.

It was, in the end, my words to the Colonel which alerted us. Unbeknown to me he had listened to me and booby-trapped the wire. The wire itself was neutralised but one of the booby traps was triggered some hundred yards to our right. The sky was lit up and I saw bodies flung in the air. Then a Very Light soared in the air. The sight before us was terrifying. Less than thirty yards from the slit trenches before us was a wall of white-coated Communists. They had not used their trumpets and gongs. I cocked and fired my Thompson as Lofting's first bullet struck an officer who had his hand raised. Our whole front erupted in a wall of bullets and mortar shells began to drop into the Chinese ranks. Their front ranks were scythed down but there were more to take their place. Ashcroft used his rifle like Lofting and picked off leaders. Hall's Bren gun sent short bursts towards the enemy.

Inevitably guns jammed or men fired too many bullets at once. It was easy to understand, for some of the American infantry had not fought in a battle before. A few of the forward trenches were overrun. I saw deadly battles. Lofting showed his cool by aiming his gun to hit the Chinese head which was so close to the American he was fighting that the American was covered in bone, brains and gore but he cleared the trench which was under attack in six bullets.

"Well done, Lofting!"

Then the artillery kicked in and we heard the shells screaming from behind us. They were ranged to fall three hundred paces from the wire. With our bullets slaughtering the ones close to the wire so the pressure diminished. The Colonel must have called a halt to the artillery after fifteen minutes and we saw that the attack had failed.

From the trenches, before us, we heard the cry, "Medic!"

My three medics did not hesitate but raced forward to tend to the wounded. Behind us, the Colonel sent stretcher-bearers and a Very Light soared into the night sky to make it day. It was like a scene from Dante's Inferno. Other medics did the same. I watched an American Corporal kneel next to a machine gunner who had been hit in the head. As he did so an apparent Chinese corpse rose and raised his rifle. Lofting had been watching and a single shot ended the killer's life.

"Ashcroft, come with me. Let's make certain these Chinese are dead. Lofting, keep watch."

"Right sir."

I left my Thompson in the gun pit and took out my Colt. "Hall, cover us!"

"Sir!"

We walked past the grisly gun pits. In one all of the men were dead. A Chinese grenade had exploded in the bottom and the men were shredded by the shrapnel. The Chinese who had thrown it also lay dead. He was obviously dead as his face had been torn away but all the ones who did not have the clear marks of death we kicked. One grunted and I hauled him to his feet. As I did so a second one, just ten feet away, rose and raised his rifle. Ashcroft shot him and the man I had hauled to his feet slashed at me with a dagger. It did not connect; my Colt hit him in the face and took away the back of his head.

I heard the Regimental Sergeant Major shout, "Shoot the Chinese corpses!" As bullets poured into the dead some of the apparently dead Chinese leapt to their feet. Hall and Lofting helped us while Ashcroft and I shot another three and then it was all quiet. Men were sent to the edge of the wire to throw grenades in case any were lurking there.

Sergeant Major Thorpe came for us, "The Colonel has ordered you back to your gun pit, sir. He is worried about you. All the wounded have been evacuated and replacements are here."

"Right Ken. The men?"

"Not a scratch!"

We had barely been in our trench for fifteen minutes when the gongs and trumpets sounded and the Chinese and their allies launched another massive attack. The attempted attack on the medics had not only hardened all of the defenders it made them impervious to the trumpets and gongs. As the mortars and artillery decimated their attacks the men who made the wire were mown down by rifle and machine-gun fire. Rifle grenades were used to ensure that men did not shelter behind the mounds of snow driven into drifts by the blizzard which raged on, unabated. When dawn broke the attacks were over and the white snow was covered in a sea of bloody bodies.

When we were told to stand down, we left our trenches and made our weary way back to our tents. The sun came out and a short while later we heard the scream of Sabre jets as they roared overhead. We had air cover once more. We could smell the bacon and eggs. We would forego the shower until we had eaten. We had had a victory and the food would be a celebration.

Chapter 14

The Colonel sent for me just after one o'clock. He and his officers were in the command tent. "Just wanted to thank you, Major. I am putting you in for a citation, that was damn brave."

I shook my head, "No need, sir. I have enough fruit salad as it is. Are the Chinese likely to attack again tonight?"

"That, as they say, is the $64-dollar question. I thought that after the first attack was repulsed then they would have given up but they came again."

His officers nodded and I said, "Without tanks."

They stopped and stared at me. "Say again, Major? What do you mean?"

"The last attack was made by infantry and damned little artillery. The air force and artillery knocked out the tanks that they intended to use before they got here. I noticed was that there were no tanks. If they had had them, they would have used them. I think they either have no petrol, sorry, gas, or they haven't the tanks. We all know that the roads in Korea are awful and it is a long way from China. They have not captured any South Korean ports. Ipso facto, they are having supply problems."

I had set them thinking and we debated for a couple of hours. It was a tiny chink of light but a chink nonetheless. The bodies on the battlefield had been cleared and buried and the burned-out tanks blown up and destroyed. We went out on a chillingly cold January afternoon and used field glasses to view the battlefield.

"The trouble is, Major Harsker, that we have no eyes on them yet. The Sabres which were sent out this morning were just shooting up their artillery and tanks and their pilots did not have the opportunity to look at their dispositions. The Chinese are masters at disguise and their men were hidden. We just don't know their situation." The Colonel smiled, "You have given us a dilemma. You and your men can stand down tonight. If we are attacked then you will be our reserve but you and your men fought like lions last night and after what you did at Seoul you deserve time to recover."

"But…"

The Colonel came over to me and spoke quietly so that only I could hear, "I am not sure yet if last night was sheer courage or the actions of a man who was close to the edge and had a death wish. I would be happier if you took a couple of days off." He smiled, "And that is an order!"

My men were delighted to have a night in their beds but, like me, they slept dressed, and with their guns close to hand. The Chinese did not come. We heard that there were attacks, further east towards the British and Australian units and that Wonju had fallen. There were no attacks that night, nor the next night on our sector. The American defences had held. The bad weather, however, had returned and aerial reconnaissance could not deliver effective results.

I was summoned again after four days of silence from the north. This time the Colonel and I were taken well south to the headquarters of the 1st Corps and its commander, General Frank W. Milburn. Also there, was Colonel David Hackworth. His regiment was known as Raiders, similar, I think, to Mosby's Raiders of the American Civil War. His men, the 27th Infantry had a good reputation. I learned all of this in the jeep ride south. Colonel Coulter was a mine of information.

There were just six of us in the room, A stenographer and an officer from General Ridgeway's staff made up the numbers. I never did discover his name but when he spoke, I heard authority in his voice. "Gentlemen, I am General Ridgeway and General MacArthur has given this command a mission. We are to probe north and discover the positions occupied by the Chinese." I later learned that he was a blunt man who liked to come directly to the point. It was an attitude I liked. He lit a cigar, "Now if like me, you wonder why the Air Force can't do this then the answer is simple. The Chinese and North Koreans have air defences which are too great a risk for our pilots and we have too few of them. In addition, the Chinese are masters of disguise. Hell, they spirited this whole army through Manchuria at night! They came as a helluva shock to the 8th Cavalry. Operation Tomahawk will be a reconnaissance in force. However, Mrs Milburn did not raise any dummies! I do not intend to send ninety thousand men north into what might be a gigantic Chinese and North Korean trap so I have my own operation. In honour of Colonel Hackworth and his men, it will be called Operation Wolfhound!"

"Thank you, sir! That is an honour."

The General shook his head, "Only if you bring your men back alive." He suddenly swivelled, "And you, Major Harsker, will also go north. While the Wolfhounds head northeast towards Yangpyong you and a company of Lieutenant Colonel Coulter's men will head for Seoul. Now I am pretty damned certain that the Commies will be there but we need to know the numbers and what sort of defences they have."

I knew that he was daring us to ask questions but I would not oblige him. In the end, it was Colonel Coulter who broke, "Do I get to choose the units, sir?"

"Damn right you do but they had better be good. We need them motorised but I am not risking tanks. You get in, you see how many men there are and where they are and you get out. Firefights I am happy about but I want no Coulter's last stand! This is not the Little Big Horn!"

I smiled at the analogy; Custer, famously, had taken a small unit into what he thought was a single encampment and he discovered, to his cost, tribes of Plains Indians gathered for war.

Lieutenant Colonel Coulter coloured, "I have no intention of being associated with a disaster, sir!"

The General sucked on his cigar and said, "That is why Major Harsker will be leading the operation. He has proved time and time again that he can make good judgements under fire and as the last man out of Seoul he is in the best position to assess its defences. So, any questions?"

"When do we go, General?"

"As soon as possible, Colonel Hackworth. You will be going in different directions and you will be discreet. You have two days to get me the information I need. Operation Tomahawk will only go ahead if I think it can succeed. The start date is no earlier than January fifteenth so you can see, gentlemen, just how much rests upon your shoulders." He pointed his cigar at some manila folders. "Here are the maps and other information you will need. Major, a word, if you please."

"Sir."

He took me to a corner by the window. "I need you to be involved in this and then Operation Tomahawk but after that, the British want you back. I fought to keep you here because of your knowledge of Seoul but the Commonwealth Division need you and your men. You will be attached to 29th Infantry Brigade. You need to know that this will be your last mission under American command before you and your men go off on this mission. I will be honest, I fought for your inclusion. Everything I have heard about you and your men I like. Chuck Wilding was also a friend of mine and his men told me how much you did to try to save him and his command. I hope that you can give Colonel Coulter some pointers. He is a good officer but between us we will make him a great one!"

It was a great deal to take in. The Lieutenant Colonel had been annoyed by the General's comments; I could tell. We were alone in the jeep and, although wrapped up against the cold we were able to talk. "Sir, the General seems to be a plain-speaking man. In England, we say that someone like the general calls a spade a shovel!"

He laughed, "I can appreciate that. The thing is, Major, I am coming on this little jaunt and I can't be seen to be deferring to you all the time, can I?"

I didn't remind him that the General had made it perfectly clear that I was in charge but I had a plan to make it easier for him. "How about this then, sir? My men and I will be the vanguard and we will use the radio to let you know the situation. I can run any decisions by you."

He nodded, "I can live with that besides you know the road. You were one of the last units out of Seoul."

I didn't tell him that we had not been able to use the road when we had come south due to the number of refugees but it was a moot point anyway. "What vehicles will we be using?"

"I thought half-tracks and a couple of self-propelled guns."

"If we meet dug in guns, sir, or heavy concentrations of Chinese then we get the hell out of there. That is what the General said. I would like at least a couple of jeeps with a Browning .50. The half-tracks are a good idea but take the fastest ones we have. My men and I can try to sniff out the enemy but if we find large numbers then speed will be of the essence."

"I can see your point." We were nearing our camp. He said, "I decide when we go."

"Of course." To me, it made little difference. We were just trying to get close to them. Small groups of men we could handle. Heavy defences meant we turned around and day or night would make no difference.

"Then we leave before dawn tomorrow."

I nodded, "And one more thing, sir. Snow camouflage! The snow is not going to thaw in the next few days. Let us blend in with our background, eh sir?"

"Of course, Major. And I appreciate your advice."

I knew that when we reached his men, I would be treated like a subordinate and all my ideas would be his. I didn't mind. The Colonel was a career soldier. After this, if I survived, I was going home!

My men were sanguine about the operation. Sergeant Grant said, "Travelling in a jeep or a half-track is better than walking, sir."

Corporal Lowery nodded his agreement, "And it beats waiting for the Chinese Brass Band to come calling. I bloody hate brass bands! Sorry, sir."

I waved my hand. His words had not offended me and the others had all laughed. "I intend to have two jeeps. I will drive one with Ashcroft and Lofting. Sergeant Grant, Entwhistle and Harris will be in the other. The Lieutenant will have half of the men in one half-track and Sergeant Thorpe the other half. I intend to travel with the jeeps, half a mile in front of the two half-tracks and they will be half a mile in front of the Americans."

Lieutenant Morrison asked, "Why sir?"

"The Jeep can often be mistaken for a GAZ. The half-tracks are unmistakable. We will not be wearing helmets and I am hoping that we can trick our way close to any North Koreans we meet. They might think you are chasing us."

The Colonel had one jeep for himself and six half-tracks. As far as I was concerned this was a major incursion but they seemed to think that eleven vehicles would not even be noticed. The vehicles were brought over before dark and we examined them. I had no Fred Emerson as a mechanical whizz to give them the once over but Lieutenant Colonel Coulter had men who knew engines. The white uniforms arrived and I had my men put parachutes over the front of our jeeps. It might delay our being seen. On our heads, we wore caps we had taken from the dead Chinese. They had ear flaps and were lined with fur. Everything was about making any soldiers we met, hesitate. In a perfect world, I would have had a couple more silencers and Colts but we would have to make do with mine. That evening, after we had eaten, I pored over the maps with my officers. We would be heading up Highway 1 to Suwon and then up to Seoul. It was a straight road and there were many places the enemy could have battle lines. The fact that the air force had not seen them meant nothing. This would take eyes on the ground. Our eyes!

The land froze solid as soon as darkness fell. The roads would be treacherous and I knew that the Colonel would be wondering about my choice of vehicle. The half-track could cope with ice as well as snow while the jeep would slip, slide and slew around. I knew all of that but also knew that the jeep was our best chance to remain undetected. The Colonel started us dramatically by pumping his arm three times in the air. We drove up the road towards Suwon. Ashcroft had two jobs: he would man the radio and the Browning. Lofting would feed the heavy calibre machine gun. Mine was simple. I had to drive and to keep the jeep on the road.

I had chosen Sergeant Grant for the jeep behind us as he was a good driver and he was dependable. We virtually crawled up a black and deadly road. In many ways that helped for my two men were able to keep a watch for enemy positions. We passed the detritus of battle. The artillery had destroyed vehicles and guns. The Chinese had cleared the roads of such obstacles but the sides were littered with them as well as the remains of bodies. I saw few tanks and the ones I did see were the smaller, lighter tanks. My theory of them outrunning their supplies and fuel made even more sense now. Once we were a mile from Suwon, we slowed down even more for if the enemy had a fortified line then it would be close to Suwon which they could use as an anchor. We drove through an empty and almost deserted town. Here the roads were less icy but we still maintained our sedate pace. I was more comfortable in the jeep now and the couple of early skids were already behind me. The Colonel had a South Korean soldier with him to translate. I hoped he would stop and find someone to question. I could have used the radio for that but I wanted to maintain radio silence as long as possible.

North of Suwon the roads had fewer signs of damage. The American artillery had not pounded this area. In the houses adjacent to the road I saw smoke rising. There were still people here and the Colonel could garner valuable intelligence. Each time we approached a crest in the road I slowed, expecting to be greeted by Chinese and North Korean soldiers. We found none. As the sun showed a thin glow in the east we continued towards Seoul. I had begun to wonder if the enemy had any soldiers at all south of the Han River when sharp-eyed Lofting tapped me on the shoulder.

"Sir, I see a light next to the road about three hundred yards north of us."

I trusted Lofting and I stopped the jeep. "Ashcroft, get on the radio and tell the Colonel that we have found North Koreans or Chinese, five miles north of Suwon and we are investigating."

Grant's jeep pulled up behind mine. I did not need to tell the Lieutenant. He would be monitoring the radio and would stop behind our jeeps. I took out my Colt and fitted the silencer. My battle vest had six grenades and that would be enough.

"Sergeant Grant, there is a light ahead. Take your two men and head up the western side of the road. I will take the east. If there are less than twenty men there then we will try to take them. If there are more then we wait for the Lieutenant."

"Sir. Entwhistle and Harris, with me."

Ashcroft turned off the radio. "The Colonel has acknowledged, sir."

"Let's go!"

We left the road and headed across the fields. This road was lined with small fields. The farmhouse we passed was burned out. It could have been destroyed last summer or when the Chinese came south. The derelict building was too badly damaged to be used by the men we were hunting. I wondered why they had not heard the jeep. Perhaps they had and were waiting in ambush for us. The frozen snow crunched underfoot. There was no way to avoid it but Lofting and Ashcroft used my footsteps to minimize the sound. I smelled the fire before I saw it. The fact that Lofting had spied it from the road meant that there was likely to be some sort of structure between us and the fire. It could be harmless and might just be the South Korean family still trying to eke an existence out. Then I heard voices. They were male and there were at least four of them. It sounded to me like an argument. I could not see anyone and I realised why. There was some sort of animal byre or pen ahead. The snow had drifted against it but approaching from the east I could see it and the glow from the fire. I waved my hand to the right and held my Colt before me. Ashcroft and Lofting moved to my right and levelled their weapons. I stepped forward. As I cleared the building, I saw the fire. There were four North Korean soldiers and there was a heated argument going on. It explained why they had not heard us. They were wrapped in their winter uniform with mitts on their hands. As far as I could tell one was a sergeant.

We were just thirty yards from them when our movement alerted them. I shouted, in Korean, "Hangbog!" It was Korean for surrender.

For a heartbeat, I thought they were going to do as I asked but the door of the wooden animal byre was pushed open and an officer with a Russian submachine gun, the PPsh41, raised his weapon at me. I reacted and, raising my Colt, fired three times. The machine gun with the drum magazine fell to the ground but the four men around the fire reached for their weapons. Grant and his two men had been approaching and five guns ended the threat of the four Koreans.

I shouted, "Hangbog! Son deul-eo!"

Ashcroft said, "What did you say, sir?"

"I said, surrender and hands up. There should be more men inside."

I heard a conversation in Korean which confirmed the presence of more men. "Hangbog! Son deul-eo!"

A voice shouted, "We come! No shoot!"

Five men came out. One was wounded in the leg, there was a bloody bandage around his thigh, and he was supported by two others. "Lofting, Ashcroft, check the building. Sergeant Grant, take Harris and bring up the jeeps and, if they are there, the half-tracks."

"Sir!"

"Entwhistle, cover them." Holstering my weapon, I went to the officer and searched him. He had papers with him but they were indecipherable. They were in Korean. I might have learned a couple of phrases but I could not read a single symbol!

Ashcroft and Lofting came out. "There is a dead North Korean in there, sir. He looks like an officer. He had a stomach wound."

This began to make sense to me now. These were survivors from the battle. It explained the argument I had heard. The four men must have wanted to head north. I heard the sound of the half-tracks as they ground up the road. One jeep pulled up and a minute later the second. Sergeant Grant glowered at Marine Harris, "Sorry about your jeep, sir! Harris here is about as much use as a one-legged man in an arse-kicking contest. He skidded your jeep and bent the wing."

Harris looked embarrassed. I shook my head, "So long as it can be driven, I don't care." I turned to the prisoners. "Which one speaks English?"

The wounded Korean said, "Few words!"

"Where is your army? Where are the Chinese?"

He shook his head, "Gone!" He pointed north.

I heard the half-tracks, "Go and fetch Pike."

Harris said, "Sir!" He ran to the half-track. No doubt he was trying to atone for his error. "Ashcroft, offer them a cigarette."

Ashcroft took out the packet of Marlboroughs and offered them all one. They eagerly took one and then he took out his Zippo. The Koreans loved American cigarettes. It was why I had acquired some from the PX and given them to my men. "Where have they gone?"

The wounded man frowned. He had not understood me.

I pointed north again. "Chinese? Where?"

"Han river!"

Pike and Powell arrived with Lieutenant Morrison and half a dozen of my men. "Look after him. Lieutenant, tell the Colonel that I think the enemy has pulled back to the Han river. I intend to head north and find out if that is true. You follow us when he arrives." I handed him the papers I had taken.

"But what if there are more North Koreans north of you, waiting in ambush."

I looked at the wounded man. I had not seen a lie in his eyes. "I will be careful, Lieutenant."

When we reached the jeep, I saw why Sergeant Grant had been annoyed. The left front wing was badly dented. It was not Harris' fault. I was a good driver and I had found the road difficult. The sun had risen and the sky was clear. In the distance, I saw clouds gathering. There would be more snow before dark. "Sergeant Grant, I intend to push on as fast as I dare. I don't want to get caught in that storm. I think the North Korean was telling the truth. If there were soldiers south of the Han then they would have tried to get their wounded men to them."

"Right, sir. We will keep our eyes peeled."

There were no more occupied houses as we headed north but there were some unnatural looking mounds beneath the snow. I suspected that the local populace who had not fled south had paid the price for the withdrawal.

Seoul rose in the distance. There was a sprawl of buildings south of the river and, as we neared them, I slowed and then stopped. I took out my glasses and scanned the buildings. They did not look to be fortified and I saw no roadblocks. "Have the Browning ready!"

I drove up the road through deserted and empty buildings. Many showed damage from the fighting. Lumps of rubble and masonry littered the road but I saw no uniforms and, thankfully, no bullets came in our direction. I stopped six hundred yards from the bridge and parked the jeep where it would not be seen. Sergeant Grant did the same. "Ashcroft, you stay here and watch the jeeps. Get on the radio to the Colonel and tell him where we are."

"Sir!"

I took my Thompson and led my four men along the road. We used the buildings at the side for cover. Where we could we walked over the dead ground to the left of the road. We were aided by burned-out vehicles and the rubble from fallen buildings. Here, however, our snowsuits hindered rather than helped us. There was less snow around to disguise us.

Lofting was on my right and he suddenly hissed, "Sir! Machine gun emplacement! Dead ahead!"

"Down!"

We dived to the ground behind the remains of a shop. I slowly raised my head above the brickwork. If anyone saw me, they would see the same kind of hat worn by the North Koreans and Chinese. It would buy me enough of a delay to save me. I saw, just a hundred yards ahead of me, sandbags across the end of the bridge and there were two machine guns there. I took out my glasses and scanned the bridge. The parapet and the sandbags prevented a good view but I saw a barrel. There was either artillery or a tank there.

"Well done, Lofting. I guess we can go back to the jeeps and give the good news to the Colonel." I heard the rumble of the half-track. The Chinese must have heard it too for a trumpet sounded and the machine guns opened fire.

"Sergeant Grant, have you a smoke grenade?"

"Yes, sir."

"When I give the word we rise, give them a volley and you throw the grenade. Then we high tail it back to the jeeps. We have seen enough." We just had to distract the machine guns and whatever the barrel could fire and that would allow the half-tracks to take cover.

I cocked the Thompson and shouted, "Now!"

I stood and sprayed the machine gun left and right. I heard Lofting's rifle and saw one gunner slump forward. Then Grant's grenade spewed smoke and I shouted, "Run!"

A loud crack from north of the river told me that they had fired their heavy weapon while the other machine gun sprayed the rubble behind which we had hidden. As we ran back to the hidden jeeps we kept under cover. I saw that the half-tracks were now under cover but there was damage to one of them. As we neared the jeeps, I spied the Colonel and the rest of the half-tracks. I hoped he would realise there was artillery or a tank ahead.

"Any damage Lieutenant?"

"Not to the vehicle but Lake and Bridges were hit by shrapnel."

That was ironic. They were both medics. "See to them and then pull back south. Don't expose yourselves. I will wait for the Colonel!"

The Chinese gun and the machine guns were still firing. They had no targets as all of our vehicles were off the road.

Marine Lofting said, "Do you mind if I have a pop at them, sir? There is a snowdrift over there I can use."

I nodded, "But, for God's sake be careful. We have achieved what we came for. Let's get home safe!"

"Sir!"

I watched him head to a broken wall between which snow had been blown. Wrapping the end of his rifle in parachute silk he lay down. The Chinese gun fired and I saw why. The Colonel was roaring up in his half-tracks. A shell exploded just in front of the first half-track and, as men spilt out a second landed a little closer, the explosion throwing the half-track on to its side.

I shouted, "Get the half-tracks off the road!" Even as the Colonel's jeep slewed next to the half-track, I heard the crack from the gun. "Take cover!" The Colonel and his two men barely made it behind the nearest half-track before their jeep was destroyed.

There were four Americans who would not have to move for they lay crushed beneath the wrecked half-track. Behind me, I heard Lofting's rifle as he sniped at the enemy. Lieutenant Colonel Coulter was looking around as though dazed, I waved my arm, "Over here, sir!"

The other half-tracks had seen the fate of the first and were sheltering behind buildings. Eventually, the gun would shift targets and they would be at risk.

The Colonel ran up, "We heard the firing and thought you were under attack, Major."

"We were but we were not exposed, sir." I realised then that if the Lieutenant Colonel had led the reconnaissance then we would have had serious losses. I pointed to the bridge, "The Chinese have the bridge defended. There are machine guns and at least one artillery piece. The prisoner was correct, at least here in Seoul, the Chinese have fallen back to the Han River."

I saw him rub away a patch of blood. Shrapnel had caught him. "Any chance we could rush the bridge, Major?"

Machine gun bullets struck the walls above Lofting. I sighed, "You saw what they did to your half-track. Even now they may be bringing more artillery here or they might blow the bridge. We have done our job, sir. Now we get the hell out of Dodge!" The Chinese gun fired again and this time part of a building was struck and fell into the road. A few bricks flew perilously close to our heads.

"I suppose." Lofting's rifle barked again, "What is your man doing, Major?"

"Annoying the Chinese and keeping their heads down." Just then there was a double crack and the shells hit the wall close to Lofting. "Lofting, back to the jeep. It is time we left." I looked at the Colonel, "It is time we all left!"

"You are right! Back to the half-tracks! It is time to go home." He shook his head as he looked at the bodies of the four dead men, "Damn shame!"

We made it back to our camp before dark and I helped the Lieutenant Colonel to write the report. He would deliver it. I did not mind. One more mission and I would be returned to the British and that pleased me. Our two wounded medics were not seriously hurt although they became the butt of many jokes. It was always the way with British soldiers. Humour was a way of getting through each day!

Chapter 15

The Wolfhounds had a similar story to tell except that they suffered no casualties. The Chinese had withdrawn their main units to the Han River and whenever aircraft could take to the skies then their supply lines through North Korea were bombed. High Command had seen a weakness and we would exploit it. Operation Tomahawk was planned for the twenty-fourth of January. Over ninety thousand men seemed to me to be a large number for a reconnaissance but as the plan was General Ridgeway's and he was a cautious man, I was optimistic. Along with the Wolfhounds, the 5th Cavalry and four companies of the 95th we were to be a fast-moving screen which headed for Kumnyangjang-ni. We, along with a Turkish division, were to take the crossroads on Highway 20. I knew that too long a period had elapsed since our initial recce and that the Chinese would have moved men south but I hoped that they would not have had time to dig in.

It was a good plan for our tanks could move across country and we had air support. The air force had not seen large numbers of Chinese but that did not mean they were not there. The Chinese and North Koreans might not have many tanks but they had plenty of anti-aircraft guns and our pilots were wary of them. We had the same vehicles as on the original recce. We were happy with them. This time, however, as we were making an extended recce, we took more supplies with us and they were in the half-tracks. We were close to the Turkish battalion and next to the 95th and Lieutenant Colonel Coulter. I suspected that the Colonel would be happier this time as he was in command of his own sector. We had found a minor road between Highway 1 and Highway 55. We took it, leaving

the Turks to use Highway 1 and the Colonel and the Wolfhounds
to use Highway 55. I knew we would have to leave the road
eventually and go across country. To that end, we acquired some
rope for the half-tracks which would be able to pull us out if we
were stuck.

We left after dawn to enable the USAAF to give us air cover.
We headed down the minor road which we hoped would be both
quiet as well as allowing us to avoid detection. Nothing had been
down it for some days and the only indication of its direction was
the shape of the snow. The jeep had good tyres and it was actually
easier to drive than it had been on the slick and icy road. This was
also rougher land and there were many places for us to be
ambushed. Ashcroft kept his headphones on as reports were passed
back to Headquarters. Other units were heading up the main road
and Suwon was taken without a fight; we grew hopeful that this
recce would be as fruitful as the first one with the singular
difference that we could hold on to what we had. Just before noon,
we realised that the Chinese had reinforced the land south of the
Han River and intended to make us bleed for the land. The
difference was that they had not had time to dig in nor had they
heavy artillery and tanks to support them. We knew they had come
south since our first recce when we heard gunfire from the east and
the west. Small explosions indicated grenades and the louder
cracks the mobile guns the Lieutenant Colonel had brought. We
had no such problems and I began to wonder if they thought we
would not use this narrow track. Once again Lofting's hunter's
eyes spotted the ambush.

"Sir, at two o'clock. I saw a flash. It might be nothing."

"We heard firing to the east and west, let us assume it is
something." I braked gently and leapt from the jeep. The other
vehicles stopped behind me. "Sergeant Major Thorpe, I want you
to be bait. Head slowly up this road in your half-track and we will
ambush the Chinese and North Koreans up ahead. The rest of you
will be with me."

"But sir, I might be wrong!" Lofting was appalled that we
would act on his slight sighting.

"Then regard this as an impromptu run. Let's go!"

I hefted my Thompson over my shoulder and set off up the slope. In the summer this might have been harder but the snow had frozen and evened out some of the cracks and crevasses. My men naturally fanned out on both sides of me. Lieutenant Morrison was on the far right and Sergeant Grant on the far left. We had four Thompsons and two Bren guns. We had firepower. Lofting was next to me and eager to prove himself correct. His eyes scanned the slopes above us. We moved somewhat obliquely so that we were constantly climbing.

When Lofting dropped to his knees, I knew he had seen something and I held up my hand. He used his left hand to point across the slope. The North Koreans and Chinese were not all wearing camouflage white as we were and I saw them. They had heavy machine guns and what looked like mortars ready to attack anything coming up this narrow track. I pointed to the mortars and Lofting. He nodded and unslung his rifle. I could leave him to deal with them. I pointed up the slope and led my men to approach the Chinese and North Koreans from above. It was hard work for here the frozen snow was quite slippery. The sky was filled with white and we blended in. We did not stand out along the skyline. A hundred and fifty yards below us I could now see the full extent of the ambush and I heard the half-track as it lumbered along in low gear. An officer shouted something and I saw the mortar crews prepare their shells.

I waved my men to the ground, "Choose your targets." I knelt and, resting my gun arm on my knee I shouted, "Fire!" Lofting must have had good hearing or perhaps he anticipated my command for he fired his first shot and hit the Chinese soldier who was about to drop a mortar into the pipe. Our automatic weapons came as a complete shock to the enemy. They managed to fire one shell and then Bert Entwhistle opened up with the Browning heavy machine gun. I emptied one magazine and reloaded another.

Lieutenant Morrison shouted, "Sir, they are breaking and heading north."

"Down to their camp. I want papers."

There were still sporadic shots as Lofting and my men who were armed with rifles picked off the enemy who were fleeing. There were at least seventy dead and dying. From their uniforms, they were a hotchpotch of different units and a couple looked to be civilians. Perhaps they were South Korean sympathisers. We took all the papers we could find from the officers and the heavy weapons then headed back to the vehicles.

We loaded up and continued on the road. When it turned north-west, we left the road and I allowed the half-tracks to lead. Long before they had had proper roads here, they had used ancient paths to cross the higher areas. We followed one of these. It was not easy and we did not make good time. Twice the half-tracks had to pull us free but we reached the top of the ridge and looked down on Highway 20; it was three miles away. There were men preparing defences which straddled the road but I did not think they had seen us as there was no road down from the peaks and we had parked our vehicles in dead ground. I saw that there appeared to be a sort of trail heading down the slope but the snow made it hard to correctly identify it. I took my binoculars out and scanned the men below us. They had some small calibre artillery pieces but it was mainly infantry. I estimated their strength to be that of a regiment. They were fortifying half a mile of the road.

They had to be preparing to take on the 95th which was to our right. "Ashcroft, get on the radio to the Turks and Lieutenant Colonel Coulter. Tell them there are men digging in on the road between them."

"Sir!"

Our lofty eyrie meant he had a good signal. I looked at my watch. It was almost three in the afternoon and the sun would soon drop like a stone. "Officer's call!"

When my NCOs and Lieutenant Morrison were around me, I said, "I want a night attack on these positions. We will leave the vehicles here and move down during the night. We will leave four drivers with the vehicles and they can bring them down during daylight. It is too risky at night. First, we eat. I will try to find a good route down. Sergeant Major, organise the food if you please."

"Sir."

"Lieutenant, come with me."

The two of us crept to the edge and then slid down as far as we could so that we were not seen from below. The slope was not as steep as it had first looked. Once again, the frozen snow helped. As the two of us scanned the ground large snowflakes began to fall. That could only be to our advantage. I pointed to the left of me, "We can zig-zag down the slope. We have some rope and if we are roped together then we should be able to ensure that we do not lose anyone." He nodded. "I will lead one half and you the other. You should be able to follow our steps but keep the men steady; better to get down there slowly than risk a fall. I intend to make roughly two hundred-yard legs. We can cover three miles in less than two hours easily. We will still have plenty of time to attack them. If we can then you, Williams and I, will try to booby trap their guns in the dark. That will depend upon their sentries. I will use my Colt and you two lay the charges."

He nodded, "We have some explosives and plenty of grenades."

"If it takes too long to make the descent then we will just have to use firepower rather than explosives." I placed my Commando hat at the place I would begin our descent.

"Sir!"

When we returned Ashcroft said, "Sir, I have had both commanders on the radio. They have been held up and won't be at the road until mid-morning at the earliest. The air force is going to send a flight of Sabres and Mustangs if the weather permits."

I nodded and took the mug of beef tea the Sergeant Major proffered. It was warm rather than hot as we had had to use Thermos flasks. "That makes sense. We were not seen and the men who fled us were heading north. The roadblock is a response to the two flank columns. I would bet more men will be on their way tomorrow. All we have to do is disrupt them and hold them until the Turks and the Americans arrive. If we have to, we can retreat up the hill. I want Corporal Lowery and Digger Tomlinson on the radio. We can keep Headquarters informed about our progress."

"Sir."

As darkness fell, I slung my Thompson and fitted the silencer to my Colt. Lofting followed me as he had shown great skill in moving silently in addition to which he had a poacher's sixth sense which you could not replicate. In the darkness, the slope looked more intimidating. I found my hat and turned left to walk down the slope. We were all roped together. If one slipped then the others would lock the rope until the one who had slipped regained their footing. I hoped we would not need it but it was a very necessary precaution. My pistol was in my belt and I was using my hands for balance. As my eyes became accustomed to the slope and the darkness, I found the movement easier but I still kept it steady. The enemy had lit fires. No doubt they were cooking but I took comfort from the fact that I could not hear them. After two hundred steps I turned right to begin the next leg. I looked up and saw the line of men led by the Lieutenant. They were moving steadily and that was good. The falling snow ensured that we were careful. It made it hard to see and it was only when a flurry ceased that I was able to look down at the enemy position.

It was the third leg where disaster almost struck. We were passing Lieutenant Morrison's section when Wally Bridges, who was in the middle, slipped. Marine Collins was a strong lad and he locked his right arm across his chest so that Bridges fell no further. Pike was in front and he helped Bridges to his feet. They said not a word but nodded to each other. Had there not been snow then there would have been a skittering of stones which might have alerted the enemy. We had had a lucky let off. The slope was gentler towards the bottom and there was a temptation to go faster but that would have been a mistake. I estimated that the whole journey would take less than an hour and a half. We would have the opportunity to get into position and even to do some sabotage.

The ground flattened out some one hundred and fifty yards from the southern end of the defences. There were no defenders looking either north or south and the four sentries I had been watching as we descended were looking east and west. The main camp was on the north side of the road. We stopped on the slight slope two hundred yards from their defences. I untied the rope. The last man would coil it; Commandos were neat. I waved the men into a defensive line. Already Marine Lofting had found some rocks beneath the snow and he had made a snow loophole. His rifle was masked by parachute and he slid it through. He was ready before anyone else. I waved the Bren gunners so that they were spread out. Sergeant Grant took one end of the line and Sergeant Major Thorpe the other. I waited until all of them were in position and hidden before I signalled the Lieutenant and Lance Corporal Williams to join me. I laid my Thompson down between Ashcroft and Lofting, that would be my position and then I drew my Colt.

I looked at the four sentries. The two pairs had their heads together and I saw the glow of their cigarettes. They would not expect danger from the slope we had just descended. I moved forward towards the small artillery pieces. They had obligingly placed them and the four anti-tank guns back to back. It made sense. They would be able to keep the ammunition centrally. The sandbags we had seen were protecting the eight guns; that way the guns could keep up a good rate of fire east and west. We moved slowly for we had hours until daylight. The snow had been falling as we had descended and shrouded the whole camp in a world of white. I kept watching first east and then west as my two saboteurs laid booby traps and charges amongst the guns and the ammunition. The ammunition was set with timers while the guns would be triggered when they tried to load them. It took longer than I would have liked but, eventually, it was done and we moved back. I was the last man and, after holstering my gun, I used my hand to remove our tracks. It was not the best clearing up job I had ever done but, with the snow continuing to fall, nature would do it for me.

I joined Ashcroft and Lofting and pulled up my hood. I laid my Thompson and Colt before me. We now all had mitts with a firing finger although Lofting still preferred his fingerless gloves. We had some high sugar content sweets, the Americans called them candies, although not as good as Kendal Mint Cake, we could eat them while we waited for dawn and it would keep up our blood sugar. I looked at my watch and saw that it was an hour until dawn. I glanced up and saw that my line of men could barely be seen for they were completely covered in snow. I was proud of them. They had remained motionless during the snowstorm and resisted the impulse to shift.

The Chinese used a bugle to wake their men. I smiled to myself. So much for their ambush. However, they must have thought the nearest allied troops were still many hours away. The four sentries fed the fire and put a pot to heat upon it. It would be for water to make tea no doubt. My only fear was that someone would come to our side of the camp to use it as a latrine. I slid my hand on to the butt of the Colt. I still had a silencer fitted. Dawn broke and I began to feel the need to make water myself but I fought the urge. The Chinese and North Koreans breakfasted and then went to the guns. They would not load them until they had to. The choice of ammunition would be determined by the targets. We had seen both armour piercing and high explosive.

Disaster almost struck when the Chinese sergeant who had been standing by the nearest artillery piece decided to come towards us. I guessed he was coming to use the snow as a lavatory. He kept coming and I lifted my Colt to aim it at him. I hoped he would stop before he reached us but he kept coming. Suddenly I heard the distinctive sound of four Mustangs as they flew in from the sea. There were carriers there and I guessed these had come from the USS Bon Homme Richard. The Chinese sergeant heard the machine guns of the Mustangs and, as his trousers were already around his ankles, he dived towards us. He landed just ten yards away and he buried his face in the snow. The Chinese and North Koreans fired up at the piston-powered aircraft. The machine guns of the Mustangs tore through the camp. The sergeant pulled up his trousers and turned to run back towards the guns when the Mustangs climbed for a second attack. The four Sabres which followed had more firepower and they sent rockets towards the camp while firing their machine guns. Explosions showed where the rockets, shells and bullets had struck munitions. The unfortunate sergeant was sliced in two by the machine guns of one Sabre. When the Mustangs came back, they machine-gunned the camp. The Sabres just roared into the sky and headed west.

There were fires burning and cases of ammunition were exploding. I suspected that the air attacks had been coordinated with the ground attack for no sooner had the six aeroplanes disappeared than a Chinese officer pointed east. It was the 95th; they had arrived early!

There were more than enough explosions to cover the sound of my voice. "Ready lads!"

Marine Williams said, "The timers will go off in half an hour, sir!"

That was cutting it fine. I aimed my Colt at the officer and I risked a shot at a range of ninety yards. He spun around when my bullet hit him. His death went unnoticed for the booby traps on the four artillery pieces went off at the same time as the Chinese tried to load them. They exploded, sending shrapnel everywhere.

"Fire!"

I had picked up my Thompson and I fired. Every other gun opened up. At the same time, the tanks of the 5th Cavalry opened fire. When the anti-tank guns exploded, they set off the explosives hidden in the ammunition. A wave of heat and metal flew over our heads! The air was filled with the smell of cordite and the screams of the dying. The small area between us and the camp became a killing ground. I knew that some would take the line of least resistance and head west. They would be caught by the Turkish battalion. The only real escape route was north towards the river.

I heard one of my men say, "Bloody hell!" It seemed a minor curse in the circumstances. As the debris descended, I risked standing. The American tanks were less than four hundred yards away and the armoured half-tracks of the 95th were close behind them. The dazed and shaken Chinese and North Koreans surrendered. There were just one hundred of them. We had taken the first of our objectives. We had reached and secured our target, Highway 20! We had done so with minimal losses but stiffer resistance than we had expected. But for the attack from the aircraft carrier, it might not have been so.

The Americans had more men and so they began to herd the prisoners back down the road. Lieutenant Colonel Coulter was in an ebullient mood, "Helluva victory, Major. Your men take any hits?"

It had been the first thing I had checked and we had not. "No, sir. I just have to get my vehicles down from the high ground."

He nodded, "We are pushing on to the Han River. The General will be pleased. Have you been listening to the chatter?" I shook my head. I had needed every man's eyes on the enemy. "We have taken all of our objectives. The General himself flew over the battlefield yesterday and he is delighted."

"We will follow when we can, sir."

With the tanks of the 5th Cavalry before them, the 95th pushed north leaving us with the dead bodies of our enemies. The snow which had stopped briefly now began to fall again. Sergeant Major Thorpe shook his head, "We can't bury them sir, but this doesn't sit right. When a man dies in battle he should be buried."

"I agree Sergeant Major, but nature, it seems, will do the job for us. The fires are still burning, let's get some food on the go. It will do the men good to have a brew and hot food. We can't do much until the vehicles are down."

"Right sir."

"Ashcroft, tell the lads on the ridge to bring the vehicles down but take it steady."

"Corporal Dixon."

"Sir?"

I handed him my binoculars, "Get yourself a good vantage point and keep your eye on the men and the vehicles. If you think there is any danger then give me a shout!"

"Sir."

The Lieutenant Colonel had left before searching the officers and so, before the dead were completely covered, I collected the papers from the dead. Intelligence could sift through them and glean valuable information. The morning was half over when the food and tea were ready. Sergeant Major Thorpe had had our men clear the bodies away from the fires. I knew I should have thought of that. I went over to Corporal Dixon at 1030 hours. I had already drunk a cup of tea. "Go and have a brew, Dixon. Where are they?"

He handed me the glasses, "About a third of the way down. The lads are taking it steady. Sudden flurries of snow hide them and they are hard to see."

He left and I raised the glasses. There was a half-track at the front and one at the rear. The two jeeps were tucked between them. They were travelling slower than we had in the night attack. It was the right thing to do. By the middle of the afternoon, it became clear that they would not reach us much before dark. I took a decision, "Lieutenant Morrison, we will camp here for the night. This side of the road looks to be free from bodies. Have the men clear some snow to make windbreaks and when the vehicles arrive, we will pitch our tents. The men could use a night's sleep."

"Sir."

"It was shortly before 1600 when our weary four men drove the four vehicles into the camp. Tomlinson shook his head, "I wouldn't like to do that again, sir."

"You did well and I am sorry I put you and the other chaps in that position. The plan worked though."

He smiled, "Aye, sir and we had a grandstand view watching it from the ridge. I hope the Sergeant Major has a brew on. I am gagging!"

"He has and we camp here tonight. We are ahead of schedule."

The next morning, we loaded the vehicles again and followed the route taken by the Lieutenant Colonel. We found him along with the 95th and the 5th Cavalry. The Chinese and North Koreans had managed to find a patch of high ground where the tanks could not follow. With heavy and light mortars, they were able to keep the advance from moving towards its objective. As we drove up the road, we could hear the fighting.

Marine Lofting said, "Sounds like the Yanks did not get far, eh sir?"

I pointed to the high, snow-covered ground, "No surprise really. They didn't see us the other night even when that Chinese Sergeant was within ten paces of us. They can make snow bunkers to hide them. This is perfect country to hold us up." Above us, the skies were filled with threatening cloud. There would be no air support.

We had to stop half a mile from the actual fighting. The road passed between two high peaks. It narrowed to a pinch point. I saw a burned-out Patton there. There were tanks, half-tracks, jeeps and trucks closer to us. It looked like an enormous car park! A Sergeant stopped us, "Sorry Major Harsker. If you go any closer you risk the Commies hitting your vehicle. We have lost one tank and three half-tracks that way."

I nodded, "Lieutenant, take charge here. Ashcroft, come with me. Where is the Lieutenant Colonel, Sergeant?"

"Wilson, take the Major to the CP!"

A PFC signalled for us to follow. We ran along a snow wall which hid us from the hillside. I heard the whump of mortar shells and the crack of rifles. They were Chinese and not American. I saw soil lifted into the air. That told me that the mortars had cleared the snow and were hitting the ground. Two medical orderlies were running back towards the vehicles with a stretcher and a wounded American. Soldiers were pressed against the snow and they looked strained. I remembered the same looks on D-Day when we had fought alongside the Paras at Belleville. They were having to take casualties and finding it hard to hit back. It demoralized troops.

We reached the Command Post. I saw the Colonel of the 5th Cavalry. He was smoking a cigar and he and Lieutenant Colonel Coulter were deep in conversation.

PFC Wilson said, "Colonel sir, Major Harsker."

The look which Lieutenant Colonel Coulter gave me was a mixture of relief and annoyance, "Glad you are here, Major, what kept you? We expected you last night."

"We had to get our vehicles down from the high ground, sir."

The cavalryman took out his cigar and shook his head, "You brought half-tracks down that slope in snow? Well done, Major. Your men are either highly skilled or very lucky."

I smiled, "I think they are both, sir, and they are good traits for a soldier to have."

Lieutenant Colonel Coulter said, "And now we are stymied by the Chinese. They are controlling this road from above. We have tried using the tanks' guns but the angle is wrong. Every time we have sent men up, they have been repulsed."

I nodded and looked to the hills to the west. "I take it they haven't got men there, sir."

"No, thank God. If they had then we would have lost more tanks and men."

I looked at my watch. It was three hours to darkness, "Sir, we are still ahead of schedule. The General knows that without air cover our progress will be difficult. Why not try a night-time attack?"

"They would be ready for us."

I shook my head, "Not a regular attack, sir, but a raid. Use my men and a platoon of your best men. We sneak close and make an attack with grenades and machine guns from above them. If you have some of the tanks run their engines and move back and forth, they will think you are trying to run the pass. They will have their mortars ranged in on the wrecked Patton. If their attention is here then we might be able to use the slope from the south to attack. They will have their machine guns dug in but they will be vulnerable to hand grenades if we can get close."

The cavalryman nodded, "Seems like a good plan to me but then again I will just be wasting gas. It will be your men who have to attack. It is your decision, Tom."

I saw the Colonel debating then he nodded, "Captain Morgan has been itching to work with you, Major. We will try it."

I nodded, "If we wait until 2300 hours to start the tanks' engines that will give us the opportunity to get into position. Have your Captain join me at my vehicles, sir, and we can refine the plan."

Lieutenant Colonel Coulter smiled, "Even when you make a request, Major, it sounds like an order. I will send him and A Platoon."

As Ashcroft and I made our way back my radio operator said, "Always at the sharp end, eh sir?"

I laughed, "Would you have it any other way, Ashcroft?"

"No, sir, and your plans have a habit of succeeding."

I hoped he was right.

Chapter 16

I gathered my men around me. "We had a good night's sleep last night so you should all be fresh as daisies. We are going out tonight to try to get rid of the enemy on the hill." There were no groans and no complaints. "We are going up with a platoon of Americans. We are the experts and they will be the support. This is classic Commando! We move up behind them silently and use knives and saps to eliminate their sentries. Then we use grenades. With luck, they will not be expecting this. Once we are inside their lines then we should be able to roll them up."

Lance Corporal Williams said, "You make it sound easy, sir."

I smiled, "That is why I am an officer, Williams. They teach you to make the impossible sound easy!"

The men all laughed and I knew they were not worried. We heard the approach of the Americans and we turned. Normally a platoon was led by a Second Lieutenant. The fact that this one had a Captain as well as a Second Lieutenant told me that the Captain who led them was keen. There were three rifle sections each commanded by a sergeant. The senior one would be a Sergeant, First Class. There would also be a weapons section. I hoped they had the BAR and not a heavier gun for we needed speed and silence.

"Captain Morgan and his pirates reporting, Major Harsker." The Captain grinned. I guessed he liked the piratical image. I had known worse.

"Welcome, Captain. I am glad you could join us. First things first. Tonight, we move silently and we move like ghosts. As you can see, we are wearing rubber-soled shoes. I appreciate that you do not have that luxury which is why when we begin our attack tonight your men will step into the footprints left by my men. That way there is less chance of making a noise. Secondly, you need to be wearing white."

I saw his face fall. I don't know if he thought this would be a John Wayne charge up the hill with gun firing from the hip but his face showed he had not expected this. He nodded. "If your officers and sergeants would come with me, I will explain the plan. I would like to bring back as many men as possible. I do not like writing letters to mothers, wives and sweethearts!" I turned, "Sergeant Major Thorpe, if you would like to explain to the enlisted men what we expect. I daresay you will know the appropriate words."

He grinned, "Yes sir!"

I took the Americans and my NCOs to the side of the hill we would be ascending and pointed as I spoke. "We are going to climb up there after dark. If you look carefully to the left you can just make out the caps of the sentries. On the right you can see there is a natural path which zigs zags up the slope and takes us away from the enemy. We use that because I don't think the sentries will be able to see us. It is dead ground. I want to get as high as we can before we begin our attack. I will take a small team of specialists in and we will neutralize the sentries."

The Second Lieutenant asked, "Neutralize?"

Jake said, "Kill them, silently, Lieutenant."

I saw their eyes drawn to the Commando daggers we all wore. I continued, "We will be using hand signals. I will be the only one who speaks and that will be just two words, 'open fire!'" I saw the sergeants smile. "When the sentries are eliminated then we will move in closer. As soon as my men pull their grenades then yours will do the same. We all throw them at the same time and then hit the deck. I intend to be above the Chinese at that point and that means we should be safe from flying shrapnel. We rise and use our guns to kill as many as we can. The next command after 'open fire' will be 'follow me'. We move through the camp shooting as many as we can. If they surrender, fine but the enemy has proved very adept at playing dead as we found at Suwon. Better to waste a bullet than take a risk." I smiled, "Any questions?"

The Captain asked, "What happens if you are hit, sir?"

"Lieutenant Morrison will assume command." I saw his mouth open, "And to pre-empt your next question, if he falls it will be Sergeant Major Thorpe. He can't be killed; he is a Sergeant Major!"

That made the sergeants burst out laughing.

"Don't worry, Captain Morgan, our enemies have been trying to kill me since 1939. Even the SS had a go. I am a tough old boot."

He smiled, "Right sir."

"If there are no more questions then I suggest you brief your men. We will assemble here at 2200 hours."

"When they had gone, I turned to my officers, "What do you think?"

Sergeant Grant nodded, "They seem keen enough and they give us numbers."

"Lieutenant, I want you and Sergeant Major Thorpe directly in front of the Americans. Keep them in line."

"Who will you take in to deal with the sentries, sir?"

"Lofting, Sergeant Grant, Corporal Lowery, Marines Hall and Harris. We should be enough. I have my silenced Colt and that will give us an edge. Remember the Chinese should be busy trying to take out tanks!"

I managed to get an hour of sleep. When I woke there was hot food ready and it was dark. After I had eaten, I cleaned my weapons and prepared myself mentally. I lit my pipe and smoked until I just had ash left. Looking at my watch I saw that it was 2130. I went to the jump-off point. Lance Corporal Williams was there. I handed him my Thompson. "I shan't need this tonight. I have my Colt. You can use it."

He looked delighted, "Thank you, sir. I will look after it."

I shook my head. "It is not precious to me, Sam, the one I had had since the last war is with Ji-hoo." Williams nodded and I wondered how the one-armed man was surviving. He was tough but he and his men could expect short shrift if they were caught.

Sergeant Major Thorpe and my other NCOs arrived next. "How did the briefing go, Sarn't Major?"

He chuckled, "I put the fear of God into them but I reckon they will be alright, sir. They are keen and they saw what happened at Suwon. They are eager to get back at the enemy."

"Good."

We were all in place by 2150 and I went to the edge of the jump-off point. The NCOs shuffled the men into lines. It was dark but the blizzard had stopped while I had slept. I looked up at the snow-covered slope. No one had yet walked on it and it was virgin snow. I was putting a great deal on the shoulders of the five men who would come with me. I had worked out the route during the hours of daylight and identified where the sentries were. I hoped they would not change at night.

The tanks would start their engines at 2230 and so at 2215, I began the ascent. I waved my five men forward and they were followed by six more men. We would ascend in a line six men wide. Of the six of us at the front, I was the only one with a weapon. I looked at each spot where I would place my foot as carefully as if I was walking across a minefield. At 2229 I heard the engines of the Shermans and the Pattons roar into life. As soon as they did, I heard a Chinese trumpet. I held up my hand and we all stopped. The sentries on all sides would look out to see if this was a general attack. Then I heard the sound of the tanks as they began to move. The Chinese sent a Very Light up but it was on the other side of our camp, where the tanks could be heard. We remained in darkness. The first mortars sent their shells. The machine gunners in the tanks added to the illusion of an attempt to break through by firing up the slope. As the light faded, I waved my hand and we moved forward once more. The Chinese and North Koreans began to fire at the tanks. I hoped that the tank commanders would not get carried away. This was a diversion to get us close to the enemy.

I looked at the snow-covered rocks ahead. When it had been daylight, I had fixed the position of the sentries. I would not be totally accurate but so long as I was within fifteen feet then all would be well. The going was a little easier as this was a flatter part. The Chinese had chosen a place which had a natural rock parapet. They had, in effect, a fortress. I could smell smoke which told me that they had a fire. I watched a tiny glow arc over the top to sizzle in the snow. It was a cigarette butt and it meant that I was less than twenty yards from the nearest sentry. I halted and everyone else, a heartbeat later, also stopped. I turned and pointed to Corporal Dixon and the other NCOs. I held up my hand. They knew they had to wait.

I dropped on to all fours and began to crawl up the snow. The other five copied me. Now they would each have a weapon of choice in their hand. I could actually hear, when the mortars stopped firing, the sound of the men on the other side of the rocks. There sounded to be just four men. Then the sound of the tanks changed pitch. As I had asked, they were withdrawing to safety. The enemy would continue to send their mortar shells in the hope of catching infantry in the pass. I began to climb the snow-covered boulder. I saw that Lofting had his Commando knife and he was insinuating himself between two snow-covered boulders to my left while Sergeant Grant, also with a knife was like me, climbing over a third snow-covered rock. My hood was over my head and I just peered over the top. There were five men and they were seated around a fire. The snow-covered boulders had hidden the fire. There was no one else within thirty yards. We had ascended behind their highest positions. The rest of the men were a good one hundred and fifty yards away and closer to the American threat.

I looked at Sergeant Grant. He mimed diving at the men. It was a risk but I nodded. I had grenades and so long as we took these five out, I could buy the rest of the team enough time to get into position. I had to hope that the others were also in position. One of the Chinese soldiers I saw below me was a sergeant and I aimed at him. He was just twenty feet away and I aimed at the centre of his chest. Two other men faced me. The one to the sergeant's right would be my second target. I took a deep breath and squeezed the trigger. Even before the bullet hit him, I had fired a second bullet at the second man. Sergeant Grant had leapt on to the back of his man while Lofting had appeared like a wraith and slit the throat of the other man whose back was to me. The last man looked up and stared at me. My bullet hit him between the eyes.

My other three men appeared and went to the bodies to ensure that all five were dead. The tanks' engines had stopped. I turned and waved forward the rest of the men. Already Sergeant Grant and the others were using the five dead bodies as an improvised barricade and had laid out their grenades. My team of commandos came over first and they were quickly organised by Sergeant Grant through the use of hand signals. I spied a Chinese submachine gun with the familiar drum magazine. I picked it up and moved to the extreme right of the line. The Chinese below us thought that they had defeated the Americans and there was much laughter as they began to leave their mortars to return to their blankets. Sentries resumed their watch. I took my hand grenade and looked down the line. About half of the Americans were in position. I took out the pin and watched my men as the Chinese and North Koreans approached their fires. The fires were forty paces from us and below us. Soon they would see us. I pulled my arm back and was relieved to see all eyes on me and more than three-quarters of our men had their grenades ready. I threw mine as far as I could high in the air. An airburst was always effective. Then, after seeing that everyone had obeyed my orders, I did the same and threw myself to the ground. The concussion was horrific. More than forty grenades had gone off at once.

I lifted my head and I was aware that my hearing had gone. I had forgotten to cover my ears. I shouted, "Open fire!" And I sprayed the PPsh41 from side to side until the drum was empty. Enough men heard me to obey orders and the rest saw the bullets.

Soon sixty guns were pouring lead into the shell-shocked Chinese and North Koreans. When I saw the muzzle flashes from guns on the other side of the enemy, I knew that the Lieutenant Colonel had launched his own attack.

When the order to cease-fire was given more than two-thirds of the enemy were dead or wounded and the other third were happy to surrender. We had won! My assault team had lost no men and that pleased me inordinately.

It took another two days to reach the Han River. We had more firefights but nothing like the fight on the snow-covered slopes above the narrow pass. The tanks were able to use their heavy guns and machine guns to destroy enemy emplacements and our infantry winkled out the few survivors. We were the first of the units to achieve our objective. There had been stiffer resistance to the east and west of us. We were ordered to hold our position and to dig defences.

General Ridgeway himself spoke to Lieutenant Colonel Coulter. I happened to be there when the radio call came in, "You have done well, Tom, but I don't give a damn about real estate. I want as many Commies dead as you can manage. Dig in and don't try to cross the river. Let them come to us. Have the 5th dig their tanks in. I will send air cover. You stay there and the rest of the army will squeeze them against you."

I knew it went against Lieutenant Colonel Coulter's nature to fight defensively but the order had been quite clear and so he obeyed. We had had no snow for three days and, as the days lengthened and warmed up, so the snow inevitably began to thaw. We had a position between two Patton tanks of the 5th Cavalry. We had our four Bren guns there as well as the Brownings on the two half-tracks. We still had no mortars but thanks to Sergeant Major Thorpe we had plenty of ammunition and grenades. We took the two Brownings from the jeeps and used rocks instead of sandbags to make a gun emplacement. And we waited.

The first Chinese and North Korean units came in the early hours of the morning. Sergeant Major Thorpe had arranged a rota and we had men who were watching. Phil Hall was the sentry and he spotted the movement. He was too experienced to make a noise and so he sent Geoff Bates to rouse us. The enemy crept towards us but we had men already racing to our position. I ran to the headquarter tents of the cavalrymen.

"The Chinese and the North Koreans are about to attack us!"

They jumped up. Their Colonel had decided that having their crews sleep in their tanks was deterrent enough. He would soon find out that he was wrong. I had retrieved my Thompson from a disappointed Williams who thought he had a new weapon. I threw myself behind the wood we had cut to make a defence. I turned to Phil Hall, "Where are they?" He pointed directly ahead. I stared into the dark and thought, for a moment, that he was mistaken. Then I saw the subtlest of movements. "Well done, Hall, you have good eyes!" I turned to Lieutenant Morrison, "Stand to!" As he repeated the order, I turned to Sergeant Grant and said the same thing. I cocked the Thompson and took three grenades from my battle vest. I heard the Brens and Brownings as they were also cocked. The enemy soldiers were in for a rude shock.

"Stand by!" I waited until I could see their faces just one hundred yards away and I shouted, "Fire!"

The combined firepower of my whole section tore into them. The tank crews were aroused and their Brownings added to the hail of lead. Yet, still they came.

Having emptied my magazine, I lifted a grenade and, pulling out the pin, hurled it towards the enemy. I had no need to shout for we had protection and my arm had thrown the grenade thirty yards. My men emulated me and, as I reloaded, I saw the enemy physically recoil as the shrapnel shredded into them. Some would be killed outright whilst others would be so badly wounded that they would not be able to carry on. More of the 5th Cavalry joined us. The Headquarters Company picked up weapons and fought alongside the men on the line. When the tanks were fully manned, they fired High Explosive shells to break up the attack. By dawn, the first attack was over. The second attack was on the 95th and began halfway through the attack on us. We could hear it but were in no position to do anything about it. Our eyes were fixed to our front. I lit my pipe as we waited for dawn to break.

Sergeant Grant said, "They are hard men, sir. I think our lads would have given up long ago."

"Perhaps but this is not their country, if they were fighting for England then they would fight until the last man. Trust me I know."

"Can we win this, sir?"

I looked into the eyes of Sergeant Grant. I knew the answer I should give but he deserved the truth, "Realistically? No. But we will keep on because this is just the start. If Chamberlain had been stronger in Munich then who knows how many lives might have been saved? We keep on doing what we do and trust in God and the men alongside whom we fight."

"Not the politicians, sir?"

I burst out laughing, "They are the last people I would trust! They look out for number one and they always will. You show me a politician with a gun in his hand and I will change my mind. Churchill was the last politician to put his money where his mouth was. I would trust him!"

The enemy did not come again that day. We removed our casualties. Two of my men had wounds which needed attention and we reloaded our weapons. We ate and we snatched some sleep. Unless there was an airdrop then we would run out of ammo in the next four days. Just before darkness fell, I slipped out with ten volunteers and went to the Chinese and Korean dead. With the guns of the two tanks watching over us we collected as many guns and ammunition as we could. When the next attack began, we would use their guns to fight them. I liked that irony!

When darkness came so did the enemy. They were determined to shift us. Word came that our defence was helping the other elements of our reconnaissance to make inroads. We were the thorn they had to remove and we stubbornly hung on. I had a Russian submachine gun and two magazines. I was more profligate with the bullets than I would have been with my Thompson. The bullets scythed down the enemy. We were well protected. In the middle of the night, at about 0200, the attack ceased. I heard some of the tank crews breathe a sigh of relief. I hissed, "Commandos, this is not over. Keep a sharp eye out and listen for the enemy. Use your noses!" The Chinese and North Koreans ate different food to us and would smell differently.

"Yes sir!" rippled back towards me and I took out my Colt. I had a full magazine and I knew that the enemy had something up their sleeve.

Lofting had a poacher's eye and ear. I heard him hiss, "Watch out lads I can smell 'em!"

That was enough for me. I saw a patch of snow move. It was impossible and yet it moved. I had enough bullets and so I wasted one. The bullet smacked into the head of the North Korean who was just fifteen feet from me. My men saw what I had done and four dead Chinese later the enemy fell back! They were more successful on the eastern side and Lieutenant Colonel Coulter lost twenty men. The attack was repulsed but I knew the Lieutenant Colonel would not sleep easy. He would regard that as his failure.

We had six days of attacks and assault but we held on and when they gave up we had a line along the Han River. There was still a huge North Korean and Chinese enclave to the east but Seoul was within assaulting distance and we were sent back to Suwon. General Ridgeway himself greeted us. He shook my hand and that of every Commando. It was his way for he was a soldier. "Major, you and your men have done more than we could ever have expected. The traditions of the Commando have been upheld and then some. I hoped for a unit citation but…" he waved an arm "but you and I are soldiers and I will just say, 'Well done!'"

"Thank you, sir, it has been an honour,"

"And, sadly, we now lose you. You are being returned to the Commonwealth Division. Good luck, Major."

We spent another three days at the base. We had a long way to travel. The men used the PX to buy what they needed. It was like an Aladdin's cave for my men. We also waited as long as we could in the hope that we might receive some long-overdue mail. We did not and so we headed east in early February. We were not there to see Seoul recaptured for the final time. I had no idea of Ji-hoo's fate but I hoped he had survived. He deserved to. The Americans had left us our four vehicles and so we travelled east through recently recovered land and we saw the bitter result. There were hanged men in every town. They were the North Korean sympathisers and guerrillas. The Republic of Korea had been harsh in its punishment and in all honesty, I could not blame them. The men looked forward to British command. I did not disillusion them. We would have an Australian as our commander but, from what I could learn, he was a good bloke. I let Ashcroft drive and I enjoyed my pipe and a great quantity of pipe tobacco courtesy of the Americans. They had wished to reward me. I wondered if my war was coming to an end. With our air superiority and the supply problems of the Chinese, I hoped so but the Communists had a fanaticism which terrified me. I had killed more men in less than a year in Korea than I had in six years of war in Europe and Africa. It was a frightening and sobering thought.

Lieutenant Colonel Coulter was a changed man. He had lost good officers and men and he was not the gung-ho commander I had first met. He understood war. He had wanted to give me something in return for our service but I had shaken my head, "It is not necessary, sir. I fought alongside Americans in the last war and it is good to see that you have not changed. Our people share more than a common language, we share the same values and ideals. We are the same under the skin. You take care sir, and survive. America will need men like you to train the next generation! You pass on what you have learned."

We were heading first, to Wonju, which had been recently recaptured and then we would be on the Kansas and Utah line of defences. The British were defending a twelve-mile sector.

It took almost a week to arrive and, when we finally reached the British sector, we had to spend three days in Wonju while the paperwork was sorted out. I asked about our mail but I knew what the answer would be. It was still chasing us! The good news was that we were put up in a hotel. We had hot showers and soft beds. I knew it could not last but those three days were like R & R!

Chapter 17

It was while we were enjoying the comforts of a bed that we heard first that General MacArthur was about to be replaced by General Ridgeway and, a few days later, that Seoul had been recaptured. Both appeared to me to be good news. Lieutenant Morrison and I sat in the bar of the hotel enjoying a drink. "Do you think the war might be over, sir? I mean we have Seoul again and we have blunted all of the attacks so far. With better weather, we have more air support."

I shook my head, "You are clutching at straws. This war has some time to run. The Chinese have an almost inexhaustible supply of men. It is only their long supply lines which give us any hope." He nodded and I sipped my whisky. "Listen, Jake, if you want to resign and go to Israel, I will expedite the paperwork."

He shook his head, "I know, sir, but that would be like desertion. So long as you and the lads stay here then so will I."

"Very noble and, to be honest, you may not have to be here that long as this unit is due to be rotated back to England. We have exceeded the expected time here. Don't forget you and the ones who came with you were replacements but the unit has been here since last summer. That means that you could resign when we are back in Blighty."

"And we leave tomorrow for our new posting, sir?"

"Yes, we are heading north. There is a push across the whole front." I smiled as I had garnered that information from an American Major who was on his way home. He had been more than a little indiscreet. He was one of MacArthur's men and resented Doug's removal. "I think that the plan is to envelop large numbers of the enemy. We are heading for the Imjin River."

"And what is the make-up of the brigade sir?"

"The Royal Northumberland Fusiliers, they are a good unit, are brigaded with the Glosters, Ulster Rifles, a Belgian unit and the Royal Irish Hussars who have the 7th Tank Regiment attached to them. They have all been here for some time. Then there is the Royal Artillery support. It is a good division."

We left the next morning and drove with the flow of traffic to the Headquarters of the 29th Brigade. That the enemy would know an attack was imminent was not in doubt. Despite the scourging of the south in February there were still North Korean sympathisers and there were too many loose-lipped officers like the Major of Intelligence I had met. The constant traffic heading for the north could only presage one thing, an attack. However, the Chinese and North Koreans had been badly hurt during the Korean winter and I hoped that their morale would be weakened.

Brigadier Tom Brodie came from Northumberland. Our paths had never crossed as he had spent the latter years of the war in the Far East, Burma, but I knew of him. He had stayed in after the war and was a professional soldier. He was old fashioned too and I liked that. He made a point of meeting me personally and his words told me that he had done his research. He had also met my father during the war. All in all, I felt comfortable after meeting him. He was no glory hound and he cared for his men. He was also resolute. I had been told that when the Chinese had begun their New Year Offensive his orders had been quite clear. The staff sergeant who took me to him quoted the Brigadier's order, *'I have no intention that this Brigade Group will retire before the enemy unless ordered by higher authority to conform with general movement. If you meet him you are to knock hell out of him with everything you got. You are only to give ground on my orders.'*

Men appreciated such commanders for they knew where they stood!

"So, Major, you and your unit are due to be rotated but we have this one operation first. We move up to our jump-off positions in the next three days. Our task is relatively simple. We have to take a ford on the Imjin River and hold the high ground close to Highway 11. We have Republic of Korean units on one side and Americans on the other. I intend to use the skills of your section to our best advantage. You will be our eyes and ears as we advance." He had smiled, "I know you and your lads have had a hard time but, remarkably, your losses have been lower than any other unit. That speaks well of your men's skill."

"We have been lucky, Brigadier, and we both know the value of that."

"Quite so. You have a day or two to settle in and I will send over Lieutenant Machin, one of my aides, with the maps and the aerial photographs. We will begin the attack at dawn so that we can have good air support. As I say once we have the ford then your work is done and I expect that you will be taken from us fairly quickly. Your men have played their part already."

"Thank you, sir."

After the hotel, the tents were a comedown but one we understood. We were close to the Hussars and our men went to chat with them. Sergeant Major Thorpe had found some packing cases and we had those as seats. The snow had gone while we were in the hotel. Although it was hardly balmy, we were able to sit outside in battledress protected by the windbreaks which were our tents! Ken had brought us a brew and I gestured for him to join Jake and myself.

"This next action might well be our last, Sergeant Major. We are overdue a rotation. You might spread the word. It is not gospel but as the Argylls have just been rotated and we have been here longer, you never know."

"That will please the lads with families, sir." I lit my pipe. Sergeant Major Thorpe asked, "Do you mind if I try some of that baccy, sir? It has a nice smell."

"Of course." I wondered how long it had taken for him to pluck up the courage to ask.

As he filled his pipe he asked, "How does it smoke, sir?"

"It is a moist tobacco so slowly. It is not too hot a smoke. I like it. I prefer a bar tobacco like Condor, soaked in navy rum but..."

The Sergeant Major laughed as he put a match to his pipe, "Aye sir, that would be nice." We had our pipes going and Lieutenant Morrison had learned that our silences were necessary.

Eventually I broke the silence, "Any plans when this is over, Sarn't Major?"

"Aye, sir. I have served my time and then some. I have grand bairns I haven't seen yet and more than seven months back pay. I will put in my papers when we get back to Blighty. I doubt they will fly us back and we will have at least a month at sea."

"And you, Lieutenant?"

"The same as I told you before, sir. Nothing has happened to make me change my mind, sir. If I am going to fight, I would rather fight for something worth fighting for. What about you?"

"I was only brought back because they were short of senior officers. I will go back to the territorials and play at soldier for two weeks every summer. For the rest I will enjoy building up the company and seeing my children grow." The Sergeant Major and I spoke of his grandchildren and my children. I saw the wistful look on Jake's face, that was a journey he had yet to make.

This was a major operation. I visited Headquarters each day and learned more on every visit. An American liaison officer told me, in confidence, that Major Rogers and his Rangers would be making an attack not far from our position across a vital reservoir. The ninety-odd thousand soldiers from Operation Thunderbolt would be dwarfed by this operation which also involved almost half of the South Korean forces. General Ridgeway was a planner and he would not take unnecessary risks; slow and steady were his watchwords.

I was summoned to a meeting in the last week of March. I was not the only relatively junior officer there. Major Rickford commanded the Ulster Rifles and Major Huth represented the 8th King's Royal Irish Hussars. The Brigadier had a map before him. "Gentlemen, we are going to take part in Operation Rugged." He pointed to a line which was about two miles north of the 38th Parallel and went from the east coast of Korea to Seoul. "This is the Kansas line and it is our objective. There are a number of Chinese and North Korean Divisions facing us but, as you no doubt know, they have had supply problems and the increasingly benign weather means we have air support. Our particular target is the Imjin River and Highway 11. This operation, if successful, will be followed by Operation Dauntless which will take us here." He pointed to another line which looked to be sixteen or so miles further north. "This is the Wyoming Line but that is for the future." He looked directly at me, "We now have some Commandos under the command of Major Harsker. He has been acting as a recce for the Americans but we now have his men and I intend to use them. They will be supported by the Hussars. It will be good to have tank support. We need their Centurions and armoured cars."

Major Huth, of the Hussars, raised his hand, "Sir, A and B Companies are due to be rotated. Our tanks are already being loaded onto tank transporters." He looked apologetically at the rest of us. "C Company will be taken to Japan when the tank transporters return."

The Brigadier shook his head in dismay, "Not your fault but which half-brained pencil pusher came up with that idea? Well, of course, C Company will have to stay. We need tanks."

"Of course, sir."

"Who is the commander?"

"Captain Peter Ormrod. A good chap!"

"Then have him liaise with Major Harsker." I could see that the Brigadier was unhappy with the situation and he glowered around the room. "Is there any other joyous news for you to share with us, gentlemen?"

We all shook our heads and he proceeded with the briefing. Afterwards, he called me over. "Sorry about this, Major, but as you might have gathered, I knew nothing of this."

"We both know, sir, that this was a regular occurrence in the last war. We will manage. To be honest the American half-tracks are probably better than Centurions in this sort of action. Just so long as we can call in their firepower if we get in trouble then we should be alright."

"Remember, Major, you will have four battalions to support you."

"But we don't know the numbers we will be facing, sir, nor the defences they have in place."

"A good point but aerial photography suggests that they have no tanks there and have yet to put artillery into the line. It will be the sheer weight of numbers."

I returned to my men and told them of the operation. When they heard the start date, the 2nd of April, some found it amusing coming as it did, a day after April Fool's day.

Captain Ormrod roared up with another of his tank commanders, Lieutenant Hurst; they drove in a borrowed jeep. The Captain had lost an eye in the last war and wore an eye patch which gave him a piratical look. He later told me he had a prosthetic but it had a habit of falling out and so he kept it for, as he called it, best. He and the young Lieutenant saluted.

I nodded to Lieutenant Morrison and Sergeant Major Thorpe, "Lieutenant Morrison and Sergeant Major Thorpe. As you can see, we are a small unit."

"I shall fetch some tea, sir."

"Thanks, Sarn't Major."

The Captain smiled and took the packing case I offered, "And we are not much bigger. I know that Major Huth is less than happy to be leaving one squadron to do the work of three."

"The Centurion is a good tank. I know that."

"It is the best but we both know, sir, that if we are surrounded by overwhelming numbers then they can destroy us!"

"And we will be with you so leave the infantry to us!" My pipe had gone out and so I loosened the crust with a match. "The thing is, Captain, it would be easier for us if we operated ahead of you and called you in when we needed heavy armour. They can hear you coming."

They both laughed, "Quite right, sir. The Centurion is a good tank but it is a noisy bugger! And, of course, the terrain does not suit us. Still, we have incredibly thick armour and our only fear is losing a track. The Commies have nothing that can come close to damaging us. We have discovered that they are intimidated by dragons. We have painted dragons on our tanks. The Yanks told us about it. You never know, it might work!"

We spent a pleasant hour talking. The Captain and I had some shared experiences. He had been at Normandy although not with the first wave. The hour was amongst the most productive I had had in a long time. I felt as though I knew the Captain; more than that, I trusted him.

The timing of each attack was left largely to the individual commanders. It was a mark of General Ridgeway's style. He trusted his officers. Having looked at the maps, the Brigadier decided to have the Hussars advance up the main highway to the Imjin River. We, supported by the Glosters, would head up a side road which twisted through the mountains. The Centurions would have struggled in the terrain anyway but Brigadier Brodie anticipated that the sound of the tanks' engines would draw the enemy like flies to the main road and we might be able to ambush the ambushers. The Glosters had one half-track and the main body of the regiment used lorries. We left at dawn. By now we had perfected our technique and the two jeeps kept half a mile ahead of the noisier half-tracks and lorries. We had rigged up two of the Bren guns to augment the firepower of the Brownings in each half-track. Sergeant Major Thorpe had also used the men's Bergens to provide some sort of protection from shrapnel. While we waited for the actual attack, we augmented our armament. We acquired two grenade rifles and a mortar.

We had learned much in our time in Korea. The enemy used mines and minefields but they were not very good at doing so. They rarely hid them well enough and four miles up the twisting road we saw the crude attempt to mine the road. I was careful when I made it safe but any of my men could have done the same. We had just given the signal for the column to move when we heard machine guns from the east. The tanks and the main column had been attacked. In many ways, it was a relief because I had feared an attack from the west. The fragmented nature of our advance made it hard to predict the direction from which the enemy would attack.

The message came through from the Brigadier and our plans went into action. We were to ambush the ambushers. The main road was less than two miles away and the ground between us, whilst rough, could be traversed by jeeps and half-tracks. A Company from the Glosters left their lorries to follow us as the four vehicles turned to go to the aid of the main column. We managed more than three-quarters of a mile before the going proved to be impassable. We left our vehicles and made our way through scrub and rock. We could hear the Besa machine guns in the Centurions as the tanks and armoured cars tried to fend off the Chinese and North Koreans. There was no point in using their big guns. The firing drew us to the point of attack. A Company was just half a mile behind us. They had two mortars with them as well as six Bren guns.

I spied the first of the Communist soldiers. It was the Headquarters section. I saw the antenna of the radio as well as the other signs of such a company. There were more officers and non-coms than men! I waved my men into a line. The enemy was a hundred yards from us. "Lofting, when we begin our attack, I want one bullet in the radio, then the operator and after that every officer you can kill!"

"Sir!" He went to get a good vantage point.

"Lieutenant Morrison, take ten men and flank them to the south.

Sergeant Major Thorpe take another third and flank them to the north. Begin your attack when you hear our guns!"

"Sir!"

Major Delaney who was in command of A Company appeared. I pointed ahead, "We are going to attack the enemy. Use your men to back us up."

"We can go in with you if you like?"

"To be honest, Major, we are a well-oiled machine and we know how we work. Next time, eh?"

He did not seem offended, "Whatever you say. You are the experts at this sort of thing."

I looked at my men, "We don't fire until Lofting has knocked out the radio. I want to take out their command post and then use the confusion to our advantage."

"Seems like a sound plan."

I cocked the Thompson. "Over to you, Lofting!"

We ran. He would judge the moment. He had learned to look for the signs and, as an officer began to turn, he fired five bullets so quickly that I thought five men had fired. The radio was hit and three men fell. I fired my Thompson and my men used their rifles. There had been ten men in the Headquarter's party. None survived. I waved the Glosters forward as my men scrambled up the rocks to enfilade the Communists below us.

"Ashcroft, search the officers for papers."

I scrambled up on to the rocks. There had to be a regiment, at least, below us. I did not need to give the order to fire. Lieutenant Morrison and Sergeant Major Thorpe had already begun their attack and the Glosters, eager to join us also found good vantage points. It did not take long to end the ambush. The enemy were surrounded and more than half of them surrendered.

Major Delaney came over to me, "Textbook piece of work."

I nodded, "This time, but next time? We take one step at a time. We still have twenty miles to go to reach our final objective. When we reach it, I will rest easier!"

It took most of the day to clear the ambush site and to begin to march the prisoners south. We made our vehicles not long before dark. I knew that we were close to the Imjin River and so I just travelled two more miles before we made camp. While the food was prepared, I spoke with Major Delaney. "I intend to take out a patrol before dawn. I want to scout out the river. If they had an ambush waiting for us back there then I am certain that they will have another one at the river or, at the very least, they will be preparing something for us."

"What if you hit trouble?"

"I have Ashcroft with the radio. I only intend taking eight men. I want to see and not to fight."

I chose the men and while the rest busied themselves, we got our heads down for a couple of hours sleep. We were awake at 0230 hours and I led the eight of them along the crude road. After a couple of miles, it began to twist and turn down to the valley bottom. It would be an interesting descent but my drivers had already endured a more challenging drive. As we began to negotiate the slope, I could smell the smoke of Korean cigarettes. They had a distinctive aroma. I held up my hand and, drawing my Colt, tapped Lofting on the shoulder for him to follow me. We were both wearing our rubber-soled shoes and we were both silent.

The sound of the river was ahead and the trail flattened out as it joined the road which crossed the river at the ford. We had blacked up, Harris had not been awake or else he would have sung, '*Mammy*'. It was Lofting who spotted the sentries and his arm came across me to arrest my progress. I dropped to one knee and levelled the Colt. I saw movement on the other side of the river. We both dropped to our bellies and crawled along the side of the trail close to the river. There was lush undergrowth here and we were well hidden. There were North Koreans guarding the ford. I recognised their language if not the actual words. I saw the glow of their cigarettes and the occasional flash of flame from their brazier. We kept moving forward. Even if they had turned their gaze to look across the river it would not have been to the ground. Grass and weeds flourished close to the river and we were hidden as we peered through them at the north bank.

There were sandbags and I saw guns. They looked like a Chinese version of the British seventeen pounder anti-tank gun.

They could hurt the Centurions. I took the time to see what other defences there were. To the side of the anti-tank guns were heavy machine guns hidden in the undergrowth. I looked at my watch. It was almost 0415 and soon the camp would be waking. I tapped Lofting on the shoulder and we slid backwards. Once we were safe, we rose and went back to the others. I gestured for them to join me further up the slope where we would not be overheard.

"Ashcroft, get on the radio to the main column. Tell them that there is an ambush at the ford with anti-tank guns. We will deal with it and they should wait for my signal to attack! Then ask Lieutenant Morrison to bring the men on foot to the river, and for Major Delaney to prepare to support us with his men and the tanks of Captain Ormrod." I did not want the enemy alerted by the sound of the tanks.

While Ashcroft passed on the messages I spoke with the others. "Williams, I want you to wait up the road for the Lieutenant and the rest of our men. When they arrive bring them down here."

After they had left us, I began to work out a plan. The danger was the anti-tank guns. The machine guns could not harm the tanks. "Lofting, I want you to get to the place where we hid. I will distract the machine gunners while you eliminate the sentries and then the men on the anti-tank guns. Sergeant Grant, you, Hall and Smith will get close enough to the western machine gun to destroy it with grenades and small arms fire. Collins, Carter and Harris, you will do the same to the eastern machine gun."

"Sir!"

Grant asked, "And the anti-tank guns, sir?"

"When the six of you have disabled the machine guns then take cover and try to hit the machine guns on the other side of the crossing. By then we will have the Brens and Brownings in place. I intend to use our firepower and then six of us with hand grenades."

Sergeant Grant said, "You, sir?"

I smiled, "You think I am too old, Sergeant?"

"No, sir, too valuable! Let some of the young lads take the risk."

"I have done this too long to change. I will be leading one of the teams, now get in position. Lofting's rifle will signal the attack. Use the mortar and the rifle grenades to hit the enemy further back. As soon as the alarm is sounded then they will rush to their defences. That is when they will be vulnerable."

They moved, albeit reluctantly, to their attack positions. I also chose myself because, when the others came, I would join Lofting. I still had my Colt with the silencer and I would use it! I was left alone to await Williams and our men. They did not take long and I could tell that they had run.

"Campbell, Haynes, Entwhistle, Moore and Corporal Dixon, you will be with me. I want us hidden as close as we can get to the anti-tank guns. That means we occupy both sides of the road. We need to be in position in the next five minutes. When Lofting opens fire with his rifle then hurl grenades into the gun emplacements. Lieutenant Morrison, you and the rest of the men will use small arms to shred the enemy. Ashcroft, as soon as you hear the grenades then send for the cavalry." I smiled, "Quite literally! And when the Glosters arrive have them support Lieutenant Morrison."

"Sir!"

"Now move!"

I tapped Haynes and Campbell on the shoulder. They would be with me. I glanced at my watch. It was 0445. The Chinese and North Koreans would be sounding reveille soon and I wanted the attack to begin before then.

The sentries were still talking and they must have thought the allies were many miles hence. I pointed to my left. I knew that Lofting was hidden there and Corporal Dixon took his two men to the other side of the crossing. I had my pistol out and I had it aimed at the four sentries. They were shadows and more than thirty yards from me but I hoped I could drop at least two and that would give us a chance. When my men were hidden, I dropped down between Lofting and Campbell. I took a bead on the sentry to the left. I said, "Whenever you are ready, Marine!" He would be the trigger which set off this ambush. When I heard the breath escape from his mouth, I squeezed off the first bullet from my Colt. The crack of the Lee Enfield sounded deafening. Even as I squeezed the trigger a second time, I heard the sound of the detonators on the grenades springing in the air. My second shot and Lofting's cleared the sentries. A head appeared from behind the sandbags guarding one of the antitank guns. Lofting hit him. I laid down my Colt and took the pin out of a grenade. Haynes and Campbell had already hurled theirs and as soon as mine was thrown I dropped down.

All along the river, I heard the sound of grenades exploding and then the sound of our Bren guns, Thompsons and rifles as they shredded the undergrowth. The mortar's whump was reassuring and when I heard the sounds of explosions further back from the river then I knew that the two rifle grenades were enjoying some success. Far in the distance, I heard the unmistakable sound of the Rolls Royce engines in the Centurions as they lumbered down the road at a sedate twenty miles an hour. They would not be quick in getting here. I hurled another two grenades in quick succession. Corporal Dixon had been even luckier. One of their grenades had managed to set off the ammunition for there was a huge explosion.

"Open fire with everything you have!"

I picked up my Thompson and fired blindly across the river. I knew there had to be Chinese racing to face this latest threat. We had to keep firing as long as possible to give the tanks the chance to arrive. I heard the sound of the 84 mm gun as Captain Ormrod announced that he was close by firing a shell behind the ford. The effect was dramatic. We heard the trumpets sound. This time they did not herald a charge but a retreat. We kept firing until the lead Centurion appeared and majestically sailed across the ford. We had taken our objective and we had made the Kansas line! Soon we would be able to go home.

Chapter 18

General Ridgeway did intend, eventually, to advance further north but the main aim of this advance had been to secure a defensive line which was north of the old border and to allow the pockets of resistance behind us to be mopped up. He was a cautious man and we were told to dig in. Brigadier Brodie himself organised the positions. We had a twelve-mile front to guard. The Belgian contingent was given the most hazardous duty as they were north of the river at a place called Hill 194. The Glosters were a mile east of the South Korean 1st Division and a mile from the ford. They had a good position, overlooking it. Two miles to their east came the Northumberland Fusiliers and the Ulster Rifles were our reserve, guarding the important Route 11. The 25 pounders and 4.2 mortars of the Royal Artillery gave support and the tanks under the command of Captain Ormrod were our mobile support.

"And what about us, sir? Where do you want us?"

The Brigadier smiled, "You have done your bit, Major, and, besides, I expect you to be rotated soon enough. The last message I had was that you were to be sent back to Seoul at the start of May. There are more units due to arrive then and you can be relieved. You have just three or four weeks left here. You and your men can bivouac here with the Headquarters unit and the Rifles."

I confess that it felt like something of an anti-climax. It was as though our war had just petered out. It would have been better if they had just sent us back to Seoul but my unit had been something of a lucky charm and the other officers were keen for us to stay.

Major Huth was recalled from Japan to take command of the single squadron of tanks. Captain Ormrod's independent command was over but I think the one-eyed veteran was happy for someone else to take command.

Life in the new camp was the easiest we had had since we had been in Korea. For one thing, the weather had improved. The Korean winter was over. It would never be what one considered balmy but it was pleasant and we did not need to move around encumbered with greatcoats, mittens and as many layers of clothes as we could manage. We were issued, a week after we had driven the enemy from the river, with new uniforms. They came with a delivery of much overdue mail. It had chased us around Korea and now that we were, albeit temporarily, settled it had finally reached us. That was what we all thought of as a good day. With clean uniforms and a sunny day, we sat outside our tents and read and re-read our mail from home. Little Samuel had apparently had a growth spurt and William and Izzy were finding him a handful. Reading between the lines I deduced that Susan was too; she wanted me home. When I read the letters from Mum, I discovered that Mum and Dad were spending more time at my home than their own. I was lucky to have them and I knew it.

Lieutenant Morrison was the one who appeared most disturbed by his mail. He had a letter from his brother and discovered that the Arab states and Palestinian guerrillas were making life hard for the settlers. I noticed his agitation for he smoked more heavily than normal. "The thing is, sir, since we had our little talk, I have sort of committed myself, at least inside my head, into resigning my commission and joining my brother. While we were doing something useful it was easy but knowing that we are just waiting here to be sent home makes me impatient."

I nodded, "Listen, how about I put in a call to Captain Warwick. He is the only name I have but he might be able to expedite your return to England. You are quite right. We are in reserve here and if you are unhappy then we can solve that."

He shook his head but his eyes told me he wished me to make the call, "I don't want to make a fuss, sir."

"And you aren't. I am also frustrated to be sitting idly by when I am not needed."

I used the radio at Headquarters and left a message for Captain Warwick. While we waited for a reply, we watched the vapour trails of jets heading north to bomb North Korea and were reassured by the sorties carried out by the USAAF. After the tribulations of the New Year offensive and a winter war, we seemed, finally, to have some sort of stability.

It was in the third week of April when Captain Warwick finally sent a message back. Lieutenant Morrison could head back to Seoul on the 23rd of April. Sergeant Major Thorpe was also allowed to return early and take a well-deserved retirement. We planned a party to celebrate and we held it on the 21st of April. The only alcohol we had was our beer ration but that did not matter. The men had saved their ration so that they could enjoy the party and everyone was in good humour. During the late afternoon, they had contests and games. There was a tug of war and three-legged races. It was like a children's party really. After we had eaten, Harris led them in a sing song. He had a good voice and the men enjoyed singing. This was almost like a goodbye party for the Commandos as, when the Lieutenant and the Sergeant Major had left, we would be following. I saw men exchanging addresses. When the regulars returned to Blighty the likelihood was that they would be separated; we all knew how the military worked.

Marine Lofting joined me, "Sir, I will clean your rifle and sight and return it to you. It has been a good weapon."

I shook my head, "You keep it, John. I doubt that I shall ever need it again. You are a far better shot than I ever was and it will be something to keep after you have left the service." He nodded absentmindedly. "Or are you going to re-enlist?"

He shook his head, "No, sir, I have got the need for adventure purged from my system and I shall follow my dad's footsteps and become a gamekeeper. He is getting on and I know that his lordship would like someone to take over. When I get back, I can give them both a date so that they can plan."

And so, like every other marine, we made plans. Mine were just to spend time with my three children. The company could run itself and they would not need me, although I would still fly for I enjoyed being a pilot. I knew that Dad would not mind. He always put family before the company. In his eyes, the company was just there to make us comfortable and to give us an income. However, as Robbie Burns had once written, '*The best-laid schemes o' mice an' men oft gang aft a-gley*'. That was certainly true of us for, what we did not know as we went to bed on the 22nd of April, preparing to say goodbye to two of our own was that there were three Chinese armies totalling seven hundred thousand men about to launch their Spring Offensive.

We were all in our beds when the Chinese artillery began to open fire and, in the distance, we heard the trumpets and gongs which inevitably marked a Chinese attack. We needed no bugle to make us leap from our beds. We were one of the few units in the 29th Brigade which had experienced a Chinese attack and we were dressed and armed before any others.

"Lieutenant Morrison, organise the men and I will go to the Brigadier."

"Sir!" He grinned, "I am guessing I won't be leaving tomorrow as we had planned!"

The Brigadier was half-dressed as were most of his officers. He gave me a wan smile, "You know something we didn't Major?"

"Let us just say, sir, that I have experienced a Chinese attack before and know how to dress quickly."

He nodded, "Well, Captain Tucker, report."

Captain Tucker was the only officer fully dressed as he had been the duty officer. In the time it had taken me to dress he had been on the radio. "The Chinese have attacked along the whole front. They have caught us, sir, with our trousers down. The Belgians, Fusiliers and Glosters are all under attack. Their sentries were killed in the first attack. I am sending a Philippine Combat team to go to the aid of the Glosters. Even the cooks are going to have to fight!"

The Brigadier looked at the map and the positions. "Have Lieutenant-Colonel Crahay pull his Belgians back across the river. The Belgians and Luxembourgers are too exposed there. Ask Lieutenant Colonel Young to use his guns to support their withdrawal. Then I want Major Huth to bring the Hussars up closer to the front. When we have daylight and a better idea of the opposition, I want options. Major Rickford, Major Harsker, your two units are our only reserve. Have your men ready to move out as soon as possible."

I nodded, "Mine are ready, sir, and we have the two half-tracks!"

"Good, then when we see what is what I will send you out first. Wait at your vehicles, Major."

The Lieutenant and Sergeant Major Thorpe had organised the men and were waiting for me. To the north, we could hear the fighting. The Northumberland Fusiliers were the closest to us and we could hear the small arms fire.

"The Chinese have attacked down the line. We are being used to help those units in the greatest danger. Have the two Brownings brought from the jeeps and fitted to the half-tracks. We are using those only."

Sergeant Major Thorpe said, "They will be a little crowded, sir."

"Can't be helped, Sergeant Major. The jeeps are just too vulnerable. Besides, we won't be fighting in them. They will be mobile forts and we will use them just to get where we are needed. Ashcroft, we need you to be on the radio and in constant touch with Headquarters."

"Sir!"

It was daylight before we received our orders and they were dramatic ones. The Belgian Contingent was trying to fight their way back across the river and the Fusiliers had already lost some of their forward positions. The only bright spot was that seventeen men of the Glosters had held off eighteen times their number at the ford we had secured.

Captain Tucker, himself, brought us our orders, "Sir, the Brigadier wants you to get to the river and cover the withdrawal of the Belgians. They are heavily pressed and have already lost three of their vehicles. When you have them safe then the Brigadier wants you to join the Fusiliers; they are going to try to head west. We are in danger of losing touch with the Glosters."

Debate and questions were irrelevant. We had to move and move quickly. We had three miles to cover to the river. Lieutenant Morrison commanded the other half-track with Sergeant Grant. I had divided the men equitably so that we both had a balance. Sergeant Major Thorpe would be my driver. The Lieutenant had one more man than I did. That was deliberate; I did not want him to be at risk on his last mission.

We headed up Highway 11. To our left, we could hear the small arms fire of the Fusiliers. The Rifles were already hurrying to aid them. The 25 pounders kept up a steady barrage and they would slow down the enemy. I knew we would not have as much aerial support as we needed. This was an attack by three armies. We were one brigade in the midst of much larger armies. The fact that we held a crucial river crossing and a vital road were immaterial in the greater scheme of things. Ambulances were already racing down the highway towards headquarters bringing the casualties from the front. There was a makeshift hospital there and from the overloaded vehicles, they would soon be busy.

Ashcroft shouted, "Sir, the Brigadier is sending a company of the Ulster Rifles to support us. They are in lorries on the road behind us. The Brigadier has suggested we use Hill 257. It overlooks both the road and the river!"

"Head for it Sarn't Major." We led and Jake would simply follow us. We saw the first of the Belgian vehicles in the distance. They were under attack from the Chinese who were swarming all over them. They seemed to totally disregard the sheer number of bullets. Then I heard a flight of Sabres which raced in from the south and sprayed the ground beyond the Belgians. "Get up that slope! The aerial attack has bought the Belgians time."

Sergeant Major Thorpe pushed the half-track up the slope. His experience came to the fore as he chose the flattest area he could. It meant we had dead ground behind the half-tracks. Even as he swung us around, I was shouting orders. "Set up the mortar and rifle grenades. I want this side of the river to become a killing ground. Gunners, your target is any Chinese you can see beyond the Belgians. The rest of you spread out along the slope. Lofting, you know what to do!"

I stayed in the half-track with the gunners and Ashcroft. Lance Corporal Williams was on the heavy calibre Browning and Sergeant Major Thorpe was acting as the loader for our most powerful weapon. The Brownings from the jeeps would also add to the firepower at our disposal.

"Yes, sir!"

The Sabres had raced off home, their ammunition depleted. The twenty-five pounders were still firing but they were merely slowing down the seemingly endless wave of Chinese troops. Brigadier Brodie had told us that in our sector it was only the Chinese who were attacking. We had left the bazooka back at our camp as the Chinese were using men and not tanks to attack! The river was nine hundred yards from us and the road was less than two hundred.

"Ashcroft, tell the artillery that they can now target the river. By the time they adjust the Belgians will be over it."

"Sir!"

I knew that it was a risk but I could see the command jeep of the Belgians at the rear of the column of trucks; that marked the last of our men north of the river. We were impotent until the Chinese came a little closer. The leading vehicles were level with our position and I guessed that they were safe. The shells from the artillery began a rolling barrage which drew closer to the river. The gunners knew their job and the effect was dramatic. The Chinese who had been massing for another attack suddenly found huge holes in their lines. The command vehicle raced across the river and the column passed along the road. Just then the lorries of the Rifles appeared and they began to disgorge their men.

I began to hope that we might have stabilised our lines when Ashcroft shouted, "Sir, the Chinese have got between the Fusiliers and the Glosters. They are threatening the road behind us!"

I nodded. Ken Thorpe and I exchanged a look. We were in great danger now of being trapped. There were at least ten thousand men across the river and we had less than one hundred and fifty men to slow them down. There was little point in bemoaning our fate. I saw some of the younger lads look nervously at each other.

Lance Corporal Williams asked, quietly, "Are we trapped, Sarn't Major?"

In answer, Sergeant Major Thorpe suddenly began to recite:

When first under fire an' you're wishful to duck,
Don't look nor take 'eed at the man that is struck,
Be thankful you're livin', and trust to your luck
And march to your front like a soldier.
Front, front, front like a soldier . . .

Lance Corporal Williams said, "What's that, sir?"

"Rudyard Kipling. It is a poem about a young soldier. It just shows that in over a hundred years war has not changed that much. He is saying that even when things look black you face your front and do your duty! That is all you can do"

He said, quietly, "I will fight, sir, but I don't want to die!"

Ken Thorpe was a grandfather and his voice had a reassuring quality about it, "None of us does, son, but worrying about it will make it likelier that it will happen. It is a long way off that yet!"

"Sir, they are in range of the mortars and rifle grenades."

I looked and saw that thin lines of Chinese soldiers were now racing across the river. "Wait until there is a large block of them. We can deal with the others using our small arms."

As if to prove my point Lofting fired at the officer exhorting his men to close with the Belgians. The flag bearer next to him fell a moment later. Then they were in range of our men with rifles and the Brownings on the half-tracks. The enemy began to fall as the heavy machine guns rattled out death. The Chinese were packed together and our bullets could not miss. The artillery shells thinned out the advancing Chinese and then when larger numbers crossed the river our mortar and two rifle grenades began to thin them out even more. I felt like the little boy with his finger in the dam. Even if every bullet we sent hit and killed a Chinese soldier there were another fifty to take their place. Then they were close enough for the Brens and Thompsons. The air was filled with a cacophony of noise which actually hurt our ears. As each gun clicked on empty we reloaded and fired again. By noon even the Chinese had tired of the losses and retired. I heard the sound of the Centurions coming up the road. I knew it would not be the whole squadron. The Glosters needed support too.

Ashcroft said, "Sir, Major Huth says he and his tanks will stay on the road. He wants to speak with you."

I went to the rear of the half-track and took the microphone and headphones from my radio operator. "Major?"

"This is for your ears only, Major Harsker. We are cut off. The Chinese are behind us. The Americans are sending tanks to relieve the Glosters. We have lost contact with them. The Belgians are holding the road open for us. As soon as we can extract the Fusiliers then we are falling back."

"And we are the rearguard?"

"Pretty much. I have five tanks and armoured cars with me, Captain Murray, Lieutenant Boyall, Lieutenant Hurst and Lieutenant Radford. Captain Ormrod has the rest further down the road. When I give the command, the Rifles will fall back and then we will follow." There was a moment's silence. "If you fall behind..."

"I know the form, Major. Thank you for the honest assessment, I appreciate it."

I handed the microphone and headphones back to Ashcroft and went to the other half-track. I waved over Jake and told him what I had been told. He looked unhappy and so I reassured him, "It is not doom and gloom. They have no aerial support, no tanks and, as far as I can see damn little artillery. These half-tracks are well armoured."

"I know sir. What will happen next?"

"I am guessing that they will make a night-time attack. We may have pulled back by then but, if not, then it could be a hard withdrawal. We can go cross country. The Rifles can't so, unlike them, at least we have an option."

The artillery had to stop firing as their ammunition would be limited. The Chinese were wary and did not show themselves again. Brigadier Brodie radioed us in the middle of the afternoon to tell us that we could leave and the Rifles loaded their lorries and headed south. The tanks were to follow and then it would be us. Two companies of the Rifles were halfway down the road we would travel already and were preparing a defensive position in case we were followed. We kept our guns, mortars and grenades trained on the river in case we were needed. We could load and leave in moments. The lorries pulled out and the tanks drove towards the river so that they could turn around. We watched.

Our vigilance paid off. Lance Corporal Williams was on the Browning and he had been looking to the east. It was he who saw the Chinese who had scaled the heights there and now launched an attack at us from behind us. It was Williams who saved the section. Even as he shouted, "Stand to!" He let rip with his Browning and the huge calibre bullets tore through the Chinese. I leaned on the side of the half-track and opened fire with my Thompson. When Lieutenant Morrison's Brownings joined in then the attack was slowed. The mortar and the rifle grenades switched targets and it was they which broke up the attack.

"Everyone back in the half-tracks. Ashcroft, let headquarters know what is happening."

"Sir."

"Well done, Williams." The ground was littered with the bodies of the Chinese and, as we turned, I saw more follow us across the river.

Bates had one of the rifle grenades and he said, "Sir, we are down to twenty grenades between the two weapons."

"They saved us back there, Bates, but we had better be more careful from now on."

I went to the rear of the half-track. Lieutenant Morrison was ahead of us with what we had termed, Red Team in the Red half-track. Mine was the Blue half-track. We had been lucky, thus far and lost no one but I had a feeling that our luck could not last forever. The road ran between high ground and the Chinese had managed to infiltrate our thinly held lines. There were few Chinese but the attacks began within half a mile of the river. Marine Collins was hit in the shoulder. We had two medics each in our half-tracks and he would be treated but that meant three fewer guns for defence. We were travelling at just over twenty miles an hour, the top speed of the Centurion, and it made us sitting ducks. It was when the Chinese began to lob grenades in the dark at the tanks that I began to worry. One grenade in the back of a half-track could spell disaster. Powell was also wounded by a stray piece of shrapnel. He could still fight but he was wounded and needed evacuation. I took a risk and used our Very gun to send a flare high in the sky. As soon as they were seen, the waiting Chinese were struck by a hail of bullets. The journey to the defensive position seemed a lot further than a couple of miles! The Rifles had used their lorries as static obstructions; they were almost like a wagon train in the Old West. We added the tanks and the half-tracks so that we had a wall of steel around us.

"Sergeant Major Thorpe, get some food organised and then a rota. One man in two sleeps. Two hours on and two off."

"Sir!"

I joined the other senior officers for a hurried officer's call. It soon emerged that the situation was chaotic. The Belgians and half of the Rifles were waiting a further four miles down the road. The Fusiliers were heading east to join us but all around were elements of the three Chinese armies. American and South Korean units were heading north to relieve the Glosters. We were all majors and the decision we took was by consensus. We decided to leave as soon as the Fusiliers joined us. No matter what time of night or day that was, it would be the trigger for our retreat.

No-one managed more than an hour of sleep at any one time. The Chinese were relentless. Had they had heavier weapons then we might have suffered more than we did. They kept coming even though we were watching and we used our machine guns to scythe through them. Even so, there were casualties. Marine Carter died when a wave of Chinese broke through on one side; he was using the lighter Browning and it had jammed. He fought like a maniac using his Lee Enfield like a club yet he died and Hall and Smith were both wounded in the attack. All twenty Chinese died but that did not compensate for the loss of a Marine. We buried him in a cleft between two rocks. I was not sure if we were in North or South Korea but, if I could, I would have his body repatriated. His family deserved the closure of a grave that they could visit.

The last attack before dawn was defeated by the Fusiliers. Lieutenant Colonel Foster led his men in and they destroyed the surprised Chinese who were trying to get at us. They had not expected to be attacked in the rear. We now had a senior officer but he was in no condition to make sound judgements. He had lost too many men and had gone too long without sleep. He concurred with our plan and he led the column south. The tanks and a lorry load of the Rifles were in front of us and we were tail-end Charlie. Our three wounded men were all in a lorry at the front of the column. None wanted to leave us but I was adamant for they could hinder us and I would be happier if they were relatively safe. Lieutenant Morrison had got over his depressed humour and he joked and bantered with Red Team. We had survived longer than he had expected and the confidence survival gave him was most welcome.

As we headed down the road, at a sedate twenty miles an hour, we enjoyed forty minutes of relative peace. Then, when dawn broke, all hell joined it! The high ground was covered in Chinese; they must have been moving all night to get ahead of us and now they waited all along the road we would take. They were able to fire down with impunity and were too widely scattered for our jets to inflict casualties. Men began to die. It was not just rifle and machine-gun fire, the Chinese had mortars and they rained down on the road. Our artillery continued to send shells at the enemy positions but without spotters the effects were random. Lieutenant Colonel Foster was leading the column when his jeep was struck by a mortar shell. It exploded, killing him and the others in the jeep. Worse, it blocked the road and a lorry of Fusiliers was also hit. The twenty-five pounders tried to hit the mortars but they were hidden. That was the beauty of mortars, they could fire over obstacles.

As it happened, we were relatively safe from attack as, when we stopped, we were next to a piece of high cliff which afforded us some protection from the Chinese. Marine Ashcroft gave me the news that we were held up and that it was almost impossible to clear the road because of the fire from the Chinese. "Tell them that I will take some men up and try to distract the Chinese."

"Sir!"

"Haynes and Moore, fetch your mortar. We are going for a little hike. Lofting, your rifle. Marine Campbell, I shall need you and your grenade rifle. Corporal Dixon, organise them while I go and have a word with Captain Robinson." The Captain commanded the detachment of Ulster Rifles.

He was a young officer with a broad Irish accent. "By, but it is lively eh, sir?"

I nodded, "I need a good sergeant and ten men who know how to handle rifles. I want to go up into the rocks and try to dislodge the Chinese."

"Of course, sir, Sergeant McIlroy, the ten best riflemen with Major Harsker."

"Take charge here, Captain. If the column can move then don't wait for us. We will catch up with you."

"Are you sure sir? This is Indian country."

I smiled, "I know!"

The Sergeant and the ten men were ready and eager. They had the look of veterans and they wanted the chance to hit back aggressively and not just defend. "I have a mortar and a rifle grenade. I intend to annoy the Chinese and make them come after us. Your job is to protect us."

The Sergeant nodded, "No problem, sir!"

I turned, "Lofting, lead the way. I want to get above the enemy mortars and take out the crews." I waved at my men as I cocked my Thompson. Up the road, I heard the firefight. Had we bitten off too much this time? We were close to the rest of the Brigade, just a few miles, but it might as well have been the moon! I followed my sniper up the narrow path which had to have been made by animals.

Chapter 19

The firing seemed to be further away from us and I realised why. The path we climbed led away from the fighting but Lofting was no fool. He had seen that although it began to head north, further along, it turned to come south. We climbed at least six hundred feet before we levelled out. The path led between a high cliff wall and some boulders which had tumbled down from above. We could not see too far ahead but Lofting had a sixth sense and when he lowered his rifle and then fired, I was ready with my Tommy gun. As I hurried to join him, I saw that we had stumbled upon eight men and a 4.2-inch mortar. I sprayed them with my gun. Sergeant McIlroy had a Bren gun and he finished off the couple I had missed. We now had a much more powerful mortar.

"Lofting get in a position where you can see down below us; act as a spotter. Corporal Dixon, join him. Sergeant, see if a couple of your lads can fire this mortar. Swing it around so that it faces due south!"

"Yes, sir. You heard the officer. Murphy and Harrington, you went on a mortar course. Show me you didn't spend all the time in the boozer!"

"Right, Sarge."

I went to the edge of the rocks. Below us, I could see Chinese mortar and machine crews but they had the smaller mortars. Beyond them, I saw the column of tanks and lorries, they were still not moving. The Besa machine guns on the Centurions were keeping the Chinese at bay. I saw our two half-tracks. They were belching fire too. Then I saw the barrels of the Centurions swing around. There were Chinese on the other slope too.

I pointed to the Chinese below us. "Haynes, Campbell. There is your target."

Lofting fired his rifle and Corporal Dixon shouted, "I can see another two mortar pits, sir."

"Then tell these lads the coordinates. Sergeant, have your men join us here. We have a little shooting gallery!"

As the Centurions fired at the other side of the valley and left this side alone the Chinese became emboldened. Captain Robinson had his men with mine and they were pouring bullets into the Chinese. I wondered if we were too late, "Open fire!" We had an elevated position and there was no shelter for the Chinese. We kept firing and reloading as quickly as we could. Haynes and Moore destroyed all of the mortars below us and Campbell's grenade launcher accounted for three machine guns. It was, however, the Rifles who achieved the greatest success. Their first shell with a Chinese mortar fell well short but by the time they had fired their third they had their eye in or, to be more accurate, Corporal Dixon had his eye in and six of the heavy mortars were destroyed.

Lofting shouted, "Well that has upset them, sir. The buggers are coming up here for us!"

"Right Sergeant, one last mortar shell and then destroy the weapon."

"Sir, the column is moving!"

"Okay lads, we go directly down this slope. I will lead with Sergeant McIlroy, Corporal Dixon you bring up the rear. Set a few booby traps before you descend."

"Right sir."

The mortar fired one last time and I heard the two men destroying it.

I looked over the side. There was a drop of about five feet and then it looked as though there was a path we could pick out. It was the safest way to go as we had cleared it of the enemy. I could see Captain Robinson loading his lorry and the tanks were moving, still firing at the western side of the valley. I began to move quickly down the slope. The Sergeant had his Bren at the ready too. We were halfway down and had not been attacked when I heard an enormous explosion. The

Sergeant grinned, "That is what Irishmen like, blowing things up."

We had about four hundred yards to go before we reached the road but it had rocks and scrubby shrubs which could hide the enemy. I could see the lorry and two half-tracks approaching. I risked turning and saw Corporal Dixon and Marine Lofting. They were turning and firing at targets I could not see. Then there was an explosion behind them. The Chinese had set off a booby trap. Suddenly half a dozen Chinese rose as I turned. I fired instinctively. The Sergeant did so too. There was a shout from one of his men who had been hit but we had killed the Chinese.

"Let us try some grenades. I want every man to throw one grenade as high as he can and drop down. There may be more men hiding ahead of us!"

Twelve grenades flew high into the air. A couple of the Rifles were big lads and they lobbed them further than I could ever manage. We dropped down and then heard the rippling explosions as they spread shrapnel through the air. When we rose, there was smoke and dust before us and unprotected ears were ringing. The wounded man was supported by two of his men and we made our way to the road. There had been Chinese waiting to ambush us but they had been killed or wounded by the grenades. The Rifles shot the ones who looked as though they might still be a threat and then we reached the road. I waited until all of our men were aboard before I climbed in to the Blue Team half-track.

Sergeant Major Thorpe shook his head, "You should know better, sir!"

I laughed, "Yes, mother!"

We were still in danger. The mortars were no longer ranging in on us but the Chinese on the slopes were firing their weapons and, being above us, we were exposed in the open half-tracks. Ricocheting bullets could be deadly. Haynes, who had done such sterling work with the mortar was hit in the face by shrapnel. Lance Corporal Lake treated him as well as he could but he feared he would lose the eye and wanted Haynes to be seen by a doctor. Powell was the closest we had to a doctor but he had been wounded himself and was at the front of the column. Haynes had to take his chances. When the firing along both sides began to diminish, we knew that the rest of the brigade was close by. Haynes was sent directly to the doctor and I was summoned along with the other surviving senior officers to an officers' call with Brigadier Brodie.

"Lieutenant, see to the men. You know the drill."

He smiled, "I didn't three months ago sir, but I have learned! Sergeant Major Thorpe, have one of the lads get on a brew eh?"

"Right, sir!"

The Command Post was a tent with a few sandbags around the entrance. It showed the depth of the Chinese attack. They were all around us. Our leader had aged since I had seen him last. Brigadier Brodie gave us a wan smile, "I am glad you made it, gentlemen. You did well and now we have the majority of the Brigade together. We are in a parlous state. The Glosters are cut off. There is a column of tanks and elements of the South Korean Army trying to get to them but as the Chinese now have the rest of this Highway the tanks are having to use a narrow defile. Our orders, at the moment, are to stay here."

We all looked at each other. Major Rickford gave voice to the inner thoughts we all shared, "Sir, we have had to fight for each yard of ground. A journey which should have taken less than half an hour has taken half a day. If Major Harsker hadn't managed to eliminate the Chinese mortars then we would still be stuck. We would either be dead or in the bag."

"I know. I know." He looked and sounded weary. "The Chinese have attacked along the whole front and we are desperately outnumbered. General Ridgway has men preparing lines of defence but that takes time. The longer we can slow them up the better."

I took out my pipe. It seemed a lifetime since I had enjoyed a pipe, "And the Glosters, sir? What are the chances of the tanks getting to them?"

"Better than average, Major, although they have lost almost half of their men both wounded and dead. Lieutenant Colonel Carne and his men have performed above and beyond the call of duty. We have to do the same. Major Huth, your tanks are our best offensive weapon. I need you to keep them facing the slopes. Fortunately, they are not as steep here as further north and south which is why we chose this as the holding point. Get some food. Captain Williamson will assign you your defensive points."

"And the wounded, sir, can they be evacuated by air?"

"There will be an attempt before dark to get the most severely wounded away but the walking wounded will have to stay with us, Major Harsker."

Haynes was one of the lucky ones. He would lose an eye but he went out with another five men who were placed aboard the three helicopters which made it. A fourth was destroyed by the Chinese.

We had food and it was most welcome. We were now a smaller unit and that made us much closer. We had been confined inside the steel walls of our American half-tracks and, huddled together, it made us like a family. The Lieutenant and the Sergeant Major sat with me, Corporal Dixon and Sergeant Grant. The Sergeant Major shook his head, "You know, sir, I have never seen such fanatical enemies. Jerry didn't have these sorts of numbers in the last war. If he had then we would have lost. They don't seem to care if they live or die."

I remembered Blair; he had been a clever man but he had been indoctrinated by the Communist ideas, "They are all taught to believe in the greater good of their country. They see themselves as part of a greater whole."

Sergeant Grant said, "We all think about our country too, sir! My Uncle Billy gave his life for England in the last war but we wouldn't do what those Chinamen did! It was unbelievable."

He was right and that worried me. We still had many miles to go to reach safety and I knew that, inevitably, there would be one attack which would breach our defences. "Make sure the lads keep their knives handy. If they manage to get aboard the half-tracks then it will be bloody."

Sergeant Major Thorpe tapped his holster, "Like you, sir, I still have the Colt I was issued with during the last war."

I saw the others looking at the Colts. Their rifles and machine guns would be of little use in the close confines of the half-track. I thought of the German pistols I had left locked in the cupboard at home. I had not thought I would need them. Now they might make all the difference. Only Lieutenant Morrison had a handgun and his weapon was the service Webley. With just six bullets it was better than nothing but only just. My Colt had the ability to stop a man and eight others!

I had an early duty and it was quiet. That worried me as it meant the Chinese were preparing something. I went around the men to speak to each one. Many of them were young and worried to the point of terror. Nothing in their training could have prepared them for this. I joined Lance Corporal Williams. "I bet you couldn't have imagined this six months ago, eh Sam?"

He shook his head, "No sir, but I think it will make me a better Commando. Lieutenant Morrison wants me to become a demolition expert. He says I have a real skill."

"And you do."

"The trouble is I am not sure I want to stay in. The Lieutenant is getting out, isn't he sir? You and the Sergeant Major will be leaving. With you three in charge, well, I feel safe somehow. Even when we were being attacked on all sides, I thought we would survive. The Sergeant Major is like a rock. He is so calm. If you weren't leading us…"

"You know, Sam, I joined the Loyal Lancashires as a private. I was on a retreat just like this one. Then the Germans were using Stukas to bomb us and I was sure I would die. I didn't and I began the journey that brought me here. You are right this will be my last war but, in your case, it is your first war and you have done well. You will become the one like the

Sergeant Major. You will be the one that men will feel safe fighting alongside."

"You think so, sir?"

"I know so."

I was roused from my bed by the Lieutenant, "Sir, the Brigadier needs to see you. Something is up. I have been told to have the men stand to!"

I reached the Brigadier before the other senior officers. He shook his head, "Bad news, Major. The attempt to relieve the Glosters has failed. They are on their own."

He looked distraught and I knew why. They were his men and they were being abandoned. It was not his fault; the terrain and the overwhelming numbers of our enemies were the reason but he would lose sleep long after the war was over wondering if he could have done anything to save them.

When the rest of the officers had all entered, he said, "Headquarters have been in touch. Plan Golden A has been put in place. We have to withdraw south." Major Rickford looked as though he would say something and the Brigadier shook his head, "I have already told Lieutenant Colonel Carne that he is on his own and whatever decision he makes has my support."

Major Huth said, "That means either surrender or try to fight his way through God knows how many Chinese!"

"Major, that is out of our hands now. I have ordered the camp to be roused and we will head south. Your tanks will guard the rear of the column along with Major Harsker and his men. We have Royal Engineers with us and they will lay charges behind Major Harsker's vehicles. We will, hopefully, deny them the use of this road. The Royal Artillery have already been withdrawn. We will have no more artillery support. If yesterday was anything to go by this will be as hard a journey as any of us have ever undertaken. We do not stop for anyone. We keep going until we reach the nearest United Nations unit." He looked around us and we saw in his eyes the resignation. He knew that many of us would die. "Gentlemen, rejoin your units. We leave in an hour as soon as the charges have been laid.

Our men had not been idle. The Bergens, greatcoats and anything else which could be used were packed around the inside of the half-tracks to give some protection. Men were making miniature bunkers in the vehicles. Lance Corporal Williams had found a hard hat from somewhere and he had fastened his Bergen to the side of the steel shell. I threw him my Bergen and greatcoat. "Use those too, eh Williams. You are the most exposed man."

He grinned, "Thanks, sir. I feel a fool but who cares so long as I survive!"

"That is the spirit."

The Captain of Engineers knew his business and the road and rocks behind us were mined and set with charges. If the Chinese were careful, they might be able to dismantle them but I expected them to come through as recklessly as they had in every attack up to now. When they returned to their lorries, we waited for the column to move. I stood at the rear with my Thompson. I was not sure how many magazines I had left but I knew it would not be enough. With just four grenades I might be down to my Colt. We set off and made a mile before the first attack. It came at the head of the column. The Centurions opened fire with their big guns. They were firing relatively blindly for it was still dark but because they were using high explosive, shattering rocks could be as deadly as shrapnel. We kept on moving.

When dawn broke, we passed the men who had been attacked. The survivors jumped on to the Centurions. Three were hauled aboard Red Team's half-track. It was when we were attacked at the rear that we heard the distant explosions. The Chinese must have attempted to bring vehicles down the road and had paid the price. The Engineers' demolitions had done the trick. Lofting and his rifle hit every face they saw. Williams' Browning cleared one side while the Brens and my Thompson cleared the other. The other Browning had been destroyed when Carter had been killed. We had one lucky escape when a grenade was thrown from on high. It must have had a longer fuse than we used for it bounced off the side of the half-track, hit the ground and the explosion rattled off the steel hull of Blue Team's half-track. Soon the Centurions were covered in the survivors from the attacks.

Ashcroft said, in a brief lull, "One of the tank commanders has just said that they have to stop firing their Besa for fear of it seizing up and the others have had to changed barrels." There was desperation in Ashcroft's voice. Alone out of all of us he could hear the battle ahead and knew that we were losing.

I could see a pattern emerging. There would be frenetic attacks which would hurt us and they would withdraw only to return a short while later to attack somewhere else. We were forty yards behind Red Team and they were a hundred yards behind the tanks. The tanks were completely covered by the survivors they had picked up. I knew what was coming and yet I could do nothing about it. The Chinese would attack the tanks which would not be able to fire their machine guns at the Chinese for fear of hitting our own men. There must have been a thousand Chinese soldiers who rose from the side, where British bodies lay, and hurled themselves from the slopes above. It was almost suicidal and yet it worked. They landed on the British and Belgian soldiers who were clinging to the tanks and a bloody battle ensued. It could only have one outcome, a Chinese victory. The tanks would not be harmed but the men who had survived the early attacks would all die.

The Lieutenant could not help himself. He had Grant accelerate to go to their aid and therein lay his downfall. The Chinese could not hurt the tanks but their grenades could hurt the men in the half-track. Even as we fired at the Chinese who threw their grenades, I knew we could not stop all of them, and one exploded inside the half-track. We now had no choice and Lieutenant Morrison had forced my hand.

"Sergeant Major get us close! Pike get inside the half-track and see if any are alive. The rest of you I want every gun to hit a Chinese soldier!"

I fired my gun and reloaded until the barrel burned my hand. I drew my Colt and fired bullet after bullet into the lemming like

Chinese. Campbell's grenade launcher was in the Red Team's half-track and, if that had been in our half-track, it might have saved us. As we neared the wrecked vehicle, I saw that there were only Chinese left on the Centurions. The tanks were now the focus of the Chinese attack. We drew next to the half-track.

"Sarn't Major, give Pike a hand. Williams, clear the tanks."

We were just a hundred yards from the tanks and he could not miss yet no matter how many men he killed more swarmed on board. I kept clearing the hillsides. Suddenly, the tanks all turned their guns to face each other and I wondered what they were doing. When their Besa machine guns began to hose down their fellow tanks I realised. The bullets would not harm the tanks but they turned the Chinese soldiers into mincemeat. It was effective and it ended the attack.

The survivors of Red Team were hauled on board. There were three of them. Sergeant Grant was just slightly wounded but Lance Corporal Lake and Lieutenant Morrison were more seriously hurt. Everyone else was dead. Sergeant Major Thorpe handed me a handful of dog tags.

I said, grimly, "Get us underway again. Sergeant Grant, are you fit to fight?"

"Too bloody right sir! Let me at the bastards!"

We had a spare Bren and I handed it to him. "Everybody, the priority is to hit men with grenades. Sergeant Major put your foot down!"

"Sir!"

The tanks had moved off and we were a good four hundred yards behind them. I hated leaving the bodies but I had to. The Chinese withdrew. It was not a surprise. Between them, the tanks must have slaughtered more than four hundred men. I dropped next to Lieutenant Morrison. He had a stomach wound. I saw Pike shake his head.

"See to Lake."

"Sir!"

I took one of Morrison's cigarettes and lighting it for him, placed it between his lips. Sergeant Grant looked down, "Sir, the Lieutenant tried to throw himself on the grenade. It was the bravest thing I ever saw."

I shook my head, "Jake, what did I say about keeping your head down?"

He smiled and a tendril of blood came from the corner of his mouth. "I saw Jimmy Cagney do it in a film once, sir. I'll get it right next time."

I nodded.

"Did we lose many?"

"You saved three of you, Jake, and that will have to be enough."

Although Pike had put a dressing on the wound it merely slowed the blood and more blood spurted from his mouth when he coughed. "Sir, in my battledress pocket is a letter for my family, will you…?"

"Of course." I took it from his pocket. It had spatters of blood on it and there was a hole where some shrapnel had gone through. In the movies, this was where the hero would tell his wounded man that he would live and the man would smile. This was real life and we both knew that young Jake would never get to Israel. He was going to die.

He took a drag on the cigarette, "I learned much from you, sir, and it has been an honour. I hoped that when I got…" That was all that he said. His head lolled to one side and the half-smoked cigarette fell on to his battle dress. It was such a tragic mistake. If he had held back then he would not have been attacked. The Fusiliers, Rifles and Belgians would still have died but Red Team would still be alive. I took his tags and put them with the others.

"How is Lake?"

"Stable sir. He was wearing his Bergen and his back was facing the grenade. It saved him."

"Sir?"

"Yes, Ashcroft?"

"The advanced elements have reached the UN lines. We are just a mile shy."

I shouted, "Don't take anything for granted. Keep a good watch. This last mile could be the worst."

As if to echo that Sergeant Major Thorpe said, "Aye sir, and when we reach our lines we will be driving on fumes. A bullet must have hit the tank."

"Here they come again, sir!"

Lance Corporal Williams' voice made us all look up. Ahead of us, the Chinese were attacking the Centurions. They were using hand grenades and what looked like a bazooka. The tanks had some open space and they drove at the Chinese. Once again some had hurled themselves at the tanks and clung on. I watched as one tank drove deliberately through the wall of a house to dislodge one such man. The sudden charge took the Chinese by surprise and one of the bazooka teams was squashed beneath the tank's tracks as it twisted and turned. The tanks were now less than a mile from safety and artillery shells began to rain down on the valley side. When a flight of Sabres roared in to drop bombs on the high ground it looked as though we might make it. Then, with less than three-quarters of a mile to go the last Chinese bazooka sent a rocket at us. It hit the engine block and the whole vehicle rose and fell.

"Everybody out and on me!" I grabbed my Bergen and jumped out of the back. I ran to the cab. We had the half-track between us and the main body of the enemy. The Sabres had cleared the hill to the west. I had time to evaluate the situation. Sergeant Grant was dead but Sergeant Major Thorpe was alive. He was unconscious but he was breathing. Pike and Williams carried Lake from the half-track.

Lofting and Hall, along with the rest of my men, appeared at my side, "What now, sir?"

"This is not the place for a sniper, John, sling your rifle and hoist the Sarn't Major over your shoulder. Hall, take the Sergeant Major's Tommy gun. We will flank Lofting." I raised my voice, "Blue Team it is a long time since we had a decent run. Let us see how fast we can make the finish line!"

"Aye, sir!"

"You ready, Lofting?"

"Aye, sir!"

"Let's go!" I threw a grenade into the back of the half-track. The steel shell would confine the blast and I did not want the enemy to have the use of the Browning.

As we burst from the cover of the half-track, I saw six Chinese to our right. I sprayed them with a short burst. Only three of my men were not firing and they had the two injured men. It was hardly a sprint for the Sergeant Major was a big man but my men behaved magnificently. They did not panic but chose their targets. Behind me, I heard my grenade go off and smoke poured from the half-track. When I ran out of bullets, I took one of my four grenades and hurled it high and to the right. It exploded behind us and I quickly reloaded my Thompson and then emptied the magazine into a wall of Chinese who rose from before us. There had to be at least a hundred of them and even with Hall and I firing seven hundred rounds per minute, they were getting through. We had to get through them if we were to reach safety and that would be an impossible task. One ran at me with a bayonet. I swung the Thompson like a club. It hit the rifle and bayonet up into the air. As I smashed it across the Chinese soldier's head the gun broke in two and I drew my Colt. Two Chinese were charging with bayonets at Lofting and Thorpe. I shot them both and then emptied the magazine at the others. We were still two hundred yards from safety but it might as well have been two hundred miles.

Then I heard the sound of wild Irish yells and saw Captain Robinson and Sergeant McIlroy leading a company of the Rifles to charge into the back of the Chinese. It proved too much for them and they broke. With the Rifles protecting our backs I led the survivors through the tanks to the cheers of the rest of the Brigade. We had made it and our war was over. For me, it was bigger than that. War would finally be over for me.

We laid Sergeant Major Thorpe on the ground. As the Rifles' medic dropped next to him, he opened Sergeant Major's right eye. He examined Ken's head and then nodded, he said, "Looks like a concussion, sir. I will put him in the recovery position and then get some stretchers." He smiled, "Thanks for watching our backs, sir! We owe you and your lads."

I looked back and saw the smoke rising from the half-track and, beyond it the wreck of Red Team. We had done our job but at what a cost.

I heard a groan and Sergeant Major Thorpe rolled onto his back, "I am getting too old for this game, sir." He patted his breast pocket and said, "And the buggers have broken my favourite pipe!"

I laughed and shook my head, "Luckily I have a spare and, Sergeant Major Thorpe, it is yours!

Epilogue

There was a continuous convoy taking the wounded to the coast and we were sent with them. We did not have to wait for a ship to take us home. Our actions had merited a flight to Japan. When we were airlifted to Japan, I used some of my father's old contacts to get us a ride on a military flight heading to the Middle East. A telegram home ensured that there would be a company aircraft waiting to take us to our airfield back in England. I did not feel guilty for it was the least I could do for my men. I had with me just fourteen men left from my command. Lake was the most seriously injured but we managed to persuade the doctor in Japan to allow him to come with us. We had more than twenty-four hours in aeroplanes and that gave us the opportunity to talk and reflect on the battle of Imjin River. We had learned, while in Japan, of the heroism of the Glosters who had bought the Brigade the time to escape. They had paid a huge price. Only two hundred and seventeen men escaped from the regiment and Brigadier Brodie had told me of some of the recommendations that had been made.

Lieutenant Colonel Carne and Lieutenant Curtis had been put in for the Victoria Cross. In Curtis' case it would be a posthumous award. Four men were recommended for the DSO and three, including Captain Ormrod, were put in for the Military Medal. The Brigadier wanted to put in for another medal for me but I talked him out of it. "Sir I have more fruit salad than enough and we both know that the War Office is parsimonious with their medals. I would rather the others were rewarded. I am going home now and my war is done. Give one to Lieutenant Morrison. He deserved it." He concurred and Jake's mother would get to meet the King when he was awarded the Military Medal posthumously.

What I did ensure was that all of those who had survived would be promoted. If nothing else it would guarantee a bigger pension and they deserved it. As we landed at our small airport and before the doors were opened, I spoke to them all, "We shared a great deal in this Korean winter. I for one will not forget it. I want you all to promise to keep in touch and we will have a reunion, once a year, to remember the dead. I know I shan't forget them."

I saw from their faces that they all agreed. Sergeant Major Thorpe said, "And with the money I have saved, Sir..."

I shook my head, "I am out of the army now, Ken, it is Tom and that goes for all of you."

"Aye, well, as I was saying, Tom, I intend to buy a little pub. When I get one that shall be where we hold the reunion. What do you say, lads?"

They roared, "Aye, Sarn't Major!"

The doors opened and there, on the tarmac, were our families. I only had eyes for mine. My wife, children, my mum and my dad. As I stepped down and ran to them, I could not control myself. All the emotion of the last months got to me

Izzy shouted, "Mummy, why is Daddy crying, is he hurt?"

Susan ran to me and threw her arms around me, "If he is then I know the best cure. Welcome home, Tom."

Dad and Mum put their arms around me and hugged me too as the three children clung to my legs.

I heard Dad say in my ear, "It really is finally over, son. Now you can start to live."

He was right but I knew that my dreams would be haunted by the men who had died and would never be coming home. I had to make my life meaningful for them. I would live the life they could not.

I bent down and picked up my three children. "Sorry about that, children, it has been a long flight and Daddy is just pleased to see you."

Samuel kissed me on my cheek, "And I planted tomatoes! Can we go and water them?"

I laughed, "Of course, we can do whatever the three of you want. Daddy is home and home for good!"

Dad nodded and gestured behind me. I turned and saw the remains of my command standing at attention. I put my children down and drawing myself to attention, saluted them. It was a soldier's farewell. I held the salute and then all of us dropped our arms at the same time. I waved and they cheered. I could now go home.

The End

Glossary

AP- Armour Piercing Shell

ATS- Auxiliary Territorial Service- Women's Branch of the British Army during WW2

Birome- the world's first commercially produce biro (using the two inventor's names- Bíró and Meyne)

Bisht- Arab cloak

Bob on- Very accurate (slang) from a plumber's bob

Bombay-Mumbai

Butchers- Look (Cockney slang Butcher's Hook- Look)

Butties- sandwiches (slang)

Caff- Café (slang)

Capstan Full Strength- a type of cigarette

Chah- tea (slang)

Comforter- the lining for the helmet; a sort of woollen hat

Conflab- discussion (slang)

Cook-off- when the barrel of a Browning 30 Calibre overheats

Corned dog- Corned Beef (slang)

CP- Command Post

Dhobi- washing (slang from the Hindi word)

Doolally tap- Going mad (slang- from India Deolali- where there was a sanitorium)

Ercs- aircraftsman (slang- from Cockney)

Ewbank- Mechanical carpet cleaner

Formosa- Taiwan

Fruit salad- medal ribbons (slang)

Full English- English breakfast (bacon, sausage, eggs, fried tomato and black pudding)

Gash- spare (slang)

Gauloise- French cigarette

Gib- Gibraltar (slang)

Glasshouse- Military prison

HE – High Explosive shells

Jankers- field punishment

Jimmy the One- First Lieutenant on a British warship

Katusas – Korean soldiers attached to American units
Killick- leading hand (Navy) (slang)
Kip- sleep (slang)
Legging it- Running for it (slang)
LRDG- Long Range Desert Group (Commandos operating from the desert behind enemy lines.)
Mao Tse-tung- Mao Zedong
Marge- Margarine (butter substitute- slang)
MGB- Motor Gun Boat
Mossy- De Havilland Mosquito (slang) (Mossies- pl.)
Mickey- 'taking the mickey', making fun of (slang)
Micks- Irishmen (slang)
MTB- Motor Torpedo Boat
ML- Motor Launch
Narked- annoyed (slang)
Neaters- undiluted naval rum (slang)
Oik- worthless person (slang)
Oppo/oppos- pals/comrades (slang)
Piccadilly Commandos- Prostitutes in London
Pom-pom- Quick Firing 2lb. (40 mm) Maxim cannon
Pongo (es)- soldier (slang)
Potato mashers- German Hand Grenades (slang)
PTI- Physical Training Instructor
QM- Quarter Master (stores)
Recce- Reconnoitre (slang)
RSM- Regimental Sergeant Major
SBA- Sick Bay Attendant
Schtum -keep quiet (German)
Scragging - roughing someone up (slang)
Scrumpy- farm cider
Shank's Pony- walk (slang)
Shooting brake- an estate car
Shufti- a look (slang)
Skiver- those who avoided conscription
SOE- Special Operations Executive (agents sent behind enemy lines)

SP- Starting price (slang)- what's going on
SNAFU- Situation Normal All Fucked Up (acronym and slang)
Snug- a small lounge in a pub (slang)
Spiv- A black marketeer/criminal (slang)
Sprogs- children or young soldiers (slang)
Squaddy- ordinary soldier (slang)
Stag- sentry duty (slang)
Stand your corner- get a round of drinks in (slang)
Subbie- Sub-lieutenant (slang)
Suss it out- work out what to do (slang)
Tatties- potatoes (slang)
Tommy (Atkins)- Ordinary British soldier
Two penn'orth- two pennies worth (slang for opinion)
Wavy Navy- Royal Naval Reserve (slang)
WVS- Women's Voluntary Service

Historical background

Royal Marine Commandos did operate in Korea. However, I have Tom and his men arriving early. The North Koreans did race through the South Korean army and by the time the Americans arrived the South Koreans and the Americans held just an 80 by 50-mile corner of south-east South Korea. The attack by MacArthur at Inchon was a masterstroke. The North Koreans lost not only all of their gains but elements of the American and Allied forces reached the border with China. Had China not intervened then who knows how history might have been altered but invade they did and the war which might have lasted months dragged into years and the peace talks lumbered on into the next millennium!

I have tried to use the names of the places as they would have been in 1950. Mumbai was Bombay then and Busan was Pusan. Beijing was Peking!

The Royal Marine Commandos and the Rangers both operated in North and South Korea. Most of their missions were behind the enemy lines. My raids are all fictitious but reflect the sort of work that would have been carried out.

Radio protocol from:

https://www.globalsecurity.org/military/library/policy/arm y/fm/24-19/Ch5.htm

There was an attempt, in October 1950 to try to rescue POWs before they were spirited across the border but the 187th was also tasked with capturing North Korean politicians. The attempt was only partially successful.

Stalin used Soviet Advisers to aid the North Koreans and he was less than pleased at the sudden collapse of the North Korean defence. He allowed his MiGs to operate but only in North Korea. MacArthur reached the Chinese border and wished to invade. What he did not know was that 200,000 Chinese troops were poised to come to the aid of North Korea and that Stalin had authorised the

Russian air force to intervene. The Chinese marched at night and every time an aeroplane flew overhead, they froze! When they attacked the American 8th Cavalry regiment and the 1st Marine Division at Chosin Reservoir it came as a complete and devastating shock.

Operation Thunderbolt was a reconnaissance in force but as the General had over 90000 men it could have been called an attack. The General was being cautious. It took just two weeks to reach the Han River and although Seoul took a week or so longer to recapture the allies had regained the 38th Parallel and begun to eat back into North Korea.

Soviet MiG in the Smithsonian at Dulles
Author's Photograph

American Sabre in the Smithsonian at Dulles
Author's Photograph

Battle of the Imjin River

Captain Ormrod's tanks had forced their way down the last lap of the valley through milling Chinamen. They could see what was estimated at 2,000 more, swarming down the western hillsides, from the heights where they had been held up all day. The Centurions came through, crushing enemy under their tracks. Sgt. Cadman found a Chinaman battering at his turret to get in, and directed the tank straight through the wall of a house, to brush him off, and then ran over an M.G. post beside the road. Cornet Venner, who had behaved with great gallantry at every stage of the day's fighting, lost his scout-car, but guided one Centurion out of trouble and escaped, wounded, himself. Captain Ormrod was wounded in the head by a grenade. Three platoons of Infantry suddenly appeared, in parade-ground order, out of the river bed – and were blown to confusion with some of the last ammunition the tanks carried. Some tanks took to the paddy and were ploughing-in Communists, crouched under every bank. The firing was a continuous iron rain on the outside of the tanks, and only a small proportion of the Infantry on the top survived this death-ride. The tanks came out of the valley to see the Belgians leaving their ridge, that all day had guarded this southern opening.

8th Hussars Regimental Journal

Richard Napier who was a tank commander at the battle wrote a book. He said that, as he was unable to use his weapons, he withdrew, allowing infantrymen to hitch a ride on his tank. The Chinese had infiltrated behind them and were swarming around them, shooting at the infantrymen on the tank. The crew resorted to lobbing grenades out of the hatches at the mass of Chinese infantry. On one occasion, the Centurion tanks of the 8th were swamped by Chinese soldiers who were attempting to prise open the hatches to throw grenades inside. The response of the Irish Hussars was to turn the turrets of their tanks towards each other, and "hose" the enemy off with their Besa machine guns. On their return to the British Lines, it was said that these tanks "ran red with the blood of dead Chinese." Human detritus was also caught up in the tracks as the tanks had run over a number of Chinese and (unfortunately) some British dead.

Timeline of the Korean War

This is adapted from Encyclopaedia Britannica.
June 25, 1950
A massive artillery barrage from the North signals the beginning of the Korean War. Roughly 100,000 North Korean troops pour across the 38th parallel, and, although South Korean forces are driven back, they retire in good order.

June 27, 1950
The United Nations Security Council adopts Resolution 83, authorizing UN member states to provide military assistance to South Korea. Seoul falls the following day.

September 12, 1950
North Korean troops reach their farthest point of advance. Although thousands of UN troops have arrived to reinforce South Korea, months of fighting have reduced the area under their control to a 5,000-square-mile rectangle centred on the critical south-eastern port of Pusan. By the time the North

Korean invasion force reaches the "Pusan Perimeter," its strength has been nearly cut in half and it is almost entirely lacking in armour.

September 15, 1950
X Corps, a force led by U.S. Maj. Gen. Edward M. Almond, stages an audacious amphibious landing at Inchon, some 150 miles behind enemy lines. The plan, conceived by UN commander Gen. Douglas MacArthur, is an unqualified success; 10 days later Seoul is liberated.

October 25, 1950
Having destroyed the bulk of the North Korean army, UN troops have pressed on into North Korea and are now approaching the Yalu River. Chinese People's Volunteers Force (CPVF) troops under veteran commander Gen. Peng Dehuai cross into North Korea and inflicts serious losses on the lead units of the UN advance. The sudden appearance of Chinese forces sends the main body of UN forces reeling back to the south bank of the Ch'ŏngch'ŏn River.

December 6, 1950

The U.S. Marines at the Chosin Reservoir begin their "attack in a different direction" as they engage in a fighting retreat to the port of Hŭngnam. Two entire Chinese armies have been tasked with the destruction of the 1st Marine Division. They succeed in driving the American force from North Korean territory but pay an enormous price: as many as 80,000 Chinese troops are killed or wounded, and the CPVF Ninth Army Group is rendered combat-ineffective for months.

January 4, 1951
Chinese and North Korean forces recapture Seoul.

March 14, 1951

Seoul changes hands for the fourth time when UN forces once again liberate the South Korean capital. The city has been devastated by fighting, and its population has been reduced to a fraction of its pre-war size.

April 11, 1951
U.S. Pres. Harry S. Truman relieves MacArthur of command. He is succeeded as UN commanded by Lieut. Gen. Matthew Ridgway.

April 25, 1951
Vastly outnumbered UN forces check the Chinese advance on Seoul at the Battles of Kapyong and the Imjin River. 4,000 men of the British 29th Brigade stage a successful delaying action against nearly 30,000 troops of the Chinese 63rd Army at the Imjin River. Some 650 men of the 1st Battalion, the Gloucestershire Regiment (the "Glorious Glosters"), engage in a Thermopylae-like stand against more than 10,000 Chinese infantry at Imjin. Although the overwhelming majority of the Glosters are killed or captured, their sacrifice allows UN forces to consolidate their lines around the South Korean capital.

July 10, 1951
Truce talks between the UN and the communists begin at Kaesong. The negotiations do not mark an end to the war, however; the fighting continues for two more years. In October the peace talks relocate to the village of P'anmunjŏm.

I had to keep referring to the timeline whilst I was writing the book as events seemed to happen too quickly to be true. The actual war lasted just 13 months and considering the numbers of men who were killed it was a too bloody a war to be called a police action!

Reference Books used

- The Commando Pocket Manual 1949-45- Christopher Westhorp
- The Second World War Miscellany- Norman Ferguson
- Army Commandos 1940-45- Mike Chappell
- Military Slang- Lee Pemberton
- World War II- Donald Sommerville
- The Historical Atlas of World War II-Swanston and Swanston
- Churchill's Wizards: The British Genius for Deception 1914-1945- Nicholas Rankin
- The Korean War 1950-53 -Thomas, Abbot and Chappell
- Military Small Arms of the 20th Century- Hogg and Weeks
- Jane's Fighting Ships of World War 2
- Jane's Fighting Aircraft of World War 2
- World War II tanks- Grove

Other books
by
Griff Hosker

If you enjoyed reading this book, then why not read another one by the author?
Ancient History

The Sword of Cartimandua Series (Germania and Britannia 50 A.D. – 128 A.D.)
Ulpius Felix- Roman Warrior (prequel)
Book 1 The Sword of Cartimandua
Book 2 The Horse Warriors
Book 3 Invasion Caledonia
Book 4 Roman Retreat
Book 5 Revolt of the Red Witch
Book 6 Druid's Gold
Book 7 Trajan's Hunters
Book 8 The Last Frontier
Book 9 Hero of Rome
Book 10 Roman Hawk
Book 11 Roman Treachery
Book 12 Roman Wall
Book 13 Roman Courage

The Aelfraed Series
(Britain and Byzantium 1050 A.D. - 1085 A.D.)
Book 1 Housecarl
Book 2 Outlaw
Book 3 Varangian

The Wolf Warrior series
(Britain in the late 6th Century)

Book 1 Saxon Dawn
Book 2 Saxon Revenge
Book 3 Saxon England
Book 4 Saxon Blood
Book 5 Saxon Slayer
Book 6 Saxon Slaughter
Book 7 Saxon Bane
Book 8 Saxon Fall: Rise of the Warlord
Book 9 Saxon Throne
Book 10 Saxon Sword

The Dragon Heart Series
Book 1 Viking Slave
Book 2 Viking Warrior
Book 3 Viking Jarl
Book 4 Viking Kingdom
Book 5 Viking Wolf
Book 6 Viking War
Book 7 Viking Sword
Book 8 Viking Wrath
Book 9 Viking Raid
Book 10 Viking Legend
Book 11 Viking Vengeance
Book 12 Viking Dragon
Book 13 Viking Treasure
Book 14 Viking Enemy
Book 15 Viking Witch
Book 16 Viking Blood
Book 17 Viking Weregeld
Book 18 Viking Storm
Book 19 Viking Warband
Book 20 Viking Shadow
Book 21 Viking Legacy
Book 22 Viking Clan
Book 23 Viking Bravery

The Norman Genesis Series
Hrolf the Viking
Horseman
The Battle for a Home
Revenge of the Franks
The Land of the Northmen
Ragnvald Hrolfsson
Brothers in Blood
Lord of Rouen
Drekar in the Seine
Duke of Normandy
The Duke and the King

New World Series
Blood on the Blade
Across the Seas

The Anarchy Series England 1120-1180
English Knight
Knight of the Empress
Northern Knight
Baron of the North
Earl
King Henry's Champion
The King is Dead
Warlord of the North
Enemy at the Gate
The Fallen Crown
Warlord's War
Kingmaker
Henry II
Crusader
The Welsh Marches
Irish War
Poisonous Plots

The Princes' Revolt
Earl Marshal

**Border Knight
1182-1300**
Sword for Hire
Return of the Knight
Baron's War
Magna Carta
Welsh Wars
Henry III
The Bloody Border

Lord Edward's Archer
Lord Edward's Archer

**Struggle for a Crown
1360- 1485**
Blood on the Crown
To Murder A King
The Throne
King Henry IV

Modern History

The Napoleonic Horseman Series
Book 1 Chasseur a Cheval
Book 2 Napoleon's Guard
Book 3 British Light Dragoon
Book 4 Soldier Spy
Book 5 1808: The Road to Coruña
Book 6 Talavera
Waterloo

The Lucky Jack American Civil War series
Rebel Raiders

Confederate Rangers
The Road to Gettysburg

The British Ace Series
1914
1915 Fokker Scourge
1916 Angels over the Somme
1917 Eagles Fall
1918 We will remember them
From Arctic Snow to Desert Sand
Wings over Persia

Combined Operations series
1940-1945

1. Commando
2. Raider
3. Behind Enemy Lines
4. Dieppe
5. Toehold in Europe
6. Sword Beach
7. Breakout
8. The Battle for Antwerp
9. King Tiger
10. Beyond the Rhine
11. Korea
12. Korean Winter

Other Books
Carnage at Cannes (a thriller)
Great Granny's Ghost (Aimed at 9-14-year-old young people)
Adventure at 63-Backpacking to Istanbul

For more information on all of the books then please visit the author's web site at www.griffhosker.com where there is a link to contact him.

Made in the USA
Lexington, KY
12 September 2019